A SEAT AT THE TABLE

"Michelle tells an important story and she does it with heart. You can tell she has a deep love for her reader and for all of the Joys of the world!"

BRAD PAUQUETTE
BEST SELLING AUTHOR OF *THE NOVEL MATRIX*

"This inspiring tale of spiritual awakening will resonate with fans of Sharon Garlough Brown's *Sensible Shoes*. Rich with characters and situations both complex and relatable, the story hooked my interest to the point that I twice overcooked food because I ignored timers in favor of just a few more pages. This book offers those hungry to explore themes of lived-out faith and the authority of Scripture a seat at the table."

EMILY CONRAD
AUTHOR OF *THE RHYTHMS OF REDEMPTION ROMANCES*

"This story of Joy juggling what she believes with how much that should affect what she does resonates with today's challenges. I was so drawn into the novel, I stayed up until 2:00 a.m. to finish it! I can't wait to share this book with my twenty- and thirtysomething daughters. Michelle has written an engaging story, but more importantly embedded a message we all need to hear."

SUSAN MACIAS
AUTHOR OF *FINDING HOME* AND *UNCEASING*

"A well-told story is a gift. A reminder that God's Word is our most solid foundation is an even greater gift. In *A Seat at the Table*, Michelle has given us both. I was gripped from the opening chapter. I was challenged—and encouraged—by every chapter that followed. After reading the last paragraph, I immediately thought of several people I need to give copies to. Simply put: Read it…then share it."

KEITH FERRIN
SPEAKER, *YOUR BIBLE COACH* ON YOUTUBE
AUTHOR OF *HOW TO ENJOY READING YOUR BIBLE* AND
***THE SCRIPTURE JOURNEY SERIES* OF BIBLE STUDIES**

"*A Seat at the Table* is both thought-provoking and inspiring, filled with godly wisdom that can truly transform your life. The impact of this book will extend far beyond its words, leaving a lasting imprint on your heart."

RACHEL CASH
AUTHOR OF *MIXTAPE THEOLOGY*

"*A Seat at the Table* explores matters of Christian thought, ethics, and action through the ever-evolving lens of a young professional discovering where she fits in the world. As Joy navigates hurdles of betrayal and belonging, her journey invited me to reflect on God's Word as the foundation of a truly rewarding life. The invitation is open for you, too. I encourage you to take it."

CHRISTINA HUBBARD
WRITER AND FOUNDER OF
THE CREATIVE AND FREE COLLECTIVE

A SEAT AT THE TABLE

MICHELLE NEZAT

HERON HAVEN
PRESS

Developmental Editor
Brad Pauquette

Copy Editor
Noah Matthews and Vella Karman

Book Designer
Alli Prince

Cover Designer
Levi Matthews

Ebook ISBN: 979-8-9914441-1-8

Paperback ISBN: 979-8-9914441-0-1

Hardcover ISBN: 979-8-9914441-2-5

Printed in the United States of America
1 3 5 7 9 10 8 6 4 2

To my husband, Ron,
whose unwavering support means this book exists.

And to my daughters, Emily and Meredith,
who promised me they'd read it.

• • •

CHAPTER ONE

THE BELLS JINGLED as I opened the door, a familiar song welcoming me into a familiar place. I took a deep breath, willing the smell of the fresh-ground coffee to infuse me with courage. I slid my cardigan off and simultaneously attempted to shed the feeling that I had something to prove.

I didn't have anything to prove to Beth. She saw my visit as a favor for an old friend and had said as much. No. I was still trying to silence the voices in my head that said I was stupid for taking the risk.

Beth waved at me from behind the counter. I waved back and slid into a booth just inside the door. She greeted a customer at the counter with a "Welcome in." Her light brown ponytail swished as she swiveled toward the espresso machine. Her hot pink beaded drop earrings stood out against her dark uniform shirt and black apron.

I glanced around the café. While every Cup O' Joe was outfitted with the same collection of leather booths, high-top tables with stools, and intimate round tables for two with café chairs, the walls reflected the community. Mountain Home, Idaho, was home to an Air Force base, and the old and new photographs of air shows, family picnics, archery contests, and other base activities filled every square inch of open wall space. A bright blue Air Force flag draped from the ceiling above the door, and I noticed the seal of the 366th Fighter Wing shining through the epoxy on the tabletop in front of me.

I pulled out my phone to translate the Latin phrase in the banner under the multi-colored shield—*Audentes Fortuna Juvat*—"Fortune favors the bold."

Am I being bold or reckless?

The bells jangled again. A young man, no older than twenty, tied his apron over a wrinkled Cup O' Joe collared shirt, ran his fingers through his hair, and shuffled behind the counter. Beth glanced at him sideways before offering the woman at the counter a steaming hot cup of coffee.

As the customer walked away, Beth turned her attention to the young man, who leaned against the counter and stared at his shoes. I couldn't tell what she said, but she didn't draw attention with loud words, and eventually the young man lifted his head and gave a half smile. Beth patted his shoulder, untied her apron, and hung it on a hook before grabbing a notebook and heading over to my table.

Beth set her notebook on the table but didn't sit down. "I'm gonna get us some coffee. Black?" she asked with a wrinkled nose.

I smirked and shrugged, "What can I say? I actually like the taste of coffee."

A minute later, Beth set a white porcelain mug and a plate with a fresh blueberry scone in front of me.

I tilted my head toward the counter, "So, what's the story with that guy?"

Beth's eyes softened. "He's a work in progress." Raising a finger, she added, "But there is progress. Small baby steps of progress. But it's there. And I don't want to give up on him just yet."

Classic Beth. She hadn't given up on me yet—and we'd been friends since kindergarten. She would do anything to help me overcome my insecurities. Like in first grade when she made her mom curl her straight hair every day for a month because I thought my curly hair was ugly. Or that poster she made me in fifth grade of all the famous people with fair skin and chocolate brown eyes like me. In seventh grade, when she was still straight as a pole and my curves made me feel fat, she joined me in wearing a T-shirt over our swimsuits all summer. And in high school, she signed us up for a career discovery weekend at the local community college when I flipped out one afternoon because I didn't know what I wanted to do when I grew up.

But today she needed me to help her overcome her insecurities, and so I tucked away my own anxieties and turned my attention to Beth's. For the next hour, we pored over her list of questions about managing a Cup O' Joe location.

"Thanks, Joy," Beth repeated. "I can't believe you came all this way to sit with me. And for this!" She patted her notes. "I feel like I have a plan now."

"Anything for you." I leaned in to catch her gaze, "You're going to make a wonderful store supervisor."

"I can only hope Marshal agrees with you," she said, averting her eyes. "I'm sorry. I didn't mean to mention him."

I reached over and placed my hand on top of hers, "It's okay. I'm in a good place now. Honestly, I couldn't have planned it better. If I had been given the general manager position, I wouldn't be embarking on this new adventure."

"You seem really excited."

"I really am." I tucked a curl behind my ear and twisted the ring on my right hand.

"But…"

"But, I'm anxious, too. It's really risky."

I gazed out the window at the various shades of yellow and orange dancing across the sky—the sunrise brought all the hope contained in a new day.

"But you said Maggie believes in you. She wouldn't have loaned you the money if she didn't, right?"

"And that's the part I'm most afraid of. What if I don't have what it takes, and then I can't pay her back, and then all I'm left with is debt, hurt feelings, broken relationships, angry accusations, and—"

"Whoa, Joy," Beth grabbed both of my hands and gazed into my eyes as they glistened with tears on the verge of spilling over. "Where's all this coming from?"

"Family history. Pressure overload. All of the above." I waved my hand as if to clear cobwebs from in front of my face.

"Why all this doubt today?" Beth prodded.

"I don't think I've ever wanted something more. Especially after my visit to Coates."

• • •

A week earlier, I had checked in with the guard at the gate at Maggie's office in Boise. It was my first time visiting her office, even though I'd been welcomed into her home on many occasions during our mentor sessions for my master's program. The campus of Coates Incorporated, founded by a woman I admired, sat on a hill overlooking the city. A physical representation of success, it boasted the guard at the gate, a three-story modern open lobby, and glass offices with professionals running around looking very busy and very important.

John, Maggie's boss, radiated charm as he raved about the university accounts they were trying to acquire. His straight white teeth could have been featured in a toothpaste commercial, and his hazel eyes blazed with passion. His gray hair only made him look distinguished as he leaned on the corner of his desk with his ankles crossed. He and Maggie could have been in a magazine ad—he in his fitted modern blue suit, classic tie, and camel-colored oxford shoes, and she in her fitted sheath dress, designer heels, and every short, blonde hair in place. Maggie glowed as they shared work stories with humor and cheer—"Remember that time when," and "You'll never believe this one." I soaked up the camaraderie.

Periodically, John's assistant, Mateo, would bring in something for him to look at or to sign. At one point, John showed me two different ad options for Coates's flagship tracking camera and asked for my opinion. I made some suggestions to update the wording and font choices and melted when he told Maggie I was something special. I wasn't sure if he was joking when he suggested I abandon my consultation business to come to work for him in Coates Inc.'s marketing department.

After meeting John, Maggie guided me to a small conference room. Mateo brought me a latte from the coffee station while Maggie and I worked on the initial phase of my project for the contest with Berean Christian Academy. Just like during our mentor-match days, Maggie challenged me, celebrated moments of insight, and filled the gaps of my inexperience with her wisdom. Throughout the afternoon, each member of Maggie's team dropped into the conference room to introduce themselves and offer their video, graphic, and copywriting skills for BCA as needed.

"When you win the retreat with Julia Coates and a feature story in *Marketing Trends Magazine*, you'll remember us little people, right?" Mateo had teased when he walked me out.

• • •

After I described the scene, Beth smiled broadly, "That sounds amazing. Everything you ever wanted. So what's the problem?"

I nibbled at my scone trying to decide if I should give voice to my deepest fear. "What if I'm not worth the investment?" I blurted.

"Are you kidding me? You're unbelievably talented, Joy. You have a gift. If you do with them what you just did for me, you'll be a tremendous success."

"Thanks," I said with a sigh.

"I'm serious," Beth added with a frown.

"What if—I mean—I know how to run a Cup O' Joe. What if I don't have what it takes to win this contest?"

"Believe in yourself, Joy. God has prepared you for this moment. You've got this."

CHAPTER TWO

AS THE DOOR to Cup O' Joe closed behind me, a gust of wind blew errant curls into my face. I tucked them behind my ears and scanned the block for traffic before crossing the street to jump in my Jeep.

Mountain Home was hometown Americana—a quaint mixture of old and new, renovated and falling apart. A historic newspaper building with peeling paint sat across the street from the "new" low red brick structure from the 1970s. The crimson roof and awning on the hardware store drew my eye as a young man in a red apron held the bags of an elderly woman padding across the street behind her walker. She raised her walker, slammed it down, then grated the wheels forward inches at a time—thwack, scrape, shuffle, thwack, scrape, shuffle.

I turned to step off the curb, and then I saw them. My feet grew roots and refused to move. Maggie and John stood about a block away in an embrace. The sign above them read "Sunny Ridge Boutique Hotel."

My mind flashed to dinner the week before with Maggie and her husband, Peter. Peter was a treasure. His unrestrained adoration for

Maggie was evident in every touch of her waist, every kiss on her forehead, and every chance he took to brag on her. When we settled on the patio after dinner with steaming hot cups of tea, Peter told me about how a meal train for Maggie's fellow board member at Berean Christian Academy fell apart. He teased Maggie for spending the weekend prepping enough freezer meals for a month. I had laughed because it sounded like me—always taking things to the extreme.

• • •

Maggie and John continued to stand close together. His arms looped around her waist as if to keep her from blowing away. Maggie's head tilted back in laughter. John leaned over and kissed her neck and then her lips. Like a Broadway scene where the characters came on stage and then froze, time stood still. Bit by bit, the scene came back to life. A bird chirped—a robin with the largest red breast I had ever seen. A car passed—a black rusty stepside truck like my grandpa used to have on the farm. I felt myself let out a trapped breath.

With John's back toward me, Maggie perched on the tips of her toes to give him another hug. She kept her eyes closed, her chin rested on his shoulder, and a gentle smile graced her face. Then she opened her eyes and saw me.

Her eyes, dazed and dreamy, widened with recognition as her face clouded with horror.

I held her gaze for a moment, then rushed to the safety of my driver's seat. I sat motionless with my hands on the steering wheel, staring at my knees, trying to catch my breath.

My phone vibrated with a new text. It was Maggie. *What are you doing in Mountain Home? I thought you had a meeting with BCA today?*

It got canceled. I replied with shaking hands.

Why are you here?

I banged my thumbs against the phone screen. If it had been my laptop keyboard I would have pounded the keys. *I spent the night at my aunt's house for a change of scenery to work on my business plan and stopped at the coffee shop to help a friend.*

Another text. *I need you to keep what you saw to yourself.*

I stared at the crumpled silver gum wrapper on the floorboard. I wanted to say I hadn't seen anything. I wanted to say I planned to text Peter myself. I wanted to say I quit. I wanted to say it's not the first time I've been asked to keep a secret like this. Instead, I settled for—*I can do that.*

I started my Jeep, shifted into gear, and headed home.

CHAPTER THREE

THE NEXT TIME I heard from Maggie was to remind me of the barbecue, and to ask me to bring my "famous" banana pudding. She acted like nothing had happened. And there I stood, in her driveway with a beautifully layered banana pudding in a glass trifle bowl, acting like nothing had happened.

I had actually dug my old vision board out of the closet the night before. I stared at it for an hour, running my fingers across the picture of people sitting at a table. Not a conference table. A kitchen table. I had carefully written my vision in block letters with a black marker below the photograph cut from a magazine.

I could still see Maggie rolling her eyes at the idea, but I believed in it. You can learn more from people at their kitchen table than a conference table. There are too many masks around a conference table. It's hard to put on airs when you're in flannel pajama pants slathering butter on a fresh biscuit.

I shifted the trifle bowl to the other hand and rehearsed the hand-lettered vision: "Private meeting with the CEO of a major corporation." This contest was a custom-made ticket to fulfilling this dream. Despite my fresh distaste for Maggie, everything about this project with Berean Christian Academy was still true. It was still a contest sponsored by Julia Coates between her west and east coast marketing departments to benefit two organizations she believed in. I was still the marketing specialist hired to create a video that simultaneously promoted the school and the Coates tracking camera. I still desperately wanted the weekend retreat with Julia at her Lake Tahoe vacation home—and being featured on podcasts and in *Marketing Trends Magazine* was pretty irresistible, too. I still had access to an amazing team of professionals to pull it off. And with Maggie's loan, I still had the money I needed to work on the project pro bono while building my portfolio and making connections to launch my business.

The money.

I shook my head.

I am not my mom. This is not family. This is business.

I heard music, conversation, and laughter before I pushed on the gate to reveal at least thirty people milling about in small groups in the backyard.

"Joy!"

My attention snapped to see Peter waving and coming toward me.

"Hi, Peter," I said with a shy smile.

Peter reached around my shoulders and gave me a firm side hug. "You finally get to meet some of our BCA family."

His wide grin and sparkling eyes only deepened the ache in my chest. I wished I could share his buoyant anticipation, but all I could think about was the look on Maggie's face in front of that boutique hotel and how duped I was by John's engaging white smile.

Peter's eyes widened as he spied the bowl in my arms. "Is that what I think it is?"

"Of course," I replied. "It's your favorite."

"Let me take this off your hands."

I watched him take the bowl into the house, unsure if it would make it back out again.

The ache remained, inducing a flurry of mixed emotions—the familiarity of the Hensleys' home now strangely comfortable and uncomfortable at the same time.

The lawn looked like it was ready for a baseball opener. The bright green grass lay cut with precise lines creating a crisscross pattern. Standing tables lined the perimeter with long white table cloths kissing the grass at the edges. A fresh floral bouquet of bright yellow sunflowers and white lilies graced each table and battery-operated candles flickered beside them. A group of teenagers tossed bean bags in a game of cornhole on the right side of the yard. The grill and tables filled with food flanked the left side of the yard. The back covered patio featured Maggie's custom outdoor furniture Peter had purchased for their anniversary last year.

Peter practically gleamed as he flipped burgers, told bad dad jokes, and helped people find common ground for conversation. I spotted Maggie moving from group to group with a smile and an hors d'oeuvre tray. She wore a long white dress with tulip sleeves and a V-neck. Her wide pink belt accented the dainty flowers sprinkled across the fabric in a spring pattern—a stark contrast to her usual attire of pencil skirt, suit jacket over solid-colored blouse, and Christian Louboutin pumps.

I made my way to the patio and slumped into my favorite chair. I remained unnoticed by a man who muttered something about not wanting to be preached at as he fiddled with the phone attached to the speaker system. A country playlist replaced the Christian soundtrack that had been playing, and the man slipped away. I tapped my foot to the familiar tune while building my courage to mingle.

Peter called out to everyone as he pulled Maggie to his side with his hand around her waist. "Time to eat! Dig in!"

Maggie's smile looked as genuine as ever as she spotted the almost empty jug of tea on the serving table. She didn't see me as she snuck into the house, reappearing within moments with two full jugs in hand.

I stood quietly in line for food behind two women in simple, knee-length sundresses and sandaled feet. In a low voice the blonde woman said to the brunette, "I miss the days when Mrs. Verity used to insist we all hold hands and pray before we ate." When they stepped forward, I could no longer hear what they said in hushed tones.

After I filled my plate, I made my way to a standing table in the corner of the yard. Another group of women stood nearby. These ladies were decked out in designer outfits, full make-up, and sparkling jewels around their necks and on their fingers. "Don't you love Ashley's new dress?" one woman said, pointing to a group of teenagers huddled on the other side of the yard.

I spotted Ashley right away because she was the only one in a dress. The flirty frock was completely open in the back with three wide triangles cut out in the front. I had envied the designer look in a recent magazine spread. The article featured several East Coast trends like Ashley's dress, accessories that several of the moms wore, and even an overpriced tote I spied laying in the grass at the feet of one of the teenage girls.

My dinner entertainment turned out to be the boys playing cornhole. With each toss they either cheered or groaned, with a bit of smack-talk sprinkled in.

Ashley and a few of her friends brought plates of food to the table where the ladies stood. "We need this table," Ashley demanded.

"Of course, dear," three-carat-ring mom responded. And the women shuffled away.

I overheard Ashley say, "I can't wait to get out of here." Another girl whined, "I know. It's so lame."

I smiled to myself, remembering how much I hated extended family events. I supposed even the BCA family fell into the teenagers' same category of contempt.

On my way back to the food table for another scoop of baked beans, I overheard a guy in a green BCA polo shirt talking to Peter about football. "I'm tellin' ya, turf is what we need. That and an athletic director who can recruit players."

"It's not really legal to recruit," Peter offered.

"You know what I mean. Get out in the community and build relationships so kids want to come play for the Eagles."

Peter patted him on the shoulder, "God will bring the right players." Peter missed the man's frown as he turned to serve up another burger patty.

I felt someone touch my elbow and turned to meet Maggie's dancing eyes, "Joy, I didn't see you arrive." She took my plate and set it on a table and guided me by my elbow toward a group of people that included both of the sundress ladies. Maggie said, "Everyone, this is Joy, the one I've been telling you about. Joy, these are some of the committee members who will give input on the video you're going to create for the contest."

Next came a flurry of handshakes and names most of which slipped through my mind as soon as they floated toward me. The last name, Millie, belonged to one of the sundress ladies.

Millie put her hand on my forearm and said, "We have so many ideas."

Maggie patted my arm and slipped away toward another group. I felt as if she just deserted me in the wolf habitat at the zoo.

I hoped my tone wasn't as plastic as my smile, "I can't wait to hear them."

Green polo guy had sauntered up during introductions. "Athletics is a big draw. We should feature that," he suggested.

That comment opened the floodgate of ideas from everyone.

"Well, I was thinking the video should highlight academics. We are a school after all."

"We should use the preschoolers. They're so cute."

"But we're trying to grow the high school."

"No one ever features the arts. The drama club would make the perfect actors for the video."

I maintained my smile as I scanned the yard and caught Maggie's attention with my eyes. I tilted my head and hoped she would get the message that I needed saving. It must have worked because she made her way back toward the group.

Millie placed her hand on my forearm again and bemoaned, "I wish you could've met Mr. Easton tonight."

"Yeah, where is the *esteemed* Mr. Easton, anyway?" green polo guy asked.

"He had a family conflict," Maggie explained as she rejoined our circle.

"Who's Mr. Easton?" I asked.

"He's the Bible teacher," Millie said.

"And he's head of the committee," Maggie added.

"He's just so wise," Millie continued. "You're really going to like working with him. He's calm and measured and so dedicated to his faith. He really cares about the kids and has a deep understanding of things. I mean—he's a pillar of BCA, wouldn't you say?" Millie looked around, and a few people nodded in agreement.

"That's a little overstated," green polo guy grumbled.

The sky lit up with heat lightning, and the conversation shifted to oohs and aahs with heads tilted.

"Well, let's make sure we eat dessert before we're forced to break up this party," Maggie said as she turned and walked toward the house. Looking over her shoulder she added, "Joy, can you help me set everything out?"

"Sure thing. Nice to meet all of you," I whirled around and scampered up to Maggie's side.

"Let's get you scheduled for a meeting with Mr. Easton," Maggie said as I followed her into the house.

A variety of dessert trays lined the kitchen bar in addition to my banana pudding. Maggie dug in a drawer for serving spoons. I grabbed a tray of cookies and removed the plastic film. I skipped down the back steps toward Peter and set the plate of cookies on the buffet table.

I loaded my arms with the mostly empty food platters to make room for the desserts and turned only to have Peter blocking my path back into the house.

"You know, I noticed that we had a lot of desserts in there. I'm wondering if that pudding is just too much for tonight," Peter said.

I tilted my head with a smirk and blinked twice. I looked at the trays in my arms and then toward the kitchen door. Peter put his hands up in surrender and stepped aside with a grin.

My foot slipped on the steps heading back into the kitchen and Maggie rescued the teetering tower of food platters. "Whoa. Careful.

I got these." Maggie deposited the stack on the counter, near the sink and tilted her head toward the desserts. "Those are ready to go out."

I grabbed two trays and headed back out to the yard. I watched my feet as I descended the rear steps so as not to lose my footing again and nearly ran into the back of a man at the base of the stairs.

"Oh, I'm so sorry! I didn't see you there."

"No worries," he said. The blood drained from my face as John Clarke turned with that bright smile—that "you're-gonna-love-me" smile. Well, I didn't. I couldn't. Not after Mountain Home. Then he recognized me, "Joy! It's good to see you again. Let me take those from you."

What was John doing here?

I turned to look at Maggie who had followed me down the steps with trays of her own. She displayed the same look of horror as when I saw her and John in Mountain Home. In an instant, the alarm disappeared and a plastered smile took its place. "John! So glad you could make it."

John leaned over and kissed the air near her left cheek, careful to balance the trays he had taken from me. "And miss Peter's baked beans? Never!"

He's had Peter's baked beans?

"Our famed Booster Club President has arrived," Peter shook John's hand and leaned in for one of those guy-hugs where they keep one hand in the shake and slap each other's back with a loud clap.

Booster Club President?

"Joy, go grab your pudding and a serving spoon," Maggie instructed.

I glanced at Peter. He shrugged.

As I stepped back into the kitchen, I walked to the sink, clutched the side of the counter and bent over with my head down. My rapid breaths in and out of my nose did not give me the oxygen I needed to think clearly. I reached up and turned on the hot water. I stood upright and let the water pour over my hands and took a deep breath and exhaled in rapid, staccato puffs.

I took another deep breath, still unable to calm the shaking that seemed to come from my core. I did not feel safe. This so-called family was riddled with disunity and deceit. It was not worth the risk. I'd be setting myself up for failure for sure.

The soothing water turned scalding and I jerked my hands away from the stream. I looked around the kitchen suddenly desperate to escape. I turned off the water, dried my hands, and patted my pocket to confirm that my key fob and phone were still in there.

I left out the front door—the banana pudding on the counter my parting gift to Peter.

CHAPTER FOUR

I EXITED THE GLASS DOORS of my bank, stopped on the sidewalk, and looked at the cashier's check in my hands. $50,000 for a fresh start seemed a pretty steep price. $50,000 for freedom from Maggie's runaway train? Totally worth it.

I had spent the morning at home staring at my two business plans side-by-side. Plan A used my savings to launch my own company—a high-risk endeavor that still raised my blood pressure. I had developed Plan B after Maggie convinced me to take on the pro bono project for BCA, offering a $50,000 loan to make up for the lost time I would have spent on launching my new firm. She insisted winning the contest would jump-start my business in a way that pounding the pavement never could. She said I had talent worth betting on.

That and she offered a contest custom-made for my heart's desire.

A desire I would have to fulfill in some other way.

I knew where this was headed, and it was nowhere good. Money messes up everything. I learned that when our whole family blew up because mom couldn't pay back a loan from her brother. I would not make the same mistake.

I climbed into my cherry-red Jeep and retracted my soft-top to let in the sunshine. I sat still for a moment with my head back and eyes closed.

I thought back to my vision board. It mocked me this morning, propped up on the sofa. So, I had turned it over.

Now you see your dreams coming true in ways you never dreamed possible. Now you don't.

I looked over at the check I had laid on the passenger seat. *Am I really going to walk away from the chance at a kitchen table experience with the CEO of a major corporation?* And not just any CEO. Julia Coates.

I reflected on the research paper I had written about Mrs. Coates for an entrepreneurship class during undergrad. I loved everything about her. She beat the boys in a male-dominated industry by pioneering the development of a smaller tracking camera and opening new markets. She received equal acclaim for her philanthropic efforts—not something I could picture for myself anytime soon since the only donation I currently made was to round up to the nearest dollar for whatever cause they were promoting at my local Safeway. And she was classy. She was always so put together in every interview I had ever watched—from her clothes, to her posture, to her eloquent speech.

That's why I took Maggie's money and said yes to the contest. It wasn't the podcast interviews and a feature in an industry magazine—although those opportunities couldn't hurt. No, what intrigued me most was the personal retreat with Julia Coates.

I shook my head. Time to back out.

With fresh resolve, I put the Jeep in reverse and backed out of the parking spot. I drove forward to exit the lot and noticed a gray minivan backing out in front of me. They didn't have room, so I shifted into reverse, but somehow my foot slipped and I gunned it. The Jeep lurched backward like a rocket, and I felt the vehicle bounce up and heard crunching.

I sat completely still with my hands at ten and two on the steering wheel. At first I didn't remember where I was. I peered at the sign towering above me—*Horizon Trust Bank*. Red taillights in the distance drew my attention, and I watched a gray minivan pull into traffic. My mind formulated a replay—minivan, reverse, crunch.

My hands trembled as I pulled on the door handle to get out. When I slid both feet to the ground, the Jeep felt off balance.

I pressed my left hand onto the side of the Jeep to steady myself. I staggered to the back of the vehicle and saw it teetering on a short cement post guarding the pedestrian entrance to the bank. The smell of hot metal mixed with concrete dust assaulted my senses.

My mouth watered and I swallowed the bile rising in my throat. I raked my hands through my hair and let my chin fall into my chest.

I felt a hand softly touching my shoulder. "Are you okay?"

I looked up into a familiar face. Mateo, John's assistant from Coates Inc., stood before me. "I'm fine"—a tear escaped and dripped down my cheek—"but Scarlett isn't."

Mateo's eyes widened and he leaned to look inside the Jeep.

"Oh, no," I sniffed, "there's no one else in there. Scarlett's the name of my Jeep."

Relief washed over Mateo's face as he smiled softly and patted my shoulder. "I remember you from the other day. Joy, right?"

"Yes."

"Okay, Joy. Do you have a mechanic?"

"No," I sniffed some more.

A man and woman in matching navy blue pantsuits and gold name tags emerged from the bank, walked up to us, and began asking questions. Mateo stepped in to answer. The muted conversation echoed in my ears, and my eyes blurred with tears. I knew I should be paying attention to what they were saying, but I couldn't focus. I took mental assessment of my body and determined that beyond the unsteadiness and shaking, I hadn't been hurt. I looked around to make sure no other vehicles were involved, and sighed with relief when I verified only Scarlett and the post were impacted. I watched Mateo pull at his short beard, nod his head, and shake hands with the workers as they returned to the bank and he turned back toward me.

"Do you always wear a bow tie?" I asked.

"I'm sorry, what?" Mateo clipped.

"You were wearing a bow tie at Coates the other day and you're wearing one today, too."

"Scarlett's all torn up and that's what's on your mind?" Mateo asked with a smile.

I shrugged.

"Yes. It's my signature look," Mateo said pulling on the edges of the tie with an exaggerated tilt of his head.

I looked up at Mateo with misty eyes. "What'd they say?"

"Who?"

"The bank employees."

"They were checking on you."

"Oh, that's nice," I said. I felt distant from my own body—like I was watching the scene unfold from afar.

"And making sure you knew they weren't liable for the damage to Scarlett," Mateo added.

The floating feeling dissipated, crashing me back to earth. "Oh, right."

"My uncle has a mechanic and body shop. I can call him to tow Scarlett in."

I looked at him blankly.

"Do you want me to do that?" Mateo asked.

"Yes, please."

"Okay. Let me text John to tell him I won't be in this morning."

My stomach tightened at the mention of John. "Why?"

"Because I'm going to help take care of you."

"Oh, that's nice," I said. "Has anyone ever mentioned you look like Lin Manuel Miranda?"

Mateo tilted his head back and laughed, "A time or two." Then he turned away from me to talk on the phone.

I retrieved my purse from Scarlett and tucked the cashier's check inside. I sat down on a patch of grass and rested my head between my folded knees.

Mateo sat down next to me and said, "They're on their way."

"I don't know what I would've done without you."

"Glad I could help," Mateo replied.

We sat in silence as I watched butterflies and bumblebees flit from bloom to bloom in the manicured flower bed to my right.

"I don't know anything about repairs. Your uncle won't take advantage of me, will he?"

"Nah. That's not the way Gonzales men were raised."

"I can see that." I hoped my lopsided smile would convey the gratitude I felt.

I stayed in the grass when the tow truck arrived because Mateo jumped up to greet the driver. The crunching and scraping and clunking only served to heighten my anxiety. Scarlett's front end was intact, so they towed her with her broken tail-end suspended in the air. She looked as sad and hopeless as I felt.

Mateo let me ride in silence to the body shop. His uncle, gracious and kind, conducted an initial damage assessment and assisted me in contacting the right people at my insurance company. All said and done it amounted to thousands of dollars in damage. Not to mention, I would have to cover the cost of a rental for at least two weeks—maybe more.

"Can I give you a lift to the rental place?" Mateo offered.

"Yes, please. But first, can we stop back at the bank? I need to deposit a check."

CHAPTER FIVE

I PIDDLED. I swept the kitchen floor—which took all of two minutes. A good four sweeps and the whole of the expanse was touched. I walked into the guest room and adjusted the blanket on the foot of the bed that had not been slept in for months. I turned and straightened a pencil on the desk I never used—always opting for the counter-height bar separating my postage stamp-sized kitchen from the living area.

I rounded the corner from the guest room into the bathroom to check my hair and makeup in the mirror. I plucked a rogue intruder growing between my eyebrows. I reapplied my lip gloss and fluffed my curls.

I gathered trash from baskets around the house into a large, black bag and took the half-empty sack to the can tucked in the corner of my backyard. I went back inside, wet a paper towel, and walked back out to the makeshift patio I had made out of sixteen concrete squares. It created a pad big enough for a small, wooden bistro table and two chairs. I wiped the dust from the tabletop I never sat at because I always felt claustrophobic in the backyard. A fence loomed on two sides of the house and created a dog-run-sized area no wider than two and a half passes of the lawn mower.

I returned to the kitchen, refilled my coffee, propped myself on a stool at the bar, and opened my laptop to review my notes for today's meeting with Mr. Easton. The game plan Maggie and I had mapped out before—

Before.

Everything from here on out with Maggie was going to be measured by before Mountain Home and after Mountain Home.

Don't look back, Joy. Just keep moving forward.

I grabbed my phone and called Beth.

At the sound of Beth's greeting, I hurled my anxious thoughts at her. "Why am I so nervous?"

"Good morning to you, too," she replied with a laugh.

"Sorry. Good morning. I'm—it's—I'm a wreck, and I'm not normally a wreck."

"Talk the crazy out, girl. Actually, wait a sec. Let me refill my coffee." After a moment of silence, Beth returned with an, "Okay. I'm ready. Go."

"I'm never going to be able to please everyone."

"Who is everyone?"

"The committee."

"Is pleasing everyone the goal?" Beth always knew the right questions to ask.

"I guess it's my hope," I admitted.

"Are you meeting with the committee today or something?"

"No. I have a meeting with the Bible teacher, Mr. Easton." I stood up and started pacing. "He's head of the committee," I added.

"So you're nervous about meeting Mr. Easton?"

"Not really. Well—maybe. I don't know what to expect with him.

I haven't met him yet, but from how he's been described, I'm picturing an old theologian who likes to smoke cigars and drink whiskey. You know the kind. Set in his ways and not very open to all these newfangled ways youngsters do things these days."

Beth sat in silence. I could picture her quietly sipping her coffee laden with cream and sugar and patiently enduring the crazy I heaved at her.

"There are so many obstacles," I whined.

"Could you drum up support from the committee?" she asked.

"A committee is always a bucket of obstacles on its own. Everyone has their own ideas. And the people I've met so far are a minefield of conflicting opinions."

I walked back into the bathroom and stuck my nose close to the mirror looking for flaws.

"Can't Maggie help?"

I stood straight up and watched my face turn into stone. "I'm not going to ask anything else of Maggie." My tone matched the hardness of my reflection.

Beth's voice softened with caution. "Is there something going on with Maggie?"

"Nothing I can't handle."

"Okay, let's back up," Beth transitioned. "What is your very next step?"

"Meeting with Mr. Easton in…" I glanced at my watch, "an hour."

"Do you know what you're gonna say?"

"Yes. I have a solid plan."

"And you think he'll reject it?" Beth asked.

Boom. There it was. If he rejected the plan, I'd have to start over. And I was done starting over.

"It's possible."

"But you won't know until after this meeting with Mr. Easton."

"Right."

"Okay, then. Let's pray right now."

I knew better than to object. First of all, Beth never gave any space to object. Second of all, I could use the prayers.

Beth was the only person I believed actually prayed when she said she would. I believed her because she always stopped and prayed in the moment. I think it was her way to get me to pray with her, too. She was on to something. Because pretty much the only time I prayed was when I prayed with Beth.

"God, Your Word says we are not to be anxious about anything, but should present our requests to You with thanksgiving. First of all, we thank You for this opportunity for Joy to create something that will help a Christian school shine like a light on a hill in their community. We lay Joy's concerns at Your feet and ask for Your favor as she meets with Mr. Easton today. And—"

A knock at the door snatched my attention. "Um. Sorry, Beth. We're gonna have to say 'Amen' because someone's at my door."

"Oh. Okay. I'll keep praying. Give me an update after your meeting."

"Will do. And thanks. As usual."

I slipped on my heels, wiped the wrinkles from my light tan suit skirt, and made my way to the front door. I peeked through the peephole to see what looked to be a delivery person in a bright blue button-up shirt and matching ball cap with a logo I couldn't distinguish.

I opened the door to a man holding a leash to a dog that looked familiar.

"Joy Swallow?"

"Yes?" I replied with a question in my voice.

"Delivery from Mimsy Thompson. Sign here, please."

I took the clipboard because he handed it to me. I signed on the line because he asked me to. When I handed the clipboard back, he handed me the leash.

"The *dog* is the delivery?" my voice raised to one notch below shriek.

The man looked straight at me, tapped the red logo on his shirt that read "Pet Porter," and turned to walk back to his truck.

I looked at the dog, who sat practically motionless with rump on the ground, straight front legs, a tilted head, and a dripping tongue. Pant. Pant. Pant.

"Wait!" I cried.

"Not leavin' yet," he proclaimed without turning around. He retrieved a dog crate from the back of the open transport truck and a large basket wrapped in cellophane and tied with a bright red bow.

He set the crate on my stoop. The dog didn't move other than to lean over and sniff the crate.

The man held the basket out with both hands. "Pet Porter would like to be the first to rejoice with you and—" The man stopped to look at the tag on the basket, cleared his throat, and started again with stilted words, "Pet Porter would like to be the first to rejoice with you and Piper. She and this basket of necessities have been delivered for your delight. May her presence enrich your life with endless happiness and cherished memories."

I stared at the basket in my face because Mr. Pet Porter's head was hidden behind it. He kept his arms extended and tilted his head to the side to look at me. "Well, aren't ya gonna take it?"

I blinked. And I must have been holding my breath, because air rushed into my lungs waking me from my stupefied stance.

"No," I declared, holding the leash out toward him with a

straight arm.

Mr. Pet Porter shrugged, ignored my extended hand, and set the basket down on top of the pet carrier. He turned to walk back to his truck.

"Wait!" I called out again. "I said I don't want the dog!" My voice matched the frenetic feeling that washed over me.

He reached into the back of the transport truck and held up the clipboard. "You already signed." And with that, he closed the back doors. One bang. Two bangs. The driver's door slammed, the engine revved, and he drove away—the company's tag line on the back declaring "Your pet's journey is our priority."

But it's NOT my pet!

I looked down at Aunt Mimsy's dog. She sat there looking expectant as she panted. She wasn't a big dog, but she wasn't small either. Her straight fur seemed like it would be soft if I wanted to touch it. She looked like cinnamon-hued watercolor paint had been spilled all over her white fur. And her eyes were different colors—one blue and the other hazel.

I grunted as I dragged the basket-topped crate inside and closed the door. I looked at the leash in my hand and decided against letting go as I retrieved my phone from the kitchen counter. Piper trotted along with me then sat, stared, and panted. Pant. Pant. Pant.

I searched for Great-Aunt Mimsy in my contacts, tapped her mobile number, and prayed she would pick up.

"Oh, hey, darlin'," Mimsy answered. "I don't have time to talk. They're herding us onto this bus like cattle. Did Piper get there okay?"

"Yes. About that," I began.

"Oh, good. I can't bring her to Oregon with me, and I knew you'd take good care of her."

"Oregon?" I asked confused. I could hear indistinct voices and shuffling on the other end of the line.

"I bit the bullet and decided to move to that assisted living place with my friend, Cheryl. No pets allowed, though."

"Aunt Mimsy, I love you, but—"

"I love you, too, sweet girl. Check on the house from time to time, okay?" Before I could respond, I heard talking but it was too muffled to understand. Then her voice came back full force and startled me as she snarled, "I'm comin'! Hold your horses. Okay, I'm about to get left behind. I'll call you when I get settled." And she hung up.

I closed my eyes and rubbed my temples. *I need another cup of coffee.*

Piper remained by my side as I poured the coffee into a travel mug. I left the top off to cool a bit, holding it in my right hand as I looked at my watch on my left wrist. I needed a plan to do something with the dog so I wouldn't miss my meeting with Mr. Easton.

Just then, an alarm went off on my phone. Piper barked at the alarm and jumped up on me. The entire cup of coffee spilled down my dry-clean-only skirt, filling my shoes with hot liquid, too.

"Ouch, ouch, ouch!" I dropped the cup and the leash and kicked off my shoes. Piper jumped back as the metal cup clanged on the floor. She ran to the living room and hid under the coffee table. In shock, I stared at the small lake of coffee on my kitchen floor with the alarm on my phone still sounding.

Growling with disgust, I turned off my five-minute warning to be thirty minutes early and ran to my bedroom. All my other suits were at the cleaners, so I slipped on the jeans spread out on my bed—the only pair of clean pants available. I grabbed a suit coat to dress up my blouse, slid on a pair of flats, stomped into the living room, and grabbed the dog crate.

After putting the crate in the back seat of my rental, I stormed back into the house, grabbed the leash, and practically dragged Piper to the car. Luckily, she jumped right in the car and into the crate. I flung the crate door shut and latched it, then slammed the door.

CHAPTER SIX

I ALTERNATED WATCHING THE ROAD, the clock, and Piper in the rearview mirror of my small rental sedan. She lay in the crate, her head resting on folded paws like a proper lady. A sorrowful lady.

My racing heart slowed as I pulled onto the peaceful tree-lined drive leading to Berean Christian Academy. Dappled sunshine danced through the trees as the leaves clapped in the gentle breeze. I had fifteen minutes to spare before my appointment with the "esteemed" Mr. Easton.

The tunnel of trees ended at a large fountain, boasting what appeared to be the Ten Commandments etched into large stone tablets embedded in boulders. Sheets of water sparkled as they cascaded over the rocks. A stucco-and-brick chapel towered in the background. The large stained glass window near the peak of the front facade boldly displayed a golden cross with rays of blue emanating from it.

A sign indicated the cross street would take me to the gym toward the right and the front office to the left. Maggie told me Mr. Easton's classroom was above the gym, so I headed that way.

I pulled into a spot near the doors of the two-story metal building, put the car in park, and opened all of the windows. I turned with a pointed finger and as stern a voice as I could muster, "Stay here. Be good."

As soon as I walked away from the car, Piper started barking. I glanced at the car, around the mostly empty parking lot, then at my watch, and pulled on the gym door.

It was locked. The sign on the door instructed me to check in at the front office. I stomped my foot with a grunt and scrambled back to the car to head back the way I came.

As soon as I got back in, Piper silenced. I glared at her in the rear-view mirror. "Really? This is how it's gonna be?"

The "Main Building" didn't match the chapel or the gym. It was a long, narrow, one-story building with siding and an aging shingle roof. The large letters on the glass doors in the middle of the building indicated I had located the front office. I parked at the far end of the parking lot under a tree—less for the shade and more for the distance from anyone else visiting the office. I feared Piper's clamor drawing attention more than someone stealing my car from a closed private campus, so I left the car running this time—with the AC on and windows shut tight. As soon as I exited the vehicle, Piper resumed her protest. I refused to look at her, and shut the door to muffle the commotion.

This door was locked, too, but I pressed the buzzer, and the door unlatched. I located the reception area immediately inside the door to the right, and the sign on the front desk read "Mrs. Molly Carrol—Receptionist." Molly's face puckered as if biting into a lemon as she looked me up and down.

I glanced at my jeans, still seething about the dog. Blessing Molly with a broad smile, I chirped, "I'm here for an appointment with Mr. Easton, and the sign on the gym said I needed to check in here first."

She tapped a clipboard, picked up a phone receiver, and punched the number pad. "Mr. Easton, you have a visitor."

I retrieved the pen on a chain and filled in the boxes requesting my name, phone number, and time in. I set the pen down and wiped my damp hands on my jeans.

Replacing the receiver with a clatter, she grunted. "He's expecting you. Go back to the gym. From the lobby, take the stairs on the left, and his classroom is the third door on the right."

"Okay, but the gym door was locked."

"Yes. That's our safety protocol." She slid a key card across the counter. "You'll need this to get in the building, but you must return it to me before leaving campus." She turned away and dug in a filing cabinet.

"Thanks. I'll be sure to do that." I grabbed the key card and slid it into my back pocket.

"Wait," she said with her back toward me. She swiveled on her office chair, rolled toward me, and slid a piece of paper across the counter. "It looks like you need this as well." The heading read "Campus Dress Code."

My neck flushed with heat. "Thanks, Molly."

"We use last names on this campus."

"Oh, um…thank you, Mrs. Carrol."

She turned back to her computer and clacked away on the keyboard.

I tapped the counter twice and turned away. *Good talk.*

Piper was still barking when I returned to the car. Only this time, she didn't stop when I slid into the driver's seat. "I can't bring you with me to this appointment." She stopped barking and begged me with pleading eyes. When she started barking again, I sighed to myself, "But I obviously can't leave you in here either."

Backtracking toward the gym, I passed the tree-lined drive. I longed to use it as an escape route from further disaster. My only hope was that this great mentor of Berean Christian Academy would be a dog lover.

Why not double down and bring a dog? How much worse can it get?

Pulling into the same spot as before, this time with only two minutes to spare, I opened her crate and clipped a leash to Piper's collar. She hopped out in silence but immediately pulled on the leash to explore.

I yanked the leash. "Piper. I'm in charge here. Don't mess this up for me."

I walked up to the door and paused for a moment with my eyes closed. I took a centering breath and swiped the key card, entered the lobby, and located the staircase to the left. It led to a hallway with a brick wall on the left and closed doors on the right. Signs hung above each door with the teachers' names on them. I spotted Mr. Easton's sign three doors down as Mrs. Carrol had promised. Light poured from the open door into the dim hallway.

I wrapped the leash around my right hand to keep Piper by my side. I peeked into the classroom. The modular desks, all triangular in shape, neatly fit together in groups of four, forming squares. I counted six groups outfitted with rolling chairs. A big-screen TV filled one wall, and I caught sight of the Coates tracking camera mounted to the ceiling. The other wall featured a large digital whiteboard. I saw the back of a man in a navy sport coat and khaki slacks digging in a set of repurposed lockers in the back corner.

I cleared my throat and knocked on the open door.

"Come on in," the man called out, his back unmoving as he beckoned me inside with rapid waves of his left hand.

Piper pulled at the leash, and I jerked back and tightened the leash around my hand. Thankfully she remained silent.

I sucked in a breath as the man closed the locker and turned to greet us. This was not the old balding Bible teacher I had envisioned. He looked to be my age, was over six feet tall, with a trim build, dark hair, a pressed shirt and tie under his navy sport coat, and brown business sneakers.

We closed the distance between us enough that I could see that his thick black glasses framed blue eyes the color of Piper's right eye—eyes that lit up when he noticed the dog.

"Mr. Easton?" I choked out, my mouth bone dry.

"Call me Chance," he said, squatting down to pet Piper. "And who is this?" He scrubbed her head between her ears. I never understood why people changed the tenor of their voice when talking to dogs.

"This is Piper. I'm so sorry. I just—well—it's a long story. I just couldn't leave her in the car. She was losing her mind."

Piper reveled in Chance's attention. She flung herself on her back, coaxing him to rub her belly. I wiped my open hand on my jeans. I finally discovered one benefit of the dog—Chance's hands were otherwise engaged, so he didn't try to shake mine.

"I can only imagine having a dog on campus is way worse than my dress code violation."

"So, you met Molly."

"Yes. I met *Mrs. Carrol.*" I waved the temporary key card.

I loosened the leash a bit and wriggled my fingers. My hand tingled as the blood began to flow again.

"Her bark is worse than her bite," Chance looked up with a crooked smile. "So to speak."

"Clever."

Chance smirked. "I know Piper's name, but I still don't know yours."

My face flushed as I started to untangle the leash to offer my hand, but I reached down and patted Piper instead.

"I'm Joy. Joy Swallow."

"Nice to meet you both," he said, standing. Piper jumped on him with paws on his midsection. I cringed as she licked his face. "She's beautiful."

Do you want her?

"I have a Border Collie at home, but I've always thought Australian Shepherds were gorgeous."

Ah. So Piper is an Australian Shepherd. I would have to do an Internet search when I got home to see what a Border Collie looked like.

Chance crossed the room and closed the door. "Here you go, Piper. Sniff away!"

"Are you sure?"

"She's fine." He motioned to a group of desks, "We can sit here." I let go of the leash, and Piper began inspecting every nook and cranny of the room.

I must have bumped the chair as I sat down because it almost rolled out from under me. My less-than-graceful plop into the chair reflected the entire morning—off-balance at every turn. "Thanks for meeting with me. Maggie—er—Mrs. Hensley said you're heading up the committee approving the video and could help me."

"What'd you have in mind?"

I launched into my prepared speech about how the video could promote the school and the Coates camera in a way that would benefit both institutions.

"I only need a live classroom setting. I can handle the rest with my videographer."

"We could use my classroom."

I pushed my shoulders back. "Is the science lab set up with a Coates camera?"

"Yes." Chance tucked his hands in his front pockets and leaned back slightly.

"I think science sells better."

"But we're a Christian school."

"And Christianity and science don't mix?" I replied with a hint of mockery.

"Touché," Chance's sly smile conceded my victory.

I tossed my hair and giggled, then froze and blinked. I had a job to do, and flirting with the Bible teacher was not in the description.

"Okay. Miss Swallow. It's obvious you have a vision." He smiled. "Or is it Mrs. Swallow?"

"Oh, no. It's Miss. Definitely Miss." *Definitely Miss? Joy, what the heck?*

"Obviously, you have a vision, and I am but your humble servant," Chance bowed with one arm across his midsection and the other spread out. His eyes flickered with playfulness.

I smirked—willing a threatening blush to remain at bay. "Actually, Maggie suggested someone." I pulled out my phone and tapped my notes to find the name. "Jackson?"

At that moment, the door opened, and a teenage boy and girl entered. Piper scampered across the room and ping-ponged back and forth between the two.

"Piper!" I shrieked.

"Well, hello, Piper," the boy said, laughing. Piper continued bounding between the two, trying to lick their faces. They changed their voices, too—oohing and aahing about Piper's kisses. *Why would they let her lick their faces?*

"So, you've met Piper," Chance said. "And Miss Swallow, this is Jackson and Olivia."

I raised my hand in a meek wave. They waved back, giggling and attempting to pet Piper.

"Actually, Jackson, Miss Swallow was just talking about you."

Jackson raised his eyebrows.

"She's putting together a promotional video for the school, and Mrs. Hensley said you'd be willing to be the star."

"Always," Olivia responded for Jackson with a grin and an elbow nudged into his side. He shrugged and looked at me.

"I want to film in the science classroom," I explained. "Is there a flashy experiment you could conduct on camera?"

"Elephant toothpaste would be awesome," Jackson said with bright eyes and voice. Piper lost interest in the kids and started sniffing around the classroom again.

"Elephant toothpaste?" I asked.

"It's an experiment that uses hydrogen peroxide, dish soap, yeast, and food coloring. It foams up like crazy."

I doubted I would forget the name of the experiment, but logged it in my notes app anyway. "Perfect."

"Is it something the homeschool kids can try, too?" Chance asked.

Turning to me, he explained, "We have students taking our classes live from home." He pointed at the Coates camera mounted on the ceiling, "That camera follows the teacher around the classroom." He pointed at the big screen at the back of the room, "The teacher can see the students logged into class on that screen."

"So, can they follow along?" Chance asked Jackson again.

"Oh, yeah," Jackson assured. "There's nothing toxic or anything."

"One more thing," Chance said. "How can we make it from a biblical worldview?"

"Sorry, Mr. Easton. I'm not in class right now," Jackson said, grabbing Olivia's hand. "We'll leave that to you," he turned with a smile and a wave.

Chance grunted and looked at me. "Did you see that? And I don't even know why he stopped by," he laughed.

Jackson and Olivia left the door ajar, and Piper looked up from across the room and dashed for the opening. I grabbed the leash as Piper ran by. Chance jumped up and flung the door closed. The momentum from Piper's sprint jerked me toward him. Her exodus blocked, Piper circled around us until the leash pulled us together in an awkward jumble of arms and dog.

In my wordless haste to step out of the leash, I lost my balance and fell against Chance with both hands flat on his chest and knocked him against the wall.

"Whoa," he laughed, steadying me with gentle hands around each arm. His touch sent sparks through to my fingertips.

I avoided eye contact as I untangled myself.

Chance asked, "Where do you take Piper to play?"

"I—I'm not sure," I mumbled. I took a few steps back and resisted the urge to yank the leash as punishment.

Chance looked at me questioningly.

"Like I said, it's a long story. I just got Piper today."

"I take Ruby to the dog park in Morrison Park."

"I'll check it out," I said, with eyes averted as I wiped invisible dirt from my jeans.

"Maybe I'll see you there sometime."

This time I blushed and returned his gaze, "I'd like that."

CHAPTER SEVEN

THE VAST LOBBY of Coates Inc. boasted soaring ceilings, stained concrete floors, and modern furniture. The four groupings of four white leather chairs created a runway to the receptionist.

As I approached the receptionist desk floating in the modern expanse, my gaze landed on a familiar face. Mateo looked sharp in his light gray suit and neon green bow tie as he casually leaned against the tall counter. He stood upright as I drew near. His bright white smile stood out against his neatly groomed black beard and mustache. "Hey, there!" He gave me a side hug and directed me to scan my ID and pose for a photo for a visitor badge.

At least I have one reliable friend in this place.

"I didn't expect a welcoming committee," I said.

"John asked me to meet you and bring you to his office for a minute before your meeting with Maggie's team."

My stomach sunk. I hoped to avoid John and Maggie. I knew it was naive, but I still hoped. "I didn't plan for that in my schedule."

"I'm sure he won't take long," Mateo assured me as we began the trek up the stairs. "In other news, Tío Eduardo says your Jeep should be done next week."

"And for that, I am grateful. I sure miss Scarlett," I smiled. "I can't thank you enough for helping me that day."

"So you said in your thank you note. Nice touch."

"It's the least I could do. We don't know each other that well, or I'd offer to cook."

"I'm a fan of homemade meals, but I can't cook and neither can my girlfriend," Mateo said. "So let's be friends." His eyes sparkled.

I laughed out loud. "Done."

We stopped at the coffee station. "Coffee?" Mateo offered. The shiny black coffee maker looked like it belonged in a high-end bistro. It featured a touch screen menu that suggested I could choose a flat white, cortado, cappuccino, and more. Mateo placed a clear, glass mug with a Coates Incorporated logo on the tray and waved his hand like it was a prize in a game show.

"Always," I said. I tapped on "americano," heard the grinder, then watched my brown liquid prize drip into the mug. "I could get used to this," I said.

Mateo reached under the cabinet and grabbed a container of beans. "It's a nice perk, I'm not gonna lie," he said over the sound of the whole beans clattering into the reservoir.

"So, how long have you worked for John?"

"Right out of college. I went to a job fair and met with someone else from Coates. Somehow my résumé ended up on John's desk." He snapped the lid back on the container and put it back in the cabinet. "I'll never forget my interview with him. We met in a downstairs conference room. I was already equally impressed and intimidated by the lobby—"

"I can see that," I interjected.

"—and he was sitting at the end of a huge conference table and leaning back in his chair like a boss. I knew right then I wanted to work for him."

"Because he was lounging in a conference room at a fancy office?" I sipped my coffee.

"No. Because I could feel his power and control."

That bit of information did not bring me comfort. Powerful, controlling, and a cheater—not someone I wanted my new friend to emulate.

"Could you show me where conference room number three is?" I asked. "I want to put my bag down and see the space before my meeting with the team." I hoped to delay having to see John until after the meeting and then have something come up and make a quick escape.

"Sure, it's right over here." Mateo's pace slowed and brows furrowed as we walked up to a glass room filled with people. "There must be a scheduling error. Let's go ask Maggie."

I swung my arm to dramatically look at my watch, plastered on an expression I hoped would display nervousness, and fumbled with some folders in my bag careful not to spill my hot coffee. "I'll wait here. I only added a few minutes of buffer to look over my notes and—"

"You'll do great," Mateo said and guided me by my elbow away from the conference room. "I'll go check with Maggie for you."

"Oh, thank you," relief washed over me as Mateo continued guiding me down the hall. "I'll just—"

I stopped when I saw John through glass walls sitting at his desk and tapping on his computer. Mateo reached in and knocked on the open door. He turned to me with a smile, "He only needs a minute. I'll go check with Maggie about the conference room."

John took off his glasses as he looked up with a smile. "Joy!

Thanks for stopping in," he waved at me to come in and motioned toward the chair across from his desk.

I sat on the edge of the seat with my arms clutching my bag like I was at the principal's office.

"Let's talk about this video," John said with a take-charge tone.

I raced through various possibilities in my mind, attempting to decipher his intention. "I'm ensuring the Coates Camera is a notable aspect of the—"

John waved his hand like he was shooing a fly. "I'm sure all that will be fine. I'm talking about how my son, Jackson, will be portrayed."

I sucked in a quick breath and started to choke and cough. *Jackson is his son?* I sipped my coffee to buy me some time. I mustered as much confidence as possible and replied, "Jackson has provided us with a great experiment that will be impressive on video. The specific details are getting nailed down in today's meeting."

"Jackson is a strong athlete and athletics is how BCA will attract new students. Play to that as much as you can."

"Mr. Easton also wanted—"

"Mr. Easton is a one-trick pony," he snapped.

My mouth and my eyes widened.

John added, "But Maggie says you are a brilliant marketer, so I'm sure you can incorporate all interests seamlessly."

"I'll do my best."

"I have faith in you."

I winced—a reaction to the combination of his blindingly flashy smile, the weight of his expectations, and my growing dislike of this charming man.

I heard a knock behind me. I turned to see Mateo leaning in the doorway. "Joy, I found the right conference room."

I jumped up and sloshed some coffee on my leather bag. I looked up to see John working at his computer again. *I guess we're done. Thank goodness.*

CHAPTER EIGHT

I PACED AT THE FRONT of conference room #5. Mateo said he'd make sure the team knew about the location change and I awaited their arrival. I added John's request to highlight athletics in the video to my notes—in pencil—a passive aggressive nod to the overtly aggressive feelings I had about John and Maggie and their ties to—and continued influence over—the BCA project.

I sat at the head of the table and then shifted to one side. I wanted to lead from the middle—an active member of the team, not simply the leader of it. My knee shook under the table. I dug my heels into the carpet. I wiped my hands on my suit pants and tucked my hair behind my ears.

Nervcited.

Nervcited is how Beth always described a combination of nervousness and excitement. I was nervous because there was so much at stake for me with this project. I was excited because I'd never worked with professionals like this before—especially ones with expensive software and equipment and years of experience to produce something prizewinning.

Oh, and those new feelings of dread lay over all of it like a weighted blanket since I discovered the brilliant mentor I looked up to was—well, wasn't who I thought she was. I dreaded working on this project with her and I dreaded working on this project without her.

Maybe I should say a prayer. Dear God, keep me from looking foolish, and may this be a team I can connect with and lead well—without Maggie—to win this contest. Amen.

One by one, the three-person team assigned by Maggie joined me in the conference room.

A woman in her mid-twenties walked in. Her strikingly straight black hair cascaded over her shoulders framing a serious face with Asian features and large, round glasses. With a firm handshake she introduced herself as Lan, the copywriter, choosing a chair next to mine.

A young man strolled into the room. His kind white smile contrasted with his smooth black skin and brightened not only his face, but the room as well. He gave me a fist bump and I noticed a slight southern accent when he said he was Roderick, the videographer.

Roderick was still taking his seat directly across from Lan when the final member of the team sauntered in. His confident demeanor told me he knew how handsome he was with his short blond hair, dazzling blue eyes, and crooked smile. "Let's get this show on the road!" he declared as he flung himself into the chair adjacent to Roderick. At my questioning look he added with a salute, "Greetings! I'm Andrew. Graphic designer extraordinaire!"

Maggie called this her crack team. When I asked about other projects they collaborated on, I discovered they worked together almost every time. As a new leader, I knew I needed to get to the root of what motivated them—something Maggie drilled into me during our mentor-match days.

"I'd like to get to know you a little better," I appealed. "Bring me up to speed on a project you were most passionate about, and how your efforts were critical to its success."

Andrew leaned over the table and placed his palms face-down in front of me. "We don't need your master's program psychology. We've been doing this together for years. Lay out the project, and let's get to work."

My stomach recoiled as I willed my face to remain neutral. "We can do that. It's just that I'm as committed to you as I am to the project. If I can arrange things so we can all work from our strengths and passions, the end result will be better."

Roderick's benevolent smile and southern charm warmed the room as he added, "I think what Andrew is getting at is you'll discover our strengths and passions as we work on the project. We're ready to do our jobs."

I felt my authority slipping away. I wondered what Lan thought as she sat there in silence, but I didn't want to turn to look at her and make it seem like I wanted her to rescue me.

I wished for a moment that I had created a plan with Maggie to hold this introductory meeting. I needed her wisdom to walk this road with her team. That thought repulsed me because I didn't want to have anything to do with Maggie. I was hoping to take this team, finish the project, and ride off into the sunset. I hated that I needed her.

The meeting continued to go downhill. I struggled to explain my vision and the requirements from various stakeholders. When I indicated the video must come from a biblical worldview as Chance had requested, Lan asked me to define that and I couldn't really answer her. All three of them argued that the science experiment didn't have anything to do with athletics.

I pretended to get a text. "It looks like Maggie needs me for a minute," I lied. "Can you continue brainstorming options while I'm gone?"

"Sure," Lan said. She took the dry-erase marker from my hand and stood in my place at the whiteboard.

I retreated down the hall to Maggie's office and rapped my knuckles on the open glass door.

Maggie's flawless makeup, contemporary hairstyle, and trendy attire corresponded with every other time I'd met with her. I don't know what I expected. Perhaps part of me wanted her to look flushed or apprehensive since having her moral failure exposed. A larger part of me wanted to continue to act like it never even happened and refocus on the tasks at hand.

"Good morning, Joy." Maggie took off her reading glasses, smiled, and motioned for me to sit across from her.

"Sorry to intrude."

"You're not intruding. How did your meeting with the team go?"

"It's still in progress," I said, tucking my hair behind my ears. "That's what I came to talk to you about."

I filled Maggie in on the team meeting and my approach thus far. Maggie tapped the arm of her reading glasses on the desk as I explained. I detected slight tension around the edges of her persimmon-colored lips.

"What do you need from me?" She wasn't going to make this easy on me.

"I guess I'm uneasy about the team. They don't seem to be enthusiastic about the project at all. How can I inspire them?"

Maggie leaned back in her chair and paused before replying, "Actually, Joy, let's start with you. Do you believe you are capable of handling this project?"

"Yes," I hesitated, then added, "I really do."

Maggie flung herself forward again and placed her elbows on her desk. She leaned toward me and said, "Okay, good. So what traits and skills do you possess that give you that level of confidence?"

I thought for a moment, straightened my shoulders and asserted, "I am driven. I am willing to work at something until it's perfect, but I'm also eager to improve."

Maggie smiled. She seemed pleased with my answer.

"Perfect. Use all of that to move the project forward. Keep the end goal front and center. You want that feature in *Marketing Trends Magazine*. In fact, grab a copy of the most recent issue and put it somewhere where you'll see it every day. Keep your focus on that."

My mind wandered to my vision board. I could almost feel the breeze flowing off of Lake Tahoe as I sat with Julia at the retreat. Maggie was right. If I focused on the prize, everything else would fall into place.

Maggie reached into her desk drawer and pulled out a marker and some sticky notes. She wrote elegantly on three squares and handed them to me.

Driven.

Hard worker.

Continuously improving.

"Here," she said. "Add these to your magazine cover. Rehearse them every day. Use your skills and traits to keep you confident and motivated. This is what matters most."

"Thanks, Maggie."

"My pleasure," she smiled as she put her glasses back on. "Oh, and Joy"—she tilted her chin down and peered at me over the frames—"I suggested you because of your amazing talent. You have the power within you, but if you can't get the job done, I WILL take you off this project."

I stood stunned as she pushed her glasses up her nose and went back to work as if I had vanished.

I took methodical steps back to the conference room.

What have I gotten myself into?

I forced my thoughts to settle on Maggie's encouragement before the threat. I had no guarantee that future client situations would not be equally messy—albeit hopefully in different ways. I may have taken this job because of the contest, but I went out on my own because I believed my skills, talents, and driven nature would ensure my success.

You know what you're doing, Joy. You have what it takes. Stop looking for Maggie's approval. Stop looking for the team's approval. Listen to your client.

With renewed confidence I returned to the team meeting. I held my hand out for the marker from Lan. "So far I've laid out the mosaic pieces of this project and then listened to a bunch of complaining about the color and shape of the pieces. However, the voice of the client is the only voice that matters at this table. They've hired us to use these mosaic pieces to create a masterpiece. That's the job. So, let's finish up this proposal so we can celebrate."

As if on cue, Mateo stuck half his body inside the conference room door at such an angle that he would tumble to the floor if he released the door frame, "Did I hear a call to celebrate? I'll plan it! Salsa, chips, and margaritas at The Outpost downtown after work." He then snapped his body upright and walked away.

Everyone around the table laughed.

"Was he serious?" I asked.

"Mateo is always serious about getting together," Roderick confirmed.

"Live for each second without hesitation!" Andrew burst out with a finger raised to the ceiling. At my raised brow he added, "Mateo says that all the time. I think it's an Elton John quote or something."

"Okay, then. Now that we have something to look forward to, shall we get back to work?"

By the end of the day, the entire project was mapped out, scripted, and ready to email to Chance for approval. The team even incorporated my input and included me in their easy banter. I had never been more exhilarated at the collaboration and proud of the end result.

Mateo bopped back into the conference room. "It's quittin' time! I reserved the high-top table at The Outpost. Let's go!"

CHAPTER NINE

I SQUINTED AT THE BRIGHT BALL of fire in the sky putting "sun" in Sunday. I smiled at the greeter who welcomed me at the glass doors of my church. I wove my way through small clusters of people throughout the lobby as they laughed, talked, and hugged each other. I didn't really know many people, so no one stopped me to chat as I entered the sanctuary.

A full band filed onto the stage in the front as the lights dimmed. Two large screens flanked either side of the stage. I climbed the stairs at the back of the room to my favorite spot in the middle of a row about halfway up.

I prayed Piper would be fine in the backyard for the morning. I didn't have time to babysit and I couldn't pay for doggy daycare on the weekends, too. Plus, I needed to hear from God today more than ever.

The curt email from Chance late Friday evening said, "Tacking on a Bible verse does not make it from a biblical worldview. Try again."

A little harsh, Mr. Easton. I pictured a bright red F on our video proposal.

I knew I couldn't rely on Lan to adjust the copy I needed. She made it pretty clear during the meeting that not only was she agnostic, but she grew up in an agnostic home and had no language for the project. Although Roderick said he grew up in a home that attended church semi-regularly, he wasn't really trained in copywriting. Andrew was all over the place quoting Buddha and cliché phrases feigning substance. I figured I'd stick to relying on his graphic expertise.

Starting over once again.

I felt like when I was a kid and tried to build a tower made of playing cards. I would hold my breath as each card wobbled precariously until I could place another to stabilize it. With a ginger touch, I added layers until it inevitably fell. For hours I would try over and over again, sure that this time it would stand.

Is this persistence or delusion?

As the countdown clock clicked down to the start of the service, the lights flashed, the band played, and I let the music take me away. I closed my eyes and focused on the songs about God helping me fight my battles, to see my victory. The music swelled and shivers went down my spine. The hair on my arms stood on end and a lump rose in my throat.

The songs ended, but the pianist and drummer continued to play. The pianist's hands moved across the keyboard with a confident, sweeping motion as the intensity and volume of the notes increased. Simultaneously, the drummer brushed the cymbals and then increased the vigor and swiftness of each strike. My anticipation expanded in unison with the musical swell that reached its peak as piano and cymbals synchronized with electric force.

The pastor walked to a center microphone and podium with arms stretched wide and the auditorium erupted in applause.

"As we begin today, I need to remind you…you are…very powerful," Pastor's dramatic pauses only emphasized the stomach flip I felt.

I clapped with everyone in agreement as I recalled Maggie's words—"You have the power within you."

Pastor encouraged everyone to sit. I bounced a little in my seat as he continued.

"By entertaining feeble thoughts such as, 'This problem is too big,' or 'My dreams are beyond reach,' you nullify your own power."

I normally didn't take notes, but today I snatched my phone out of my purse and opened the notes app. Like the fireflies I captured in jars on summer nights as a kid, I recorded each idea as a treasure of light to me.

I practically skipped to my car at the end of service. I couldn't wait to meet up with Beth for lunch.

CHAPTER TEN

BETH AND I GREETED EACH OTHER with a tight hug. Our friendship stood strong against both liking strawberry-blond-haired-blue-eyed Benjamin in the second grade, middle school angst, her mom's betrayal of her family, moving states apart for college, and her working for me at Cup O' Joe. To be honest, Beth was better than me at breathing life into our relationship—always putting on my oxygen mask before her own.

"What're you doing in Boise?" I asked as we made our way to a quiet table in the courtyard.

I'd been enamored with courtyards since a trip to Savannah in high school. I would peek through the iron gates and envision classy dinner parties and rich conversations under twinkling lights. The Boise Bistro courtyard brought my visions to life with a slate patio and redbrick walls. Patio lights swooped over intimate tables for two. Oversized terracotta pots graced each corner, filled with fountain grass and hostas. Smaller pots, grouped around each base, spilled over with white patio roses.

Beth's cadence matched the bubbling fountain in the center of the back wall, "I promised Mom I'd meet with a girl from her church who's considering attending Multnomah next year. I made a weekend of it to spend some time with Mom and Dad and go to church with them."

I cringed a little on the inside thinking of Beth's dad.

Poor Mr. Carmichael.

I tucked a rogue curl behind my right ear and bent over to dig my phone out of my purse. "I have so much to tell you!" I started eagerly.

"But first, let's order!" Beth smiled knowingly. It may have happened once or twice that we had to take our lunches to go because once I got started, we forgot to order and ran out of time.

After the waiter retreated to submit our order, Beth put both hands flat on the table, leaned toward me slightly, looked me straight in the eye, and said, "Okay, go!"

I told her all about the rough start and collaborative ending of the team meeting, and carefully selected highlights of my encounter with John and chat with Maggie respectively. I hadn't told Beth about Maggie's affair with John—partially because I didn't want to give Maggie any more space in my mind than she already captured, and partially because I didn't want to dredge up painful memories for Beth. If they were painful for me to endure, I could only imagine how Beth would respond.

I opened my mouth to tell her all about the sermon when the waiter delivered our food.

When the server walked away, Beth asked, "Who are you up against in this contest?"

"The East Coast marketing department of Coates Inc. Their project is for a microloan company. Both Berean Christian Academy and Ezra Micro Loans use the auto-tracking cameras. It's innovative, really. Julia Coates chose two organizations she wants to support, they both get a professionally produced marketing video, and Coates walks away with two pieces highlighting their flagship camera in real-world settings."

I could feel myself getting more excited, and I started talking faster. "But the crazy thing is that this contest is tailor-made for me. Remember the vision boards we made in high school?"

"Of course. I remember you thought mine was way too sparkly," she remarked.

"Everything you did in those days was too sparkly." We both laughed. "Well, I kept mine, and added to it in college. I literally put 'Private meeting with the CEO of a major corporation' on my board under a picture of people sitting around a kitchen table."

Beth's eyes widened. "No way."

"Way," I bounced in my chair a little.

"But I thought winning the contest was more about helping you launch your new company and get clients through that magazine feature."

I shrugged, "Industry recognition will definitely beef up my portfolio. But you know me, I think finding the right people to learn from is most important. From what I know about Julia, the weekend with her at her lake house in Tahoe seems more life-changing." I shoved a huge forkful of salad into my mouth.

Beth moved her fork around her plate without actually eating. "I hate to even ask this—"

Her prolonged pause made me mumble a "what?" with a mouth full of lettuce.

"What happens if you don't win the contest?" Her eyes quivered as she held my gaze.

I swallowed hard and shook my head. "I'm not even going to think like that. I believe this is a 'promised land' moment for me, and I'm going to go in with a promised land mentality."

Beth wrinkled her nose and creased her brow in a question.

"That's what I was getting ready to tell you. The sermon today was EXACTLY what I needed to tap into my own power and take the next step in this project."

I barely paused long enough to take a sip of my water before continuing to babble on. "I was so stressed this morning heading to church because Chance—er, Mr. Easton—emailed me on Friday rejecting the video proposal. I had no idea where to start to fix it, but then when I got to church today, the sermon was on the power within us to do great things."

"Where did the pastor say this power comes from?"

Beth always wanted all the details.

"He said it comes from magnifying your greatness and minimizing your weaknesses. He said to play a new recording in your mind. Rather than playing the recording of our weaknesses and failings, change the recording."

"Give me an example," Beth prodded.

I tapped my phone to look at my notes. "Let's see, he said instead of saying, 'I'm unworthy, I'm not good enough,' say, 'I'm amazing. I'm marvelous. I'm wonderful.' He said that comes from Psalm 139."

I paused when the waiter approached our table and refilled our glasses. We murmured our thanks and he walked away.

Beth looked down at her salad and then slowly lifted her eyes to meet mine. "I'm familiar with that Psalm, but I always thought it was more about God than us."

"Well, anyway," I continued excitedly, "it's a strategy to rewire how you see yourself." I stabbed at my lettuce and took another bite.

"So, how's this going to help with your proposal?" Beth asked.

I explained how Pastor brought a telescope on stage. He looked through it the right way to talk about magnifying our potential and looked through it the wrong way to talk about minimizing our negative thoughts.

"That got me thinking that we could still use the science lab scene I had planned, but use a microscope to talk about magnifying the greatness God placed within us. Then I'm going to keep the magnification theme to tie in magnifying the abilities of BCA students in the classroom and athletics."

I took a few bites of salad and chased it with iced tea before continuing. "I needed the message this morning as much for me as for the project. I realized I had some pretty negative messages playing in my mind. I need to lean into my own greatness and get the job done, win the contest, and step into the future of my dreams—my very own promised land. I. Am. Able!" I made my declaration with a little too much verve. I knocked over my glass of tea and spilled it all over the table and myself.

The waiter rushed to my side with extra napkins and helped sop up the mess. Thanking him, I excused myself to the restroom to clean up and dry off.

When I returned to the courtyard, a man and woman stood at our table talking to Beth. Their backs faced me, but Beth looked up at them with a broad smile. She saw me approach and declared in a sing-song voice, "There's Joy."

The man and woman turned toward me to reveal Beth's parents. Mrs. Carmichael tilted her head and opened her arms wide, "Oh, Joy. It's been a lifetime since we've seen you."

Six years and counting, actually.

I stood stiffly as Mrs. Carmichael enveloped me and squeezed. I leaned in for Mr. Carmichael's silent side hug and patted his arm.

"Mom and Dad drove into Boise after church to meet some friends for a late lunch a few restaurants down," Beth explained.

Mrs. Carmichael talked about the preschool class they helped in at church, the pastor's main points in the sermon that morning, and the friends they were meeting down the road. Mr. Carmichael stood there with his hands in his pockets dutifully listening to his wife prattle on. I bent down and grabbed my purse.

"I can't believe we haven't seen you since you girls graduated high school," Mrs. Carmichael said.

"It's been a minute," I mumbled and slipped the strap from my purse over my shoulder.

"I guess I thought we'd see you when you moved back for your master's program, but I know how busy you were. And then when you two worked at Cup O' Joe, we missed you every time."

Hmm. Wonder how that happened?

"But here we are. And you're so beautiful. And Beth tells me you started your own company—"

"And got a dog. That I have to go see about. I'm so sorry I have to cut this short. It was good seeing you," I said to the Carmichaels. I looked at Beth and said, "I'll find the waiter for the check. I've got this one. Thanks for listening."

CHAPTER ELEVEN

I HEARD PIPER barking as soon as I put the rental in park under the carport.

I wonder how long she's been doing that? My neighbors are gonna hate me.

When I opened the gate to the backyard, she jumped up on me with muddy feet. There were holes where she had been digging all along the fence line, and one of the legs of my bistro chairs had gnaw marks.

I flung my head back with an exasperated cry, "Piper!"

She sat upright and panted, with her head tilted like, "Did I do something wrong?"

"Stay there," I said with a pointed index finger practically touching her nose. "We're going for a walk."

I stomped into the house, dropped my purse on the bar in the kitchen, and picked up Piper's leash. I locked the door behind me and attached the leash to Piper's collar. I yanked her across the street toward the park a few blocks away.

I had calmed a bit by the time we entered the park. Piper trotted beside me. An exhilarated squeal mixed with fear drew my eyes toward the merry-go-round. An older boy grabbed a bar and shoved hard. The merry-go-round spun faster and faster. A younger child held firm, braced with feet apart and a white-knuckled death grip on the arched bars that ran from the outer edge to the inner circle. Giggles and smiles transitioned to tears and begging "Bubba" to stop. With a toothy grin, Bubba pushed harder. A figure flashed onto the scene, snagging Bubba's arm and pulling him off the wheel of death. Did Dad come to the rescue? With one hand gripping the older boy's arm tightly, the father hampered the rotation by allowing each bar to slap against his other hand. Slap. Slap. Slap. The wheel slowed while Bubba pouted and his brother's lament transitioned to ragged breaths.

I drew in a deep breath and the cool air stung my lungs. I wished a father figure could step in and slow this spinning wheel of death I had jumped on. It thrilled me at first. Each spin of a new season held greater expectations and greater delight. Now my grip tightened as I contemplated hopping off.

Maggie's indiscretion dredged up all of the old feelings towards Mrs. Carmichael. I thought I hopped off that ride in time to avoid getting dizzy, but here I stumbled along filled with nausea at the reminder of it all.

Should I have kept the secret?

Piper tugged against the leash dragging me toward a man walking a goldendoodle on the path ahead.

I heard Beth's voice behind me. "Joy, wait up."

Her arrival didn't surprise me. We'd shared our phone location since we took that safety class years ago. I tried to sound casual. "I'm glad I left when I did. You should have seen the disaster Piper made in the backyard while I was gone."

"I see that." Beth pointed at the dirty paw marks on my pants. "But that's not why you left."

I turned and strolled down the path. Beth joined me on my left and Piper meandered on my right. I studied the cracked asphalt of the walking path. "No, really. I knew I needed to get back to Piper."

"That wasn't it. When you got back from the restroom, you were a different person."

I ran my fingers through my hair. "It's Maggie," I lied.

"What about Maggie?"

"Let's just say she's not who I thought she was," I mumbled. We stopped to let Piper sniff a pile of leaves.

"Go on."

"Maggie's having an affair with her boss." The admission whooshed out like a deflating balloon. I felt a weight lift from my shoulders.

"How do you know this?"

"I saw them. In Mountain Home," I slumped. "When I came out of Cup 'O Joe after meeting with you, I saw them kissing in front of that boutique hotel across the street."

"Do they know you know?"

"Yeah. Maggie saw me." I felt my neck heat up as my words flowed out like a faucet on full blast. "I don't think John saw me, but she definitely did because she had the nerve to text me almost immediately to ask me to keep it a secret."

I felt my heart race as I relived the memory. "As if that isn't bad enough, I keep thinking of her poor husband, Peter. I've spent time with him, and he's so kind and attentive to her. It's all so shocking and discouraging and brings back all of the awful memories of your—"

I stopped and covered my mouth with my hand, eyes wide with horror.

"Of my mom's affair?" Beth suggested.

"You knew?"

"I knew." Beth smoothed her skirt, then looked at me and added, "But I didn't realize you knew." Before I could respond, she continued with a distant voice, "It all kind of happened as I was moving away, and I felt such shame about it. I didn't know how to bring you into my pain." My eyes matched Beth's as we both welled up with tears. "But how?" she whispered.

"I was at your house one day, and you were in the downstairs bathroom when I needed it, so I ran upstairs to the hall bathroom. I heard a giggle as I came around the corner."

I pictured the taupe carpet and light blue walls. A series of framed school photos of Beth lined the hallway—kindergarten Beth, first-grade Beth, second-grade Beth…

"Your mom stood in the hall cupping the telephone to muffle the conversation. I heard her say something like, 'Oh Frank, don't say that!' When she saw me, the blood drained out of her face and she ended the call."

We stopped at a balance beam along the walking path. I sat down and let the leash out a little for Piper to explore. Beth sat beside me. We both looked out at the green space rather than at each other.

"As I normally do, I asked a question without filtering first," I fiddled with the end of the leash. "I asked, 'Frank? Are you having an affair with your accounting partner?' I don't even know why that was the first thing that popped into my head, but it hit the bullseye, because shock and guilt washed over her face. She begged me not to say anything to anyone—especially you. I didn't know what else to do, so I agreed."

"Oh, Joy," Beth reached out and placed her hand over mine. "I never understood why you withdrew from our family. I chalked it up to the fact that we were graduating and I was leaving and life was changing so fast. Plus, I blamed myself."

Beth jerked her body to face me with wide eyes. "You catching her must have been the catalyst for Mom to confess to Dad."

How could that be?

"I'm sorry I withdrew, Beth. I didn't know what else to do. I was glad she asked me to keep the secret because I didn't want your life to blow up with the truth, but I felt sick inside every time I talked to your dad." I turned to look away from Beth again. "And you're right. Things were changing so fast anyway. You moved away, and so did I, so I didn't even have to bump into them."

"*Aah.* So that was the change when you came back to the table," Beth said.

I don't know why I thought I could keep the truth from Beth. I dropped my chin to my chest in shame.

"Is that how you're feeling now? You want to keep Maggie's secret so Peter's life doesn't get blown up?" Beth asked.

How does she do that?

I turned to look at her again with tear-filled eyes. "I wish I could avoid Maggie like I did your folks. I don't understand how you move on from something like that without divorce. I don't want to be a part of that end-result for Maggie and Peter any more than I wanted to be a part of it between your mom and dad."

I tucked some rogue curls behind my ear. "How in the world did it NOT end in divorce for your parents?"

"Mom confessed and repented. That's a huge step." Beth leaned over and flicked a leaf from her shoe. "Also, it wasn't physical.

Not that an emotional affair is okay, but there were some lines she hadn't crossed yet. Like I said earlier, I wonder if God used you to protect her."

A gust of wind swirled a pile of leaves into a small funnel. They tossed and twirled like my memories. I thought because Mrs. Carmichael had asked me to keep it a secret that she kept the affair from everyone. To think that God might have used me—it didn't compute with how everything played out in my head over the years.

"Forgiveness for my dad was a process. It was an even slower process for me. You know, the thing that helped the most was to replace negative thoughts with the truth of God's Word."

"Like we talked about this morning."

"Sort of," Beth said. "Jesus said, 'My grace is sufficient for you, for My power is made perfect in weakness.' My counselor said that she did a study of the Greek words and the part about Christ's power being made perfect in weakness is better said, 'Christ's supernatural influence over reality is accomplished through my lack of physical or natural qualifications.'"

Beth paused and I shuffled my feet in the dirt.

"I wasn't qualified to fix my parents' marriage," Beth continued. "Heck, even Mom and Dad weren't qualified to fix their marriage. We needed the power of Christ—His supernatural influence over our reality."

"So, what'd you do?"

"First, we stopped trying to force it. Then counseling—lots of counseling for all of us to learn how to walk through the cycle of confession, repentance, and forgiveness where God brought restoration."

"I'm not sure Maggie's the repentant type."

"Maybe you'll make a difference in her story, too."

I doubted it. Truthfully, I hoped to get out of Maggie's story sooner rather than later. If I stayed on the merry-go-round longer than this contest for BCA, it might pick up speed, and I would never be able to get off.

CHAPTER TWELVE

I DIDN'T KNOW where to put my hands. I put my right arm on the door frame at the base of the open window. That felt weird, so I put both palms flat against my thighs. I started tapping my hands to the rhythm of the music playing from the radio. I stole a glance at Chance, pretending to check on Piper and Ruby in their crates in the back seat.

How did I let him convince me to do this?

My revised video proposal still did not meet Mr. Easton's standards. After a few emails back and forth regarding adjustments, we reached an impasse. Chance's next email to me asked for my cell phone number. He called immediately and said he sensed my frustration and had an idea. He asked if I was up for a drive with the dogs, and I agreed before I thought better of it.

Once we were on the road, Chance explained we were headed to Idaho City to meet Nanette Verity, the founder of Berean Christian Academy. He said he didn't do a good job of explaining the heart of the school and that once I heard from Nanette, the video would be the masterpiece he knew it could be.

Great. Another voice to incorporate into this project.

"You're gonna love Mrs. Verity," Chance said over the wind and radio.

I nodded with a forced smile. "Tell me about her."

"She's hard to describe. She's wise and kind. She loves God's Word. And she has a real knack for people. It's like she can scan your soul."

Chance's phone rang. He muted the radio, rolled the windows up and answered, "This is Chance. You're on speaker."

"Chance," a woman's voice came through the speaker. "It's Nanette."

"Hey, Mrs. Verity. How are you?"

"I'm blessed. But, Chance, I told you to call me Nanette. You don't work for me anymore." Nanette didn't have a Southern drawl, but her voice held the same cadence.

"I'm not sure I can do that, Mrs. Verity," Chance glanced at me with a grin.

"Well, I wish you would. Anyway, I'm checking on your ETA so I can be sure my dip is hot and fresh when you arrive."

Chance looked at the map displayed on his dash and replied, "It looks like we're about twenty minutes away."

"What a blessing. Okay, well, drive safe and I'll see you soon."

Chance babbled on about Mrs. Verity's cheese dip, a trail near her cabin he wanted to take Ruby down, his pastor's sermon on Sunday, a new song he added to his Favorites playlist, his lesson plan for Monday, and a book he was reading. Periodically, he asked for my opinion or feedback, but I was too nervous to say much.

Mostly I looked out the window and tapped my hands to the music. We turned down a narrow road with the wall of a mountain on our right and a steep ravine to our left.

The road curved to the right and we came face-to-face with a giant logging truck. Chance took his foot off the gas and tucked the car against the mountain wall. As his sedan rolled to a stop, the logging truck careened forward missing us by inches.

Chance turned his shoulders to face me. "Are you okay?"

I couldn't find breath to respond verbally, so I gave a slight nod of my head and peeled my fingers from the edge of my seat.

"Those logging trucks think they're the only ones on the road," Chance said as he eased his way back onto the asphalt.

"I can't believe you're so calm," I squeaked.

"It's my superpower," Chance grinned.

"Avoiding head-on collisions with logging trucks is your superpower?"

Chance laughed, "Staying calm in unexpectedly stressful situations."

We traveled a few more miles before Chance slowed and pulled onto a steep driveway leading to a log cabin that looked like it came out of a painting. The rounded logs were a golden hue and fit together perfectly with white chinking in between. The high peak of the roof boasted small windows on a second story. The green metal roof blended in with the mix of towering pine trees and clapping aspens.

A woman stood on the large deck that spanned the front of the cabin. She waved with a wide smile as our tires crunched to a stop on the gravel drive.

"That's Mrs. Verity," Chance said and waved back. He put the car in park and hopped out to release the dogs.

Mrs. Verity's short blonde hair allowed her pearl earrings to peek out through wisps of hair over her ears. Her rust-colored blouse highlighted her flawless skin and engaging copper eyes. Her pressed capris complemented her petite frame.

I don't know what I imagined. Maybe someone more traditional. Not necessarily older, because though she held it well, she must have been in her sixties. I thought she'd be frumpy. I had no idea why. Maybe because she used the word "blessed." I pictured the older ladies at church on potluck night—the ones wearing floral tops and matching polyester pants while plopping globs of mashed potatoes on my plate and telling me to "be blessed."

Ruby raced up the steps of the deck and went straight to a row of shiny silver dog bowls. Two held water and two held fresh food. Piper got the memo and followed.

I wiped my palm on my pants before reaching it out. "Good morning, Mrs. Verity. I'm Joy. Joy Swallow. It's nice to meet you in person."

"It's Nanette," she said shaking my hand. She stopped shaking and gave my hand a strong squeeze, "I insist."

"It's nice to meet you…Nanette," I tilted my head and smiled.

We hooked the dogs to light chains so they wouldn't run off. Then, for the next thirty minutes we sat inside enjoying Nanette's cheese dip Chance loved so much. We made small talk about the cabin, Idaho City, the dogs, and the gala Chance was charged with planning at BCA.

"Enough of all that," Chance said as he jumped up, gathered the plates, and put them in the sink. "Ruby and I are gonna check out that trail."

"Oh. Okay." I wished he would stay.

Nanette encouraged me to make myself at home while she cleaned up the dishes. I walked around the living room and admired the paintings adorning the walls. They depicted landscapes that looked very much like places I had seen all over Idaho, featuring pine trees and boulders with creeks running through each scene. I noticed "Verity" in the bottom right corners.

"Is this your work?" I asked.

"My husband, Ricky. I wish you could have met him. He's away on a business trip."

I made my way around the room to look at some photos on display on the log mantel. I saw a photo of Nanette smiling adoringly at a man I assumed was Ricky. A large group photo showed Nanette and Ricky among a small crowd of all ages including children and babies.

"Does your family live around here?" I asked.

"Spread throughout the Northwest, I'm afraid."

Another frame featured two photos side-by-side. The faded photo on the left displayed two young girls with matching "Camp Cascade" T-shirts hugging one another with heads tilted in full laughter. The photo on the right featured Nanette standing next to a tall woman with jet-black Afro-curls in a pixie cut that framed her dark, strikingly sculpted face—a face I had seen before.

"Is this Julia Coates?" My heart picked up speed.

"Who?" Nanette turned to see the picture I was pointing at. "Oh! Yes. That's Julia. We've been dear friends since middle school summer camp."

No. Way. This woman is friends with Julia Coates?

"She's sponsoring the contest that the BCA video is for." I tried to sound casual.

"That's what Chance said." She dried her hands on a woven cloth and draped it over the dishes drying in a rack next to the sink. "The sun has finally moved a little so the front deck is shaded. Let's take our iced tea and sit out there to chat."

Nanette let the screen door slam closed behind us and set two glasses of iced tea on a picnic table on the deck. I walked to the far side, sat, and swung my legs over the bench. Nanette settled onto the bench across from me. As soon as we sat down, Piper scurried to the table for attention.

"Chance tells me you're a brilliant storyteller," Nanette began, petting Piper's head with long smooth strokes.

"Oh? I didn't get that from him," I admitted.

"Oh, yes. He simply asked me to help infuse it with God's heart and said it will be the best marketing piece BCA has ever had."

She sipped her tea and looked at me. I smiled. She smiled back.

"So, tell me about Mrs. Coates. I think it's amazing that she's offering this kind of opportunity for marketing professionals like me and BCA."

"Yes, I think it's amazing, too. She's amazing, so it fits." Nanette scrubbed Piper between the ears. "I try to keep a wall between myself and BCA these days, but if Julia is sowing into Berean Christian Academy in a bountiful way, I'm blessed to be part of reaping a bountiful harvest!"

I didn't realize people talked like that anymore, but I was completely on board with getting bountiful results from my efforts. Maybe it could be even more abundant if Nanette could give me insight into how to impress Julia.

"I think having the video feature BCA and the Coates camera is a smart move. It's like killing two birds with one stone," I said.

Nanette sipped her tea.

"Something my mom used to say," I added.

"Just so. Before we get to the video, Joy, tell me about yourself," Nanette leaned forward with her elbows on the picnic table.

A wave of nervousness surged through me. I'd felt this way in every interview I ever participated in.

This isn't an interview, Joy. It's only a conversation.

"Well, I was born in Boise, but grew up in Nampa. I recently earned my MBA to complement my undergraduate marketing degree from Pepperdine. It's always been my dream to work for a corporation and sit at tables with innovators like Mrs. Coates, but I decided to go out on my own, so this contest is a dream come true for me. Well, could be a dream come true if I win. Of course I really care about BCA, too, it's just—"

Hello foot. Meet mouth.

Nanette's eyebrows raised as she continued to softly smile. Her eyes held a "bless her heart" look to them.

"I mean, of course I'm dedicated—no matter the task," I stammered. "I guess I meant…"

"I think I know what you meant. Let's say this project means a lot to everyone," Nanette said, patting my hand.

"Yes," I blushed and pulled my hand away to tuck my hair behind my ear.

"Are you a Christian?" Nanette asked.

I blinked and shifted in my chair. "Yes," I replied.

"Tell me about that."

I blinked. A barrage of possible right answers crashed around behind my steady gaze. I swallowed.

"Tell me your Jesus story," she prodded.

My Jesus story? What kind of question is that?

"I believe that Jesus is my Savior," I began timidly. "I attend church weekly, though we went a lot more than that when I was younger. Is that what you mean?"

"Sort of. Let me ask this—you attend church, what did your pastor teach or preach on this Sunday?"

This question I could answer. I threw my shoulders back and said,

"He talked about magnifying the promise not the problem. He used a telescope in his sermon. Visual props always help me remember."

"How wonderful. What promise was he talking about?"

I couldn't decide if Nanette was like Beth, wanting all of the details, or if she had some sort of agenda. Either way, what I really wanted was to talk about the project and how to get it back on track. I decided to play her game a little longer.

"He mentioned many. Mostly about the blessings God has for us. He talked about God making a way when there doesn't seem to be a way through—like the splitting of the Red Sea. He reminded us not to focus on what we don't like about ourselves—that it will block the amazing future God has for us. We should remember that we are God's masterpiece and focus on what God has said about us—that God has many good thoughts about us."

I searched Nanette's face for a response. I felt like I was in a classroom waiting to see if the teacher approved of the answer I had given.

"God's masterpiece," Nanette said pensively. "Don't you love that idea? It reveals so much about God. Only a master artist can create a masterpiece. As a master artist, God has the vision, creativity, skill, and ability to bring the masterpiece to life."

I immediately thought of the art hanging in Nanette's living room. Her husband really brought the scenes to life. You could almost hear the water trickling across the boulders in the creeks he painted.

"I never really thought about it like that."

"We have a distinct advantage as followers of Christ. We serve a God who has revealed Himself to us in His Word. We don't have to worry about distorting God's image by making up things in our own mind of what He is like. He told us all about Himself in sixty-six books through forty authors from three continents over fifteen hundred years. And not only that, but He protected it and preserved it to remain without error." The twinkle in Nanette's eyes matched the sunlight reflecting off the leaves of the aspens behind her.

"I get so passionate about God's Word," Nanette continued. "But don't worry, I'm not off track. The biblical worldview Chance wants from you comes from looking at the world through the lens of Scripture. So, with that, tell me about your experience with the Bible."

"My experience?" Once again, I had no idea what she wanted.

"You mentioned God has many good thoughts about you. What are your thoughts about His Word?"

I felt like I was back in beginner sessions on the balance beam in gymnastics class. With one question, I successfully completed a cartwheel, feet firmly planted. Then the next question sent me off balance, wobbling with my arms grasping at air for stability.

"I'm so sorry," I faltered. "I'm not really sure what you want to know."

"Let's start with who introduced you to reading the Bible?"

"James," I replied as memories long shoved down came flooding in.

Nanette sat in silence with an expectant look on her face.

"James was the camp director at a summer youth camp I interned at the summer between high school and college." Then with a dramatic wave of my hand, I added, "But, of course, other people taught me the Bible. I had Sunday school teachers, and pastors, and youth pastors, and—" I fidgeted with a small pinecone I picked up from the bench next to me.

"Tell me more about James and what he taught you. I'm a sucker for a good summer camp story."

"I remember the first time James invited me to The Table. The Table was a room at camp where the leaders and interns gathered. James always talked about how being invited to the table in the world meant that you were given a seat of influence and power. He said that people wanted to be at the table because it made them an insider—someone who was in the know."

Nanette's eyes never wavered from me. Even though I couldn't seem to say the right things in front of her, I felt a shift in our conversation. There was something about her I hadn't seen in anyone since… well, since James.

"James said that it was completely different at The Table, because at The Table we opened the ancient holy text of knowledge. He said that we were now *in the know* but for different reasons. He said that studying the Bible at The Table planted seeds of knowledge in our lives, but that our job was to take the seed we'd received and sow it in the lives of others, not feel more important because of the knowledge we obtained."

I paused. Struck by the language I used. Language I had not used in years. Words that now felt foreign though they were so familiar at one point in my life.

Nanette seemed content to sip her tea and let me ramble on.

"That summer I would sit at The Table and highlight my Bible, jotting notes in the margins. I filled notebooks with James's teaching. A couple of weeks into the eight weeks of summer camps, James asked me to start leading small group devotions for middle school girls. He said it was time to sow the seeds I had been given into the lives of others.

"I would spend hours looking for the right Scripture to make my points. Actually, that's when I got to know Kent better."

A flash of uncertainty flitted across her eyes and I realized I was talking about people Nanette didn't know.

"Kent was James's assistant director," I clarified. "James was the director of the camp and the main communicator, and Kent brought the fun. They were both so magnetic in their own ways. James had a passion and intensity, and a love for God and the Bible. Kent really knew how to connect with the kids on topics that mattered to them. And he could tell a story!"

"I love a well-told story!" Nanette interjected.

"I suppose that's where my love for marketing came from. Kent taught me how to influence people through story."

I paused, forgetting I was talking to Nanette. I said to myself, "I don't remember one lesson I slaved over, but I'll never forget how it felt to be at The Table."

Then we sat there. In silence. As if we were in the hallowed halls of a great old church. Lost in my memories, I didn't look at Nanette. And she left me there, undisturbed.

Finally I looked up and reconnected with her gentle gaze, "Wow. I haven't thought of that story in a long time."

"Thank you for sharing it with me. This was a holy moment."

Holy. Yes. That's what I was feeling.

I hadn't felt that since a few special times at The Table. It didn't always feel like that at The Table, but it was the only place other than today I had ever experienced that sensation.

"So what has your experience with the Bible been like since then?" Nanette asked.

I blinked and wobbled inside—off-balance again.

"To be honest, I brought my Bible with me to college, but eventually set it aside. I follow along on the screen at church and repost verses my best friend Beth shares with me on social media, but I can't say I 'experience' the Bible much outside of that."

"Thank you for being so forthright. That helps me a lot."

Helps you?

"I think the next step is to take a walk," Nanette swung her legs over the bench, stood up, and reached for a walking stick propped against the cabin wall.

I felt a distinct shift in the energy between us. Maybe I said something wrong. Or maybe I passed the first test. Maybe I was overthinking it. Perhaps we merely shared pleasantries and were ready to dig into the project. But none of it mattered. All I could see was Nanette leading the way, so I did the next logical thing. I followed.

CHAPTER THIRTEEN

NO WORDS PASSED BETWEEN US as Nanette, Piper, and I took our walk down a well-worn path through the woods. If you could call it a walk. It was more like a stop and stroll. Every few feet Piper nearly yanked me off my feet as she spotted some new rock, or log, or flower, or bug, or blade of grass she wanted to sniff.

On the hundredth stop, I jerked Piper's leash, growling her name under my breath.

"Let her explore," Nanette said like a grandmother correcting a mom who keeps wiping her baby's hands as they play in the dirt.

We came to a clearing and Nanette explained, "This is an old pioneer campsite. I've found a few treasures buried in the dirt here—a glass ink bottle—a broken saw blade."

Nanette pivoted in silence. Her face held a sense of awe—seeing something I couldn't see. I looked around and didn't even see a campsite. I saw a bare space in the middle of towering lodgepole pine trees with a few boulders circled up in the center.

"I can't imagine how hard it would have been to be a pioneer—no map, only a dream," Nanette mused.

I didn't need a field trip, I needed insight, but I didn't want to be rude either. I quoted from something I pasted on my vision board, "Eleanor Roosevelt said, 'The future belongs to those who believe in the beauty of their dreams.'"

"Just so," Nanette's eyes twinkled. "Some of the pioneers sought fortunes, others sought better health, some cheap land to build a better life, many would give all of those reasons. No matter what motivated them, once they set their feet and wagon wheels on the journey, they were in uncharted territory."

"That's how I feel about some of the elements of this project," I said. I hoped to swing Nanette around to the matter at hand.

It didn't work.

Nanette continued, "Early expeditions hired guides. The more reliable the guide, the better chance of survival and fulfilled dreams."

Don't I know it. Still searching for that.

"Eventually a well-worn path emerged. The ruts are so deep and long-lasting that there are places an hour south of here where you can see the remnant of the Oregon Trail—a trail followed over one hundred and fifty years ago."

"Wonder why there's a camp here then?" I asked.

"Following the crowd may have led the pioneers to a geographical destination quicker, but it also made them more vulnerable to attack and robbery. I like to think the people who camped here discovered the direction they had been heading may not have been the right way to fulfill their dreams after all. I mean, Oregon is nice, but Idaho is God's country, don't you think?"

Nanette's contagious smile and twinkling eyes prompted me to offer a smile in return. I gazed up at light beams filtering through the trees like a magical woodland scene in a fairy tale. Squirrels and chipmunks scurried around, birds chirped, and serenity infused the site.

"So, Joy, where do you think you went wrong with your proposal?" Nanette asked as she motioned for me to sit on a boulder next to one she sat on.

Like cold water in the face, the peace I felt disappeared in an instant. It's the conversation I came for, but the abrupt transition caught me off guard.

"Well—er—I guess—well, I'm assuming the right answer is that I didn't include a biblical worldview."

"Where do you think you should go from here?"

"If I knew that, I wouldn't be here," I replied sharply. I took a deep breath of desperation and added, "I'm sorry. I guess I'm not sure what Chance is looking for because I'm not sure what a biblical worldview is, how I missed it, and where to find it."

"What do you think it is?"

I wanted to groan. "Earlier you said it's seeing the world the way the Bible does."

Nanette nodded in agreement. "Just so. And it's deeper than that because your worldview is the way you interpret the world around you. That then leads you to act on that interpretation. It changes your behavior. Your worldview even impacts how you dream and where you aim your life."

A shrill sound came from above us and we tilted our heads to see a hawk fly overhead. Piper barked at the hawk as it soared higher and higher until it was just a black dot. Far, far away like the actual solution to my problem.

"So, how do I fix the video?"

"A biblical worldview is developed over time by a deep commitment to knowing what God's Word says and being open to seeing things differently and acting differently."

"But I don't have the luxury of 'over time' to get this project right," I spouted. I usually reserved that kind of snarky tone for those closest to me. I couldn't believe I let it slip with Nanette.

"Everyone has to start somewhere," Nanette replied calmly.

I heard a rustle in the bushes behind Nanette. Piper heard it too because she took off and ripped the leash out of my hand, but not before pulling me off balance and off of the boulder onto the dusty ground.

I gathered myself, stood up, and dusted my rump and legs with my hands. I finally glanced up to see Chance standing in front of me with a smile.

But I wasn't in a smiling mood. "Argh, that dog!"

Chance looked startled as if being pulled into the dirt by a dog wasn't a big deal. I caught him looking at Nanette with wide eyes.

"Chance, be a dear and take both dogs back to the house. We're not quite finished chatting."

I couldn't even look at Chance. Neither he nor Nanette seemed bothered by Piper's terrible behavior. Another meeting ruined by that dog. Chance could take her away and never bring her back.

"Can I make an observation?" Nanette asked as Chance and the dogs disappeared over a rise on the trail.

"Sure," I sighed and plopped back on my boulder.

"You're frustrated with Piper's curiosity."

"She's a distraction I don't have time for right now."

"I think it's you who is distracted," Nanette stated.

I hoped the flame in my cheeks didn't leap up into my eyes. "That's presumptive," I said flatly.

Nanette ignored my accusation. "You're worried about the destination when God wants to get your attention to show you things along the way."

Who does she think she is? She asks me a few questions and now she can see into my soul?

"I'm not distracted, I'm focused. I'm beginning with the end in mind and keeping forward momentum toward that end." I pursed my lips and clenched my fists. "I'm like the pioneers taking risks for my dreams."

Nanette continued as gentle as a snowflake sailing to the ground. "On our walk you kept correcting Piper because you thought she was distracted. Piper is curious. She's noticing the miraculous in the seemingly mundane things around her. I don't want you to miss the miraculous."

My clenched fists released and my shoulders slumped. "I don't have the pleasure of meandering and sniffing every flower I see at this point in my career." I didn't want to fight with this kind woman, I wanted to connect. "Honestly, Nanette, right now, I just need to know if you'll help me with this script," I pleaded.

Nanette leaned forward and placed her palm on my knee. "I'll help you. But I don't want you to miss what God wants to teach you through this project. Don't be afraid to stop and examine the unexpected things around you."

I offered a microscopic shrug, "I'll try."

"So, at camp you read your Bible, but now, not so much." Nanette's statement held no judgment. I nodded, my head still tucked into my chest. I picked up a stick and poked at the dirt.

"Do you remember when you set it down?"

. . .

I'm not sure why I went. I didn't really know James's wife or kids. I think I had hoped to find a place to get rid of my fear and anger. Any place near James should do that, right?

Actually, I hoped James would burst through the door saying, "I'm healed! Nothing's impossible with God!"

He always talked about being God's friend. Surely God would show up for his friend now.

The bitter coffee burned my tongue.

I guess bad coffee is a rite of passage for hospital waiting rooms. Even though I could no longer taste the bad coffee, I held onto the hot cup for comfort.

Relief washed over me when I saw Kent walk in.

He was different than I remembered.

He was always a nice enough looking guy, but today he looked like he came out of a magazine ad. His quarter-zip sweater was a little bit nicer and his brown leather shoes looked like they were actually leather. Something about him had changed. He seemed crisper. Like his image was as pressed and starched as his high-end slacks.

He didn't see me at first. He went directly to give Shelly a big hug. He handed each of the boys a stuffed animal. That was a nice gesture. I wish I had thought of something like that.

I watched Kent squat down and get eye-to-eye with the boys. He stroked the hair of one. He gently tickled the other under his chin. He must have said something funny because both boys giggled. The laughter of the children made the air lighter.

When he stood to speak to Shelly, their interaction breathed a sort of freshness into her. He reached out to her crossed arms and gently grasped her elbows. I couldn't hear what he said, but that small touch raised her shoulders from a burdened slump and she lifted her eyes to his with an attentive tilt of her head. It was as if he surgically removed some of the weight of her burden through words and touch.

I desperately wanted him to come and lift my burden too, and yet I stood mesmerized by his interactions with the people in the room. He sat on the couch next to a lady I assumed was James's mother—talking and touching. He moved to the corner where a few men were gathered—talking and touching. Kent dispersed sorrow one conversation at a time.

I wondered how James would respond if the tables were turned—if Kent were lying on an operating table with a giant hole in his skull while doctors worked for hours to remove the tumor threatening to consume him.

And that's when I realized what was missing. Kent's Bible.

Because if James were in this room, he would be talking and touching, but he never missed an opportunity to point people back to the Bible.

At last, Kent's eyes made contact with mine.

He made his way across the room toward me. "Hey there, Sadness," he said and gave me a side hug.

He remembered the nickname he had given me! After two years, I thought he would have forgotten.

I shrugged my left shoulder, "Hey."

"Joy, this is crazy, right? I keep thinking, 'Where's James? He should be here comforting everyone.' He was always the one bringing others peace."

"I know," I said. "It's all so surreal. I'm not really sure why I'm here myself. I just—he just—he meant so much to me and showing up is the only thing I feel like I have control over."

Kent took the paper cup from my hand. He held it away from him as if it held radioactive materials. He dropped it in a trash can and said, "Let's go get some real coffee."

We stopped at a coffee cart at the edge of a courtyard around the corner from the waiting room. Kent pointed to a bistro table with two chairs under a vine covered pergola, "How about over there?"

"This coffee is so much better than the vending machine," I said as I sat at the table. "Thanks for picking up the tab."

"It's my pleasure. So what have you been up to lately? How long has it been—two years?"

"Yep. Two years. I recently finished up my sophomore year at Pepperdine majoring in literature. But I have no idea what I'm going to do with that. I don't really want to teach, but what else can you do with a literature degree?" Turning the conversation away from my pathetic life, I added, "I heard you got married! That's exciting!"

"Yes. Very. Helen's an amazing woman. She's my biggest fan."

"So, what do you do, exactly?" I was pretty sure it wasn't ministry anymore. Not with shoes like that.

"I own my own marketing company. In fact, I wrote a book about marketing your business through telling stories."

"Really? You wrote a book? That's so cool!"

"Thanks. I think it's pretty cool, too. It's doing really well. It made the *New York Times* Best Sellers list and I'm flying to New York in the morning to promote it on some morning news shows."

"Oh, wow!" I almost spit out my coffee. "That's amazing!" My heart skipped a beat. *I know a* New York Times *best-selling author!* "Is it a Christian book?"

"It's a business book, but truth is truth. I learned how to tell a riveting story through ministry. Jesus was a storyteller and so am I. I'm just using His techniques in business instead of youth camp."

We continued to talk about Kent's transition into business, how he met and married his wife, and his audacious plans for the future. The thought of using words to influence others intrigued me.

"You should consider marketing, Joy. You love words or you wouldn't have majored in literature. With a well-told story I can influence others to buy things they didn't even know they wanted. Harnessing that has led to a very successful business and fulfilling life."

"Do you miss the impact you had on kids?" I asked.

"I learned all of my storytelling techniques through my time at camp. It will forever leave a lasting mark on my life."

A squirrel ran up to our table, sat on his hind legs, nibbled something between his paws, then scurried away.

"Do you and James talk often?"

"Not really. Every once in a while I'll get an encouraging text from him. Now that I've moved beyond the camp-life into bigger venues and different messages we don't have much in common. How about you?"

"He stays in touch. I guess I'm your typical self-centered teenager. Well, young adult," I smiled and tucked a curl behind my ear. "It's always him reaching out to me. He wanted me to serve at camp again last summer, but I had an opportunity to go to Europe with some friends. I didn't feel like I could pass that up." I ran my finger around the rim of the black lid on my coffee cup. "And he texted a couple of weeks ago about this summer, but—" I paused as I fought the tears welling up in my eyes.

Kent reached out and touched my arm. "Your sadness is deep because your love is deep." Talking and touching—dispersing sorrow one conversation at a time.

. . .

Later that day, I hung my keys on the hook in the kitchen—glad my mom was away for the weekend with her boyfriend. I needed to be alone. With James's surgery taking longer than expected and Kent heading home to pack for New York, I had decided to leave, too.

God, I'm angry and confused. James is a good man. He loves Shelly and the boys. He is faithful to them. He is faithful to YOU! He's given everything to teach other people about You. He lives out everything he taught us. He speaks the truth. He lives an honorable life. Please don't let him die.

I went to my small desk and pulled some books out of the lower cubby and reached to the back to grab my Bible. I wished I hadn't left all my journals from camp in my college boxes in storage in California. I knew James' words would have comforted me.

Instead, I turned to his favorite Psalm.

Psalm 119:1, "Blessed are those whose ways are blameless, who walk according to the law of the LORD."

Rather than comfort I felt anger.

Blessed?!

Blessed?!

I don't know of anyone whose life is more blameless than James. I don't know of anyone who walked according to the law of the Lord with such passion and persistence. And what good did it do him?

You call a brain tumor blessed?

I took my Bible and shoved it to the back of the cubby again, grabbed my keys, and headed to the bookstore to buy Kent's new book.

. . .

Nanette's eyes glistened as she reached out and placed her hand on top of mine. "I'm so sorry. Did James die?"

"No. Actually he didn't. But I haven't talked to him since." I felt like I was under a weighted blanket as I continued candidly, "I was so angry and confused, and by the time he recovered, I was back in California finishing up my undergrad." I didn't admit to Nanette that James continued to reach out to me periodically. I stayed too embarrassed to respond. I abandoned him and now I didn't know what to say.

"And you haven't read your Bible since then?"

"I have…some. At first, I read it out of loyalty to James's memory." I drew circles in the dirt with my stick. "I know that's weird since he's still alive."

I looked up at Nanette. She sat bent at the waist with her elbows propped on her knees, hands clasped together, and eyes on me.

"Then I would pick it up periodically when I came down with a case of the 'I shoulds'."

"The 'I shoulds'?" Nanette questioned.

"That's what my grandpa used to call it when your conscience gives you a little nudge to do the thing you know you *should* be doing."

"Ah," Nanette smiled—and waited for me to continue.

"Over time, it wasn't a part of my routine anymore. Now, I don't even know if I'd know where to start again." I kept my eyes averted, afraid to take in Nanette's reaction.

"Joy, I realize you won't be able to see the world through the lens of the Bible overnight. And I know this project is what's most meaningful to you right now, but God is calling you back to a place where you seek HIS direction and guidance over all else."

Something inside me stirred.

Nanette continued, "Psalm 119:105 says, 'Thy Word is a lamp unto my feet and a light unto my path'—"

"Not a spotlight that shines a hundred yards ahead," I interjected without thinking.

Nanette stopped, her inquisitive eyes encouraged me to explain.

"It's something James used to say. Psalm 119 was—is—his favorite chapter of the Bible. He taught us that sometimes travelers in ancient times would tie a small lamp to their ankles. As they extended their foot for each step, the light would shine on the path helping them keep their footing. James was quick to point out, though, that it was a lamp for their feet, not a spotlight shining a hundred yards ahead."

Nanette chuckled, "Just so. We get a glimpse of the final chapter, but everything in between must be lived out with a dependence upon the Author of our story." Pointing her finger toward me she added, "And God's Word is our light, guiding us step-by-step."

Nanette stood and dusted her backside. I didn't want my time with her to end. I felt like she was on the verge of leading me somewhere I hadn't realized I needed to go.

Nanette put her hand on my shoulder. "Joy, let's do this. I'll take the weekend to pray about the project and ask God what the next right step should be. Let me bear that burden for you for these next few days. Your focus needs to be about you and Father God and what He's doing to draw you back to His Word."

"I don't even know where to begin," I said quietly.

"Go back to the place where you last experienced God through His Word."

After that I felt like I was moving in slow motion back to the cabin, into the car, and all the way home. My thoughts bounced against one another like bumper cars.

Go back to the place where you last experienced God through His Word.

I had filed my time with James in the he-led-me-to-Kent folder. After all, it was Kent's influence that led me to change my major to marketing. For the first time since I left the hospital all those years ago, I felt as though James may have had more to teach me.

CHAPTER FOURTEEN

I SLOWLY DIPPED MY TEA BAG in my favorite hand-thrown pottery mug. After tossing the dripping bag into the trash, I slid onto a stool at the breakfast bar, opened my laptop, and navigated to James's blog.

A photo of middle-school-aged kids in life vests helping each other into kayaks brought me back to the sunny days of camp. The title of the featured blog post said, "Counting Others as More Significant than Yourself."

That's a good idea.

As I scanned the article, a colorful block drew my eye to the middle of the page. The words read, "Do nothing from selfish ambition or conceit, but in humility count others more significant than yourselves—Philippians 2:3."

The article went on to talk about loving others well and not being so focused on the tasks in front of you that you miss the moments to champion others.

What had Nanette said? "You're too worried about the destination..."

I lifted my right foot and tucked it under my left thigh. I sipped my tea and continued reading. In the "About Me" section I noticed a recent picture of James, Shelly, and the boys. He looked happy, healthy, and strong. I hardly recognized the boys. I guess big changes happen to a four- and six-year-old over five years.

On a whim, I navigated to Kent's website. His featured article boasted a photo from a scene in *The Godfather* with the quote, "Keep your friends close, but your enemies closer." In his article he talked about how to operate in an office setting. He skillfully wove story and humor into his office politics advice.

I was taken aback by his use of foul language and the scene he depicted. He used words like "power move" and "maneuver" as if the people you work with were pieces in a chess game. He talked about using public compliments and seating arrangements to maintain control.

I bet Maggie's done that.

As I finished my tea, I thought about Nanette's advice to go back to where I had left off with the Bible. To figure that out, I needed my notebooks from camp. I grabbed a stool and reached to the top of the hall closet. I pulled down the purple plastic box marked "College Stuff," and dug through the box until I located the notebooks.

I tossed a stack of four spiral-bound single-subject notebooks on the coffee table. I dug in my purse for a note Nanette had given me, and grabbed my Bible off of a bookshelf. I settled into the corner of the couch, reached for the notebook on top, and flipped through it. Over and over I saw Psalm 119 referenced—James' favorite.

I pulled out Nanette's note with a bulleted list of ways I could interact with the Bible. She said, "Move beyond merely reading the

Bible. Start there, but move beyond it."

Start there.

I pulled my Bible into my lap and opened it to the middle. I flipped a few pages to get to Psalm 119 and read that first verse that caused me to set it aside so many years ago.

Keep going.

I didn't remember this psalm including so many activities of wicked people—pitfalls, snares, plots, and unfeeling hearts. The psalm used "insolent" to describe those behaviors. I couldn't define that word in my head, so I grabbed my phone and pulled it up in my dictionary app. "An insolent person is boldly rude or disrespectful."

My mind flipped to Kent's brazen description of making war against others in the workplace for personal gain using some of the same approaches described as insolent in the psalm I just read. I didn't understand how Kent could get to a place where he called these bad ideas good when Scripture so clearly taught against it. Impressive communication skills, humor, and shock tactics made it an appealing read, but it all felt so wrong.

One of the ideas on Nanette's list said to read the text aloud. I turned back to the beginning of Psalm 119 and read out loud. Piper came over and put her head on my leg. I let her stay there. I felt less silly reading out loud to Piper than to myself.

I abruptly halted at verse twenty-four, "Your testimonies are my delight; they are my counselors."

A host of counselors flashed through my mind. Among them, Beth, James, Kent, my favorite professor in college, Marshal, Maggie, and even Nanette.

In verse ninety-nine I read, "I have more understanding than all my teachers for Your testimonies are my meditation. I understand more than the aged, for I keep Your precepts."

I depended heavily on my counselors for guidance. Their advice led to trying new things, thinking new ways, and opportunities I wouldn't have without them. I wanted and valued their wisdom.

I grabbed a pen from a bowl on the coffee table. I underlined "meditation" in verse ninety-nine. Then I turned back to verse twenty-four and underlined the word "delight." I had never really meditated on Scripture much less delighted in it.

The problem is there's so much I don't understand.

As if on cue, the next item on Nanette's note instructed me to turn verses into prayers. Near the end of Psalm 119, the psalmist described what I wanted for myself.

Dear God, this says that the unfolding of Your words gives light, imparting understanding to the simple. Whenever I pick up Your book I feel simple and small. Unfold Your words to me so that they can do for me what they have obviously done for Nanette, Beth, and Chance. I want the light I see in their eyes when they talk about the Bible. Teach me how to meditate on it so that it can become my delight.

CHAPTER FIFTEEN

"YOU WERE RIGHT. Nanette has a way of penetrating your soul." I tossed a tennis ball. Piper ran to retrieve it, returned, and plopped it at my feet. Toss, retrieve, toss, retrieve—her favorite activity on our puppy playdates with Chance and Ruby.

Correction. Playdate. There had only been one before. So far, so good.

"I know, right?" Chance tossed a Frisbee and Ruby's black and white fur flowed in the wind as she expertly raced to snatch it out of the air. I found it curious that the dogs never tried to intrude on the other's game. Piper had her ball. Ruby had her Frisbee. Both were content.

I threw the ball again, only this time Piper didn't return it to my feet. She ran right past me and plopped it at the feet of a man I hadn't noticed behind us.

"I'm so sorry," I said to his running shoes as I bent over to pick up the ball and grab Piper's collar.

"No worries," he said. "Wait. Joy?"

I stood and the blood drained from my face. "Logan. Hi."

Chance trotted up with Ruby. "Piper wanted to include a new player in her game?"

"Yep, I guess so," I offered a plastic laugh. "See you around, Logan." I pulled Piper's collar, turned on my heels, and walked away.

"Wait," Chance said. "You two know each other?"

Yes, and I don't want you two to know each other.

Logan reached out his hand to Chance. "Logan Fisher. Joy and I used to work together."

"Chance Easton. We currently work together. Well, sort of—"

I picked up Piper's ball and threw it as hard as I could. "She just loves this game. Bye!" I gave Logan a half-wave and glared at Chance as I jogged off in the direction of my toss.

My error became immediately apparent. I threw the ball pretty far—in the wrong direction. This time, I tossed the ball onto an island in the middle of a pond. As soon as Piper jumped in the water, Ruby counted it as an invitation, and they both swam to the island.

Once the dogs made it to the mound of dirt in the center of the pond, they spotted a squirrel and started chasing and playing and completely ignoring our calls to "come."

"Oh, great," I said as I flung myself to the grass on the side of the pond.

"What was that about? Who's Logan?" Chance asked as he sat next to me, his arms wrapped around his bent legs.

"Oh, just a traitor I used to know," I said with a dramatic wave.

"There's a story there," Chance prompted.

"I worked with Logan at Cup O' Joe. It was during my mentor-match days with Maggie, actually. She helped me develop a marketing campaign that counted for one of my classes."

It was easier to talk to Chance when I wasn't staring into his penetrating blue eyes, so I intently watched Piper's every move on the island.

As we sat there on the grass and the dogs barked, I heard my voice begin to tell a story I tried to keep filed away.

• • •

Upon my arrival to Cup O' Joe, I had greeted Marshal warmly. I really looked up to him. He had taken on a father figure role giving me both professional and life advice. I saw Logan and gave him a fist bump as I grabbed an open stool at one of the high-tops.

The other teammates trickled in and grabbed chairs and stools throughout the dining area. Callie slipped in with one minute to spare. I caught her attention, smiled, and nodded toward an open stool at my table, but she looked right at me and chose a chair three tables over.

You couldn't say I didn't try. As the soon-to-be general manager I could still respect the fact that she showed up on time (barely) and did the job. Not all of my workers would be friends like Logan.

At 5:45 a.m. on the dot, Marshal cleared his throat. "Can I have everyone's attention?" I knew the meeting was going to be quick since the café opened in fifteen minutes. "I'm thankful for your prompt attendance. Thanks especially to Joy and Callie for being here on time—and with smiles since they closed last night."

What a guy. He noticed.

Callie examined her nails.

Whatever. This is it!

"As a way of making up for the inconvenience, I'm passing out twenty-dollar gift cards to be used when you're not on the clock. It's our way of saying thanks for your hard work and dedication."

The fog of the early morning lifted from the teammates as the cards were passed out. You could feel the energy in the room shift from annoyance to gratitude. I'd have to remember what a small act of appreciation could do for the team when I became the new general manager.

"Of course, this is not the reason to call you in for an all-team meeting," Marshal continued. "I have an exciting promotion to announce that is a surprise even to the recipient."

My heart fluttered.

"I am pleased to announce the promotion from valued barista and store supervisor to new general manager goes to…" Marshal paused dramatically, "Logan Fisher!"

Applause erupted. The room spun and I grabbed the edge of the table to steady myself. I looked around bewildered and caught Callie looking at me. She pinched her lips in a frown and her eyes softened.

Marshal had more to say. "Come up here, Logan!" They shook hands and Marshal put his arm around Logan's shoulder. "I have to tell you that your 'Shake It Up' campaign was genius! We not only sold more of a menu item with a higher profit margin, but the social media blitz got customers in the door to buy even more coffee and yogurt. Your talent and vision is what we want to see repeated at this company. Congratulations, son. Why don't you come on down to the corporate offices after this and we'll get all the human resources business out of the way."

"I will, thank you so much."

"In the meantime, I think your opening crew needs to get to work and you have some teammates who want to congratulate you. Meeting dismissed."

I stared directly at Logan, willing him to make eye contact with me. Which of course he didn't.

What just happened? Not only did I not get the promotion, but Logan got the credit for my campaign?

Sure, I got an A on my marketing class presentation, but this class-project-turned-real-life case study was MY idea.

I came up with the recipes.

I crunched the numbers.

I created the social media campaign.

The only thing Logan did was design the graphic images we used for the campaign and posters in the store—graphic images I *paid* him to create for my class project!

I wasn't going to let Logan off this easily. I regained my composure and stood at the back of the line of teammates waiting to congratulate him.

I grabbed his hand firmly. "Aren't you going to say anything?" I said tightly. Logan looked at the floor. "Look at me, Logan. Are you really going to take this promotion because of a campaign you didn't create? You know I want this."

Logan finally locked eyes with me. Sadness painted his entire face as he replied quietly, "Sorry, Joy. I want it, too."

• • •

Chance let out a low whistle. "That's awful, Joy. What happened after that? What about Marshal? Couldn't he work with you to find another position?"

"I didn't give him the chance," I replied tersely.

"What do you mean?" Chance pressed.

"My mentors have always been 'for a reason for a season.' Marshal was no different. I learned a lot from him, but it was time to move on. Besides, I decided to go out on my own and Maggie offered the opportunity with BCA as my first client. I figure as long as I'm continuing to move forward, I'm on the right track."

"So you never asked him what happened?" Chance's words pricked like a handful of cactus spines.

"People come and go from your life and it's better to look forward than back, don't you think?" I tugged the wrinkles out of my tank top and retied my tennis shoe.

Chance didn't respond to my question, rather he offered another one of his own. "How many mentors have you had in your life?"

"How many have you had?" I retorted, failing at *not* getting defensive.

"Actually, I've only had two that I would truly count as a mentor—a coach in high school and Mrs. Verity," Chance replied calmly.

He's just trying to get to know you.

I collected myself and attempted to soften my demeanor as I explained that my mom had always taught me that people will come and go from your life and you can learn something from all of them. I clarified that I would follow their lead as long as their advice propelled me forward or until I lost faith in them for one reason or another.

"Hmm," Chance replied.

"What's wrong with that?" I challenged.

"Don't you feel like that approach is a moving target? How do you measure if your mentor-of-the-moment is giving you wise counsel?"

"I can definitely tell Nanette is your mentor—asking me questions rather than answering mine," I countered. "Don't you take advice from others?"

"Of course, but I try to line it up with the Bible. That's how I know if they're leading me in the right direction."

"Why is the Bible the best guide? Isn't it just written by men?" I blurted.

Why did I say that? Now he's going to think I'm not a very good Christian.

Chance leaned back on his elbows, "It's recorded by men, but inspired by God. He's the author. That's why we call it the Word of God."

I'm not one of your students, Mr. Easton.

Chance picked a piece of grass and started chewing on it. "I personally think it's cool that a perfect God uses imperfect people to reveal Himself. It gives me hope that I can be used by Him as I'm mentored by his Word."

He can't help himself, can he?

Chance leaped to his feet and pulled the neckline of his T-shirt up and over his head. I stared unblinking at his bare chest. He slipped his shoes off, then his socks. He tucked his socks into his shoes before I regained my breath in time to ask, "What are you doing?"

"I'm going to get our dogs," he grinned as he tossed his glasses on his shirt, turned toward the pond and dove in.

"What are you? Twelve?" I called.

"Aren't you gonna help?" He swiveled to his back and floated toward the island with swift flutter kicks of his feet.

I looked down at my tank top and running shorts. "I'll get soaked," I argued.

"You'll dry!" Chance turned over on his stomach and flipped himself around in a somersault in the water.

I tilted my head back and laughed. I shed my own shoes and socks, tied my hair into a high ponytail, and ran into the water. Evidently the dogs thought we invited them to a swim party because they bounded off the island and swam to join us.

After about twenty minutes of splashing and laughing, Chance and I and both dogs lay panting on the bank of the pond. Drenched and delighted, I penciled this moment in the "best day ever" column.

CHAPTER SIXTEEN

WE ALL LAUGHED and gave each other high fives like we were in a movie scene as we entered The Outpost. I pretended to head to the bathroom while Roderick, Lan, and Andrew took up residence in "our spot" at the high-top table in front of the picture window that overlooked Idaho Street.

The Outpost featured curved booths lining the old brick wall on one side of the narrow room. The other side featured an antique bar the owner claimed came from a gold rush town. Stained glass inserts complemented the warm tones of the wooden backbar. I slid onto one of the round stools anchored in a line along the white marble counter-top and ordered the first round of margaritas. I looked around while I waited for my receipt. My eyes widened when I saw Mateo slumped in a chair in the furthest corner.

The bartender slid a receipt pad my way. I scratched out my signature, tucked the receipt in my pocket, and made a beeline for Mateo. "Hey, there," I said timidly.

"Joy! Hey! I didn't see you there," Mateo responded with a too-loud voice and slurred speech.

"Watcha doin' sitting in a dark corner alone?" I asked.

"It hasn't been sssuch a great day if I'm honessst."

"The gang's all here if you want to join us," I offered with a nod to the front of the restaurant.

Mateo sat up straighter and squinted in the direction of the group. "Thanksss. I think I'd rather drink alone tonight."

"Is Maria going to join you?"

"Nope," Mateo replied with extra emphasis on the "p." He downed the rest of his drink and rattled his ice in a raised glass aimed at the bartender.

I spotted his keys on top of his wallet on the table. "Do you have a ride home for later?"

"I hadn't really thought that far ahead."

"Okay, well, I'll take these"—I picked up his keys and tucked them in my pocket—"and when you're ready, I'll give you a ride home. How does that sound?"

"Soundsss perfect. You're a good friend," Mateo said and patted my hand.

When I returned to the group, Andrew declared with a raised glass, "There she is!"

Roderick looked down his nose, "You were trying to be sneaky, but the drinks you bought us are already here."

"Thanks, by the way," Lan added with a tip of her margarita. "Who were you talking to?" she asked as she motioned to the dark corner.

"Believe it or not, that's Mateo," I replied.

"Aw, man. He should join us," Andrew said as he stood and took a step toward the back of the restaurant.

I pushed my palms down in the air as a gesture for him to stay seated. "I invited him, but he said he wanted to be alone."

Andrew put his hands up in surrender and sat back down.

"But he's not doing too good, so I'm going to drive him home." I pulled Mateo's keys from my pocket and jingled them. "So, who wants my margarita?"

Andrew reached across the table and slid my glass toward himself with a grin, "I'll take one for the team."

The team jabbered about the film shoot. There was an "I can't believe we got such great footage of that science experiment," and "That kid Jackson is a natural," mixed with "Roderick, you're so talented," and "Your wordsmithing is divine, Lan," and Andrew's "You haven't seen great until you see my social media campaign." They even sprinkled in a few compliments for me—"You have such an eye, Joy," and "How did you get them to look so natural when they were so nervous?" Typically, I would have cherished their verbal affirmation, but I kept stealing glances at Mateo.

"Does he do this often?" I interrupted the chitchat.

"Does who do what often?" Roderick asked.

"Mateo," I said with a flip of my head to the corner.

"Actually, no," Lan said with a frown. "I've never seen Mateo drunk."

I made small talk with the group until one by one they left. Mateo slowed down on his refills but never moved from his corner.

Lan left last and murmured, "Take care of him," as she gave me a hug.

"I will."

I walked up to the bar and asked for two ice waters. I made my way to Mateo's table, set the glasses down, and slid into the chair across from him.

"I'm worried about you," I said.

Mateo ran his fingers through his hair. He never did that. His hair always looked glued in place. I didn't know you could run your fingers through it.

"I can't believe she doesn't believe me." Mateo's bloodshot eyes held deep sadness.

"Maria?" I guessed.

"I would never cheat on her. I love her. I told her there was only ever one girl for me."

I had so many questions, but I rubbed my fingers on the condensation on the outside of my water glass and waited.

"My abuela would never stand for that kind of foolishness. Doesn't she know I was raised better than that?" Mateo pleaded with his eyes. "I would never disappoint my abuela like that. Or Maria."

After a few more moments of silence I asked, "What happened?"

As if he'd been waiting for me to ask, he launched into the details. "Maria saw a charge on my credit card for a boutique hotel in Mountain Home."

I felt the blood drain from my face.

"I told her it was for work, but she wouldn't listen. I can't stop picturing the tears streaming down her face. Her perfect face with rivers of black tears the color of her hair."

Poetic sadness aside, I proceeded carefully.

"Did you stay at that hotel?" My knee shook under the table.

"No," he said with a blank face.

"So why doesn't she believe you?"

"Because I was in Mountain Home on that day."

The door to the restaurant opened and a large group entered, shedding jackets and laughing loudly.

"Why were you in Mountain Home?"

Mateo tilted his head to the ceiling and responded with a ragged voice, "Technically I just stopped to get gas on my way to meet John for a meeting in Pocatello."

"If you didn't stay at the hotel, who did?"

Mateo didn't make eye contact. His sorrow slipped away and in its place appeared a statue of a man with shoulders back, palms flat on the table, and a blank stare. "John," he said.

Thumping and screeching sounds came from the large group as they pulled tables together and arranged the chairs.

"Why didn't he put the charge on his card?"

"That's what Maria wanted to know."

"What did you tell her?"

"Nothing."

"Why?" I asked.

Mateo pursed his lips and his blank face hardened even more.

I thought of Maria's kind smile and how she always touched Mateo. A hand on his shoulder. Fingers interlaced with his. An arm around his waist.

Then I thought of Peter. He doted on Maggie—refilling her drink, or picking up the dishes before she could. "She's being too humble," he would say before bragging on her.

My blood began to boil. "Why is it our responsibility to keep their secrets?" I blurted.

Mateo looked up at me with raised brows and shocked eyes. "Who do you mean by 'their'?" he punctuated each word.

"You know who I mean."

Mateo stared into his glass.

"Do you want me to talk to Maria?"

"No," he snapped as his eyes flashed a warning that matched his tone.

"I wouldn't tell her anything. I would only confirm that it was business related." I heard my voice get higher and a little frantic.

"Hopefully she'll come around," he said. "Don't. Say. Anything."

I sat back in my chair.

Why is he mad at me? It's John and Maggie he should be mad at.

"Why would you lose the love of your life for—for—for him?" I pushed.

"John gave me an opportunity when no one else would. He's taught me a lot and he's offering the way to build the life I want. Hopefully Maria will come around, but another pathway to success like this one won't."

"You don't want to be like him."

"I'm not like him. I'm loyal."

After that, Mateo stopped talking. I asked a few more questions, but he only offered a blank stare in return. "You can take me home now," were the last words he spoke to me.

CHAPTER SEVENTEEN

I PULLED UP to the employee gate of Coates Inc. at 6:45 a.m. I wanted to get an early start on reviewing the footage from yesterday's film shoot. I twisted my hair, still damp from my morning shower, into a tight bun on top of my head. I still didn't like Piper, but I enjoyed our morning walks—they cut into my routine, but got my blood pumping and ideas flowing.

My goal was to avoid contact with everyone at the office except Roderick. We could hide in his video processing closet and bring my vision to life. He called it an office, but it didn't have windows and it wasn't much wider than my backyard.

I tapped my employee card to the box at the gate but it didn't open. I tapped it again. A red X appeared on the screen. A car horn beep-beeped behind me. I eyed the black SUV in my rearview mirror and tapped my card on the access point again. Another red X.

I got out of the car and walked up to the driver's side window of the SUV. The man inside rolled his eyes and then rolled down the window.

"I'm sorry. My key card isn't working. If you back out a bit I'll get out of your way," I said.

"This better not be a trick to sneak in," he grumbled.

"Nope. No trick. I'll go around to the visitor gate."

The man harrumphed and rolled up his window. "Have a great day," I mumbled under my breath as I returned to my rental car. He backed up and I backed out, careful to avoid adding a slow-motion collision to my morning.

I waved at the man as I drove away. He leaned out of his window, tapped his card, and the gate opened as it should. I noticed he stopped inside the entrance to be sure I didn't follow him in. I rolled my eyes. I bet he never snuck eleven items in the "ten items or less" lane at the grocery store.

I pulled up to the visitor gate and let the guard know my card wasn't working.

"Sorry. I can't let you in unless your name's in my computer."

I handed him my card. "I have this, but it's not working for some reason."

The guard took my card into his booth. While he fixed the card I went over my mental list of what shots I wanted to review first. I tapped my phone to pull up my favorite 80s music playlist. The Pointer Sisters started singing, "Tonight's the night we're gonna make it happen…" I tapped my hands to the beat on my steering wheel gearing up for the chorus.

The guard handed me my card back. "I'm sorry ma'am. This card has been revoked and I can only let visitors in who have been added to the list in my computer." I felt my neck get warm, but his face held no judgment—or emotion. "Please make a U-turn and exit through this gate." He pointed to the gate on the other side of his guard house. He turned his attention to the next car behind me, motioning them forward with a brisk wave of his hand. I circled around a median with boulders and natural grasses flowing in the breeze and stopped in the exit lane.

I pulled out my phone to call Maggie. Before I tapped on her number, I received a text message from Gonzales Body Shop. *Your Jeep is ready for pickup.*

I glanced at my watch.

I'm early anyway.

So much for trying to slip in and out of work undetected today. I looked down at my casual clothes and caught a glimpse of my wet hair in the rearview mirror. I figured I could go pick up my Jeep and then rush home and change.

I missed Scarlett. This whole experience taught me that I was not a four-door sedan kind of girl. I wondered if Piper would enjoy the wind in her hair as much as I did.

I pressed call on my contacts and put my phone on hands-free before turning into traffic toward the body shop.

"This is Maggie."

"Hey, Maggie, it's Joy. Listen, I tried to come in early today and my card didn't work. I'm actually on my way to pick up my Jeep. It's finally done. But can you check on my card, or at least put me on the visitor list for when I get back?"

I checked my mirrors and changed lanes and didn't notice Maggie's silence until I stopped at a traffic light.

"I revoked your access."

"What? Why?" The car behind me honked three long times. I looked around inside the car and up at the light—the green light. One more long honk brought me back to my senses and I pressed the accelerator.

"John got a call from Julia Coates with a negative report from the school. He doesn't want to risk Julia's reputation or his, and so he's asked me to take over the project from here." Maggie's words held no emotion.

"I don't understand."

"I'm really busy, Joy. Let's do lunch soon." Then the line went dead.

Negative report? Revoked? Lunch?

My head spun with Maggie's revelation. I replayed every scene from the film shoot the day before. Nothing went wrong. No one was upset—only laughter and magical moments.

Without really thinking it through, I drove to Berean Christian Academy. At the intersection by the fountain, I considered heading straight to the gym and seeing if I could sneak in to talk to Chance without a visitor pass. The rule-follower in me forced me to turn left and face Molly Carrol with wet hair, a light cardigan over my graphic tee, and hot pink, wide-legged linen pants.

Molly buzzed me in and I headed straight for the clipboard to sign in as a visitor. "I'm here to see Mr. Easton. He doesn't have a class yet, does he?"

"He's in morning devotions, but don't sign that," Molly snapped.

I dropped the pen like it shocked me and looked at Molly for an explanation as to why she sounded like she just warned a toddler not to touch a hot stove.

"You're not welcome here anymore."

I stopped breathing. So the report was true. I had done something wrong and I was oblivious to it.

"Can you tell me who said that?"

Molly shook her head.

Do I detect sadness?

"Was it—" I turned to look out the window. "Was it Mr. Easton?"

"I'm sorry Miss Swallow. Please leave," Molly said as she waved her hand toward the door.

My feet remained rooted and I placed my palms flat on the counter and leaned toward Molly. "Was it Mr. Clarke?"

Recognition flickered in Molly's eyes as she stood, came around the reception counter, and cupped my arm with her hand. She guided me toward the door and opened it for me. "Good luck, Miss Swallow."

I don't even remember getting back in the car, but the water streaming from my eyes made it difficult to see. I pulled over at the next gas station to get a grip. My head pounded and I couldn't turn off the faucet of tears.

I put the car in park and stepped out to get some air. I paced back and forth while traffic whizzed by. Maggie wasn't any help. I wasn't going to call John. Chance was at work. How else could I find out what Julia had heard?

I yanked my hair band out and shook my bun loose. My damp curls cascaded down into my face, and the pressure in my head diminished. An idea emerged and I dialed Nanette's number before I chickened out.

"Hello?"

"Nanette, hi, it's Joy." I circled the parked car with swift steps. The pace of my words matched my stride. "I'm so sorry to bother you this morning, but something tragic has happened and I was hoping you could help me."

"Oh, no, dear. What is it?" I could picture her concerned eyes and feel her gentle hand on top of mine. I could almost smell the spruce I smelled at her home in the woods. Almost. Really, all I smelled was gasoline and exhaust fumes.

"It seems as if someone has given Julia a bad report and I have been removed from the project."

"Oh, Joy. I'm so sorry." Anyone could say those words and I would have swatted them away like an errant bug. But when Nanette said them, I believed her—and they brought a small amount of comfort.

"Me, too," I pushed on. "The thing is that I need to get to the bottom of it. This project is important to me on so many levels, but right now"—I paused for effect—"Nanette, my career is on the line."

Nanette didn't immediately answer. Birds chirped on the other end of the line. I heard a chair scrape. Oh, no. Was she sitting down?

"Joy, dear. I care about you very much already, and I don't know what is going on behind the scenes, but—"

I don't really know what she said next. It didn't really matter because she wasn't going to help me either. My back slid down the side of the car until I was sitting on the ground with my head in my knees—the phone still pressed to my ear. Nanette continued to speak, "…pray and ask God to reveal the truth to you as well as a pathway forward."

"Okay, thank you," I whispered. "Sorry to bother you."

The cacophony of sound from the traffic around me muted in my ears. Everything I thought sure was slipping through my fingers like water.

As if in a trance, I got back in the car to complete the next task in front of me. I needed to pick up my Jeep. I could think about the rest after that.

I pulled into Gonzales Body Shop and saw Mateo skip down the exterior stairs of the garage apartment adjacent to his uncle's business. Clean and pressed like last night never happened, he held his head high and straightened his bow tie before scrolling through his phone. He didn't see me drive up.

"Good morning," I said with a wave.

Mateo stopped his descent when he looked up from his phone and locked eyes with mine.

"Morning." There was something missing. Oh, yes. His smile.

"I thought maybe you wouldn't make it into work today," I said with my hand over my squinting eyes to block the morning sun directly behind his head.

Mateo shrugged. "Life goes on, right?" He tapped out messages on his phone and continued down the stairs.

When he reached the base of the steps, I approached him and put my hand on his arm. "I'm here for you if you need me."

A flicker of something I couldn't quite read flashed across his eyes. "Thanks." He tossed his head toward his uncle's shop. "So, Scarlett's finally ready to go home?"

I smiled and puffed out a thankful breath. "Yes. Finally."

"Glad to hear it. See you around," Mateo said and turned away.

See you around?

Then it hit me. He just said "see you around," not "see you at work." He knew.

I marched over to Mateo as he opened the door to his car. His car that I parked in this very spot when I drove him home last night. At his apartment that I opened the door to after helping him up the stairs. The apartment that I locked as I left after he passed out fully clothed on his bed. The bed I protected by taking off his shoes and sliding his socked feet under the covers.

I grabbed his hand with the keys in them. The keys I left on the kitchen counter when I locked the handle of the door to scuttle down the stairs to a ride share to go back to my car at The Outpost. "Did you tell John I know about the affair?"

"It's my job to protect him."

"Cuz my key card's been deactivated and Maggie took the project from me because of a report from John," my voice increased in volume and my hand squeezed his tighter.

"You should've kept it secret," he said as he pulled his hand out of my grasp.

"I *did* keep it a secret."

"You told me," Mateo said as he peered down at me over his nose.

"But you already knew!" I watched Mateo look around to see if I drew attention from others with my outburst.

"I told you. I'm fiercely loyal."

I dropped my head in defeat. "I thought I was being loyal, too." I locked eyes with his. "To my friend who was hurting."

Mateo glanced at his watch then slid his sunglasses on. "I'm sorry. I have to leave now. With traffic at this time, I'm going to be late for work."

CHAPTER EIGHTEEN

ONCE I REALIZED Chance didn't have anything to do with me being removed from the Coates Inc. video contest, I decided Maggie and John didn't have the right to take away my friends, too. In the four days since I'd been removed from the project, Chance and I had two puppy playdates at the dog park. At the last date, he convinced me I could bring Piper out in public. He didn't have to twist my arm too much when he suggested we go down by the river to listen to live music.

"Are you sure she'll be okay?" I looked at Piper and Ruby in the very back of the Jeep, their chins propped up on the back seat, content to be side-by-side and not in their crates. "I really don't want Piper jumping all over strangers."

"She doesn't really do that." Chance turned to look at Piper, "You don't jump on people, do ya girl?" he said in his dog voice. Turning back to me he added, "You do realize most everyone in the world likes dogs but you."

"I like dogs."

"You're not very good at lying," Chance smiled at me, turned to look out the front window, and pushed his glasses up his nose. "I really like that about you."

I fiddled with the volume and then adjusted the AC vent to blow more directly on me—even though the top was off of sweet Scarlett.

"Speaking of that, how's work?" Chance asked.

"You think I've been lying about work?" My grip tightened on the steering wheel.

"No. But you won't talk about it. And ever since we met, that's all you talk about."

"Let's just say working for myself is more challenging than I thought. But I'd rather talk about you. Let's talk about your gala planning. I love giving unsolicited advice to others." I turned to grin at Chance and got a gob of hair blown into my face.

"Ugh." Chance flung his head back against the head rest. "I have no idea why they think the Bible teacher is qualified to do a fundraiser. The only thing I have going for me is that I believe in the school and what the money's for."

"I've worked on galas before. I could help," I offered as I tucked the curls whipping in my face behind my ears.

"You have enough with launching your own business. But thanks."

We parked Scarlett in a shady spot and opened the back. As soon as we hooked leashes on the dogs, they hopped out and each gave a good shake. Then they both sat looking at us. I swear they were smiling and asking, "Now what?"

Chance and I each slung a folding camp chair over our shoulder, locked up the Jeep, and made our way toward the sound stage. "I'm starving, but let's find a spot for our chairs before we hit up the food trucks," I said.

Chance ambled beside me—so comfortable in his own skin. And so attractive—in a nerdy sort of way. As if on cue, he pushed his glasses up on his nose and commented on the weather.

Chance was right.

Everyone loved Piper and Ruby.

People stopped and asked to pet them. Piper never once tried to jump on anyone. She ate up the attention. She was especially gentle around children. I loosened up with every interaction.

Chance read all of the food truck options aloud—funnel cakes, frozen lemonade, hot dogs; at "barbecue" I saw Mateo and Maria arm-in-arm laughing and walking toward us.

"You know what? I think I need a funnel cake." I grabbed Chance's hand and yanked him toward the food truck.

"I thought you wanted to find a spot for our chairs first."

"Changed my mind. Dessert first. Definitely." I released Chance's hand as we slid into line. I dropped my head, let my curls cover my face, and hoped Mateo and Maria wouldn't spot me.

And they didn't.

They spotted Piper.

"Hello, Piper! I thought that was you," Maria said in her dog voice. *Why do people talk to dogs like that?*

Maria squatted next to the dog, rubbed her head, and smiled up at me. "Hi, Joy! It's good to see you." She stood and gave me a hug. Maria gave the best hugs. She gave I-love-you-just-the-way-you-are hugs like a grandmother, but with a tiny frame instead of pillows for arms.

"You too," I said. And I meant it. In our few interactions I felt a connection to her, which is why I wanted Mateo to—

I guess they made up. I'm glad.

Mateo rubbed his hand along his closely cropped beard and looked at the ground. "Um, Joy. Can we talk for a minute?"

"I don't want to lose my spot in line." I pretended to study the menu.

Maria grabbed Piper's leash from my hand, slid the chair from my shoulder, and looked at Chance, "Let's go set up your chairs while they chat in line."

I begged Chance with my eyes not to leave me, but he had already turned away and trotted alongside Maria toward the grassy area in front of the sound stage.

"You two made up," I refused to look at Mateo.

"We did," he said.

"I'm glad."

"So am I."

A man with a stroller and two toddlers, with what can only be described as leashes on their wrists, came up behind us. The kids hopped up and down and ran around the man in circles while the baby cried in the stroller. He squatted down trying to read the menu to them in between "stop jumping" and "shh shh shh" as he pushed the stroller forward and backward.

"You can go in front of me." As much as I wanted to escape this conversation with Mateo, I felt for the guy.

"John and Maggie broke up."

I didn't want to share anything more with Mateo—not even a reaction—so I focused on the menu—Sugar Daddy, Funfetti, Nutella, chocolate chip, fresh strawberry.

"Did you hear me?" Mateo nudged my elbow.

"Good. They should. They're both married," I said. I stepped up to the window. "Original, please."

I don't know why people ruin a perfectly good funnel cake with all the extras. Obviously a traditional cake with powdered sugar is the only way.

While the worker processed my card I finally turned to Mateo and asked, "Why are you telling me?"

"I'm not sure. An act of friendship, I guess."

"Friendship?" I snorted. "By all means, don't break your loyalty to John for friendship."

Mateo bent over to dust off his shoes. "Maria is really mad at how I treated you."

"You told her about the affair?"

"No, but I told her how you helped me that night at The Outpost, and"—Mateo looked over my shoulder before making eye contact again—"and how I acted the next morning when Maggie removed you from the project."

The food truck worker leaned over and handed me my funnel cake through the small window. I walked over to the napkin dispenser and took out seven napkins—always an odd number like my grandpa taught me.

"Why did that make her mad? What did she want you to do?" I asked. I shoved a piece of funnel cake in my mouth and then blew out powdered sugar everywhere when it burned my tongue.

"She said a friend should have shown an act of friendship."

I asked, "Like what?" but it sounded more like "White what" from my funnel-cake-filled mouth.

Mateo shifted his weight from one foot to the other. His lips parted and then closed. His brow furrowed and he spoke in a sigh, "Like, make a call to John on your behalf."

"Oh, but you did make a call to John," I sneered. "Friend."

I enjoyed watching Mateo squirm. He hurt me. He hurt my future.

And now he thought he could make up for it with a juicy piece of gossip that only he and I knew about.

Mateo jogged to keep up with my quick pace as we headed toward Chance and Maria. "I acted hastily. I'm sorry for calling John and then not being compassionate when you lost the gig."

Right before we arrived at the seating area I stopped and turned to Mateo, "I wasn't going to share their stupid secret. It's none of my business. But you have no idea what you've cost me. Stay here. I'll tell Maria you want her to come with you to a food truck. And when you get your food"—I pointed away from the stage area—"take it to go."

CHAPTER NINTEEN

I TOOK IN the San Francisco cityscape as Maggie and I rode in the back of a black town car to the restaurant. We were to dine with Julia Coates and the other team in the contest.

I couldn't wait to meet Julia Coates. One of my favorite 80s music choruses played in my mind—"I'm so excited! And I just can't hide it!" But I did hide it, because although I convinced Maggie to let me back on the project, I had no intention of giving her access to my thoughts and emotions. She had lost security clearance to my heart in Mountain Home, and this latest act of goodwill hadn't changed that.

After Mateo had told me about Maggie and John breaking up, I called her up and asked to come back on the project. During that first call, I had tossed out a "You know I'm really good at this," a "Doesn't BCA deserve the best?" and a "The team really loves me, and I already have the vision."

She said she would think about it.

So I called Maggie's favorite nail salon and pretended I was her assistant adding a friend to her next appointment. She was surprised to see me at the nail bar on a stool next to hers, but she didn't turn around and walk out. I kept the conversation light and casual while the nail techs worked their magic.

On the way out, I put my hand with nails freshly painted in "You Don't Know Jacques" on her shoulder, looked her in the eye, and appealed, "Please let me back on this project. What do you care what John thinks now?"

She agreed.

With a caveat.

She wanted the VP of Branding position and requested my help to make her look good in front of Julia. "You'll get your chance to fulfill your poster board dreams with Julia when you win the contest. This will be a win-win," she said.

In San Francisco, we had agreed to meet in our hotel lobby at 6:30 p.m. I arrived fifteen minutes early and Maggie wordlessly whisked past me at 6:28 p.m. and exited through the revolving door into the open back door of a black town car. I scuttled along behind her and barely closed the door before the driver pulled out at her command.

Maggie tapped away on her cell phone, so I watched the city pass by through my window. I craned my neck at the soaring cathedral just outside my window and turned to comment on its majesty. White and fidgety, Maggie stared straight into the headrest of the seat in front of her. The historic architecture of Nob Hill did not capture her attention.

I started to ask if she was okay, but she spoke first. "This interview—er—dinner is really important to me, Joy."

"I know. VP of Branding here in San Francisco. You've mentioned it." *On repeat.*

"You'll get your chance tomorrow, but if you could give me tonight, that would be great," Maggie clipped.

"Absolutely, but how much influence do you think I'll have?"

Maggie's eyes grew wide. "You aren't on board?"

"That's not what I'm saying. I'm just saying I'm an outside consultant. Wouldn't an insider be more convincing?"

Maggie's jaw tightened and she turned her head and stared at the back of the headrest again.

I had gone too far.

"But you never know," I brightened my tone. "Maybe an outside perspective is more compelling. Like you said, this is a win-win situation, right? You get your VP of Branding job and I win the retreat with Julia."

"See, that's what I'm talking about," Maggie snapped. "I don't need you to be talking about the contest tonight. I need you to support me."

I felt slapped on the hand like Aunt Mimsy would do when I tried to grab a cookie before dinner. I pursed my lips and turned in silence to look back out the window.

"I'm sorry, Joy," she said, her tone gentler. "It's just that with all the changes—that I don't want to talk about—I need to impress Julia if I have any hope of getting this promotion."

I pushed down the thought of "you made this bed, now sleep in it," and welcomed a sense of empathy in its place. I actually felt a little sorry for Maggie—a little. She put her faith in John and he was no longer a reliable source of favor for her future.

Maggie smiled feebly.

That's a new look.

Maggie never let her guard down. Ever in control.

This time, I'm in control. So, what's the right call for me?

I studied Maggie's face. Extra makeup under her eyes concealed all but a shadow of the dark circles beneath. Guilt twisted a knot into my stomach. Maggie wasn't a pawn; she was a person.

"I'll do whatever I can to keep the spotlight on you tonight. I really appreciate all you've taught me, and this opportunity to fulfill a dream. It'll actually help calm my nerves to stop thinking about how I can impress Julia." I patted Maggie's leg, "I'll get my chance when we win the contest tomorrow."

"You have to be ready," Maggie insisted. "What are three things you are prepared to say about me?"

I spent the plane ride thinking about how Maggie's offer led me to relationships I treasured, but it had been a while since I thought positively about what Maggie meant to me. She was right. I needed to think about this.

I recalled the mentor-match ceremony. "From the first time I met you, I appreciated how generous you were with your time. You were a busy professional and you gave of yourself to a grad student. There wasn't even a position you needed to fill at Coates Inc. at the time."

Maggie nodded her head as her eyes darted back and forth, "Good. That's good. Julia's philanthropic. She'll value that."

Maggie turned back toward me with wide eyes, "Okay, something else."

"You passed on your end-in-mind leadership style. I used it to manage this project."

Maggie sat up a little straighter. "Thank you for saying that. I'm proud of you. It's my goal to raise up a generation of strong women. I keep that end in mind all the time."

I swallowed a grunt.

"One more," Maggie prodded. I opened my mouth to speak, but

she jumped in with, "How about you say something about how I've taught you to determine your own worth. I think it's important that women know they are the determiners of their value."

"Yeah, I'm not going to say that," I blurted.

Maggie's blinking eyes reflected as much shock as I felt in my response. I quickly recovered, "I was actually going to suggest how laser focused on business objectives you are."

Maggie paused and placed a finger over her lips in thought, "I like that, too." She folded her hands in her lap, "May I ask why you didn't like what I proposed?"

I repeated something Nanette taught me. "Because I don't believe we determine our own value. We're made in the image of God and that's what gives us value—we have worth because He says we have worth."

Maggie rolled her eyes.

I added, "Julia's a Christian, too. She will not agree with the assessment that we determine our self-worth."

At that, Maggie tilted her head in acquiescence. Staring at the back of the head rest in front of her, Maggie clasped her hands together in a clap. "Generous, end-in-mind leadership, and front-side focused—that's good."

I concluded the conversation was over when she reached into her purse, retrieved her phone, and resumed her tapping. Within minutes, the car pulled up at the restaurant.

CHAPTER TWENTY

THE HOSTESS ESCORTED US TO A TABLE overlooking the bay with a glorious view of the Golden Gate Bridge in the distance. Julia sat alone and rose to greet us.

Julia was taller than I envisioned. Her jet-black hair featured the same perfect afro-curls and pixie cut I had seen in the picture on Nanette's mantel. She wore a cinnamon-colored wrap dress with a V-neck that perfectly framed a stunning diamond pendant.

As the three of us exchanged greetings, Julia grasped my hand with both of hers, "Joy," her eyes glistened, "it is so nice to finally meet you. Nanette has bragged on you."

I felt my face flush. I wanted to jump up and down like a little kid waiting in line to see Santa, but I held it together and responded with, "Likewise. Thank you for hosting us this evening."

The other team members arrived and more greetings were exchanged. Maggie's East Coast counterpart, Denny James, jiggled my hand like he was shaking up a vinaigrette. The young woman with him smiled knowingly as she slid up next to me.

"The more nervous he gets, the harder he shakes," she chuckled.

"Good to know," I grinned.

"I'm Sylvia, by the way," she said as she smoothed her black, ultra-pleated skirt with her thin hand. I envied Sylvia's tiny frame that could pull off such a wardrobe choice as much as I envied the way her auburn hair flowed to her shoulders in soft waves my curly mop never could. We stood shoulder-to-shoulder watching the scene unfold.

While Maggie remained as still and cold as a beautifully designed ice sculpture, Denny bounced and popped like a puppy ready to play. Julia, on the other hand, floated gracefully like a fall leaf.

Denny wore a navy blazer over a white button-up shirt with the collar open and no tie. He tucked in a loose part of his shirt over his rounded belly into his camel-colored chinos. I glimpsed patterned socks peeking out from his dark oxford sneakers.

Sylvia must have followed my gaze to his feet because she commented, "His socks are his signature. He says they express his creative and fun personality."

I glanced at Sylvia with raised eyebrows. She smirked, "I would probably say quirky and amusing, but he's great to work for. How about Maggie? Is she good to work for?"

"She's a little more straightforward and no-nonsense," I said with an open palm wave of my hand toward her as proof of my appraisal. As if on cue, Maggie smoothed her signature fitted sheath dress and straightened her shoulders.

As we turned toward the small round table, Julia guided me to take the chair to her right hand. Maggie slid into the seat on her left. Sylvia took the seat next to Maggie and Denny bobbed around the table to sit between me and Sylvia.

Julia addressed Sylvia first. "How was it working with my friend, Tom?"

Sylvia prattled on about Tom and the project she spearheaded at Ezra Micro-Loans. I sipped my water and formulated what I would say if Julia asked me about Nanette.

"Joy, what do you think of my sweet Nanette?"

My prepared thoughts flitted away like a bumblebee moving on to the next flower. I swallowed hard and sputtered, "I've never met anyone quite like her."

Julia grinned as she sipped her water, "She's pretty special."

I straightened the napkin in my lap. "The thing that sticks out the most is her ability to turn everything back on you in a question. So, here's one for you," I propped my elbows on the table and asked with a twinkle in my eye and a lilt in my voice, "What's your favorite memory from camp?"

Julia tilted her head back in a glorious laugh that rivaled the musicality of a perfectly tuned wind chime. "Aah, our infamous camp days!" She continued to laugh as though we were all a part of an inside joke. "I see you're all expecting something good," she said as she assessed each of our faces around the table.

Julia launched into story after story of her, Nanette, and Tom's time together at camp. I had forgotten Nanette mentioned she knew Tom from camp as well. Julia was a master storyteller, pulling us from the edge of our seats into a well of laughter and back again. She captivated me.

Maggie broke in, "You and your friends are all so generous."

Maggie's words felt like turning on a harsh light before the credits completely rolled at the end of a gripping movie. She gave me my "cue" and it made my stomach sour.

I took a measured breath and remarked, "You know, Julia, I've been blessed by every interaction I've had with Coates Inc. First, I met Maggie when she charitably gave of her valuable time as my mentor-match through a special program for my master's degree. Then I had the honor to participate in this contest to meet you." I placed my hand on the table nearest Julia for emphasis and added, "And it has been life-changing. The contest led me in a roundabout way to Nanette. She challenged me to see life through a new lens."

I could feel Maggie's glare, but it was the best I could do—it was the best I was willing to do in that moment.

The evening continued with small talk and waiters delivering appetizers and refilling drinks. At one point Julia stepped away to take a phone call, Maggie engaged in deep conversation with Sylvia, and I learned all about Denny's long-haired dappled dachshund—ironically named Socks.

Once dinner was served, Julia asked Sylvia and I questions about Maggie and Denny. I was glad Sylvia had to go first. At this point I really didn't want to say anything else nice about Maggie. It all felt so scripted, and I was more than perturbed that she stole the moment I felt earlier with Julia.

While Sylvia raved about the fun and creative environment of their department under Denny's leadership, I talked myself out of acting like a brat. Everything I was about to say was true. Maggie took great pride in turning weakness into strength, but what she didn't know was that her greatest strengths were her greatest weaknesses, too.

"Tell me about working for Maggie on this project," Julia prompted.

"Maggie's great strength is her end-in-mind leadership style. She never let us get lost in the creative process without first getting clear on where we were headed. The trick in this project was getting to the heart of what Berean Christian Academy really wanted, while balancing the needs of Coates Incorporated, too."

I realized that comment might have sounded like I was dismissing the creativity of the other team, or worse, making it sound like our team wasn't creative. "Once that was clear, Maggie let us run with creativity. At every turn she expressed great faith in the team's abilities."

While causing me to question my own.

"Knowing that your leader believes in you really makes a difference," I looked directly at Maggie. Her soft smile indicated she thought I was paying her a compliment. What was bubbling to the surface of my heart was how damaging her on-again-off-again support of me throughout the contest really was.

One more point on my checklist for Maggie. "Not to mention that Maggie is consistently front-side focused."

There. I had done it. Maggie looked pleased. Julia looked pensive. Sylvia and Denny sat oblivious to the warring in my heart.

CHAPTER TWENTY-ONE

I HEARD THE BUZZER, but couldn't figure out where the sound came from. My eyes peeled open and focused on the numbers on the clock—6:00 a.m. *Alarm, Joy. It's the alarm. Shut it off. Shut. It. Off.*

As I willed myself out of bed, papers fluttered to the floor. I remembered reviewing the presentation notes I had put together for Maggie. I must have fallen asleep waiting for her to swing by the room after she took a call in the lobby after dinner.

I checked my phone. No texts.

I walked over to the window. If I tilted my head and squinted I could see a sliver of the Golden Gate Bridge between two buildings. I swiped wisps of curls out of my face, turned, and shuffled to the bathroom.

When I got out of the shower I checked my phone again. This time I had a text from Maggie. *I have to go a little earlier than we had arranged. Presentations have been moved up to 8:00. I'm leaving now. I'll just meet you there. No need to rush. I have everything I need.*

I checked the clock and calculated the time I had left to get ready, take an Uber to the home office, and still arrive without looking like I was sliding into home plate.

My heart raced, but my feet didn't budge as questions ricocheted in my mind. Why didn't she tell me about the time change earlier? How can she present from my notes without the prep session we planned?

Out of the corner of my eye I saw the minute number on the digital clock change. I groaned. Answers to my questions wouldn't add time to an already frantic morning.

I rushed back into the bathroom and stubbed my toe. When I put my hand on the counter to steady myself I knocked my hairbrush to the floor. I bent down to pick it up and knocked my head on the counter as I righted myself. Placing both hands on the counter I stared at myself in the mirror and took a deep breath.

Pull yourself together. You've got this.

· · ·

The presentation room had a large screen on one wall with a podium in the corner. Eight plush, turquoise egg chairs with swivel tables for note taking or laptops faced the screen. A panoramic skyline view of San Francisco began to disappear as the electric room darkening shades lowered in preparation for the presentations.

Maggie, Julia, and Denny huddled deep in conversation in the corner near the podium. Another young guy fiddled with cords and connections on a laptop.

I veered toward the refreshments table for coffee and saw Sylvia staring at the pastries.

She glanced up, smiled, and then looked at her hands. "When I first saw this table I was trying to decide whether or not I should eat one. Now I'm trying to decide which one I want."

We laughed together.

"Dinner was lovely last night," I offered.

"Wasn't it? I'm so sorry you couldn't make it down last night. Maggie and I had a great conversation in the lobby bar."

"Oh, um, yeah," I stammered. I leaned over and carefully examined each pastry—donut, danish, bagel, croissant. "Jet lag," I finally proffered lamely. *Jet lag? You're an hour different!*

Sylvia didn't seem to notice the lame excuse. "Maggie's amazing. Even at dinner she poured into me like I was on her team. What's it like working for her? Have you learned a lot?"

I turned and looked at Maggie. She furrowed her brow, shook her head at the IT guy, and pointed at the laptop screen. I wasn't even sure she knew I arrived. I thought about offering my assistance, then decided against it.

"So much," I painted on a smile. "From the first day I met her during my master's degree mentor program she had an agenda. She is laser focused, that's for sure."

Sylvia and I settled into two chairs in the back row when the door opened and John strode in heading straight for the group at the podium.

I didn't know John was coming.

Maggie's eyes widened and she pressed her hand to her throat and swallowed hard. Part of me wanted a bucket of popcorn to enjoy this show.

Maggie looked down and swiped her hand at an invisible wrinkle in her skirt, then raised her head, straightened her shoulders, and transformed from unnerved to poised in an instant.

Classic Maggie.

Then the right corner of her mouth twitched ever so slightly—twitch, pause, twitch, pause, twitch—a tiny crack in her veneer of control.

"Who is that?" Sylvia asked quietly.

"John Clarke, Chief Marketing Officer."

I watched as Maggie leaned over to say something in John's ear. He gave a quick nod and they left the room. Sylvia chattered on about all that she and Maggie talked about the night before. I tried to listen, but got lost in picturing how Maggie and John's conversation was going in the hall. Were they arguing about the breakup? Were they making up? Were they talking about me?

The more Sylvia talked, the more I realized that Maggie only had one bag of tricks. Her "pouring into" Sylvia consisted of the same advice she had given me at the start of our mentorship—some of which I no longer agreed with.

When John returned to the room without Maggie I knew something was up, but I didn't know John well enough to read his facial expression. Julia whispered in his ear. He shook his head and said something back and asked Denny something. Denny lit up like a Christmas tree and in moments they headed our way.

Sylvia and I both stood as Denny bobbed and John coasted in to greet us. Denny introduced Sylvia to John who shook her hand. John turned to greet me and flashed the same handsome smile he did the first day I met him. The same smile. As I shook his hand, I looked over his shoulder and saw Maggie return.

Maggie must have brought her plastering kit with her because the cracks that appeared in the mask she wore had been touched up. Unfortunately, the mask didn't cover her eyes. Her perfectly crafted veneer could not hide the shadow clouding the ever-present fire in her eyes.

"Well, excuse me ladies," John said. "I think the presentation is about to begin."

"He's handsome," Sylvia whispered in my ear as we returned to our seats.

"He's married," I retorted.

Sylvia turned with a short gasp, "I didn't mean…"

I kicked myself for not holding it together better. I knew Sylvia didn't mean anything by it. After all, John was a handsome and distinguished-looking man. "I know. I'm sorry. Yes, I agree. He's a very nice-looking man."

John, Denny, and Maggie made their way to seats in the front row, the IT guy handed Maggie a remote, and Julia opened the meeting.

"I am privileged to host today's presentations. While I thought a little friendly competition between product groups would inspire creativity, I am most excited about the ways your two groups have impacted the organizations through your quality deliverables. Therefore, I am pleased to welcome my friends, Nanette Verity, founder of Berean Christian Academy, and Tom Flower, founder of Ezra Micro-Loans."

As Julia directed our attention with a wave of her hand toward the presentation room doors, they opened and Nanette and Tom walked in.

Denny and Sylvia jumped to their feet to greet Tom, giving me "permission" to spring up and approach Nanette for a hug.

"I didn't know you would be here!"

"It was supposed to be a surprise," Nanette's eyes twinkled.

"It's a wonderful surprise—on a morning full of surprises."

Nanette raised one brow as Maggie walked up extending her hand. "Welcome, Nanette."

"Thank you, so much, Mrs. Hensley. It's nice to see you again." It made sense that Maggie knew Nanette, but I had been so careful never to mention Maggie in my discussions with her that it caught me off guard.

Maggie's mask cracked again—tiny fractures marring the perfectly poised face of a woman with a seemingly unlimited ability to command her emotions and expressions. The cracks were indistinguishable to those who did not know her as well as I did. I'm sure the others didn't notice any change in her. The others hadn't put their trust in her like I had. They didn't know how much she hated surprises.

The only other person in the room who might recognize the gray cloud dimming Maggie's intense eyes was John. But it seemed like it was he who cast the shadow.

John directed Tom and Nanette to join him in seats in the front row, bumping Maggie to the second row while we all returned to our seats. More cracks.

Julia continued, "Tom and Nanette are two of my oldest and dearest friends. They each founded organizations that are making lasting differences in the world today. It is my honor to utilize the talents of the best marketing departments in the nation to aid them in their efforts. I am thankful for them and the people they serve."

Julia paused and made individual eye contact with each person in the room as she spoke. "I hope it will inspire *you* to do the same in your personal lives. Like a tiered fountain, as each vessel is filled to the brim it spills over into the next. Continue to pour yourselves out for the benefit of others. Count others as more significant than yourselves. That is what this has been about."

Applause erupted from the small gathering.

Julia clapped with arms extended toward Nanette and Tom, then opened her arms demonstratively, "And as far as the competition goes, I desired it to bring out the very best in both teams. I believe healthy competition breeds creativity. And I assume we've kept it healthy, haven't we?"

Julia's raised brows and corrective tone brought snickers from the group.

"While I am sincere in my desire to pay-it-forward to my friends, I want to be a good steward of my company and teams as well. I asked that the videos created feature a Coates Inc. product to use in our own marketing and branding efforts. This is what will be judged from each team today.

"Today's presentations will determine the winner of the competition. The winning department will get a fifteen hundred-dollar voucher to take the entire marketing team out to a fabulous dinner. So much joy can be had over a good meal.

"And not only will the winning team get bragging rights at future company events, but they will go home with this!" Julia pulled out a custom glass sculpture from behind the podium.

A glass sculpture? What about the retreat? What about the magazine feature?

I immediately looked at Maggie whose head snapped toward John whose attention never wavered from Julia. More cracks.

The room felt like the teacup ride beginning to spin, but I willed myself to keep listening as Julia set the glass sculpture on a small table at the front of the room.

"As you can see, this stunning sculpture in the shape of a drop of water features waves of blue. This is a picture reminding everyone that their efforts will continue to have a ripple effect for eternity. A single drop in a still body of water can cause ripples that extend far beyond that first splash. May our impact continue to extend in wave after wave."

The only waves I felt were the waves of doubt, confusion, and betrayal crashing around me.

"If you think I'm overstating it when I say the ripple effect can last for eternity, I assure you, I am not. Tom, Nanette, it has been our honor to partner with you and your ministries. The lives you touch—the gospel you share—these *are* eternal."

CHAPTER TWENTY-TWO

"WE'RE GOING TO TAKE A SHORT technology break before our presentations. Grab some refreshments, and we'll resume shortly," Julia said.

I walked up to Maggie and whispered in her ear, "I need to talk to you."

Without so much as a nod of her head, Maggie stood and walked to the door in a trance. She exited the room and left me stunned.

I didn't want to make a scene, but I was done being dragged along by Margaret Hensley. She was going to have to answer for herself.

I shoved the conference room door open and marched out of the room. It took a few turns before I spotted her at the end of a remote hallway. She paced in front of a window and took a deep breath every time she turned. When she saw me, she motioned for me to join her with a quick swipe of her left hand. She fanned her face with her right hand and then ran her fingers through her hair.

I had never once seen Margaret Hensley touch her hair.

As I approached, she stopped pacing and looked over my shoulder with wild eyes. I turned my head only to see an empty hallway. Maggie turned her back to me, leaned over, placed her hands on her knees, and took deep breaths, exhaling through pursed lips.

I stood motionless for a moment and took in the scene that unfolded before me.

Maggie Hensley was losing it.

My internal seesaw vacillated between anger and compassion. Unfortunately for Maggie, in the end, compassion was a toddler stranded in the air while my anger had a backpack full of accusations pinning it to the ground.

I threw my shoulders back, lengthened my neck, and took the remaining steps to stand directly behind Maggie. I shoved down the internal nudge to gently touch her shoulder to let her know I was close.

I was done with her.

I didn't care why she was so upset. I wanted answers.

Still bent at the waist, Maggie tilted her head and made eye contact. Then, looking past me down the hall as if to ensure no one else was around, she took another deep breath and stood upright.

She smoothed her skirt, tucked her disheveled hair behind her ears, and blew out a slow breath. "I don't know what happened in there."

"Oh?" I responded with one raised brow.

"Joy!" she whispered forcefully. "You can't think I knew the contest was for a glass trophy!"

Anger bubbled up. "Perhaps," I replied.

A door opened at the end of the hallway. A young man in slacks, white shirt, and dangling tie pushed a cart loaded with file boxes away from us. He never even looked in our direction.

"I was completely caught off guard," she insisted.

"I can see that." I pressed my lips closed before the lava of accusations building pressure within me spewed all over her.

Maggie turned to look out the window. "We've been duped," she said as if to herself.

"What *did* you think was going to happen in there?" I seethed.

Maggie turned with an open mouth and ragged breath, "I thought I was going to make a presentation and we would win the contest, Joy."

"There's a lot more to it than that, and you know it. Otherwise, you wouldn't be having a breakdown in the hallway." I sounded unfeeling because I felt unfeeling. I was numb. How many times would I have to go through this? How many times would I follow someone's lead straight into the quagmire of missed opportunities and disappointment?

Maggie bumbled, "He…I just…I can't seem to…" And then she tilted her head toward the ceiling and started to cry.

Her act of humanity disgusted me.

"To be honest, Maggie, I don't really care about you right now. I want answers for me." I put my hands on my head and looked at the ceiling. I married a cry with a whine, "I have so many questions that don't even matter, because what I had my sights set on was an illusion."

Maggie's vacant eyes spilled tears in streams down her face. "I swear I thought the contest was for a retreat at the lake with Julia."

I wanted to throw something at her.

"Why would you think that, Maggie?"

"Because that's what John told me," she wailed.

I wasn't sure I believed her other than Maggie looked like a wilted flower. "Why on God's green earth would John lie about the contest, Maggie?"

"I don't know!" she whimpered.

My mind couldn't make sense of everything. I wanted to escape the maze, but I bumped into a dead-end with each additional detail. Turning back to the beginning, I asked, "Why am I here?"

"John told me about Julia's contest and said it was the ideal proving ground for me to earn the new VP of Branding position in San Francisco. He said he wanted me to come with him when he moved here for a promotion." Maggie began sobbing again.

I grabbed her arms and jostled her. "That's about you, not me. Why am I here?"

Maggie wiped her nose with the back of her hand. "John insisted I hire a Christian to spearhead the project with the school. I said I was a Chr—"

Maggie's eyes grew wide and looked past me down the hall.

I swiveled to see Nanette walking toward us. When she got close enough to see my red face and Maggie's tears she exclaimed, "Oh, my! Is everything okay?"

Maggie turned her back to Nanette and wiped at her eyes and tapped her cheeks to dry them.

"It's been better," I offered.

"Mrs. Hensley," Nanette said as she placed her hand on her shoulder. "Can I pray with you?"

Maggie kept her back to Nanette, sniffed, and declined with a shake of her head.

I walked Nanette down the hall away from Maggie. "Thanks for your concern, but she'll be alright."

"Shall I alert Julia?"

"No," I blurted with eyes wide. I softened my expression, plastered on a soft smile, and touched her arm, "Thanks for thinking of her. It's something personal. We just have a few more things to discuss and we'll be right back. Has the meeting started?"

"No, not yet. I just got a little turned around looking for the restroom and saw the two of you." Nanette gave me a quick hug. "I'll be praying."

"Thanks. We'll be right in."

I walked back toward Maggie and took in a deep breath. If I were in the praying mood, what would I ask for? I would ask for what was promised. That's what I would ask for.

"You needed a Christian for the project? That's a Christian," I spat with a finger pointed down the empty hall in the direction of Nanette's exit. "And she believes in BCA more than any of you." I paced back and forth in front of Maggie and added to myself, "How did I get here?"

Maggie must have thought I was asking her because she said, "John told me the other marketing team appointed a consultant over the Ezra Micro-Loans project and I should do the same. When I asked him why he cared about the project so much he"—Maggie sniffed and breathed in short rapid breaths at the memory—"he touched my hand and looked me in the eye and said he wanted to do whatever it took for me to be able to come with him to San Francisco." At that, she turned back toward the window fanning her face. It was just as well that her back faced me because I couldn't contain a dramatic eye roll.

Maggie turned to me with swollen eyes, "Looking back, Joy, he was right. I didn't understand the project the way you did. I could never have pulled off the result you achieved. I know it will attract new students to BCA."

"Don't pretend you did this for Berean Christian Academy, Maggie. Even as recent as last night it was all about you," I snapped.

Her shoulders slumped and her chin hit her chest. "I know. I'm so sorry. But when John insisted I hire a consultant, I immediately thought of you. I got excited about it, actually, because I enjoyed working with you at the university and truly believed you would be an asset to the project and the team. We talked about your natural talent and I reminded John that you were the one with the vision board I used to make fun of—that you had this silly picture of people around a farmhouse style table and it said something about rubbing shoulders with CEOs."

I knew she didn't think much of my vision board, but I never realized she thought it was silly. I tried to shake off the sting.

"Anyway, John said something about it being perfect for you then. He told me to convince you to take the job by telling you the contest was for a retreat with Julia."

"So, he just made it all up? Why would he do that?"

"I don't know!" she lamented, "I trusted him!" She sniffed and wiped her nose with the back of her hand. "I've made a fool of myself. Even this morning I begged him to take me back. He was so cruel. It's like I don't even know him. He said he never wanted me to come with him to San Francisco. He said he loves his wife. He said what we had was fun, but it was over and I needed to get a grip."

Maggie's entire body wracked with weeping.

"I'm assuming he's the real reason I was removed from the project?"

Maggie nodded. "He was furious when Mateo told him you knew about the affair. I tried to tell him that you'd known all along and hadn't said anything to anyone. But he said you were a liability to everything we'd been working toward and I had to pull you from the project right away."

I thought answers would bring comfort. Instead, my body twitched with fury. I glanced down the hall. If I slapped her right now it would be her word against mine.

"Did you really think the dinner last night was an interview?"

"I really did. John and I haven't talked much, except for business matters, but he prepped me over several different occasions to take the reins at the dinner. I took that as a sign that he really did want me in San Francisco with him." She slumped against the wall. "And all he wanted to do was neutralize me."

As her tears welled up again, my defenses fell.

Her head drooped and liquid sorrow dripped from her eyes to the floor.

It was all too much.

A web of deception tangled us all together—each person keeping their eyes fixed on what they wanted. My anger reduced to a low simmer as I yielded to the truth that it didn't really matter how I got here. The only thing that mattered now, was how to get out of here.

I caught movement out of the corner of my eye and turned in time to see Sophia at the end of the hall. "Oh, good! There you are! Julia's ready to get started. Maggie, you're up!"

Once Sophia disappeared around the corner again, Maggie wailed, "I can't!"

I put my hand on her shoulder and squeezed hard enough that she winced. "You can. And you will. Pull it together and go back in there and act like the classy lady I thought you were. Win the glass trophy. Take the team to dinner, and remind them how amazing they are. And let John go. He wasn't ever yours anyway."

CHAPTER TWENTY-THREE

RATHER THAN A DELIGHTFUL STROLL through a spring garden, the morning passed like the blur of the landscape from a speeding train. Maggie presented our video. Whoosh. Was that applause? Zip. Denny played their video. Buzz. Our video was far and away the better of the two. Flash. The lights came up and Julia awarded Maggie the prize. Screech.

Before I knew it I stood at the food table with Sophia while a professional photographer took photos. Click. Click. I popped a second almond in my mouth before I finished chewing the first one. I crunched loudly—and I didn't care. Sophia and I watched while the photographer snapped pictures of Julia and Tom and Nanette. Then Julia and Nanette. Then Julia and Tom. Then Julia and John and Nanette and Tom. Then Julia and Denny and Maggie. Then Julia and John and…

"So, we were literally just the hired help," I muttered in between crunches.

"Yep," Sophia shrugged. "But I've loved every minute of it."

Sophia practically floated and prattled on about how grateful she was to be a part of something so exciting. I, on the other hand, couldn't stop pouting. I hated my sullen demeanor sprinkled with bitterness, but I couldn't pull myself out of it.

As a kid, I was a terrible sport. As long as I was winning the board game, I lived on cloud nine, but when I lost, I couldn't help the raging disappointment. My mom got so frustrated with my bad attitude she refused to play with me. I wanted to play for fun, but I couldn't turn the ship in my heart away from the rocky shore of self-loathing—even when it was a game of luck.

But this wasn't a game. At least not to me. And even though we won the contest, my heart was in jagged pieces on the craggy banks of broken promises.

"Do you have your own consulting firm?" I asked.

Sophia nearly spit out her sip of coffee. She coughed and grabbed a napkin to wipe her mouth. "Oh, no. I work in the media department at church."

"Oh." So she had nothing to lose. This was a ministry gig to her.

Natural light spilled back into the room as the blinds inched open. I turned to really take in the view. It looked like a postcard. The cityscape looked crisp and clean from this vantage point. I knew from walking around that the view from here didn't tell the whole story. The towering skyscrapers with their shiny mirrored windows reflected blue skies and sunshine while their street-side awnings provided slight shelter for the poor and homeless.

Poor and homeless. That's what I'm going to be if I can't pull out my original business plan and make something happen.

Over the last two months, business, life, and car expenses—not to mention new dog expenses—ate a huge hole in the loan money Maggie gave me. And I needed the rest of the money plus my savings to keep living while I launched my business—from scratch at this point. I couldn't pay it back now if I wanted to. And I wanted to. I wanted to be free from this circus.

Sort of.

I still wanted a seat at the table with Julia. Now more than ever. I watched Nanette and Julia interact with one another—so familiar—so happy. Now that I'd gotten to know both of them better, I knew they offered so much more than a rung in the ladder to the pinnacle of my career.

"Do *you* have your own consulting firm?" Sophia's question pulled me from my thoughts.

"Yes. It's new."

"That's so brave. You're really talented, I'm sure you're going to be wildly successful."

I shoved a donut hole in my mouth so I didn't have to talk more. Sophia asked me something else, but I pointed to my full mouth. Then motioned that I was going into the hall.

I walked to the bathroom to rinse my fingers and get the sugar off of my face. I let the water flow over my hands. The warmth took the chill from my hands, but couldn't touch the chill in my chest. "Just get through the rest of the day," I said to myself in the mirror.

When I exited the bathroom, I looked down the hall to the right. I could sprint to reception, retrieve my bags, and head straight to the airport. But I had promised Nanette that we'd take a picture together, and I wasn't ready to give into the grief that welled up inside.

When I reentered the presentation room Maggie said, "There she is! Come on over, Joy. We're taking one last group picture."

Maggie waved me over with a big smile like we were at a family reunion. Winning the contest for a glass raindrop looked good on her.

I wanted to be happier. I told myself the video would still be in my portfolio of work. I told myself I had new contacts at BCA I could lean on. I told myself all I had to do was smile.

Everyone talked and mumbled as the photographer shuffled us around. He pulled me by my shirt and shoved me next to John whose bright smile made me nauseous. I started to trade places with someone and John grabbed my arm and leaned over to whisper in my ear.

"You may have wormed your way back on this project, but you're disposable now."

My breath caught and I turned to John with wide eyes, but he aimed his plastic smile toward the photographer. I whipped my head around to see if anyone else heard him, but with all of the commotion of being rearranged, everyone only paid attention to themselves.

"You—with the curls"—the photographer pointed at me—"big smile."

A smile felt impossible. His camera flashed and flashed. Maggie mentioned earlier how cruel John had been to her, now I felt the sting firsthand.

When the photographer took his last photo, the group broke up, and John said, "And one more thing." He grabbed my elbow—tight— and pulled me to the corner of the room.

I wanted to tell him he was hurting me. I wanted to make a scene. Instead, I stood like a statue.

"We're done with you. I don't ever want to see you again—not at Coates, not at Maggie's, not at BCA—never again."

I have never wanted to remain emotionless more, but the tears welled up on their own accord. I blinked quickly to keep them at bay while my hands remained at my side.

John turned to walk away. As if an afterthought, he stopped and tossed out words over his shoulder, "Oh, and the money you got from Maggie came from me and I'm calling the loan. You have ninety days to repay." He turned back toward me, leaned in, looked down his nose, and growled, "And don't even think about tattling to your little boyfriend. How do you think he'd feel if he knew you were more worried about singing campfire songs with Julia Coates than working with adulterers?"

This time I did run—even as Nanette called after me for our photo.

CHAPTER TWENTY-FOUR

THE VOICES BLENDED AND CLASHED, each vying to be the loudest—each attempting to seize my attention and hold it until another forcibly wrestled it down.

On the taxi ride to the airport I heard Mrs. Carmichael's voice, "Please don't tell. I'll change directions, I promise."

When I sat in the chairs waiting for the crew to arrive, I heard James's voice, "Wait on the Lord."

As I walked up to show the attendant my boarding pass, I heard Kent's voice, "A well-told story will take you anywhere you want to go."

When I made my way down the aisle to choose an open window seat, I heard Marshal's voice, "I choose Logan."

As our plane waited in line on the tarmac, I looked out the window and heard Logan's voice, "I wanted it too."

When I closed my eyes on take-off, the pressure in my chest matched the pressure I felt when Maggie said, "Take the money, Joy. Your business will flourish."

When I ordered my ginger ale, I heard Mateo snarl, "I'm loyal."

As I munched on my pretzels, I heard Chance say, "Man does not live by bread alone."

At the carousel in baggage claim I strained to locate my bright orange luggage and heard Nanette say, "The more reliable the guide, the better chance of survival and fulfilled dreams."

When I finally allowed my tears to flow as I pulled onto the interstate, John's words echoed in my head, "You're disposable."

And as I lugged my suitcase out of the back of Scarlett at home, I heard Julia say, "May our impact continue in wave after wave."

Waves.

I felt the waves—but they were the big, destructive, crashing kinds—not the endless, gentle ripples Julia described.

I rolled my travel bag across the threshold and closed the door behind me. I dropped my keys into the blue handmade pottery bowl on the counter right inside the door. Beth made the bowl in art class our sophomore year of college when I lived in Malibu and she lived in Portland. She almost didn't give it to me. It had a nearly invisible hole in the bottom which rendered it useless for anything liquid. But my best friend made it by hand, and I loved it.

The bowl reminded me of Beth's voice—always kind and encouraging. She listened to all my stories as they raged like a hurricane with only a brief reprieve at the eye of the storm. She would nod and ask the occasional question, but I never felt like she had an agenda. Then she would cover my hand with hers and remind me that God was still in control. She would tell me she would pray for me—and then she'd actually pray for me. Her voice in my head said, "Trust Him."

My mom always taught me to leave a lamp lit with a TV or radio on when traveling, "So people think you're home." As in most everything else, I took the advice to the extreme. Loud voices came at me from every room—singing voices, selling voices, arguing voices. The cacophony of sound was "enough to make your ears bleed" as Papa used to say.

I dragged my suitcase the few steps it took to get from my carport door to my bedroom and tossed my oversized purse onto the bed. I reached to turn off the TV in my bedroom. The talking heads on the screen argued about energy preservation.

Where should I put my energy?

Maggie and Kent would tell me to put my energy into the next hot thing to maximize momentum. James and Nanette would tell me to pursue truth.

I don't even know what truth is anymore.

I made my way back into the living room to turn off that TV. A man with blond hair and a bad comb-over told me to buy now. He sounded the scarcity alarm with his limited time offer, but offered the hope of an abundance of time saved if I used his product.

Mateo's words echoed, "John gave me an opportunity when no one else would. Another pathway to success like this one won't come around again." Scarcity.

Logan's pleading eyes assaulted my memory. "You're better at this than I am, Joy. You'll land on your feet. You're better equipped for the opportunities out there." Abundance.

As far as my landing, I did not have an epic Olympic dismount. My feet weren't planted with my arms raised in victory. Rather, my bloody hands and knees told a different story. The wounds still stung like crazy.

I shook my head. I didn't want to give Logan Fisher or Mateo Gonzales any more airtime in my mind.

As I made my way into the kitchen, Roxette's 80s tune, "Listen to your heart," streamed from the radio. Of all the advice I've ever been given, that was the chord strummed the loudest and most consistently.

"What does your gut tell you?" they asked. "Follow your heart," they said. "You know yourself better than anyone," they assured.

I turned off the radio, but continued to stare at it blankly as the melody reverberated, "And there are voices that want to be heard. So much to mention but you can't find the words."

My voice was the one that had been silent. My whole life I'd sought the counsel of others. I always believed if I could find the right mentor they could guide me around the pitfalls. I gave all of them voice to my life while silencing my own.

I didn't even know what my own voice sounded like. I didn't know myself better than anyone. I knew everyone better than I knew myself.

So what do you want, Joy?

"I wanna know what love is!" Foreigner wailed as I slipped into the bathroom to mute the final voice. "And I want you to show me!"

No, actually. I don't want anyone to show me anything anymore. I'm taking control of this thing.

What was that? I think I just heard my own voice.

CHAPTER TWENTY-FIVE

I SILENCED THE ALARM and slung my feet over the side of the bed before I fell back asleep. I changed into shorts and a T-shirt and slid on my walking shoes. I brushed my teeth and piled my curls high on my head. I filled my water bottle and walked to the hook where I kept Piper's leash.

Oh, yeah. She's not here.

An unexpected wave of sadness washed over me when I remembered Piper was at Beth's house. I couldn't believe I actually missed her.

I didn't want to wallow in those feelings, so I opted for a drive instead. I popped the T-top off of Scarlett, hopped in, and revved the engine. I hoped the fresh morning air whipping around me would do the trick.

When I returned, I took a shower, dried and styled my hair, and got dressed in my emerald-green power suit. The smell of freshly brewed coffee beckoned me into the kitchen after I finished applying my makeup. I poured myself a cup and headed into my guest room.

I sat at my desk and straightened some papers. I stood up and pushed my chair back under my desk. I looked at the phone in my hand, straightened my shoulders, took a deep breath, and dialed John's number.

"Hello, Joy. Calling to arrange the repayment of the loan?"

I determined ahead of time not to let John get under my skin. I guess the feeling of something crawling on top of my skin unsettled me most.

"Actually, yes. I have a proposal for you." I cleared my throat. "You have the wrong impression of me and I want to correct that."

I willed John to feel my power and conviction.

I thought back to the day I met Maggie. I felt her power and conviction. I needed to emulate that.

• • •

My hands shook as I tore into the envelope. The mentor-matching program was one of the reasons I chose the university's master's program in the first place. I had high hopes for my match. I had heard stories of unicorns and rainbows and dumpster fires alike.

I walked to the microphone and read the card, "Mrs. Margaret Hensley, Director of Marketing, Coates Incorporated." I looked out into the audience to see Maggie stand and smile. She had blonde, chin-length hair, wore a regal violet suit, Christian Louboutin heels, and an air of confidence I wanted for my own.

The room looked a little like a speed-dating venue as I made my way down the stairs toward our two-seat table. We whispered a greeting and shook hands before we settled in and turned our attention to the remaining match announcements.

At the end of the matching ceremony we were all encouraged to take the rest of the time to get to know our mentor and make a plan of action to utilize their expertise in our real-world marketing project.

"Mrs. Hensley, it's a pleasure to meet you, I'm Joy Swallow," I began.

"Call me Maggie. This is the second year I've participated in this program and I'm delighted to meet you as well."

"Second year?" I asked with a raised brow. "Isn't it a little time consuming? I know you're a busy professional. What makes you want to give of your time like this?"

"That's a fantastic question. Because you need to go into every project and every endeavor, even if it is philanthropic in nature, with an end in mind—and I definitely have an end in mind. I want to invest in the future generation of women. I've grown as a professional woman and I believe I have something to give back to help strengthen a future generation mentally."

"And I was only hoping for some real-life advice on my project and maybe a referral for a job."

Maggie offered a courtesy laugh and added, "I appreciate your candor. I like that."

I rubbed my hands on my thighs, "I'm so embarrassed I said that out loud. It seems so selfish and small."

"Actually, that's one of the main things I try to teach women. As a woman we have tendencies that many view as weaknesses. Speaking our mind, for one, is considered a strength for men, but unwelcome in women. Joy, if you learn how to speak your mind on purpose with a purpose, then it will be a strength—not to say that people won't still view it as a weakness."

I sat mesmerized.

"Let's take this conversation, for example," Maggie continued. "You have spoken your mind. I can see where you're coming from. And yes, to your point, it's a little selfish and small. But now that I know where you're coming from, I can help you expand your viewpoint and help you see possibilities you never knew existed."

I went from a fantastic question to revealing my small-mindedness. I wasn't sure if I impressed her or disappointed her, but I knew I wanted to stay at the table and talk with her. I had never met such a strong and confident woman.

. . .

I could be strong and confident.

I would be strong and confident.

John wouldn't know what hit him.

"There's more I can do for you at Berean Christian Academy," I continued.

"I don't think there is."

Thankful John couldn't see the wince on my face, I pressed on. "You're not thinking big enough."

"That's a bold statement," his flat tone blushed with intrigue.

"Jackson is graduating, you're moving to San Francisco, and your time at BCA is done. You want to leave a legacy—a lasting impression of the impact the Clarke family has made." I paused to see if the legacy play landed.

"I'm listening."

I stood and paced from the desk to the window and back again. "Hire me as a marketing consultant for the BCA gala. I know I can raise over two hundred and fifty thousand dollars, and with my twenty percent consultant fee that will pay back the fifty thousand dollars I owe you and leave the school with substantially more than the gala has ever raised."

"I just don't think you're worth it."

. . .

"You said speaking your mind is *one* of the main things you try to teach women. What other things are important to pass on?" I asked Maggie.

"Another great question! I'm proud of you for bouncing back from an awkward encounter."

I tucked a rogue curl behind my ear. *Great. She thought it was as awkward as I felt.*

"Your self-worth should not be determined by anyone else's opinion," Maggie charged on. "This is all on you, Joy. You determine your own value. As you grow in your mental strength, you will develop healthy coping skills to help you stand up to others who try to bring you down. Don't be your own worst enemy. I cannot determine your value. Only you can. Have you ever contemplated your self-worth?"

"You mean, other than right now where I'm feeling a little stupid?" I smiled and looked away from Maggie's intense gaze.

"I know you're nervous. And I know I can be a lot. I'm not real big on formalities and your thoughtful questions have let me dive right in to the heart of things. But have you? Have you thought about who gets to determine what you're worth?" Maggie leaned in aggressively and I fought the urge to lean back.

"I have. But I've never thought of it in the way you're describing—where I have the power to determine it."

"Good. Then let's start there. We're getting ready to plan a project where you'll be graded both in real-world results and by your graduate professors. I will also be evaluating the results. And don't be fooled, you are always evaluating yourself." The pace of Maggie's speech made it hard to keep up. "I realize your work is a reflection of who you are. But will your worth be determined by the results, your mentor, your professors, or can it stand outside of this and be determined by you in spite of what others think?"

"I'm thinking the right answer is that I can determine my worth despite what others think."

Maggie beamed as she leaned back in her chair with her shoulders straight. Even her posture gave off an air of control and self-confidence.

"Don't give away the authority to define who you are and who you'll become to anyone. You're stronger than that."

. . .

"It really doesn't matter what you think." I fluffed my hair and pushed my shoulders back. "What will Julia think when she finds out you were having an affair with Maggie? What kind of legacy will you leave when I share your indiscretion with everyone I know at BCA?"

John's laughter on the other end of the line caught me off guard. "You're right, Joy. I did have the wrong impression of you."

I wiped wrinkles out of my skirt, stared out of my guest room window, and waited for the verdict. A black-billed magpie lit on my neighbors fence and squawked.

"Have you told Mr. Easton of my indiscretion?" John asked.

"No."

"But you told Mateo."

"That's not exactly how it went down." I kept my voice professional and emotionless. "We came to the mutual understanding that we both knew and haven't discussed it since." Technically that was true. I didn't count his revelation that they had broken up a discussion.

"And you haven't told anyone else?"

"No." Except Beth. But she didn't count. She'd never tell anyone.

After a long pause, John spoke again. "There is something I want."

I knew it. Guys like you always have a hidden agenda.

"I want my name on the football field."

"You want your name on the field?" I couldn't hide my puzzlement. I pictured "John Clarke" spray painted in the middle of the field—puffy, neon letters like the graffiti art on the train cars that passed through town.

"Yes. I want to rename the football field 'Clarke Field.'"

"I don't understand," confusion displaced my confidence.

"There's an outdated tradition at BCA not to name buildings after people. Mr. Easton continues to stand in the way of a large donation I'm willing to make to completely overhaul the football field with turf, a new press box, improved stands, and an updated scoreboard."

Understanding rose like the dawning sun. "And you want me to convince Mr. Easton to stand down."

"Precisely."

"And I get the marketing consultant gig for twenty percent of gross funds raised for the gala?"

"Sure." I could picture his smug face. He didn't care about the gala. He probably didn't even care about me paying him back. But I uncovered his weakness and I would use it to get back what he had taken from me.

"I'll send over the contract later today."

CHAPTER TWENTY-SIX

THE MORNING SUN peeked over the blue-gray ridge of mountains in the distance. The clouds reflected yellow and orange and pink and purple in watercolor layers parallel to the horizon. On the hour drive to Mountain Home, I brainstormed ideas for the gala. John got me the signed contract late the day before in record time—his influence as the Booster Club President apparently oozed into budget-approval territory.

The sun completely crested the horizon by the time I pulled into Aunt Mimsy's driveway. Beth expected me later in the morning to hang out for the day and pick up Piper, but I got an early start to air out Aunt Mimsy's house first.

The porch swing didn't look the same without Aunt Mimsy's pillow on display—the one that said, "That's a horrible idea. What time should I be there?" I smiled to myself.

Abandoned hooks flanking the steps had me missing the bushy, green Boston ferns Aunt Mimsy always nurtured. I picked up bundles of printed ads in plastic bags from the stoop and tucked them under my arm as I unlocked the door and stepped inside.

Aside from the slight stale smell, everything looked as I remembered it. The sofa, accented with oversized pink roses, faced the front picture window. Aunt Mimsy's coffee table still held a collection of *Southern Living* magazines over a decade old. Beyond the living area, her dining chairs remained evenly spaced and neatly tucked under the matching oak table.

Upon closer inspection, I noticed a few framed photos missing from the sofa table. And Aunt Mimsy's lime-green swivel rocker looked naked without her colorful, crocheted granny square afghan draped on the back.

I opened all the windows and turned on the fans.

My phone buzzed. It was a text from Chance. *BCA hired you as a consultant for the gala?*

Surprise! I responded with a party face emoji complete with party hat and confetti.

I'm so relieved, he replied.

Then I was relieved. I had worried maybe Chance would see it as an unwelcome intrusion.

Now you HAVE to let me help. I tapped out with a smiley face emoji.

Gladly.

But seriously. I'll be in touch soon for planning purposes. I ran a finger across the coffee table and flicked the small pile of dust with my thumb.

Sounds good.

The house didn't need much more than a quick once-over. I dusted the furniture, wiped the counters down, flushed the toilet and swished it with cleaner, and made a quick pass with the electric sweeper. I sucked the bugs from the window sills, and found a neon-orange, squeaky, bone-shaped toy that I tucked into my back pocket to bring to Piper.

I pulled a few weeds and swept the porch before sending a few pics to Aunt Mimsy. I closed all the windows, turned off the fans, locked up, and headed to Beth's house.

CHAPTER TWENTY-SEVEN

ALL MORNING, PIPER LEANED ON ME. When Beth and I sat on the front porch drinking coffee, she leaned on me. When we ate a picnic lunch in the park, she leaned on me. When I stood at the sink and rinsed our afternoon coffee cups, she leaned on me. As we sat at the dining room table playing cards, she alternated between sitting on my feet and leaning on me.

"I don't know why you don't like Piper," Beth said. "She's so affectionate."

"She does give good snuggles," I admitted. "But she's also unpredictable—and expensive."

"Speaking of predictable," Beth looked down her nose at me and squinted.

I widened my eyes, pointed to myself, and rearranged my cards in my hand.

"Yes, you. I know you're hiding something."

It felt like a boulder dropped in my stomach. I tucked a curl behind my ear. "I'm not hiding anything."

"Why won't you tell me about your trip?" Beth discarded a two of hearts.

"I told you. I want a break from thinking about work. Plus, I've enjoyed hearing all about the adventures of Beth and Piper." I picked up the card and discarded my own. "Gin," I said triumphantly and fanned my entire hand on the table.

Beth's growl caused Piper to lift her head. "It's okay, Piper," Beth explained. "It's just that your mom's won three in a row."

"Aunt Mimsy's her mom." My curt tone surprised even me.

Beth dismissed my comment with a wave of her hand. She separated the blue cards from the red ones. I grabbed the blue stack and slid them back into their box.

Beth stood and put her hands on her hips. "I'm done messing around. It's time to air it out."

I picked up the boxes of cards and returned them to the drawer in the kitchen where Beth stored them. I knew I had to tell Beth something. I never kept secrets from her—well, almost never—but I didn't want her to tell me that what I was doing was wrong.

"What did you say about Aunt Mimsy's house?" Beth asked. "It smelled a little stale, but came back to life with a quick airing out and refresh? Air. It. Out." Beth guided me to sit on the couch while she snuggled under a blanket in the arm chair facing me and tucked her feet under her.

"I won the contest."

"What?" Beth's feet flew to the floor. She leaned toward me and grabbed my hands. "Joy, that's amazing! I want to see pictures."

I pulled out my phone and showed her the group picture.

She zoomed in and out on the screen with pinched fingers and examined every aspect of the photo. "You're not smiling," she clipped.

"I'm smiling. That's my soft smile."

Beth handed the phone back to me with a frown. "Did you bring the glass trophy to show me?"

"Maggie has it."

"Joy," she took on her mom tone. "Air. It. Out."

I flung myself back on the sofa with a sigh. Even Piper sensed a long story—she got up and trotted into the kitchen for some water. But I couldn't tell Beth the whole story. Not yet. I needed to be careful about what I told her because I couldn't risk her boycotting support of this next phase of my career.

"The contest wasn't for a private retreat with Julia." *Or anything else Maggie said it would be.*

"Oh, no! That's what you wanted most." Beth's whine of disappointment brought me comfort. "What happened?"

"Maggie misunderstood." I left out the details about John's deception and how the marketing departments were the actual winners and Sophia and I were only the hired help.

"No way. That's a big misunderstanding." She sounded skeptical.

Time to redirect. "I was upset at first, but I got to have dinner with Julia," my voice rose at the end as I tried to sell it as a happy alternative.

"Just the two of you?"

"No, but it was still really great. I sat right next to her and got to visit with her quite a bit. She's as delightful in person as I had hoped." I tried to put on a face that said, *It's not what I wanted, but it was still pretty great.* Beth pursed her lips and crossed her arms.

I soldiered on with forced enthusiasm. "But…" I clapped my hands together, "what I really need right now are paying clients, and winning the contest led to that." I tapped my hands on the coffee table in an extended drum roll. "Berean Christian Academy hired me as a *paid* marketing consultant for their upcoming gala."

Beth's blanket fell to the ground as she launched herself toward me with a big hug. "Congratulations. So, you get to keep working with Chance?"

"Yes. I'll still get to work with Chance," I said as if that wasn't important. But Beth nailed it. Our puppy playdates and conversation about Berean Christian Academy dominated my interactions with Chance. I feared our friendship would wane when we no longer had BCA projects in common. This way we could build on what we started. And I really needed the money to pay John back.

Beth clapped short, rapid claps.

I put my palm up and tilted my head. I stretched my words for emphasis, "Aaand, I'm already invited to a gathering of potential high-end donors. With any luck, I'll secure support for the gala and develop relationships with potential new clients, too."

I left the part out about the fact that the "gathering" was a fancy shindig at John's cabin in McCall the next day. "The people in this room are sitting at tables you really want to be at," he said. "Not some lakeside patio table." John didn't even try to be subtle with his dig at my kitchen-table dream.

"Speaking of that," I slapped my thighs and stood up, "We've gotta go."

Beth walked me and Piper to the Jeep. I placed the dog crate in the back seat, but let Piper hop into the very back. She loved riding free with the T-top off. I smiled at the shiny red exterior. Getting to drive Scarlett toward the sunset was part of the treat of staying all day at Beth's.

"You forgot your leftovers," Beth reminded.

We walked back into the house. Beth opened the fridge and loaded me down with plastic containers. She closed the fridge and placed her hand on my shoulder.

"I really am sorry about the contest."

"Thanks," I shrugged. "You know what, though? Through it all, I confirmed I really do have what it takes. I'm proud of the video. I know I couldn't have created it without the team, but they couldn't have created it without me, either. I really am pretty good at this stuff. I mean—" I let my words trail off.

"I know what you mean. And I'm proud of you, too. God has given you a gift. He expects you to open it and use it." Beth's words touched me as only she could.

I balanced my stack of food and shuffled out of the kitchen. Beth opened the front door and my warm heart turned cold as ice as soon as I stepped on the porch. Piper sat in the back seat with the neon-orange squeaky bone hanging out of one side of her mouth and a chunk of Scarlett's upholstery protruding from the other. Stunned, I loosened my grip on my food stack and the top container filled with potato salad toppled to the ground.

Beth and I both stood motionless with potato salad splattered on our feet. I could muster no words. Beth merely cried, "Oh, Piper."

It took twenty minutes to clean everything up. I resisted the urge to scream at her when I shoved Piper into her crate, but I did slam the door to show my displeasure. Beth cleaned up the potato salad before the ants descended. I filled a small trash bag with bits of foam and black leather from the back seat.

Once I finished loading up, Beth leaned on my open window as I revved the engine to drive away. "Don't do this in your own strength."

I looked at the hole in the back seat. "I can't. I'll need the strength of Gonzales Body Shop's upholstery department. I'm their new best customer."

"I'm not only talking about the Jeep. I'm talking about all of it."

"I'm just so frustrated. Every time I think things are coming together, someone comes along and tears it apart." I turned and glared at Piper for good measure.

"You'll bounce back. You always do. Promise me"—Beth put her hand on my arm—"don't do it in your own strength. God will bear this with you, but you have to hand it to Him. He won't take it by force. He doesn't expect, or want, you to make things happen on your own."

I nodded and blew her a kiss. I glanced at her again as I backed down her driveway. I knew she stood there and prayed for me. She always did. I needed it more than she knew.

Before I could back out onto the road, I got a text message from Aunt Mimsy. *Thanks for taking such good care of my house. Love you. Talk soon.*

At least one thing turned out right today. I sent her an emoji blowing a kiss.

Before I put my phone away, another message from Aunt Mimsy popped up. She replied directly to the photo I sent of me holding Piper's bone-shaped toy with a grin and a thumbs up. *I stopped giving her that toy. She tears stuff up when she plays with it.*

CHAPTER TWENTY-EIGHT

"I'M SORRY YOU HAVE TO BE BACK here so soon," Eduardo said. "But I'm glad you're trusting us again." Eduardo dug in a drawer, lifted a stack of papers, and looked behind a box on the counter. "I hate it when Cassie's out," he mumbled under his breath.

I seriously considered taking Scarlett to another shop to avoid seeing Mateo. I thought better of it knowing I would eventually see him anyway. He worked for John. It was unavoidable.

Everyone at Gonzales Body Shop showed me kindness and respect—especially Eduardo. He made me feel like family. I wondered if he treated all of his customers that way, or if it was because of my friendship with Mateo. Former friendship.

The door behind me jingled. A small lady shuffled in. Her shockingly white hair formed a helmet-like dome around her head. Her shoulders bent forward slightly and her nondescript black handbag swung slightly in the crook of her arm.

"Martha!" Eduardo's face lit up as he greeted her. He walked over and gave her a side hug. "You must've been on the road visiting those great-grandbabies to be back in here so soon for an oil change. Or maybe you just missed us."

Martha patted his arm and tilted her head with a grin. "Well, I certainly didn't miss your terrible coffee."

Eduardo made his way back to the counter and smacked his head with the palm of his hand. He picked up a stapler sitting in the middle of the counter and showed it to me. "This is what I was looking for," he said with a sigh. He stapled my receipt to the estimate of work and handed it to me. "I'm so sorry, but with a full shop and Cassie out, I have to run the desk and can't spare anyone to take you to the rental place."

The door from the shop directly behind Eduardo opened. Mateo walked in and made eye contact with me. He stopped abruptly and the door slammed into his back, jerking him forward.

"Oh, Mateo. Perfect timing. Can you take Joy to the rental place?"

I snatched my phone from my purse. "No need. I already have the rideshare app open."

I squeezed my eyes slightly to warn Mateo off, but he ignored me and turned to Eduardo and said, "Of course, Tío"—he turned and looked directly into my eyes—"I'd be happy to."

Mateo swept his arm to the front door and I huffed out in front of him. He placed his hand on the old lady's shoulder as he passed. "Good to see you, Martha. I got some new coffee for you to try."

Martha patted Mateo's hand and smiled. "You're all so good to me."

I rushed to the passenger door before Mateo could open it for me. I yanked it open, slid into the passenger seat, and slammed the door. I sat in silence and clutched my purse to my chest as if someone planned to snatch it from me.

Mateo plopped into the driver's seat and started the car. "I saw

Scarlett's back seat. Piper did a number on it," he said as he pulled into traffic.

"Mmhm." I stared out the passenger window.

"Are you going to keep giving me the silent treatment?"

I turned my head and looked at him with flames in my eyes. "Mmhm."

Mateo turned his attention back to the road with a clenched jaw. I don't know why he thought a simple apology would be enough. As if we could simply go back to being friends in an instant. No. We had history now.

When we pulled up to the rental car place, Mateo parked and turned off the car. "What are you doing?" I asked.

"I'm coming in with you."

"No, you're not," I spat.

"What if they don't have a car?"

"That's none of your concern. Tell Eduardo thanks for the ride." I got out of the car and slammed the door. I headed straight for the entrance without a glance back.

I approached the reception counter as another customer turned to leave with keys in hand. I slung my purse over my shoulder and opened my mouth to ask for a rental as the receptionist plopped a folded plastic sign on the counter—"No cars available."

"You don't have any cars available?" I kept my tone steady even as I screeched the question at her in my mind.

The receptionist tapped the top of the plastic sign and smacked a wad of gum in her mouth. She picked up her cell phone and started scrolling.

"But that guy just left with keys in his hand." I pointed to the door.

She glanced up at me, "Last one." Then she blew a bubble and let it pop.

I turned and stomped out of the building before I said something

I would regret. I blinked in the bright sun and saw Mateo leaning against his car.

"Need a ride?" Mateo asked with a smirk.

I couldn't tell if he was mocking me or tossing out some good-natured teasing. Either way, I wanted to slap the smirk off of his face. "I'm good."

"Aren't you going to McCall today?"

Of course he knew about the event in McCall. His concern wasn't motivated by friendship or chivalry—this was business.

"Yes."

"I'm going, too. Let me give you a ride," Mateo offered. At my silence he pleaded, "Please?"

I needed to get to McCall somehow. It didn't make sense for two business associates to take two cars to the same place from the same place. Plus, I needed to stop acting so petty—I missed my friend.

I shrugged my shoulders. "Can we stop by my house first? I need to change."

CHAPTER TWENTY-NINE

MATEO DROVE IN SILENCE. I had already endured thirty minutes of wrestling in my mind. Did I want Mateo as a friend again, or should I settle for business associates? Could I ever trust him again? It was less risky to just move on, but this wasn't like with Logan—I still worked with Mateo. Well, not with him, but with John, and so with him.

As the city streets gave way to endless cookie-cutter neighborhoods which gave way to rural rolling hills, I tried to empty my mind. When that didn't work, I filled it with memories.

I thought back to the games we played on this same road headed to the Paddy Flat camping area near McCall when I was young. I would pepper my mom over the two-and-a-half-hour drive with "Are we there yet?"; "How much further?"; and "I need to potty." She responded with the license plate game, the alphabet game, and the good ol' "I Spy" game.

Then I thought of John and all the games he played—with Maggie and the contest—and I wondered how he might scheme moving forward. I begged to be put in the game, and now I had a sinking feeling I didn't know the rules.

To clear my thoughts, I launched a personal round of "I Spy." I spied green rolling hills—each blade of grass a slightly different shade, like it had been colored with all the greens from the big box of crayons. I spied black cows content to methodically chew on the green grass. I spied a white clapboard homestead with a dilapidated red barn beyond and speculated the kinds of stories those walls would tell. I spied bright yellow flowers bending in the breeze and wondered what fragrance their petals held. I spied blue and gray mountains looming on the horizon and noted how different they looked from a distance than when my boots traversed a trail on the surface.

Why hadn't I appreciated this beautiful landscape as a kid? I know why. I wanted to get to the campground. I wanted to collect rocks and play hide-and-seek in the woods with my cousins. I wanted to roast marshmallows for s'mores on the campfire. I wanted to roll my pants up and wade in the icy water of the stream.

Nanette's words popped into my mind—"You're worried about the destination when God wants to show you things along the way."

I stole a glance at Mateo. He was so worried about climbing the corporate ladder that he missed the friendship I offered.

How are you any different?

The thought caused me to suck in a breath. How many times had I taken Piper on a walk in the park to visualize sitting at the kitchen table with Julia Coates? I could practically taste the strawberry jam on my biscuit as I bombarded her with questions.

With my singular focus, what details had I missed along the way? I spent so much time rehearsing how Mateo hurt me that I hadn't considered lately how he'd helped me, too. His loyalty to John damaged my career and our friendship, but every other interaction with him was kind and sincere.

Before I talked myself out of it, I took a deep breath and blurted, "I miss our friendship."

Mateo snapped his head to look at me and then turned his attention back to the road with a broad smile. "Me, too."

We drove on in silence for a few more miles. I didn't know where to go from there. Did I want him to say he was sorry again? He had done that already. Many times. The first time at the music event on the river, then several voicemails and text messages I ignored.

I caught Mateo looking at me with a sly grin.

"What?" I asked.

"I have something for you."

"Okay," I dragged the word out like a question.

"Grab those files out of my briefcase." Mateo pointed to the back seat with his thumb, but returned both hands to the steering wheel as I twisted and retrieved them.

I opened the top file to find a large headshot of a man in a business suit on the left and personal details on the right. Information like name, address, family members, business interests, favorite charities, and more filled the page.

"What am I looking at?"

"Each file is a detailed profile on the guests of today's gathering."

I flipped through the photos and names. "What am I supposed to do with them?"

"Study them. These are the people that'll make your gala successful. The more familiar you are with them, the better the chance you can get them to sponsor the gala."

"You did this for me?"

"As an act of friendship."

For the next hour I studied the files and committed the details to memory. About forty-five minutes outside of McCall, I took a turn at the wheel and Mateo quizzed me from the files. We even role-played conversations and practiced overcoming objections to investing in Berean Christian Academy.

"How did you learn to do this?" I asked as we pulled into McCall. Mateo indicated where to turn to head to the east side of the lake.

"John's a venture capitalist on the side. A really successful one. I've put together files like this for him before."

"Thank you for"—my voice cracked—"for the files, for the ride, for not giving up on me."

"Of course. And it's nice being on the same team, now, don't you think?"

CHAPTER THIRTY

I TILTED MY HEAD and opened my mouth to ask Mateo what he meant, but he pointed at a gated entrance on the left and when I turned, the long driveway lined with tall lodgepole pines arrested my attention.

The tires crunched as the gravel drive transitioned to cobblestone leading to a grand two-story log cabin. If you could call it that. I suppose the log walls deemed it a cabin, but this mansion did not compare to any cabin I'd seen before. Nanette's cabin in the woods could fit inside the garage. Payette Lake peeked through the trees at the edges of the sprawling home.

A host of men and women in black shirts and pants swarmed around white vans and unloaded crates of drinks, trays of food, tables, chairs, and fresh flower centerpieces. They entered and exited between columns of river stone supporting a soaring wooden portico.

Mateo had me park on one side of a large parking pad tucked into the woods. We exited his car and slipped in the front door among the caterers and rental people. Mateo disappeared around the corner to the left and I heard him say, "Hey, John, we're here."

I remained glued to the custom wood inlay floor in the entryway. The lake view completely captivated my attention. The back of the home featured floor-to-second-story-ceiling glass windows. Beyond an expansive paver patio, the lake glistened like a disco ball.

"Come on in, Joy," I heard John's voice from the other room.

I glanced at the two staircases that swept up to a second floor on either side of the foyer. Logs stripped of their bark, stained and sealed served as newel posts. Custom ironwork railings mimicking the look of branches curved toward an upstairs landing on either side. I skirted the round table that graced the middle of the foyer. A large vase in the center of the table showcased fresh wildflowers mixed with curvy branches that reached to the light fixture above. The modern chandelier featured three rings of dark metal dripping with long narrow bulbs.

Standing tables with white tablecloths already filled the great room. To the right, stones matching the columns out front flowed like a wide river up the wall from the fireplace surround to kiss the wood clad ceiling. My head tilted back to take it all in.

"Over here," I heard Mateo say behind me. I turned to see a kitchen decked out with honey-colored wood cabinets, marble countertops, and an array of appliances that cost more than my entire college education.

John perched on a stool at the kitchen island with a glass of iced water and his laptop. He looked ready for a golf ad photoshoot in his collared, pale lavender short-sleeved sport shirt and gray plaid slacks. "What do you think?" He waved his hand around the room.

"It's stunning."

"I'll let Mateo show you around. I'm gonna go change." John

clapped his laptop closed, took a sip of water, and left the glass on a coaster on the counter.

John stopped to talk directly to Mateo. "They're almost done setting up. Find your jacket and prep Joy. I'll see if Sarah has something she can wear."

"Was he talking about me?" I asked as Mateo pulled open a sliding glass door and led me onto the patio dotted with additional standing tables and wildflower centerpieces.

Mateo slipped into a business voice. "Now that you're familiar with who'll be in attendance tonight, you need to know that John has assembled this group of bankers, media tycoons, local sports team representatives, and famous athletes for a new venture capital endeavor he's embarking on."

Mateo couldn't have startled me more if he had thrown John's remaining ice water in my face. He hadn't helped me, he'd handled me. I focused on the flames dancing on the blue and white reflective glass in the firepit behind Mateo. I wanted to sink into one of the gray Adirondack chairs circled around the stone-clad pit.

How would he have managed to prep me if we hadn't ridden together?

"John wants you to piggyback on the fact that they want his money for this deal."

"What's the deal?"

"Not important for what you're trying to do tonight."

I felt used—and trapped. However, as Aunt Mimsy used to say, I had made my bed and now I had to sleep in it. "And what am I trying to do tonight?" I asked.

"Make connections. Get to know them and make them fall in love with you and BCA. Don't ask for money tonight. Your line is,

'There's plenty of time to talk about money. We just want you to enjoy your evening.'"

I have a script?

The fire flickered. "Who's Sarah?"

"Huh?" Mateo looked confused.

"John said, 'I'll see if Sarah has something she can wear.'"

"Oh. John's wife. Tonight is more cocktail attire"—Mateo shrugged—"but I thought you looked nice."

I looked down at my belted, floral, halter-topped dress that flowed to my ankles. I thought it had a "Hamptons vibe" to it when I bought it. When John invited me to a dressy event at his cabin, I figured it was the perfect venue to show it off.

A woman with an elegant A-line, floor-length chiffon dress with cap sleeves floated to the doorway. The forest green color of her dress matched her glowing green eyes. Her dark hair, swept up in a French twist, complemented her high cheek bones and dewy skin.

"Oh, good. Sarah, Joy. Joy, Sarah," Mateo chirped.

The image of John and Maggie flickered across my mind. Like the fire I had been staring at, I didn't dare touch the image or I'd get burned.

We heard muffled voices and John's booming welcome. Mateo straightened his bow tie. "It's showtime. I need to go get my jacket out of the car. Thanks, Sarah."

I looked up at Sarah and felt red heat make its way up my neck.

"John said, 'dressy' didn't he?" Sarah's voice was soft and kind—and knowing.

I bent my head and focused on the hot pink rose right above my knee.

"He should have said 'evening wear.'" She approached me, picked up the edge of my dress, and stretched the flowing skirt out to display the pattern. "This really is lovely. I hate to ask you to change."

I finally found my voice. "I wish I would have known. I'm so embarrassed." I glanced through the wall of glass to see guests arriving—men decked out in suits and women in cocktail dresses and more than a few evening gowns.

"It's no bother. I have a black dress that will go perfectly with your nude heels."

I followed Sarah as she slipped back into the house and through a passageway that avoided interaction with the arriving guests.

CHAPTER THIRTY-ONE

SARAH LEFT ME in the main suite to change.

The black, floor-length crepe dress covered my left shoulder down to a three-quarter sleeve. At the neckline it angled down to an off-the-shoulder cap sleeve on the right. The stylish asymmetrical design faded into the background when I zipped the back—at that point, my curves took center stage. Sarah's closet had a half-circle of mirrors where I examined myself from every angle.

I now knew what it meant to feel glamorous. I always avoided gowns like this—or rather, could never afford them, so I never even tried them on.

I wished Chance could see me in this dress.

I retrieved my compact from my purse and touched up my make-up. I wound a few ringlets around my finger and pulled them down only to have them spring back, kissing the top of my shoulders. I coveted Sarah's sweeping updo, but my curls had a mind of their own and it served me better to accept that.

I ran through the guest list in my mind and practiced my script in the mirror. I took a deep breath and repeated Mateo's earlier phrase out loud, "It's showtime."

I exited the main suite passageway that dumped me into the kitchen and saw Chance standing with Mateo. My stomach fluttered and my heart thrilled at the idea that I didn't have to endure this evening alone.

Chance wore a crisp khaki cotton suit with a bright white shirt to match his white pocket square and a black tie that only accentuated his thick black glasses. I practically ran up to him.

"Chance, I didn't realize you were going to be here," I said and gave him a side hug.

"Same," Chance held his lips in a line as stiff and straight as his back when I gave him the hug.

John walked up and squeezed us together until our shoulders touched. "There's my power duo. Let's get to work and make connections." John clapped Chance on the back hard enough that his body tilted forward and then walked away before we could respond.

Mateo looked right at me and said, "I'll be around if you need me." I nodded and he turned and edged his way into the throng of guests.

Chance and I continued to stand shoulder to shoulder with the kitchen to our backs. As we surveyed the room, I saw many faces I recognized from the files.

"Are you keeping something from me?" Chance asked without even a glance toward me.

I wheeled around and faced him. "What? No. Why would you say that?"

Chance looked down at me. "Why did I have to find out from someone else that you were hired to help with the gala?"

"I literally got the signed contract the night before you texted me," I scanned his blue eyes for understanding. I dropped my chin and mumbled, "I knew you'd be upset."

"Why'd you think I'd be upset?"

"Because you never wanted help with it." My words came out rapid and high-pitched. I hated the defensive tone in my voice.

"I never wanted to impose on you."

I put my hands on my hips, "Then why are you mad now?"

"Because I feel like you're keeping secrets. Like, why didn't you tell me you were coming to this?" Chance jutted his chin over my shoulder at the other guests.

"When you texted me about the new contract, I was in Mountain Home checking on Aunt Mimsy's and picking up Piper from Beth's. Then she ate my back seat, and long story short, I rode with Mateo here. I honestly didn't think of it." I talked fast and my hands flew through the air as I explained.

"You didn't think of me?" His eyes darkened with hurt.

"It's not like that. In fact, I was thinking of you five minutes ago when I wished you could—" I snapped my lips together.

"Wished I could what?"

I looked at my shoes. "See me in this dress," I mumbled.

I focused my eyes on a gray blob in the countertop behind Chance's left elbow. My hands kept flying in circles as I prattled on. "I made big promises to get this contract, and I've been distracted, and it all happened so fast—"

Chance stepped forward and closed the gap between us. My eyes traveled from the button on his coat, up his black tie, over his Adam's apple, his chin, and his lips. By the time my eyes connected with the deep sea of his blue eyes, my head tilted back. I fought the urge to place my palms on his chest to steady myself.

"Okay. I overreacted. I'm sorry." The cloud that darkened his eyes dissipated. He looked over my shoulder toward the sea of strangers milling from table to table and in and out of the patio doors. "I'm glad we're in this together. Where do we start?"

A wave of relief swept over me as I pivoted and stepped back to Chance's side. "Mateo actually prepped me on the way. Just follow my lead."

"I'll be right by your side," Chance said. At least I think that's what he said. I got a little dizzy when he placed his hand on the small of my back. As I floated forward, he leaned over and whispered in my ear, "For the record, you look amazing in that dress."

CHAPTER THIRTY-TWO

MY FACE HURT from smiling so much. Chance and I had successfully mingled with half of the people from the files. He connected with people in a way that made them open up. I would ask about their family or their interests—things I learned from their profiles—and Chance would get them to talk about their dreams, and sometimes their deepest fears.

"You're really good at this," I said.

"At what?" Chance asked.

"Caring about people, I guess."

John approached us at the beverage station while we waited for the bartender to hand us two bottles of water. "How's it going?" he asked. As he leaned against the counter, half of his body faced us while his head swiveled and surveyed the room.

"Pretty good. I feel like we're really connecting with people," I replied.

"Good to hear." John grabbed Chance's shoulder and shook it a little. "Aren't you glad we brought Joy in? This is better than bake sales, don't you think?"

Chance responded with a stiff, wordless nod.

John grabbed a fresh glass of champagne from the bar top, tipped his glass to us, and walked away.

I linked my arm through Chance's and placed my other hand on his forearm. "Don't let him get to you. If your superpower is staying calm in unexpectedly stressful situations, John's is to keep everyone a bit off balance."

Chance remained stiff as he tilted his head to take a swig of water from the plastic bottle in his hand. "This is all pretty pretentious don't you think?"

"It's definitely a different league than I'm used to playing in," I admitted.

"I mean, with the money he spent on all this, he could've just made a donation to BCA."

"Well—" I said and rocked my head back and forth as if weighing both sides of the argument. "Mateo said these are people John's working with on another business venture. He's letting us ride the coattails of this deal—which is a kind of donation."

"And why does he even care? Jackson's graduating this year and the money from the gala is to fund a project at the preschool." Chance seemed to coil like a snake ready to strike. The venom in Chance's tone startled me.

"Never underestimate the power of legacy," I suggested.

Chance took another swig of water, his jaw still tight. "I'm surprised he even invited me."

I raised my eyebrows in a question and hoped my face didn't give away what I already knew.

"It's no secret that I'm not John Clarke's favorite person."

"Well, I for one, am glad you're here." I tilted my head to look up at him and added, "We make a pretty great team."

Chance tossed his empty water bottle into a nearby trash can and covered my hand that still rested on his arm with his. Electricity shot through me like a bolt of lightning. I wanted to go sit by the fire in one of the Adirondack chairs and look at the stars with Chance. Listening to the gentle ripples of the lake lap the shoreline sounded infinitely better than hearing my own "networking voice."

Instead, I left my arm linked in his, pulled my hand away, and stretched my shoulders back. "Ready? We're over halfway done. I've been eying the chocolate mousse over there. Let's make that our prize for finishing strong."

Chance snorted, "You're on."

• • •

We stood with Carter Jenson the serial entrepreneur, Carter's wife Kelly, and Trevor, a rather stout, dark running back for the local indoor football league.

Kelly and I made small talk about her daughters and summer camp. I overheard Chance ask Carter, "How do you handle the pressure of so many businesses?"

"I live by a schedule," Carter explained.

I laughed at Kelly's story about her girls flipping kayaks on a camp excursion and their antics to try to get back in as moving water swept them downstream.

"I actually really struggle with the pressure," Trevor admitted. "But I'm not sure a schedule will help the kind of pressure I feel."

I asked Kelly a clarifying question about a section of rapids in the stream, yet continued to eavesdrop on the guy's conversation.

Carter spoke next, "John tells me you're planning a gala."

Now, both of my ears perked up. No one had asked about the gala all night. Literally every other group of people we talked to only talked about themselves. Chance's entire body language changed from attentive and curious to uncomfortable and self-deprecating. "Trying to. Not exactly my wheelhouse."

Kelly wrapped up the kayak story in time for me to hear Carter ask, "What's the theme?"

Chance replied, "The theme is—"

"—being finalized," I interrupted. Chance jerked his head toward me. He squeezed his eyes slightly in confusion, but didn't say anything else.

"If I sponsor the gala, can I do it in a way that all of my companies will be featured?" Carter asked.

"Well, actually, Berean Christian Academy is the spotlight—"

Chance stopped when I placed my hand on his upper arm. I turned toward Carter and said, "Rest assured the entire BCA community will know how valuable our sponsors are to the great work being done there." Chance's eyes clouded over, but I continued with a wave of my hand, "There's plenty of time to talk about money. We just want you to enjoy your evening and we'll be following up soon."

Chance reached his hand out to Carter, "It was great meeting you. If you'll excuse me." Carter shook his hand and seemed none the wiser at the steam blowing from Chance's ears as he walked away.

I wanted to rush after Chance, but I took time to unwind the conversation. "Gentlemen, I look forward to following up, soon. Kelly, I could talk about summer camp all evening."

They all gave the appropriate "It was nice to meet yous" and "Until we meet agains." I found Chance alone at a table on the other side of the room—a fresh bottle of water cupped in both hands. I fought the urge to sprint to him—as if I could in these heels.

"I thought it was our job to get people to fall in love with BCA and give us money," Chance snipped as I walked up.

"We are BCA to these people. It's our job to get them to fall in love with us," I explained. "They don't care about Berean Christian Academy—yet. People trust others when they're allowed to talk about themselves. And you are a master at getting people to open up to you," I placed my hand on his. He slid it out from under mine and shoved it in his pocket. "Plus, John specifically asked me not to talk money at this event," I added.

"You're really going to follow his lead?" Chance jutted his chin toward the other side of the room. I watched John take a swig of champagne, slap a man on the back, and laugh a little too loud.

I shrugged, "His party, his rules."

"I'll catch up with you in a minute. I'm going to the restroom."

I flew solo for the next couple of conversations. I missed Chance's ying to my yang, and hated how desperately I wanted him back at my side. I fought to maintain focus and eye contact. I scanned every table and every corner of the room. I wanted to go looking for him, but I figured he'd come back when he cooled off.

Mateo slid up beside me as I spoke with a man as tall and thin as a lodgepole pine. "I'm so sorry to interrupt, but I need to steal Joy for a minute," Mateo said as he cupped my elbow and guided me to an empty corner.

Mateo's eyes darted around the room, "Have you seen Trevor?"

"The football player?"

Mateo nodded.

"Not since earlier. Why?"

"John's looking for him. He hired him to be local talent and some of the guys hadn't been able to meet him yet. I saw you and Chance talking to him earlier, but he's disappeared."

I started to ask Mateo why he seemed so jumpy about the whole thing when John walked up with both hands on his hips. His suit jacket flared out on both sides like wings. He smiled wide, but his eyes flickered with anger. He sent Mateo away with a jerk of his head.

"I found Trevor," John snarled through clenched teeth.

"Oh, good. Mateo was just asking—"

"Chance is praying with him in the study."

My heart warmed at the thought. Chance really cared about people. I could tell by the kinds of questions he asked all night. I found myself wondering how I could get them to help BCA and then make them my client. Chance looked for ways to empathize and encourage.

"I paid a lot of money to have Trevor here. He needs to be out here working the room. And you're getting paid to get Mr. Easton on the same page."

John punctuated the word "you're" like a pointed index finger punched into my chest, but his plastic smile never faded.

"Chance is only trying to—"

"Get your guy under control or I'll tell him about our deal and pull this room full of connections from you."

John looked around with a wide smile, patted my shoulder lightly as if we wrapped up the most delightful conversation, and walked back into the room.

CHAPTER THIRTY-THREE

I GOT MY WISH—SORT OF. I sat in the Adirondack chairs under the stars, but I sat alone.

The evening ended without much fanfare. By the time I found Chance and Trevor in the study, they had just finished praying and clapped each other on the back in a brotherly embrace. Trevor slipped back into the pressure-pot and I didn't have to do anything to "get my guy under control."

But the clock had struck the proverbial midnight and my dream turned back into reality. I was back in my floral dress, Chance drove off over twenty minutes ago, and now I waited for Mateo as he shuttled people to the resort down the road. I smoothed some wrinkles out of my dress and gazed past the flames of the firepit at the reflection of the moonlight glittering on the surface of the lake.

I jumped at Mateo's voice behind me, "Hey, Joy. Bad news. John needs me to stay overnight. Sarah said she could make up a guest room for you."

"What? No!" I jumped to my feet. "I can't stay tonight. I have to get Piper from the kennel at eight a.m. or they'll charge me for another day. Plus, we have a training session scheduled."

Mateo pulled at his chin, "I'm sorry. Can you get a ride with Chance?"

"Mateo!" my voice rose in exasperation and I stomped my foot. "He left twenty minutes ago. Why didn't you tell me this twenty minutes ago?" I clenched my fists at my side.

"Mateo!" John's voice boomed from inside the house.

"Sorry, Joy. Gotta go."

My hands shook as I dug in my purse for my phone. Chance answered on the second ring. "Hello?"

"Is there any way you can come back and get me? Mateo just told me he has to stay overnight and I really need to get home."

"On my way."

. . .

I didn't want to wait by the driveway for half an hour, so I meandered down the stairs to the water's edge to kill time. I picked up three rocks representing the three big things I needed to accomplish next. I threw the first into the water. Bloosh. Get Chance to change the theme of the gala.

Splash. The next rock sent ripples spreading out. Find a way to talk about naming the football field in exchange for John's donation.

I looked at the final rock in my hand. I tossed it and caught it—tossed it and caught it. Then I reared back and threw it as far as I could. Plunk. Bury this attraction to Chance—this distraction—at the bottom of the lake with that stone.

I turned around and leaned on the railing and surveyed the house from the water's edge. The people had all cleared out. The only thing remaining were the tables dotting the patio and great room.

So many tables.

If I could prove myself with this gala, I could gain clients I never dreamed of before. Maybe my kitchen table dream was naive. Maybe conference tables—or even cocktail tables—were where my future opportunities lay.

I checked my watch and made my way back up to the patio, through the house, and paced under the portico.

Approaching headlights shone down the driveway. Chance's car pulled up under the portico and I reached for the passenger door. When he got out, I pulled my hand away from the handle and he came around the car toward me.

"Joy, I'm glad I caught you," Sarah's voice came from behind me. "Oh, and you too, Mr. Easton."

She still wore her flowing gown, but her dark hair—released from the confines of the French twist—cascaded onto her shoulders. She approached us and layered my right hand in between her hands. She released my hand and did the same with Chance. "I'm sorry I couldn't spend any time with you this evening. I hoped for an opportunity to share my gratitude for both of you."

With a slight step back, she turned her attention to Chance. "Mr. Easton, you have been a transformative influence in my son's life. He's a different young man because of you."

Sarah rubbed her hand on my upper arm. "And Joy, Jackson loved working with you and your team. He came home after his video session as excited as when he was a toddler coming back from the dock with a fish. And the video has already garnered interest from several of the colleges he's interested in attending."

"He's a great kid," Chance said.

"He really is. His future is very bright," I added.

"Well, anyway. I'm glad I was able to offer my gratitude in person. Safe travels home."

"Thank you," I said. "And thanks again for letting me borrow your gown. It was lovely."

"My pleasure," Sarah said and glided back inside the house.

Chance opened my door and I slid into the passenger seat. He got in the driver's seat and turned down the long drive.

"Well, that was nice," I offered. "And I can't thank you enough for coming back to rescue me."

"Anytime."

Chance's tone carried a warmth that filled me from tip to toe. I tucked a rogue curl behind my ear, folded my hands, and smiled to myself as I looked out the window. The pine trees looked like black stripes streaking by.

"That's what keeps me going," Chance broke the silence.

"What does?"

"Finding out I've made a difference." Chance pushed his glasses up his nose. "BCA is the vehicle by which we have access to the kids and their families. Sharing God's truth and love is transformative—every time. Sometimes God lets us see our impact, most times we just have to trust Him. Tonight, He let us see it."

"Hmm." I let Chance's words sink in. It did feel good being a part of Jackson's story. Even if only the most recent chapter.

I thought back to the influence Kent had on my life—the word *transformative* fit. He's the one who modeled persuasive storytelling techniques—techniques I used in the video I just produced. And Kent's encouragement to change my major changed the entire trajectory of my life and career.

"You really love the kids, don't you?"

"I really do. And I don't want to waste any opportunity to point them to truth, because God's love is the true picture of love."

I got the impression Chance was trying to convince me of something he thought I didn't agree with. "Okay," I prodded.

"That's why I don't want the gala to change." Chance turned his head toward me and held my gaze as long as he could before turning his attention back to the road.

"You don't think it could change and still be an opportunity to show BCA families God's love?"

Chance asked me to hold the wheel while he took off his jacket and slung it in the back seat. He untied his tie and tossed it on top of the jacket. He unbuttoned the top button of his shirt, let out a big sigh, and took back the wheel.

"But why do you want to change it?" Chance asked.

"Because if you keep doing the same thing, you'll get the same results."

Even in the dim light of the car, I could see Chance clench his jaw. "I like the results we've been getting. It's been God-honoring, and student-focused. We need to grow attendance is all."

I didn't want to start an argument. I could argue that sponsorships were where the real money came from, but didn't think Chance would understand. "You're raising money for the preschool, right?"

Chance nodded.

"How much do you have and how much do you need?"

"We need five hundred thousand dollars and we have a hundred thousand so far."

I shifted in my seat to angle myself toward him. "Where did the hundred thousand come from?"

"We've raised about twenty thousand a year for the last five years at the World Changers Gala."

"Chance," I punctuated his name for effect. "I'm talking about raising twice what you have in the bank this year."

Chance whipped his head around to look at me. "You could do that?" he asked before turning his attention back to the road.

"Yes. I can do that. I've totally done it before. And with the contacts we made in the room tonight, I have no doubt. And think about it, if we do it again next year, you've met your goal." I reached out and placed my hand on his shoulder, "That's why I want to change it."

Chance didn't respond and I lifted my hand from his shoulder. I clasped my hands in my lap and watched each dash of the center line of the road dart by.

"You're planning on being around next year?" Chance's question startled me. I just told him I could meet his goal in two years instead of twenty and he focused on the fact that I envisioned myself participating in the gala again?

"What can I say? I love—um—grown fond of—enjoy working with everyone at BCA." I turned my head even though it was too dark for him to see the heat rising in my cheeks.

After a few minutes of silence I asked, "Aren't you?"

"Aren't I what?"

"Planning on being around next year."

Chance's silence caused my stomach to lurch. "I don't know," he said.

I hated how that answer made me feel. I didn't want to think about BCA without Chance, but I needed to stay front-side focused.

"I love BCA, too." Chance scratched the back of his neck, "I really do. But I may have another teaching opportunity at Mount Horeb Bible College. They're promising to sponsor my doctorate work and future publication opportunities." Chance turned to me with eyes wide, "But I'm still praying about it. And no one can know."

"Of course."

The tires hummed on the asphalt for miles. I decided to break the silence again. "We made a pretty good team tonight, don't ya think?"

"Yeah," Chance grinned. "I think we did."

"Let's keep it up. You do what you do best—connect with students and families. And let me do what I do best—market the event and raise the money. Can you trust me to do that?"

"Yeah. I think I can."

I yawned and rubbed my eyes.

"Can you trust me?" Chance asked.

I blinked at him trying to discern what he meant. I opened my mouth to ask, but he cut me off. "To get you home safely. Close your eyes, sleepyhead. I've got you."

CHAPTER THIRTY-FOUR

LILLY CAME HIGHLY RECOMMENDED as a miracle worker when it came to training dogs. She met me and Piper at the dog park. The sky was clear and blue with no clouds in sight. The sun rose hours before and beat down on the dry ground. I noticed a few joggers on the trails. One girl laid on a blanket under the canopy of a tree with her dog curled at her side. I wished Piper liked to rest at the park. She normally acted more like the two squirrels that squeaked and twittered around a nearby tree trunk.

"It's important to use clear and distinct command words. Today we'll work on 'sit,' 'stay,' and 'down,'" Lilly instructed.

Lilly told Piper to sit and she sat. Lilly said "stay" and Piper stayed. Lilly said "down," and Piper obediently laid down and begged with her eyes for more instructions.

Maybe I should have come with a high ponytail and chipper attitude like Lilly, but Chance and I returned to Boise in the wee hours of the morning—and I regretted the 9:00 a.m. lesson more and more with every command.

"Sit," I said. Piper sat.

"Now give her the treat," Lilly instructed.

Piper stood up before I could dig the treat out of my pocket. "Sit down, Piper," I whined.

Piper remained standing and looked at Lilly then at my pocket.

"Be sure to be consistent with your commands. The common commands we've gone over today are best. And I recommend providing immediate feedback and rewards when Piper performs the desired behavior."

"Sit," I said. Piper sat.

I got a text and checked my phone. Piper ran off to greet another dog. "Piper!" I called. "See, she doesn't listen to me. One time I had to swim to that island over there to get her to come."

"You'll get the hang of it," Lilly encouraged. "The more consistent you can be, the better." Lilly tilted her chin to look over my shoulder. "Piper, come."

Piper lifted her head and bounded over to us. Lilly gave her a treat. "Good, girl. Sit." Piper sat and she got another treat. "Stay." Lilly walked off and Piper wiggled, but didn't leave her post. "Good girl. Come." Piper ran up to Lilly and got another treat.

"This is gonna cost me a fortune in treats," I grumbled.

"The treats are just to start. We'll shift to praise in the coming lessons. Piper loves affection, so that should work long-term." Lilly squatted down and rubbed Piper all over. Loose fur flew everywhere and I coughed and sputtered.

"Great. Oh, also, I can't meet tomorrow morning like we'd planned, but I could make the afternoon…" As I talked, Piper spotted a dog friend, barked a few times, and ran off.

"Are you sure there isn't another location where we can train? Piper will learn faster and respond better in a controlled and distraction-free environment," Lilly suggested.

"I don't have room at my house, and we like it here at this park." I walked in Piper's direction. "Come on, Piper," I called and patted my thighs. Piper continued to jump and play with her dog friend.

"Piper, come," Lilly hailed. Piper's ears perked and she stopped in her tracks. I swallowed a grumble when she turned and loped to Lilly's feet. "It's important to keep a routine for Piper. Structured training sessions are an important first step," Lilly said as she gave Piper a treat and patted her head.

"I'm sorry. It doesn't fit my schedule tomorrow."

"I understand. It's just that her progress may be delayed a bit, so if you could try—"

Piper jumped up and ran off. I looked up to see Chance and Ruby approach. "Lilly, thanks for today's lesson. I'm sorry to cut this short, but this is a client I need to speak with. Can we move our session to three p.m. tomorrow?" I turned toward Chance and Ruby.

"Sure," Lilly pursed her lips. "Same place?"

"Yes, thanks," I said over my shoulder and jogged off.

The dry grass crunched under my feet as I approached Chance and the dogs. "I didn't realize you were coming today." I stood with my hands on my hips watching Piper and Ruby greet each other with playful bounces.

"I thought I'd check out the training progress," Chance said.

My shoulders drooped. "She responds great to Lilly, but me? Not so much."

"It takes time."

"Maybe. But between her island adventure, my new back seat,

plus stuff at the house, I need Piper to get a grip."

Chance and I started down the path with the dogs running ahead together. I liked this—our friendship—our park routine. Sometimes we talked. Sometimes we walked in comfortable silence—two words I didn't normally attribute to myself. Today, I talked.

I gave Chance the play-by-play of the training session while the dogs romped together. They didn't need our attention or entertainment today. I guess Piper had enough of me telling her what to do. Chance and I sat on a bench and watched them take turns chasing each other. Ruby ran ahead until Piper caught up. They circled each other and yipped and jumped on each other. Then Piper took off until Ruby caught up—and the cycle continued.

I slipped into silence and watched the dogs. I sat deep in thought and didn't notice Chance's finger until it touched my leg. He made a motion on my thigh with his index finger and tilted his head back in laughter when I jumped.

"Sorry. You startled me," I said.

Chance laughed some more. "I see that."

"And it kind of tickled," I admitted under my breath.

Chance pretended he was going to stick his finger in my side. I shifted away from him on the bench and slapped his hand away to protect myself. The fear of being tickled almost tickled as much as actually being tickled.

Chance laughed and put his hands up in surrender. "I didn't mean to tickle you. It's something my sister and I used to do. We would write letters on each other's legs—secret messages to each other under the table at dinner."

"Ah. Okay. So try again."

Chance slowly moved his finger on my leg. "A question mark?"

I asked.

"You got it. What's going on in there?" Chance tapped my temple and shifted to face me with his elbow propped on the back of the bench. "Thinking about the gala?"

"Actually, I was thinking of another donation in play."

Chance raised both eyebrows. "What kind of donation?"

I spit out the words before I chickened out. "John Clarke is willing to make a one million dollar donation to BCA to completely overhaul the football complex."

Chance turned from me and stiffened. His hands gripped the bench seat on either side of his thighs like he wanted to launch himself. "Absolutely not."

I had mentally prepared for push back. "Why not?"

"The name of Christ isn't for sale." The cool tone of his words made me shiver.

"I'm not sure that's what's happening here. I've seen other Christian schools give naming rights to facilities on campus."

"We're not other Christian schools." Chance's jaw clenched and he inhaled and exhaled deeply through his nose.

I touched the white knuckles of his hand. "I didn't mean to upset you. Help me understand."

Chance stood and paced in front of me with his eyes on the ground in front him. "It's a slippery slope, Joy. Scripture tells us God has exalted Jesus and given Him a name that is above every other name. When we exalt the names of donors, especially in such a permanent way, we're exalting the names of men over the name of Christ"—he stopped pacing and looked straight into my eyes—"in a place that bears the name of Christ."

I didn't want to sound argumentative, so I measured my words. "So, how do other Christian schools justify putting the names of donors on buildings?"

"Every school has to stand by their own convictions. This has been a long-standing conviction of Berean Christian Academy. And maybe we're too conservative. But I know one thing, if we don't even put our foot on the slope…" Chance let the thought hang in the air.

"But you told me just last night that BCA is the vehicle by which you have access to students. A sports complex like this will surely attract new students and families."

Chance shook his head sharply. "The ends don't justify the means. God doesn't ever say sin's okay because it all turns out in the end."

"You're acting like it's immoral to name things after donors."

"We're called to be different, Joy." Chance's eyes pleaded. "We're called to reflect Christ. And I know this. He's God, but didn't flaunt it. He set aside all of the privileges of His deity to come to Earth as a man. He emptied Himself, He humbled Himself, and He lowered Himself." Chance tapped his finger into his open hand with every point, then leaned toward me, "We need to be an example of Christ."

The intensity of Chance's gaze caused me to look away. Chance straightened and turned his back to me. He watched the dogs and didn't turn back around when he asked, "Isn't the bigger question, why won't John Clarke give that donation without putting his name on it?"

"I understand," I said. "I'll drop it." *For now.*

Chance called Ruby and clipped her leash to her collar. "I'll see you Monday, Joy." My heart crumbled as they walked away.

CHAPTER THIRTY-FIVE

I SAT IN THE PARKING LOT at Berean Christian Academy on the phone with Mateo, Andrew, Roderick, and Lan. The camaraderie we shared energized me. I patted the white box in the passenger seat and tilted my head back to look at the sky. The open roof on the Jeep allowed me to examine the branches above holding onto leaves that had already begun to change colors for fall.

I had Scarlett back, I got to work with some of my favorite people, and my feet were firmly planted on the path to success with the gala.

"I wish you guys could see everything," I said.

"You know we designed it, right?" Andrew's familiar sarcasm brought a smile to my lips.

"I know. But there's something about seeing it printed on signs and posters."

"So, why are we all on this call?" Lan asked.

"Launch day should be special, don't you think? I wanted to mark the occasion and use it as an opportunity to tell you all how much you mean to me and how fun it is to work with you. I'm so glad Maggie and John pulled the strings to keep us together on this."

"That's sweet, but I have a meeting I have to get to," Mateo prompted.

"Okay, okay," I conceded. "Andrew, do you have the social accounts up?"

"Aye, Aye, Captain!"

"Let's go live!" I declared. I heard polite applause on the other end of the line. I refreshed my screen and the BCA website homepage featured the gala. I clicked over to the social media accounts and the new gala theme filled the profiles and feeds. "Great job, guys. Have a great day," I said and ended the call.

I grabbed the package of posters and retrieved another box that held a retractable banner from the back of Scarlett and headed to the front office to check in. I noticed cars lining up in the distance preparing for morning drop-off. The buzzer sounded and I pushed on the door.

"Good morning, Mrs. Carrol," I said in a singsong voice.

Molly tilted her chin to her chest and looked over her glasses. "You're back."

"And properly dressed, I might add." I twirled in my belted, floral midi dress, topped with an emerald-green suit jacket.

"Glad to see it," she said flatly, but didn't try to hide her smirk.

I scribbled my name on the clipboard and retrieved my visitor pass. "I need to display this banner in carline and put up these posters."

"Mrs. Hensley called ahead," Molly confirmed. "I've arranged a student escort to assist you."

The door to the reception area opened and Olivia walked in. "Perfect timing," Molly declared. "Olivia, are you ready to help Miss Swallow? She needs to get a banner set up in carline. And you know where the poster frames are around campus?"

"Sure do," Olivia said with a smile. "Good to see you again, Miss Swallow."

"Carline first," Molly instructed. "They're getting ready to start."

Olivia took the box of posters from me and we turned to leave.

"Miss Swallow," Molly called. "You might need this." She set a Berean Christian Academy travel cup on the counter. "Mr. Easton mentioned you like it black."

My mouth opened, but when I couldn't get my tongue to work, I closed it again. I picked up the cup and tilted it to Molly in a gesture of gratitude. I resisted clicking my heels together as I followed Olivia to the car line.

Olivia and I set up the banner as the first cars pulled forward to let out children of all ages, sizes, and temperaments—tall children, short children, sleepy children, smiling children, angry children, crying children, laughing children—all greeted by staff and high school students in an organized shuffle of car doors opening and closing.

"Where to next?" I asked.

"Mrs. Carrol said to show you where the poster boxes and bulletin boards are."

"Lead the way."

I discovered the campus was bigger than I had initially thought. My limited exposure to the gym and front office meant I never knew about the large lawn in the center of campus. A variety of buildings and sidewalks bordered the square with the gym situated on one edge and the chapel on another.

While the green space brought to mind a college quad, the buildings represented a mix of styles and ages. The sidewalk extended from a brick building to something resembling a beach cottage, and then onward to another structure that took on the appearance of an office trailer on a construction site. Despite the diverse architecture, the sense of peace I experienced every time I set foot on Berean Christian Academy's campus remained unaffected.

"Gridiron Glitz, huh?" Olivia asked as she pinned the corners of one of the posters to a bulletin board in the hall of one of the buildings.

"What do you think?" I asked.

"It's different."

"Different good or different bad?" I frowned.

"I don't know," Olivia shrugged. "It's been the World Changers Gala for as long as I can remember it."

"I'm hoping the changes will raise more money and attract new families to attend."

Olivia pushed on the door to exit the building. We walked up to an exterior bulletin board along a long stretch of sidewalk. Olivia unlocked the glass frame and lifted it to give us access to pin a poster inside.

"You don't like it," I grumbled.

Olivia snapped her head toward me with eyebrows raised. "Oh, no. That's not it. I don't really care about the gala." Her hand flew to her mouth and her eyes widened. "I probably shouldn't have said that."

I laughed out loud. "No, no. Go ahead. You won't hurt my feelings. What do you mean?"

Olivia shrugged, "The gala is more of a parent thing. They just use us kids like puppets in a show. It's pretty boring if you ask me."

I placed my hand over my lips to hide my smile. "That makes sense. Galas really are for grown-ups. But with this new theme, I have some ideas for activities leading up to the event that may infuse some fun you guys might like."

"Cool," Olivia smiled.

We made our way around the entire quad and saw Chance standing outside of the gym. He wore the same brown business sneakers and navy sport coat that he had on the first day I met him. He was no less handsome to me—more so now that we had built a friendship and banked so many hours at the dog park together.

I watched as Chance opened the passenger door of a car stopped in front of the gym. A student got out, threw a backpack over his shoulder, and gave Chance a fist bump. Chance closed the passenger door and leaned his elbows on the open window to chat for a moment with the driver.

We hadn't spoken since he walked away from me at the dog park. He said he'd see me today, and so I resisted the urge to reach out. I couldn't wait for him to see the updated theme and professional posters. Maybe that would smooth things over.

Chance unfolded himself from the open car window, gave it a tap, and shoved a hand in his front pocket as the car drove away. He glanced in our direction and his eyes registered recognition. He gave a short wave and pushed his black frames up his nose.

I wanted him to run toward me and lift me in the air and twirl me around. Or maybe walk resolutely toward me through the quad like Mr. Darcy approaching Lizzie in the open field as he declared his feelings hadn't changed.

That did not happen.

Chance turned and greeted other students instead. Mr. Darcy's hands may have been cold, but I just got the cold shoulder.

"Look! There's Mr. Easton," Olivia declared.

She skipped over to Chance and showed him the poster. His placid expression grew dark and my stomach twisted into a knot of apprehension. He took the stack of posters from Olivia and pointed to a group of girls in the distance. Olivia's blond ponytail swung back and forth as she jogged up to her friends.

Chance directed his eyes toward the ground and walked toward me—one hand still in his pocket, the stack of posters tucked under his other arm. I stood still and held my breath. Chance stopped in front of me and lifted his eyes to mine.

"You changed the theme." His eyes held an anguish I didn't understand.

"Do you like it?"

Chance let out a sigh and tilted his head toward the cloudless sky. "We have a theme. It's the same theme every year—BCA World Changers."

"I know, but we talked about—"

His eyes met mine again. This time anger flashed as he seethed, "This has John Clarke written all over it."

I was as stunned as the time my cousins hid in the loft of the barn and spilled ice water all over me. As stunned and just as mad. "I'm my own person, Chance. John Clarke had nothing to do with it. Well, other than—"

"See," Chance took the hand out of his pocket to swipe the air in exasperation.

"—other than he filled a room with potential sponsors." I placed my hands on my hips and measured my response—desperately trying to keep my voice low so as not to draw attention. "I evaluated our opportunity and set the theme from there. As we discussed. All those sponsors will love it," I continued, "and now it makes sense for them to give money to BCA. Their common thread isn't Christian education, it's football."

"Football is not about the kids. Football is not about a biblical worldview."

My irritation overflowed in a growl. "John was right. You are a one-trick pony."

Chance's eyes grew wide and he clamped his lips together in a tight line and turned to walk away.

"Chance, wait," I grabbed his arm and he stopped. "You said you trusted me to raise the money. Changing the theme is a big part of that. Plus, how can you say football is not about the kids? Jackson's a kid. And there are other athletes like him. We infused a biblical worldview into the video and we can do it with this theme, too."

My arguments rushed out in a wave that left me breathless. Chance stood there wordless.

"I have ideas, Chance. Let me share them with you."

"I thought we made a good team—"

"We do make a good team," I said.

"This is not teamwork. You don't want to share, you want to shove. You knew I wouldn't like it so you didn't ask."

Chance looked down at my hand still on his arm. I dropped it to my side.

"It's like at the dog park," he continued. "The trainer tells you what to do and you do it your way anyway. That's who you are. Doing what's right in your own eyes. Or worse, doing what's right in John Clarke's eyes."

"You want to grow attendance. I have ideas for that. You want to raise more money. This theme and my plan will do that. You want to include the kids. Let's work on that together." I willed him to understand.

"Together," Chance huffed. "You don't want to do anything together. You want to pull all the strings in a production of your own design."

"It's interesting you feel like a puppet," I snarled. "I guess I'm in good company since Olivia just said the students felt like puppets when you were in charge."

Chance pushed his glasses up his nose, shoved the posters at me, and turned and walked away.

CHAPTER THIRTY-SIX

THE WEIGHT OF MY CIRCUMSTANCES held me captive to the clock—if I looked at it ten times, I looked at it a hundred. Every second ticked by in slow motion after my run-in with Chance. I finished hanging posters in the designated spots in the gym and slogged to my Jeep—every step felt like I trudged through thick mud. Once I got home, I fought the urge to climb into bed, cover my head, and never come out.

I picked up my phone to text Chance no fewer than six times before I finally set an alarm for 8:00 p.m. and stashed it in my bedroom. My next conversation with Chance needed to be face-to-face and his Monday night routine meant walking Ruby at the park at sunset.

I pulled out my laptop and sat at the bar in the kitchen. I clicked on my list of questions I had for Chance about the gala. I made a few notes of who might be able to answer them if Chance continued to reject me in person.

When the alarm finally sounded, I slipped on my walking shoes and loaded Piper into her crate in the back of Scarlett. Her eyes drooped with sadness.

"Consequences of your choices," I said and locked the gate.

I felt a little sorry for Piper, so I brightened my voice. "Are you ready to see Ruby?" I asked, glancing at her in the rearview mirror as I backed out of my carport.

Piper's ears perked at the sound of her friend's name. Her tail thwacked against the crate.

As I pulled into the parking lot of the dog park, the sky already glowed with shades of red and orange. Distant wildfires made for spectacular sunsets.

I spotted Chance's white sedan and took a steadying breath as I let Piper out of her crate. If dogs could roll their eyes, I'm pretty sure Piper would have rolled hers when I attached her leash. It didn't matter that she wanted freedom. I didn't want any unexpected adventures tonight. I needed to stay in control.

Part of me wanted to drag Piper down the path and locate Chance and Ruby as quickly as possible. Another part of me gratefully let her sniff at dry patches of dirt and dead grass—the drought had transformed the park into a whole new landscape for Piper to explore.

Piper and I came up over a rise in the path and I saw them. Chance embraced a woman about my age and height. Her straight dark hair blew in the breeze as he lifted her and swung her around. She tilted her head back and laughed with glee. Once her feet returned to the ground, she squatted and let Ruby jump all over her and lick her face.

She stood and gazed at Chance with her head tilted back, then grasped him around his waist and burrowed her head in his chest. They turned and walked down the path away from Piper and me. Chance flung his arm around her shoulder and snugged her against his side.

Piper spotted Ruby and pulled at the leash. When I didn't move, she let out a yip and pulled harder. I yanked her leash and scuttled backwards down the rise. I lost my footing and landed on my rump as bits of gravel dug into the heels of my palms.

My eyes stung with tears as I stood up, brushed my backside, and swiped loose dirt from my hands. I didn't deserve this. As a professional with a job to do, I made hard choices. And they weren't even that hard—it was only a theme!

I yanked Piper's leash and wiped tears from my face with the back of my hand as I stumbled back to the Jeep.

And Chance and I made such a great team.

He obviously didn't appreciate how rare that was. One little disagreement, and he was in the arms of another woman.

Not that Chance had ever been in my arms.

And wasn't that my real problem? I took my eye off the prize. What did I want? Friendship or fortune?

Chance said he trusted me to raise the money, but he obviously didn't. He wouldn't even entertain the plans I'd sketched out—plans I designed based on his feedback. I knew I needed his input. I had a list of questions on my laptop at that very moment, for goodness' sake. I was as committed to including the BCA spirit in the gala as I was when I produced the video. And I had already learned so much through that.

Chance clearly didn't know how much I needed this. Plus, what's good for BCA is good for Chance. The real problem was that he didn't appreciate what I brought to the table. Worse than that, he didn't believe in me.

He's so stubborn he won't even take a million dollars. A million! I know John's a jerk, but really.

Piper alternated between walking beside me and pulling me backward toward Chance and Ruby.

I needed to get my head on straight. I needed to get back to my original goal. A successful gala meant raising as much money as possible while balancing the desires of the client and donors.

I created an imaginary scene in my mind. I pictured Chance and Carter Jenson standing at a cocktail table at the event at John's lake house. Chance's eyes dance as he tells Carter all about Berean Christian Academy. With every story he lays down a colored thread on the table. When it is Carter's turn, he leans in and lays down his own colored threads as he tells Chance all about his companies. I walk up to the table and notice that a red thread Chance laid down matches a red thread Carter laid down. I take the red threads and tie them together. Both men are smiling ear to ear and I turn to Chance to celebrate as—the dark-haired girl walks up behind Chance and flings her arms around his chest. He tilts his head back in laughter and—

Even in my imagination I couldn't seem to get a grip.

I opened the back of Scarlett, and Piper obediently jumped into her crate. I slammed every door I touched. I slid into the driver's seat and pitched my head back to keep the tears from spilling over.

Stay angry, Joy. That's how you'll stay in control.

Who am I kidding? I lost control a long time ago. I pulled out my phone and texted Beth. *I need you.*

She replied, *On my way.*

When I got home, I changed into my favorite plaid flannel pajamas, brewed a cup of tea, and snuggled into the corner of my couch waiting for Beth to arrive. The brick wall of willpower I built with every argument loosened and ultimately gave way in a torrent of tears.

Piper padded up to the couch and rested her chin on my thigh. The pressure of her head relaxed me like a weighted blanket. Her presence comforted me and slowed my heaving sobs to a gentle trickle of tears.

By the time Beth walked through the door, the couch overflowed with crumpled tissues that cascaded to the floor. "I used my key," she said as she tossed her purse on the bar. I nodded my head and sniffed.

Piper moved only slightly when Beth walked up and instructed me to "Scooch over." Beth took my place in the corner of the couch and I laid my head on her lap. Piper tucked her head into my armpit as Beth stroked my hair.

Beth listened as I poured out my arguments, my fears, and my feelings. Piper never moved from my side. By the time we all went to bed, my reservoir of tears was empty, and my heart was full.

CHAPTER THIRTY-SEVEN

IT WAS BETH'S IDEA to reach out to Nanette. Actually, Beth suggested I talk to Chance in addition to reaching out to Nanette, but I knew that wouldn't help. I tried talking to Chance and he walked away from me—toward her.

My client, Mr. Chance Easton, the chair of the gala committee for BCA, had indicated his priorities for the event. I incorporated those wishes into my plan. In the area I lacked insight, I now had a plan to seek counsel. The board hired me for my expertise and professionalism. I got myself sideways because I fostered feelings for a client—rookie mistake. There will be other clients I spend time with. I can't fall for all of them. I clearly understood Mr. Easton's priorities, Nanette had assisted before, and I had no doubt she would again.

Or at least that's what I told myself in the mirror that morning.

My shoulders relaxed when we turned off the logging road. Luckily, we didn't encounter any speeding beasts this time. Beth commented on the beauty of the landscape and on the generosity of Mrs. Verity for meeting with us on such short notice. Piper ran back and forth in the very back of the Jeep, looking out the left window, then looking out the right, and back to the left again.

I envied their responses—both enthralled by the beauty around them—while my anxious thoughts banged against one another like bumper cars at the state fair.

I found it as difficult to keep Nanette at a business-appropriate distance as it was for me to keep my feelings for Chance at bay. I waffled between wanting to fall sobbing into her grandmotherly arms for advice, and projecting the professionalism I desperately wanted to walk in.

I inhaled deeply and took in the turquoise sky and cotton ball clouds. The fall colors invaded the terrain with bushes that looked aflame in varying shades of yellow, deep rust, and bright orange. When we crossed a bridge, I took note of the water's glassy surface broken by the occasional boulder rising from the creek bottom.

As I navigated Scarlett up Nanette's steep drive, I glimpsed her on the front porch adding water to a bowl for Piper. She set the pitcher on the table and spread her arms wide as we got out of the Jeep.

"Welcome, ladies!" Piper reached Nanette first. "Yes, you too, Miss Piper." She laughed as she stroked her fur. Like arriving at grandma's house, Piper immediately located an overflowing food bowl and brand-new chew toy. Nanette attached a light chain to Piper's collar and ushered Beth and me inside.

The smell of fresh brownies billowed from the entry before I spotted the platter on the counter. Nanette followed my gaze and said, "Your voice sounded like a large plate of chocolate was in order."

Just like grandma's house.

Nanette grasped both of Beth's hands when I introduced them.

They exchanged "I've heard so much about yous" and ended up in an embrace like long-lost friends. We fixed our cups of coffee in the kitchen and Nanette guided us to the living room. She set the platter of brownies on the coffee table next to a stack of cocktail napkins that read, "Stop me before I volunteer again."

Beth and I nestled next to each other on the light-yellow couch amidst a host of pillows—plaid pillows, floral pillows, pillows with hand-stitched embroidery, and pillows so soft I wanted to rub them on my face. I tucked my leather satchel under my feet and shifted some pillows behind my back.

Nanette's phone rang and she glanced at the screen. "I'm so sorry. This is my daughter, I need to take it."

"Of course," Beth and I said in unison and then giggled. Then we each reached for the brownies at the same time and giggled again.

"Your dress came in?" Nanette asked her daughter.

"Oh," she said with a frown. "So you decided on the purple."

Beth and I looked at each other and both put our hands over our mouths. Memories of freshman homecoming and my hideous purple dress rushed in. We swallowed our laughter.

"Do they have free returns?" Nanette asked.

I picked up a book from the coffee table and flipped pages, not really looking at the pictures inside.

"Well, why don't you go ahead and order the blue one, too?" she said. "I know purple's your favorite color, but I really think the blue will look better. It's such a big event, I just want you to see both options."

Beth played with the beads on her bracelet. I put the book back and fanned the cocktail napkins on the coffee table.

Long pause. "Okay, good."

Nanette hung up, apologized again, and said she needed to make another call. "Hey, hon. Listen. Ann said she got in the purple dress."

I pointed at the photo of Nanette and Julia on the mantle and whispered in Beth's ear, "That's the picture I told you about."

Beth mouthed "oh!" and nodded her head.

"I know it's her favorite, but I convinced her to order a blue one just to try on. I might be wrong, but will you go over and be the voice of reason if I'm right? Okay, thanks. Love you. Byyyye."

"Sorry about that," Nanette said, putting her phone face down on the table. She grabbed a napkin and a brownie and said, "So, how can I help you ladies today?"

I scooched to the edge of the couch, straightened my back, folded my hands in my lap, and turned on my best presentation voice. "As I mentioned when I called, I've been hired as the marketing consultant for the BCA gala. I have a new theme, a list of sponsors to call on, and some directives from the committee, but I don't want to lose the spirit of BCA in the midst of my changes."

"Is that all?" Nanette asked.

I blinked. "Like, do you want to see the materials?" I reached for my bag to pull out a sponsor packet.

Nanette reached out and patted my hand. "No, no. I don't need to see the materials. Is that all you came here for? My insight on the changes?"

"What's really bothering Joy is—" Beth interjected.

"The new theme has not been well received by the entire committee," I said and cast a quick glare at Beth.

"What is the theme?" Nanette asked.

"Gridiron Glitz. I chose it to make the most—"

"Football?" Nanette placed her empty napkin on the table and clapped her hands. "I love football. Like the warriors of old, our young men clash it out on a field of battle."

"Not everyone agrees with you," I said flatly.

"Like Chance," Beth said. I kicked her under the coffee table.

Nanette raised her eyebrows in a question, grabbed her mug from the table, and took a sip.

I waved my hand in frustration and let my shoulders slump. I flung myself back on the couch and spewed, "We're back to the same song and dance of biblical worldview. He hates the theme, but all of our potential sponsors are going to love it. Every member of the marketing team I work with are excited about it. I'm excited about it. And the purpose is to raise money. But he's so principled. And we got in a disagreement, and I tried to apologize, but he was with another girl. And I need to be able to do this on my own. But I need your help." I sat up and snatched a small brownie from the plate and shoved it in my mouth.

"I see," Nanette said.

The brownie filled my mouth like a chipmunk. Both cheeks were so full I fought to keep my lips closed. Beth stared at her folded hands in her lap. Nanette sipped her coffee in prolonged silence.

"I was reading in First Chronicles this morning," Nanette began. "It's the part where David consulted with all of Israel to bring the Ark of God back to a place of honor. He was disgusted that it had been neglected, and it was time to make a change."

I raised my hand to interrupt and bring the discussion back around to the gala, but Beth grabbed my shoulder and yanked me back into the pillows. I crossed my arms in silence.

"Everyone agreed to it," Nanette continued. "Scripture even says something like, 'The people could see it was the right thing to do.' So they went to get the Ark and—let's just say, it didn't go well. God got angry, a man died, then David got angry that God was angry—it was a lot."

"What'd they do wrong?" I asked.

"They put the Ark on a trailer," Beth said.

"Okaaayyy." I stretched the word and looked at Nanette for explanation.

"In a nutshell, they didn't follow God's previously recorded instructions, and they never sought his counsel regarding the project," Nanette explained.

"I wouldn't have known you shouldn't put the Ark on a trailer," I shrugged. I leaned forward, propped my elbows on my knees, and tried to keep irritation out of my voice. "Chance is already angry. For all I know God is angry, too."

"Okay, then let's ask God for direction on how we should handle it from here."

Nanette stood and walked toward an open space between the living room and the kitchen. She turned around and beckoned us to join her. She spread her arms slightly with palms up. Beth knew what to do. She walked over and grasped one of Nanette's hands and reached for mine. Nanette gripped my free hand, closing the circle, and bowed her head.

"Father God, we come before You with adoration and humility. You are the Revealer of Mysteries, and You tell us when we need wisdom we should ask for it. Thank You for revealing Yourself to us in Your Word. Thank You for reminding us that Your standards are set, You stand by them, and You want us to follow them. Reveal to us where we have deviated from Your ways, and give us counsel as to how to reflect Your image as we use our talents and experience to work on this project. In Jesus's name we pray. Amen."

"Amen," Beth and I responded in unison.

"Now, let's sit at the kitchen table and spread out," Nanette suggested.

Nanette asked question after question as I detailed my plans for the gala. Every once in a while she would give a small suggestion, but mostly she just asked questions.

"This looks like fun!" Nanette's enthusiasm encouraged me when we got to the end of what I had planned. "What do you need from me?"

"How do I infuse the spirit of Berean Christian Academy into the event?"

"Do what you do best, Joy. Tell the story. And through that story, rehearse the goodness and favor of God."

An idea occurred to me so exciting it caused my heart to race. I didn't know how to rehearse the goodness of God. But I knew someone who did it every time I met with her.

I placed both hands on the table and leaned in slightly, "Can I interview you on camera for a feature presentation at the gala?"

"No."

I pulled my hands back as if Nanette had slapped them. I sat back in the chair and didn't hide my perplexity. "No?"

"No, honey. I promised myself, and the Lord, that the only way I would be involved with BCA is behind the scenes and as a prayer warrior."

"But you're so articulate, and you understand the spirit of BCA. Your history with the school represents everything I want to say."

I looked out the window over her shoulder. My head spun with the best turn of phrase to convince her to change her mind. Essential ingredient. Missing link. Vital component. Magic piece.

I opened my mouth and Nanette placed her hand on top of mine. Her eyes were soft and kind, but she shook her head "no" all the same.

"Can I ask why?" I whined.

"It's embarrassing."

I tilted my head and grimaced with cynicism. I couldn't imagine anything Nanette would have done that would cause her to disqualify herself. "Will you tell us anyway?" I pushed.

"A few years ago, I interfered in a matter between a precious staff member and a new administrator. It caused great disruption. I didn't have all of the information, and it damaged relationships. I prayerfully determined from that point forward that the best way for me to support BCA was directly between me and Father God."

"But that was a few years ago. Everyone makes mistakes. Maybe this could be a way to redeem yourself," I offered.

"I said I *prayerfully determined* my future involvement." Nanette's tone held a firmness I had yet to hear from her. "Until the Lord tells me different, I'm going to maintain my boundary."

"So, you're going to punish yourself and BCA," I grumbled under my breath as I pretended to write something in my notebook.

"It's not about punishment, it's about self-control." Nanette's measured voice continued with kindness, "We're all a work in progress. As a follower of Christ, I'm made holy before Father God in matters of salvation. However, I'm still working to become more like Jesus in my daily life." Nanette straightened some papers on the table. "My husband calls what I do meddling. If I discipline myself from putting my foot on the path, then I avoid meddling all together."

Nanette paused and took a sip of coffee and shrugged. "While I like to think of it as helping, my husband's not wrong." Nanette put her hand out to cover mine. "Do you understand?"

I did not understand. I felt like I was putting together a puzzle with no picture to guide me.

"So, it's okay to offer unsolicited 'help'—" I put my fingers up in air quotes, "—when it comes to your daughter's fashion choices, but when you're invited to help you won't?"

As soon as I blurted the words I regretted it. I sounded like a petulant child. I may as well have thrown the papers in the air, stomped out, and slammed the door.

Beth dug her fingers into my thigh under the table. "Mrs. Verity, thank you so much for your time this morning," Beth chirped. I plucked at invisible fuzz from my sweater and bit my lip. "Your insight today has made this plan better than Joy could have ever imagined." Beth did not release her grip, and my thigh began to sting.

I patted Beth's hand, but couldn't look at Nanette.

"Speaking of plans," Beth continued, "we hoped we could leave Joy's Jeep here to hike some trails and take a mountain picnic with Piper."

"How delightful!" Nanette exclaimed. She slid her chair back to stand, and Beth and I followed suit. "Of course you can. I know just the trail you should take."

We left everything on the table as she ushered us out the door.

CHAPTER THIRTY-EIGHT

BETH DIDN'T SPEAK of my ridiculous behavior. I didn't mind. I felt foolish enough. Honestly, Beth's silence only deepened my sense of guilt. I felt so comfortable around Nanette—like I could be myself and not put on an act of having it all together. Unfortunately, that meant I kept proving how not together I really was.

The trail began behind Nanette's cabin and led us up a steep incline leading to a plateau that fell off on the other side toward a high mountain meadow with a creek running through it. Piper took off running through the tall grasses. A few late summer blooms remained. The orange hue of a single Indian paintbrush flower and a few lonely remaining purple lupines hinted at the glory of the meadow earlier in the year.

Piper yipped and bounced when Beth and I took off our shoes and socks and waded into the creek. We splashed and laughed like children. Piper barked and jumped in and out of the water, occasionally chasing a butterfly through the meadow and back to the stream.

We sat on a boulder at the edge of the creek drying in the sunshine when my stomach rumbled so loud Beth commented, "Sounds like the lunch bell has sounded. We should make our way to that overlook Nanette told us about."

We slipped our socks and shoes back on, slung our backpacks over our shoulders, called for Piper, and headed to the trailhead that would lead us to the overlook. Nanette had mentioned a picnic-perfect flat area near the edge of a cliff.

The steep incline near the top sent my lungs into overdrive, but my huffing and puffing ceased when we crested the summit. The awe-inspiring panorama of untamed natural beauty literally took my breath away. The rugged terrain unfolded like a tapestry of evergreen forest. Layer upon layer of mountains receded into the distance—rolling mounds of green occasionally interrupted by a rocky outcrop of towering granite. A layer of haze masked the hills to our right, but straight ahead my eyes followed the swells of mountains like a boat dipping and rising in gentle waves until a distant, snowcapped mountain commanded my attention against the canvas of the sky.

"Wow," Beth whispered.

"Yeah. Wow," I agreed.

We spread our blanket and reclined in the sunshine and cool breezes of the summit. We devoured our sandwiches, fruit, nuts, and crackers. Even Piper stretched out in the sun and took a nap.

"I'm glad we did this," Beth said.

"Me too. I love views like this, where you can see everything all at once."

"I've enjoyed all the small things along the way, too. Like the smell of water before we crested the ridge of the high meadow. Or the dots of color in the sea of grasses. The ice-cold creek water and the ripple of your and Piper's laughter when you first splashed in it."

"Piper's laughter?" I questioned, blinking.

"She definitely laughed. All those yips?"

"I guess," I shrugged. I swept my arm to span the panoramic view. "And this is the big payoff."

"That's what I'm trying to say, Joy. This is *part* of the payoff, but there are gifts along the way that make the entire journey worth it. Don't miss the significance of the seemingly insignificant."

I replayed the scenes from our hike in my mind, then heard Nanette's admonishment, "You're worried about the destination when God wants to get your attention to show you things along the way."

But I have to keep the end in mind.

I picked up a loose rock and scratched at a patch of dirt near the edge of our blanket. I lifted my head and surveyed the panoramic view again. "If we didn't have the goal of this overlook, we wouldn't have taken this path," I argued.

"True. I'm simply saying you can enjoy both."

We lingered in silence, propped on our elbows with legs extended and ankles crossed. Birds soared in the distance and clouds floated by. When Piper stirred, we gathered our containers and blanket and headed back.

My phone dinged for the first time in hours when we regained cell service on the plateau near Nanette's cabin. I stopped to read a message from my favorite fast-food joint offering a deal of the week, a notification of a missed call from Aunt Mimsy, and a text message from Nanette sent hours before.

You were right. I meddled. I've called to confess to both of my daughters. Thank you for your boldness. A Work In Progress, Nanette.

I smiled at the fact that she signed her name to her text. Aunt Mimsy did that sometimes. Then I reread the text.

You were right? Reckless and rude, maybe. But not right.

Thank you for your boldness? Belligerent and bratty, maybe, but not bold.

I watched Beth lean over to stretch the backs of her legs while Piper sniffed and explored. I spotted some rocks that gave me an idea.

"I want to mark this day," I announced. "Let's leave the year and our initials here."

"Huh?" Beth asked with a wrinkled brow.

"We used to do it as kids up at Paddy Flat." I picked up a rock the size of my palm. "We'd gather stones like these and arrange them to spell out our initials and the year. Then every year, we'd come back to the woods and see if we could find them again."

"Craft project!" Beth rejoiced and started gathering rocks.

We nestled each stone into the dry dirt to form the numbers and then letters. I had placed the last stone needed to form the letter J when my phone dinged again.

Another message from Nanette displayed on the screen. *Work in progress.*

I heard a distant bark and Piper jumped forward, stiffened her body, and perked her ears. At a second bark, she lunged down the steep incline and her leash flapped on the rocks behind her. "Piper!" I called.

I saw Ruby first as she and Piper jumped all over each other and worked their way up the path. Then Chance's brown hair emerged, then his black glasses, then his fitted forest green T-shirt, khaki hiking shorts, tan legs, and finally his hiking boots. He stood with his hands on his hips and took deep breaths. "Those last few steps are steep!"

Beth and I looked at each other and blinked rapidly. Then Beth crouched down and lodged a stone in the earth. "Done. I need to go wash my hands." She hopped down the incline and headed straight to the cabin.

I stood and stared at her with lips parted for a moment, then turned my face to Chance. "What are you doing here?" I asked more with surprise than accusation.

Nanette.

"Can we sit?" Chance motioned toward a large, flat-topped boulder.

I sat on the boulder and looked at my feet. He sat on my right — so close that our legs touched. I shifted to insert space between us.

"Nanette showed me your plan."

I looked up and scanned his expression for approval or disdain.

"I admit it. I was hasty and harsh," Chance said and rubbed the palms of his hands on his thighs.

I blinked.

"You haven't called or texted since Monday," Chance said.

"Neither have you."

Chance tilted his head back with a sigh. "You're right. I've been so distracted with my sister's surprise visit—"

"Sister?"

"Yeah, she showed up at the dog park on Monday night and surprised me. She only stayed for a few days—" Chance shrugged, "—but I guess time flies when you're having fun."

The girl was his sister. I threw myself into an uncontrolled tizzy because of his sister.

He's still a client.

My wandering mind slowly emerged from a fog to recognize Chance was in the middle of saying something, "—but, like I said, I've seen the game plan and I'm one hundred percent on board."

Chance reached out and placed his hand on top of mine. "I want to be a team."

I drew my hand back and slid it under my thigh as I shifted my knees away from him. I blinked away the tears that welled in my eyes and angled my shoulder away from him. I examined a pine cone hanging from a branch near my left shoulder. Its compact, spiraled scales formed a tight, protective embrace around the heart of the cone. Each scale resembled a miniature wooden shield. "You didn't even give me a chance," I whispered.

His finger on my thigh startled me. My vision blurred as my mind registered that he was writing me a message. I—M

He moved his finger slowly but I struggled to focus on the letters, distracted by his touch. S—O—R—R—Y.

When I swiveled my head to look at him over my shoulder, he looked like Piper when she'd chewed something—head bent with sad yet hopeful eyes.

"Do you forgive me?" Chance asked.

Like Piper, he was impossible to stay mad at. I sighed and nodded.

As if on cue, both dogs came up to our knees, sat on our feet, and swished their tails back and forth in the dust. I was pretty sure Chance would wag his tail if he had one. He bounced a little on the boulder.

Chance bent over and grabbed two sticks — one for each hand. When he got up, the dogs stood and eagerly waited. He bent his knees and both elbows back and hurled the sticks over the edge of the steep incline. Piper and Ruby bounded down the trail.

I looked up at Chance, "Where do we go from here?"

"I think I should add my C to this rock project," Chance said with a grin. He gathered an armful of stones and bent to nestle them into the earth.

CHAPTER THIRTY-NINE

RODERICK STOOD AT THE READY with his video camera. Chance said we could get some good footage of students at today's academic pep rally. The gym buzzed with conversation as kids in hunter-green polo shirts filed in and took their seats in the bleachers that flanked one side of the gym.

The wood floors reminded me of an old bowling alley. The narrow, honey-colored planks filled the space, overlaid by the occasional painted line. Oversized photo banners of seniors from various sports hung on the walls at both ends of the gym. State championship banners draped from the ceiling amidst the silver, domed light fixtures. A massive inflatable tunnel with a screaming eagle on top graced the center of the gym. Two sections of chairs flanked each side of the tunnel facing the students in the bleachers.

I spotted Chance on the far side of the gym. He guided students to their sections and gave fist bumps along the way. He smiled and waved when he noticed Roderick and me. I loved seeing him in his element.

He's gonna miss this if he takes that other job.

A bell rang and music blared from speakers. I nudged Roderick to start filming as cheerleaders ran from both sides of the gym, hand-springing into clean back tucks before standing in formation in front of the students—their legs shoulder width apart, wrists crossed behind their backs, and chins tucked into their chests. A new song began and the cheerleaders' arms sliced through the air. Their legs kicked high in perfect unison and their bodies twisted and turned with effortless agility as the students all stood in the stands and started singing along with a fight song. It all ended with two of the cheerleaders flying through the air with legs spread wide touching their toes and everyone screaming, "Fly, Eagles, fly!"

Roderick gave me a thumbs up and kept filming as the girls transitioned to a cheer that ended in a chant—B-C-A! B-C-A! A stream of students appeared from the dark mouth of the tunnel and shuffled into the rows of chairs. I recognized Jackson and a few other students from our previous film shoot on campus. Some waved to their friends in the stands—most looked like they would rather be in the crowd than on display.

A man in a gray suit with a green tie the color of the eagle mascot stood behind a wooden podium with a microphone. "Each week we gather in a rally to support and honor our athletic warriors on the court and field. Today we have the privilege of celebrating the academic achievements of our BCA Eagle champions in the classroom."

As the program droned on, Roderick turned off his camera, leaned against the wall, and scrolled on his phone. I wished we would have left after the grand entrance of the students, but I didn't want to draw attention by leaving in the middle of the presentation— the very long presentation.

I watched Chance as he sat in the front row and gave his full attention to the ceremony. When he glanced my way, I sucked in my breath and averted my eyes back to the podium. I could feel my neck burning. I tucked a curl behind my ear and wondered how long I had been staring at him.

"And now, I am going to turn over the microphone to Mr. John Clarke, BCA's very own Booster Club President, for a special announcement."

I perked up and nudged Roderick. I didn't know what John had planned—I didn't even know he was on the agenda—but I wanted to record it in case I could use the footage later.

"Thank you, Dr. Scott. I love celebrating champions—conquerors. The academic elite in front of you will go on to conquer the world of—er—academia. But now our real Eagle champions, our esteemed football team, will come up for a special unveiling."

I cringed. Did he say "real" champions? I glanced furtively toward Chance to see if he noticed. He arched his back and bit his lip. Then he glanced at me. I raised the corners of my mouth slightly, lifted my hand, and wriggled my fingers in a wave. He nodded his head almost imperceptibly and looked away. I wanted to slap my head and melt into the floor.

The cheerleaders returned to form a line in front of the bleachers with their backs to the crowd this time. They rustled their pom-poms as a grunge rock song played over the speakers. A stream of boys in dark sport coats, gray slacks, white shirts, and green ties emerged from the tunnel. They lined up in front of the students in chairs and stood facing the bleachers. Jackson and a few other boys from the academic program got up to join them, forming a wall between the stands and the previously honored students.

"These brave warriors of the field have battled against all odds to emerge victorious, showing us what true determination looks like. And—"

As if on cue, the cheerleaders riled up the crowd with a fresh wave of B-C-A chants.

John smiled wide and clapped the backs of a few of the boys who stood closest to him. After a hearty round of chants, John motioned with his arms for the students to calm down and be seated. "And their future is even brighter now that we have finally filled the vacant athletic director position. So, stand and give your loudest BCA welcome to Mr. Jacob Vidal, BCA's new AD."

The fight song played again and a man emerged from the tunnel wearing the same dark sport coat and green tie as the football players. His over six-foot frame and wide shoulders suggested he had played football himself at one time. His ears flared slightly from the side of his head and his short, dark hair ended in a V-shaped dip on his forehead. His tan face only served to highlight his bright-white teeth and broad smile.

Mr. Vidal shook John's hand and slapped him on the shoulder with the other. He ran down the row of football players and gave them each double high fives with loud slaps. When he finished one row of players, he turned and high-fived down the other row and pivoted and raised his arms to egg on the crowd to greater frenzy. His grand entrance crescendoed with the fight song and he joined the crowd in a grand finale of "Fly, Eagles, Fly!"

I watched Chance stand with the crowd in the bleachers. He clapped his hands and his lips moved as if he joined the song, but the corners of his lips remained flat. Even from across the gym I could see a veil of reservation shadowing his eyes.

"Thank you, Mr. Clarke. I'm excited to be here and proud to be called a BCA Eagle. It's been a great day already, but I have one more presentation to make. Boys, if you could turn to face the back wall, and students if you could turn your chairs around. Jimmy, go ahead and kill the air pump."

Chairs screeched against the floor as students turned them to face the other direction. The eagle melted into a flat pile of rubber. The tunnel had obscured the opposite wall of the gym—now that it lay deflated, it revealed two sets of giant canvas banners covering the back wall—a narrow one beneath the set of windows hugging the roof line, and another larger canvas beneath.

Mr. Vidal stood at the microphone. "At BCA we want you to tap into your leadership potential and push your limits to become the best versions of yourselves. That's why our new motto is—"

Two cheerleaders stood at the ends of ropes attached to the top canvas. On Mr. Vidal's cue they pulled the ropes and the canvas fell in a heap. Bold, green words broadcast "INSPIRING GREATNESS WITHIN."

"This will serve as a constant reminder for every BCA Eagle to tap into their leadership potential and strive for greatness. It's a new day at BCA where personal growth, motivation, and leadership development are fostered and celebrated. Every time you read these words, be inspired to push your limits and become the best versions of yourselves."

The cheerleaders rushed to formation under the new motto and led a cheer. Every time they paused, the crowd thundered their response. "We are the—EAGLES! The mighty, mighty—EAGLES! We're gonna win! 'Cuz we are the—CHAMPIONS!"

"I have one more thing," Mr. Vidal nearly screamed into the microphone to quiet the crowd. "My first leadership assignment is for you to convince your parents and the booster club to vote yes for Clarke Field."

Two more cheerleaders pulled the ropes of the second covering to reveal a full-color rendering of a completely renovated sports complex with the words VOTE YES FOR CLARKE FIELD in bright red letters across the top.

The kids oohed and aahed and the cheerleaders chanted EAGLES! EAGLES! I glanced around the gym—Dr. Scott, John, and Mr. Vidal all clapped and chanted along with the crowd. I focused on Chance—his face no longer displayed reservation. No. His face read anger all the way. He stood, shoved his hands in his pockets, and exited through a side door.

CHAPTER FORTY

I ARRIVED EARLY for the gala-planning committee meeting at Chance's house. I hadn't seen him in days, and I'd never been to his home before. I slowed to locate the black house number against the white clapboard siding of Chance's small house. Rows of boxwood hedges ran along the front of the house and edged the sidewalk leading to the charcoal-colored craftsman-style front door. The dense foliage was cut low and with right angles and sharp precision, putting the "box" in boxwoods. I couldn't wait to see if the inside was as orderly and precise as the outside.

Chance had been in meeting after meeting since the big announcement at the academic pep rally. It turned out John hadn't clued Jacob Vidal in on BCA's traditions when he convinced him to unveil the details of Clarke Field. Chance embarked on a mission to make sure those traditions were not overturned.

I tucked my curls behind my ears and shifted my blouse. Then I pulled my hair back in a low ponytail and checked my makeup in the rearview mirror. I got out and walked around Scarlett to the passenger side to retrieve my banana pudding from a crate on the floor. I locked the doors and changed my mind about my hair. I balanced the trifle bowl of pudding on the hood of the Jeep and let my hair down again and fluffed it. I wiped my hands on my jeans and took a deep breath.

I couldn't pinpoint the source of my anxiety. Chance and I had made up. I'd met with planning committees before. I'd made the banana pudding a thousand times. I felt confident in my wardrobe choices. And Chance called all of the committee members ahead of time to ward off any discussion of the academic pep rally or Clarke Field—tonight's meeting would remain gala focused.

I shook my hands at my side, grabbed the pudding, and made my way to the sidewalk leading to Chance's house.

Per Chance's instructions, I left Scarlett parked in front of his matching detached one-car garage. I turned down the sidewalk toward the house when a blue Toyota Camry drove up and pulled in behind my Jeep. A woman got out and waved before she reached into her car and retrieved a casserole dish. She slammed her door, locked it, and half-walked half-skipped up to me. I recognized her as Millie, one of the sundress ladies I had met at Maggie's BBQ.

"Good to see you again," she exclaimed.

"Nice to—"

"Is that what I think it is?" she pointed to my trifle bowl.

I tipped the bowl toward her and said, "Banana pudding."

"I had some of that at the BBQ at the Hensley's and I searched and searched for you to get the recipe." She linked her arm in mine and practically dragged me to Chance's front walkway. "You do share the recipe, don't you?"

"Um—"

"Cuz I have an aunt who makes the best salsa—like, the BEST—and she refuses to share the recipe."

Before I could respond, we found ourselves walking up the steps. Chance stood at his open door with a wide grin and twinkle in his eye.

"Mr. Easton," she declared, "thank you for hosting. I saw a poster for the gala and noticed the new theme, so I brought my game-day sliders."

She shoved the casserole dish into Chance's arms and started to walk inside when she noticed a white minivan that pulled up. "Oh, look. There's Liz. I'll be right in. I'm gonna go see if she needs help."

I practically felt a breeze as she swept by in the same half-skip-half-walk from before.

"So you met Millie."

"Oh, we're good friends. We share recipes."

"Oh, recipes. Wow. I didn't realize you had gotten so close." We both laughed and wove through extra chairs circling the small living room toward the U-shaped kitchen with a wooden dining table in the middle. Chance set the casserole on one of many placemats sprinkled on the tabletop.

I eyed stacks of red cups and a large silver bowl filled with ice next to beverage dispensers on the counter.

"Well trained in hosting a committee meeting I am," Chance said in Yoda-speak.

Adorable. A little nerdy, but adorable.

I offered a faint laugh, "I can see that."

The room filled with people. They hugged and laughed and ate and laughed some more. I remembered Chance calling this committee "his people" and I could see why. Peace, love, kindness, and laughter marked this gathering. They told stories of their families—home, school, and church—and many of their experiences intersected. Church overlapped with school overlapped with home overlapped with each other.

When we finally all moved to the living room and sat in the circle of chairs, Chance gave a nod to a man named Jeremy. Everyone seemed to know what was coming because they all stopped talking and bowed their heads and closed their eyes. Jeremy asked for God's favor and wisdom on the meeting in a prayer that felt like he was talking to someone in the room.

Jeremy turned the meeting over to white-mini-van-Liz who pulled out her Bible and read from II Kings 4 about a widow who asked a prophet for help after her husband died.

"Look here, in verse three it says, 'Go around and ask all your neighbors for empty jars. Don't ask for just a few,'" Liz said. "And you'll notice that the oil flowed as long as they had jars. If they had asked for more, the oil would have flowed more. If they had gathered fewer, the oil still would have stopped on the last one."

I looked around the circle to see some people holding their own Bibles in their laps. Others were looking at the text on their phones. Liz concluded, "So, let's gather as many jars as we can and watch God fill them."

Millie gasped, "I never thought of it like that before." Others murmured their agreement.

Chance sat with his hands folded in his lap and nodded in agreement as well. Unease crept up on me as I realized I felt more composed at the cocktail tables at John's gathering than a setting like this one.

"That is the perfect introduction to what we're going to discuss tonight. I've invited Miss Joy Swallow to join us to give us our marching orders. BCA has hired her as a professional marketing consultant to take our gala to the next level."

I smiled and nodded as everyone around the circle verbalized their "welcomes" and "great to have yous." The group's enthusiasm waned, however, as I passed out materials and discussed the different ways they could help bring my vision to life. By the time I finished my presentation, apprehension replaced the atmosphere of peace and joy. I even tied in Liz's jar analogy to encourage everyone on the committee to participate in gathering silent auction items.

"This is a lot," Millie blinked at me.

Shift the momentum, Joy.

"That's the plan, but none of it will hold meaning if we can't capture the BCA spirit. So…talk to me about the Berean Christian Academy spirit."

Awkward silence filled the space. Some shifted in their seats, others stared at their feet, one lady twirled her hair.

"What about Javier and his mom?" Jeremy blessedly broke the silence.

Faces lit up around the circle as several folks tossed out details of a football player whose grandfather died. Javier and his mother had lived with her dad, but the landlord kicked them out at his death. They had nowhere else to go, so they had been living in their car. One BCA family offered a two-bedroom home rent-free for six months for them to get back on their feet. Another family coordinated an anonymous meal train delivered to BCA and discreetly distributed to the family for the first month. Another family encouraged Javier and his mother to get involved in their church and invited them to family dinner after service every Sunday.

Tears welled in my eyes. I had never heard of such sincere generosity.

"And stuff like that happens all the time," Liz said.

"It used to happen more," Millie grumbled.

A few people nodded and murmured agreement.

"We can't stop praying," a man named Charles interjected.

Charles looked at me directly. "I go on prayer walks on campus every day."

"Prayer walks?" I asked.

"You know, I just walk around the campus praying."

"Oh," I said, trying to keep my face from displaying how strange that sounded.

"BCA is still God's school," Charles continued. "One day, I was on one of my prayer walks and I asked God to bless the campus with His presence. I felt the Holy Spirit tap me on the shoulder and say, 'Charles, I'm already here. This is my school. I've invited you to be a part of what I'm doing here.'"

I heard a "mmm" and a "that's good" from the group.

"And I know it's true. I always feel the presence of God when I drive on campus. It's a peace that passes understanding."

Now, *that* I could agree with. I attributed the peacefulness I felt on campus to the serene landscape, but maybe it could be the presence of God.

Chance closed the meeting with a prayer and everyone gathered up their belongings and left one by one. He politely declined my offer to help clean up and reset his house. Instead, Chance escorted me and Millie to our cars.

"Thanks again, Mr. Easton. And Joy, don't forget to get me a copy of that recipe," Millie said. We both waved goodbye as she got in her car and drove away.

"That was pretty special," I said.

Chance leaned against the Jeep and smiled. "Yeah, I call them 'The Remnant.'"

"The Remnant?"

"Those left over from a larger group. There used to be more families like that at BCA, but don't underestimate what God can do with a small group devoted to Him."

I reached for the passenger-side door of Scarlett to put my empty trifle bowl back in the crate on the floorboard. A slick substance smeared onto my hand when I pulled the handle. I yanked my hand back and examined it in the dim glow of the streetlight.

"What's wrong?" Chance asked. He grabbed my hand to inspect it and ran his thumb over the slick substance on my palm.

"There's something slimy on the handle."

Chance pulled out his phone and turned on the flashlight to get a better look. Clear and yellow-orange gunk oozed down the side of the door. As his flashlight highlighted the ground, we saw eggshells.

"Scarlett's been egged," I exclaimed. Chance groaned and made a thorough inspection of the Jeep with his flashlight.

"We've got to get that off before it eats the paint," Chance said. "I have a hose in the garage."

Chance walked to the side door of his garage and unlocked it. He stepped inside and flipped a switch that illuminated the garage door and the area where I had parked Scarlett. I stood there stunned with my mouth open. Chance hooked up the hose and walked back toward me.

"Now what?" he asked.

"Oh, Chance," I said and pointed at the garage door.

Words in white shaving cream covered the charcoal-colored door—"Vote yes for Clarke Field."

CHAPTER FORTY-ONE

"WHAT DID HE SAY?" Beth asked.

"He didn't say anything. He just handed me the hose and went back into the garage to grab a bucket and sponge. I hosed Scarlett off while he scrubbed in silence. Once we were sure she was egg free, he put everything back in the garage, gave me a hug goodnight, and went back inside."

"Have you talked to him today?"

"I texted him, but I'm only getting one-word answers."

As we pulled out of the Gonzales Body Shop parking lot, Beth asked, "What are these again?" She waved envelopes in the air.

"Free oil changes. Mateo's uncle donated them and I'm going to use them to inspire the committee members."

"Inspire?" Beth asked with a tilt of her head, "or bribe?"

"It's not a bribe," I insisted. "It's a token of appreciation for their service on the committee." I turned at the light. "And a nudge to help me out."

Beth raised her eyebrows and twisted her lips.

"I'm only one person and I'm gonna need as many people as I can to get auction stuff."

Beth sighed and pulled down the visor to look in the mirror. She fixed her bangs and snapped it back.

"Thanks for taking your Saturday to run around with me," I said.

"It's a nice day to spend in the Jeep." Beth raised her arms through the open T-tops like she was on a roller coaster. "You should have brought Piper. She would've loved riding around with us."

"Yeah, or eating my seats in between stops," I grumbled. "She likes the doggie daycare just fine. They have other dogs for her to play with."

Our first stop was Liz's house. Her white minivan in the driveway confirmed we were at the right place. We noticed her kneeling in front of a flower bed, pulling weeds as we walked up to the front door.

"Hi, Liz," I said. "Your flower beds are gorgeous. What are these—yellow daisies?"

"Black-eyed Susans—and thanks," Liz replied. She stood, took her gloves off, and tossed them at her feet.

"This is my best friend, Beth. We won't stay long, but I wanted to drop this gift off to you as a pre-gala thank you for all of the hard work you're getting ready to do."

Liz smiled, shook Beth's hand, and took the envelope from me. She opened the flap and read the voucher.

"Isn't this the kind of thing we're supposed to be gathering for the silent auction?"

"Sure, but you're going to be going all over town. It's the least we can do," I said.

"Well, thanks, but I think I'll just donate it back to the gala."

I clasped her hands and the envelope in between mine and said, "I insist. Really. It's inspiration to go gather those jars."

She opened her mouth and I added, "Tell Beth about the jars. What you said the other night was so good."

Liz recapped her thoughts about the widow and her sons gathering jars. Beth responded like the others with an "oh, that's good."

When Liz finished, I said, "We won't keep you. Thanks again—in advance." I placed my hand on her shoulder and added, "Use the oil change. I insist."

Beth and I got back in the Jeep and I beeped the horn as I leaned out the window. "Gather as many jars as you can," I called with a wave.

"I like her," Beth commented.

"Yeah, me too. But now that I've heard the jar thing again, I wonder if the widow and her sons regretted not pushing harder to ask for more."

"I think the story is more about the limitlessness of God than the efforts of the widow and her sons," Beth suggested.

"Maybe." I thought of the list I put together of BCA families who owned businesses, and my upcoming appointment with John to call on the potential donors I met at his lake house. If I pushed harder and asked more, God might fill my jars.

When we stopped at Millie's house, I gave my pitch about the oil change and gathering jars, but she wanted to talk about the pep rally.

"I wanted to go, but Thomas had a doctor's appointment. And my Shelly tries hard, bless her heart, but she didn't quite make the cut to be honored. But her best friend got the English award. You were there weren't you? You probably saw her friend, Jill—gorgeous red hair. But anyway, I heard those football boys stole the show—as usual. And when they uncovered that banner of Clarke field, I heard Mr. Easton walked right out. I wanted to ask him about it at his house the other night, but—" Millie tilted her head and raised her hands in surrender.

I pulled an envelope out of my back pocket and said, "So, here is the—"

"I just can't get over that motto," Millie continued. "I'm not too sure about Coach Vidal. Inspiring Greatness Within just doesn't sound right."

I looked at Beth who held eye contact with Millie and nodded. Beth leaned toward Millie and asked, "How so?"

I wanted to roll my eyes, shove the envelope into Millie's hands, grab Beth, and make a run for it…not encourage more commentary.

"Oh!" Millie clasped her hands and her eyes brightened. "Back in the day, it was all about Jesus. He was the center of everything. We taught the kids to pray and ask God for strength." Millie waved her hand with a huff, "Now we're telling them to dig deep and find it in themselves."

Coach Vidal's exhortation that the students tap into their leadership potential sounded like a good idea to me. I rapped the envelope on my palm, "Well, we—"

"Yep," Beth interjected. "That sounds about right. It's the way the world's going, and good Christians don't even see it. Human reason, personal experience, and individual effort overshadow the power of the Holy Spirit and the authority of God's Word."

Millie nodded in agreement.

I tapped the envelope in my hand again. This time a little harder.

"And don't get me started on putting John Clarke's name on—" Millie continued.

"Oh!" I slapped my forehead. "I almost forgot. I brought that recipe you wanted. Let me go grab it." I jogged to the Jeep, opened the door, reached toward the console, and snatched the recipe card I had written out the night before.

When I returned, Beth stood on the stoop alone. "Millie went in to get you a recipe, too."

I leaned over and whispered, "We've really gotta move on. We have more soldiers to recruit."

Millie reappeared and I handed her the banana pudding recipe. She gave me a huge hug and handed me a print-out of her game-day sliders recipe. I earned another hug when I told Beth how amazing the sliders were. I gave Millie the oil change coupon.

As we turned to walk away, Millie called out, "You know, I think I'll give this coupon to a lady at church."

Beth and I slid back into our seats and slammed our doors. "So, that's Millie," I grinned and backed out of the driveway.

"I think she's delightful. Sounds like BCA is—or was—a special place to her."

"Mmhm," I replied as I merged into traffic.

"What do you think of this Coach Vidal?" Beth asked.

I shrugged. "I didn't really meet him. He seemed like a dynamic guy."

"What does Chance think?"

"We haven't really talked about it." *And when we do, I get myself in trouble.* "His standards are pretty high, so if Millie has all of those opinions, I'm sure his are even stronger."

"So, whose greatness does Coach Vidal want to inspire?" Beth asked.

"Okay, Nanette, with all your questions," I shoved her.

She flopped her body dramatically like I had shoved with the force to push her out of the Jeep. "Nanette? I'll take that as a compliment."

"Today, I want to inspire *our* greatness and recruit an army of volunteers to fill the gala with high-end silent auction items. Though I have a feeling I'll get more crocheted blankets than Breckenridge ski trips with this group."

CHAPTER FORTY-TWO

AFTER THE THIRD DROP-IN with John, I'd had enough. If I heard one more fake compliment, one more football story, or one more promise I had to fulfill, I would explode.

"I've always told my team to keep an eye on how you do things. We can learn a lot from you," he flattered.

"There were thirty seconds left, and with the injury to his hand in the previous play he had to throw with his left. The other team didn't know what hit 'em. We won by six," he bragged.

"Joy here is a master storyteller. Your sponsorship of this gala is not just a good deed, it's a good investment in your company," he pledged.

I nibbled at my salad while John took a third phone call during our brief lunch before we dropped in on two more potential sponsors.

"Don't we want sponsors who believe in Berean Christian Academy?" I asked when John slid back into his seat after his call ended.

He placed his napkin in his lap, picked up his fork, and looked down his nose. "You're not happy with the sponsors?"

"I feel like we've been bribing them with media coverage."

"That's business, Joy. Nobody gives out of the goodness of their heart." Then he snorted, "I thought you wanted to sit at tables with these guys."

"I do, it's just—"

"Maybe you're not ready for the conference table. Perhaps you really are better suited for kitchen tables."

I felt my neck flush with heat.

"You can mock me," I said as I straightened my shoulders. "I just think the pretense is unnecessary."

"How's it going with Mr. Easton's bake sale committee? I'm sure you're learning a lot from their kitchen tables." John's chewing noises reminded me of a cow and grated against my nerves.

"You know what, John? I've learned a lot from the committee. I've seen more love and heart from them than you."

"And what does that get you?" he sneered. "Some lamps for the silent auction?"

I poked at my salad and took a sip of iced tea. I smoothed my napkin in my lap and looked out the window. For playing such a big man all day, John Clarke looked small.

"I'm trying to leave BCA better than I found it," John said.

"Why do you want your name on it?" I pressed.

"It's called legacy." He tore off a piece of bread and shoved it in his mouth.

"According to your wife, Mr. Easton has left his legacy on the heart of your son and doesn't need his name on a building."

"It's fine if Mr. Easton doesn't want to make a name for himself. But I do."

My heart raced. I stabbed at slivers of lettuce on my plate. I knew better than to align myself with John Clarke. I should have known that day in Mountain Home when I caught Maggie in his arms.

"Well, you don't know everything. Mr. Easton has dreams, too," I retorted.

"Like what?"

"Like getting his doctorate from Mount Horeb Bible College and getting published." I spoke as if I had laid down a four-of-a-kind to his full house—smug against ego.

John tipped his fork. "Bravo, Mr. Easton."

I dabbed my napkin to my lips, then folded it, and tucked it under the edge of my plate. I leaned over and dug in my purse for my lip gloss.

"How about you?" John asked.

I abandoned my search and straightened in my chair. "What?"

"Do you want to make a name for yourself?" John challenged with squinted eyes.

"Yes," I said firmly.

"Then let's talk about the tale of two Carters." He shoved another bite of lettuce into his mouth.

I tilted my head and frowned—partly because I didn't know what he meant, and partly because I could hear him chewing again.

"What does Millie Carter get you? Love and heart? A new recipe?"

I shifted in my seat and unfolded and refolded my napkin.

"And what about Carter Jenson?" John continued. "He has multiple companies—and you heard him, he's interested in hiring you as a consultant for all of them."

I still couldn't believe it. When we walked into Carter's office today, he introduced me to his assistant by name and told John how much his wife raved about me on the way home from McCall. He added with a belly laugh, "I'll be in the doghouse if I don't hire you, Joy. This gala business can be your test run."

John set his glass down on the table with a thud. "The thing is, Joy, you have to help your client accomplish what's important to them." John raised his glass again and audibly gulped his water. "And what's important to me is getting approval for Clarke Field."

I winced.

"You can build a business or you can have a boyfriend. You can't do both here," John said flatly.

My head swiveled to the sound of shattered glass. I watched as a bus boy dropped to his knees to pick up the pieces of a broken plate. My stomach wrenched. John's influence and connections came with a price, and I had already made my choice. My desire to balance the wishes of everyone lay shattered around me.

CHAPTER FORTY-THREE

"POWER STORY INCORPORATED where we help you rise to power through story." The receptionist's voice sounded like a scene from an 80s movie. I pictured her in a headset with a cheek microphone, smacking her gum and filing her nails.

"Um, yes. May I speak with Kent Kingsley?"

"Mr. Kingsley only takes calls by appointment. May I take a message?"

"Can you tell him Joy Swallow called?" I gave her my number and slumped in my chair.

Of course Kent Kingsley wouldn't take a call from me. He's THE Kent Kingsley now—best-selling author, top-rated podcaster, and multi-millionaire. He's long forgotten the spindly intern from summer camp.

My phone buzzed in my hand. A number with a "646" area code displayed on the screen.

"Hello?"

"How ya doin' Sadness?"

Kent. THE Kent Kingsley called me back. Himself.

"Kent. Hi. Um—thanks—um—thanks for calling me back."

Get a grip, Joy.

I pictured a common scene from my days with Kent at camp. I would sit in one of the beanbags scattered around the common room. I always wore leggings with an over-sized T-shirt and piled my hair on top of my head in a messy bun. I would bring my spiral notebook and keep a pen in my hand ready to log the ideas Kent would fire at me as he paced in front of the large stone fireplace.

I sat up straight and shifted the phone on my ear. "I need your help. Are you up for a mindstorm session?"

Kent's belly laugh blasted through the phone. "I forgot we called them that. I'm going to have to bring that back to life. Watcha got?"

I took a deep breath. I was glad I had dialed his number before I overthought it, but wished I had practiced what to say.

"There's more back story here than you probably have time for, but I'll hit the highlights. I changed my major because of you. And now I've gone out on my own as a marketing consultant. I took on a fund-raising gala for a Christian school. The Booster Club President shared his contacts with me and we've secured more money in sponsorships than I dreamed. In exchange, he promised all the sponsors I would work miracles with my storytelling prowess and I'm a bit stuck."

"Wow," Kent replied.

That's all he said.

Then silence. Complete silence. No rustling papers. No clearing his throat. No squeak as he leaned back in his chair.

"It's too much. I'm sorry. I shouldn't be wasting your time," I spouted.

"No, no," Kent reassured. "You're not wasting my time. I remember our sessions and would be honored to help you. Did you really change your major because of me?"

"I really did."

"I'll make time now if you want," he offered.

I shared the spirit of BCA I learned from Nanette, Chance, and The Remnant. Then I detailed each of the sponsors and their companies including their goals.

"Wow. How did you land all these sponsors?"

"Some of them are BCA families, but most of them are contacts from the Booster Club President."

"I know some of these guys. I've tried to get some of them as my own clients. Who's the Booster Club President?" Kent asked.

"His name is John Clarke."

"John Clarke, the venture capitalist?"

I sat back in my chair and let it sink in that Kent knew about John from the business world.

"I've always wanted to meet him," Kent said.

"I'm sure I can make that happen."

For the next thirty minutes we tossed around ideas to weave all the sponsors with the BCA story in a compelling way. I shared my frustration with the warring elements at the school. "One group wants everything the way it's always been. The other group wants everything to change."

"You have the outside perspective and that means you can clearly see what's best. They're too close to it all," Kent said.

"That leads me to another area I could use your advice," I said. "If you have time."

"Shoot."

I took a deep breath and rattled off the details of John's proposed donation and requirements, the convictions of Berean Christian Academy—leaving out that few people still held them—and the pep rally reveal.

"My best advice?" Kent asked.

"Please."

"Keep your eye on the prize—your cut of the gala proceeds and future client contacts."

"But John said I had to convince—"

"John doesn't need you for that. With that stunt he pulled revealing the rendering of the field—audacious move, by the way—he's thrown it into the court of public opinion. You can just fade into the distance on this one."

"So, your advice is to do nothing?"

"Yup. Does your contract say anything about getting the school to agree to his donation?" Kent asked.

"No. That was more of a verbal agreement."

"Okay then. At this point John needs you to make the sponsors happy so he won't break the contract before your family day and gala. You don't want to get in the middle of his dispute with the school. Keep your head down and eyes on the prize."

I couldn't tell if I felt relieved or saddened. I didn't agree with Chance's philosophy on the naming rights, but I knew how important it was to him. I wanted to be a part of the growing Remnant, but I had a career to develop and Kent was right—it wasn't my fight.

CHAPTER FORTY-FOUR

I TOOK A DEEP BREATH and looked around the room. Every detail reflected the hard work and preparation of the committee and volunteers. Tables of silent auction items bordered the large banquet space—each item meticulously entered into the live silent auction app catalog.

The white tablecloths and white napkins, folded into fans and set atop the white china, stood in contrast to the gold flatware, gold chargers, gold rimmed glasses, and six gold chairs tucked under every round table.

Each table featured a wreath of greenery with a gold wire-framed football-shaped centerpiece with an artificial flame candle flickering inside. Who knew The Remnant would be as classy and creative as they were prayerful?

And they were prayerful.

Earlier in the afternoon, with the final touches complete, we had stood in a circle and held hands. Each person prayed for God to bless the event. Some prayed for money to be raised. Some prayed for the food to be good. Some prayed for laughter. Every person in the circle prayed for God to reunite BCA into a family that honored Him above all else.

When it got to me, I thought about saying "ditto" but remembered what Miss Sally taught us in Sunday School about how "amen" means "so be it," so I simply said, "Amen."

Each person scattered home to change. With Piper at the kennel, I had booked a room at the hotel next door to make it easier to get ready for the event.

Now I stood in the ballroom in high heels and a solid green floor-length gown with narrow straps and a wide belt. I couldn't think of any facet of the gala left undone.

Thank you, Lord.

The room filled as fast as a time-lapse movie. Men wore suits and ties and women wore gowns of every length and shade. Student "waiters" mingled with trays of mocktails that shimmered with cocktail glitter.

My smile faded and stomach dropped when Millie walked in wearing a dress better fit for a picnic in the park than a gala.

"Oh, my," she said. "I've never been to such a fancy event. When you said 'glitz' you meant it."

That's what formal attire means.

"I felt like a movie star walking down that red carpet out there. This is the nicest thing I think I've ever been to. I love it all!" Millie looked around the room with a wide grin and a canvas tote on her shoulder that read, "I'm not a regular mom, I'm a cool mom." She spotted a friend and gave her a fierce hug and oohed and aahed over her dress. "I'm off to take my shift at the registration table." She skip-walked toward the registration area with a giggle and wiggled her fingers in a greeting to friends along the way.

I caught sight of Chance in his fitted black suit that set off his black-rimmed glasses. His white dress shirt provided the perfect back-drop for his BCA Eagle-green tie. He stood with Trevor, the football player from the event at John's lake house. They laughed and clapped each other on the arms like old fraternity brothers reuniting.

I flitted from the check-in table to the red-carpet photo spot, to the student servers, to the silent auction tables, and back again. The amount of money the silent auction items brought in rose every time I refreshed the app on my phone. As the money accrued, so did the pride and joy in my heart.

My euphoria evaporated when I saw John and Sarah arrive with Maggie and Peter.

Together.

I watched them work the room like two power couples. I wondered if Sarah knew of the affair. Peter certainly didn't know—no way. Sarah and Peter stood talking as clueless and naive as The Remnant praying for family unity.

John moved from conversation to conversation with confidence and charm. He called each person by name as he approached them, and one by one they lit up like a Christmas tree. I could almost hear their inner voice, "John Clarke knows my name!" I wanted to warn them to run away as fast as they could.

I observed John place his hand on the small of Maggie's back and whisper in her ear. She nodded and laughed with the familiarity of old friends. I nearly wretched. I swallowed hard, twirled toward the opposite direction, and nearly knocked Chance over.

"Whoa, there," Chance laughed, his hands grasping my arms to hold me upright.

"Oh, sorry," I shifted in my three-inch heels to stop my ankles from wobbling.

Chance lifted my chin with his index finger. "Everything is going wonderfully."

"Mmhm," I said. I swiped my phone again to see if the rising totals could bring my spirits back up.

"I'll keep this for now." Chance grabbed my phone with his thumb and forefinger and tucked it in the inside pocket of his suit jacket. "Everyone is doing exactly what they said they would do. Everything is going according to plan."

"But I—"

"The program starts in twenty minutes. And if anyone needs us, they can easily find us."

I started to argue more, but a student approached us. I recognized him from a previous video shoot as one of Jackson's teammates. "Mr. Easton, tonight isn't awful at all! I just met Trevor Arnold! He says he knows you. I didn't know you knew Trevor Arnold. He plays for the Idaho Horsemen. He's a running back like me. He gave me advice on how to get recruited for college."

"Trevor's a great guy," Chance replied.

"Anyway. I'm really glad I came," he said and walked away.

My joy meter creeped up.

My eye caught Olivia as she made her way through pockets of people toward us. Her long blonde hair cascaded over her shoulders in fat curls. The green sequined top of her dress contrasted with the flowing mesh skirt. The color of our dresses almost matched. She looked lovely—I had never seen her in anything but a ponytail.

"I'm so glad I found you," she paused to catch her breath. "You were right about Family Day, Miss Swallow. Like, I hope we do that every year. Jackson said he'd help me use my soccer skills to win the field goal event. Oh, there—" Olivia caught sight of

Jackson walking by and grabbed his arm. "Let's all four go take a picture together."

Jackson stumbled along like Piper when I unexpectedly changed directions. The four of us took pictures on the red carpet. Olivia insisted Chance and I take a picture with just the two of us. *Thank you, Olivia.* Then she grabbed our hands and dragged us to the 360-degree photo booth and told us how to pose. By the time Olivia finished with us, my sandcastle walls of concern washed away with the tide of our laughter.

"I haven't laughed like that in a while," I admitted with my hands flat against my stomach.

"I love those kids," Chance said as he straightened his tie and smoothed his suit. "And I owe you another apology."

"Oh?"

"I'm sorry I didn't believe in you. You took a theme I hated and used it to incorporate everything that was important to me and the committee."

"And the donors," I added.

"And the donors," Chance smiled and tilted his head with deference.

"I have to get out of these heels," I said. I wiggled my toes and rolled my ankles around to stretch them. I remembered going to formal events in high school and college. I always took off my shoes immediately after the photographer snapped our picture. I didn't suppose I could walk around the gala barefoot—even though I wished I could.

"I saved a spot for you," Chance said.

"Oh, I shouldn't sit. I need to make sure—"

"It's a special spot."

Chance guided me by the elbow toward a round table near the presentation stage. I continued to look up at him and speak words of argument when a singsong greeting reached my ears—a voice I had heard only one other time.

"Joy, how delightful to see you again." My head spun toward the table in time to see Julia Coates rise to her feet to greet me. Nanette sat beside her and smiled wide with the mischief of someone who had pulled off a grand surprise. "Please. Sit next to me. Nanette gloats about all of the time she gets to spend with you. I've been waiting for another chance. Tonight is my turn."

Am I dreaming? I floated to the chair.

Before I could completely lower myself into my chair, a wave of distress welled up in me. I shifted in my seat one way and then another as my head swiveled around the room. Chance caught my eye as he took the chair next to Nanette and said, "Joy. Relax. The team's in place. You've done your job to prepare them. Don't steal their blessing by doing things for them."

I took a deep breath and nodded in agreement. I shifted to the edge of my seat, straightened my shoulders, and embraced the opportunity. I peppered Julia Coates with questions I had pent up since undergrad and didn't get the chance to ask in San Francisco. She answered every one and Nanette sprinkled in accounts of the many adventures that spanned their long friendship.

Moments before the program began, I heard a male voice over my shoulder. "Are these seats taken?"

John and Sarah waited to be welcomed. A power move if I'd ever seen one. Chance pursed his lips in a thin line, stood, and motioned toward the open chair next to him. I rose and gave Sarah a hug.

"Joy, good to see you again. You look lovely," Sarah slid into the seat next to mine.

"Thank you. So do you. I'm assuming you know Mrs. Coates and Mrs. Verity?" Nanette tilted her head in a mock glare. "Er—Nanette."

"Of course." Sarah and John said in unison—Sarah's tone gracious and John's curt.

Chance's phone vibrated in his pocket. He retrieved it and said, "Welp. There's my reminder to get this party started." He walked to the stage with confidence and charm—the kind that held allure, not motive.

After Chance called people to their seats, he opened in prayer. Like every time I prayed with The Remnant, I felt the energy in the room shift. Chance thanked the attendees for their support of BCA and blessed the food before returning to the table.

The peace I felt after Chance's prayer dissipated as John dominated the conversation during dinner. I pretended to listen, but shifted my attention to the committee members who scuttled around and fulfilled all the tasks of the evening. They helped people at the silent auction tables, they directed the student workers, and they served as spotters during the live auction portion of the evening.

Julia, Nanette, and Sarah showered me with praise after the "Spirit of BCA" video played. Chance didn't have to say a word. The look of pride on his face told me he liked it, too.

"See. You didn't need me after all," Nanette winked.

"On the contrary," I said. "It wouldn't have come together without your insight and the advice I got from Kent."

"Who's Kent?" John asked. He leaned back in his chair and surveyed the room, half-listening to my response.

"Kent Kingsley. He's an old mentor of mine."

John snapped upright in his chair. "You know Kent Kingsley?"

"Mmhm. In fact, he said he'd like to meet you, too."

John flung himself back into his chair. "You continue to be full of surprises, Joy Swallow."

Like lint from the cloth napkin in my lap, I chose to flick away the contempt I held for John Clarke and focus on the unexpected blessings in front of me.

I sat at a table with Chance Easton. I couldn't have hoped for a friendship like his before walking into this new project.

I sat at a table with Nanette Verity. Another surprise. Her quiet strength and vulnerability inspired me. Her wisdom and grace left me uncomfortable yet longing for more.

I sat at a table with Julia Coates. A dream come true. Again. Not exactly the kitchen table I hoped for, but frankly more than I ever thought possible.

The live auction delivered robust competition among the guests. The auctioneer skillfully reminded the audience of all the elements I had highlighted in the video. The silent auction closed before dessert to give time to calculate the money the gala had raised. It turned out Mr.-Prayer-Walk-Charles himself worked as a comptroller for a regional corporation and served as the committee member in charge of the fundraising calculations.

When the sponsorship and Family Day money had inched its way toward the $200,000 mark, Chance insisted Charles cease sharing financial totals with me until the night of the gala. He wanted it to be a surprise. Chance didn't know I desperately needed it to be at least $250,000 to break free from John Clarke.

Charles walked up to Chance, whispered in his ear, and placed an envelope on the table. I couldn't discern anything from either man's expression. Chance gave a sharp nod and shook Charles's hand.

Chance stood with the envelope in hand. He pushed in his chair and walked up the stairs to the presentation stage without once making eye contact with me. I held my breath and placed my hands on my knotted-up stomach.

"Before I speak the benediction over you this evening, I have an announcement to make. Charles Morrow, our Fundraising Calculation Chair, just handed me a very important envelope. The number inside reflects the amount of money raised at this year's gala, including our Family Day event leading up to this marvelous evening."

I wished he would open the envelope already. I couldn't breathe until I heard the number. I felt lightheaded.

"There are many people to thank, most of whom we've honored throughout the evening. But a number cannot adequately reflect the gratitude I have in my heart for our loving Father who supplies our needs according to His riches in glory in Christ Jesus.

"The author of Hebrews instructs, 'Do not neglect to do good and to share what you have, for such sacrifices are pleasing to God.' You have not neglected to do good tonight, and now we can share in the delight of our God."

Some of the football boys scattered throughout the room started a drumroll with their hands on the tables. Chance smiled and opened the envelope.

CHAPTER FORTY-FIVE

"THREE HUNDRED AND FIFTY thousand dollars?" Kent bellowed. I held the phone away from my head to protect my eardrum from his enthusiasm.

"It's unbelievable, really," I admitted.

Everything that happened after Chance read that number aloud felt like it happened to someone else—like I remained outside of my body looking in. Every person at my table embraced me with congratulations and thanks. I didn't even cringe at John's grasp—nor at his self-adulatory words.

Various sponsors who had attended came by the table to greet John and me. Questions like, "Ready to start on my project?" and compliments like, "This was magical," filled my head.

The preschool director rushed me with a hug she refused to release as she covered my shoulder with tears. She kept saying, "We're so close now. We're so close. Thank you. We're so close now."

Nanette squeezed my hand as she and Julia said goodbye. "You did it. You truly captured the spirit of BCA. God was glorified tonight."

Joyous chatter never ceased as committee members shed their gala attire in exchange for jeans and T-shirts to pack up decorations and unclaimed silent auction items. My heart soared as I basked in the success of the event.

I slept in fits all night after the gala, but awakened to Kent's call to check on my results.

"I want to have you on my live radio show—" Kent said.

I sat straight up in the bed, now fully awake.

"—but I want to make it special. Let's do this. I'll fly you out to my offices here in New York. I'll interview you in the studio about the fundraiser, and we'll get to tell our story, too. I think my audience will love the history we have," he continued.

"I—that—"

"And we'll pull together a photo shoot. We've recently launched a business magazine. We can do a feature story in there and on the blog and tie all the channels together."

I let out the breath I had been holding in. "Oh, my gosh, that all sounds so fun." I felt like the spindly teenager sitting at Kent's feet.

Kent's laugh rumbled, "It'll be loads of fun."

I flung myself back into the tangle of sheets and pillows as visions of the big city and flashing lights filled my mind. "Thank you, Kent. For everything."

• • •

I settled into the first-class seat Kent's office had booked for me. I sipped the glass of water the flight attendant handed me and pondered how I had gotten here. Kent Kingsley functioned at breakneck speed, and his timeline for this trip reflected it.

I had only a matter of days to arrange for Beth to help me pack and stay with Piper. Her excitement for me was only tempered by her concern about Kent's tactics. I assured her this opportunity reflected God's blessing. "Kent wants to tell our story. God's a big part of that," I reasoned.

I hadn't seen Chance or The Remnant since the night of the gala, but had received many texts and a few phone calls of praise. The morning after the gala, I had barely walked in the house when the front doorbell rang and I received a large flower arrangement. The card simply read "Well done" and had a large paw print in ink that had smudged at the edges signed "Ruby."

I pulled out my phone to turn it on airplane mode and saw I had two text messages.

I rolled my eyes at Beth's two-word message, *Stay alert.*

I'll be fine. I tapped back.

Chance's message, *We'll all be watching,* caused my heart to warm and stomach to twist simultaneously. The love and support offered by my new friends at BCA changed my life, and this interview had the potential to change my future. The possibilities towered taller than the skyscrapers of the City of Dreams I headed to.

I replied to Chance's message with a heart emoji. Another message popped up. *And praying.*

Thank you. I need it. I turned off my phone and turned my head to watch the landscape blur as the plane picked up speed and took off.

• • •

A man in a black suit, black shoes, white shirt, and black tie held a digital sign with my name in bold at baggage claim. He brought me into the city in a black town car like in the movies. I resisted craning my neck like a first-time tourist. The driver's only interactions with me were short and professional. "Mr. Kingsley instructed me to bring you directly to the office." And, "Mr. Kingsley instructed me to deliver your suitcase to your hotel. Do you need anything out of it?"

When I arrived at Power Story Incorporated, Kent's team whisked me to a greenroom area where they styled my hair and freshened up my makeup and offered me several jackets to choose from to put on over my blouse. I joined Kent in a photo studio staged with a white backdrop and a professional photographer who barked orders on how to bend, or turn my head, when to smile, when not to smile, and how to smile or not smile. I floated in a sea of excitement like a toddler being held by the hand—every so often I'd get yanked over another wave.

After the photo shoot, the team scuttled me into a small room with black acoustic panels lining the walls. They placed me at a wooden table with two microphones facing each other and a camera crew at the ready. Kent swept into the room with less than a minute to spare. He kept his black hair cut short along his neck and ears with longer locks styled in waves on top. His black bushy eyebrows shadowed his dark brown eyes and the short stubble on his chin kept him from looking like he took himself too seriously. He wore a dark fitted suit with no tie. His bright white teeth matched the white pressed shirt that he wore open at the collar.

Kent started the interview making a big deal of the increase in fundraising over previous year's efforts. "That's the benefit of working with a professional, people." While Kent cautioned me to keep my attention on him, he worked the camera like a pro. He knew right where to look, and his confidence and cadence brought drama to the discussion.

"Let's talk about the theme—Gridiron Glitz—how important is a good theme?" Kent asked.

"The theme is a framework you build the overall messaging on. In our case, many of the potential sponsors were related to sports in one way or another, so I chose a football theme. Your theme won't make your fundraiser successful, though. It's just the scaffolding," I explained.

"Brilliantly said," Kent lauded. I felt like he had given me a gold star in front of the whole class—only it was a nation of his followers. I tucked my curls behind my ears and rubbed my hands on my pants under the table. I willed myself to remained focused on the questions not the audience I couldn't see or the cameras I could.

"And you turned this into a much more formal event than in the past, right?"

"Absolutely."

"How did that turn out for you?" Kent prodded.

"Well, some people didn't quite bring the 'glitz,' but overall it was a huge success. People love to dress up."

"You needed an explainer video for 'formal attire'?" Kent snickered.

I laughed, "I might try that next time."

"I have to say, Joy, I watched the video you produced for the gala. You're a master storyteller," Kent praised.

I felt my cheeks burn. "I credit a lot of that to our shared history, Kent. I fell in love with a well-told story at camp and I've continued to learn a lot from you through the years."

"Aw. Shucks. Thanks," Kent replied in his radio voice. "We worked together on this video, folks, but tell the audience, Joy—the video played and then the live auction immediately afterward raised how much?"

I leaned into the microphone for dramatic effect. "Over one hundred thousand dollars."

"You heard her, folks. The live auction portion alone raised five times more than this event raised in total the year before. That's the power of using emotion rather than facts to persuade people."

Stay alert. Beth's warning flashed in my mind.

"Well, actually, Berean—"

"We made sure the video used loaded language like God and country and featured kids, too, right?" Kent picked up the pace.

"Well, yes, it's a Chr—"

"The proof is right here, folks. It's what we talk about all the time. A well-told story will get people to part with their money—whether they want to or not."

I could feel the interview spinning out of control. I thought of Chance's text. *We'll all be watching.* My stomach tightened. Then I thought of his next text. *And praying.*

With renewed courage I leaned into the microphone and added, "What's great is the story we told is a true story and effectively represented the spirit of the school while linking it to the shared values of the sponsors."

At a commercial break, we went off air. "This is so fun, Joy. You're doing great. I've purposely cut you off a couple of times because I find when I get too specific with my audience about the names of the institutions, they turn off. And when they turn off, they won't receive the best stuff. They start thinking it doesn't, or can't, apply to their specific situation."

I relaxed a bit. I'd watched dozens of Kent's live interviews in preparation for this day. I reminded myself that a student isn't prepared to teach the class on the first day. "That makes total sense. I'll keep it broad and applicable to the masses," I said. I could follow his lead and still remain true to what was important to me.

The makeup team swooped in and powdered our faces and straightened our collars before the producer hollered the countdown for the cameras and audio to go live again.

Kent continued to ask questions about the mechanics of the fundraiser before transitioning to our shared history. We laughed about camp pranks and how he's the only one who ever called me "Sadness." Kent teared up when I recounted a story of a girl from our middle school group who had a breakthrough after one of his talks. He shook his head in disbelief when I told the audience he was the reason I changed my major in undergrad to pursue marketing.

"One more question before we wrap up today. I know we've talked about collaborating with a talented and unified team, we've talked about the power of good mentors who are a few steps ahead, and we've uncovered your gift of storytelling and your addiction to the thrill of asking for money. But my last question is—what is the best question you asked in this project?"

"That's a good question," I said and we both snickered. I tilted my head toward the ceiling in thought. My heart rate increased as my mind went completely blank. I wished he would have prepared me for this question ahead of the interview. Suddenly the exact moment came to my mind.

"It wasn't a question, really, it was more of a prompt," I said. "I asked for an example—a story—that represented the spirit of the institution. The committee offered it up and then I pulled that common thread from the institution and all the sponsors to weave it into the tapestry of the video and gala as a whole."

"And a big and beautiful tapestry it was."

"I'd like to think so," I smiled.

"And she's got the receipts to prove it," Kent looked directly into the video camera. "So, folks, if you're looking to harness the power of story for your next fundraising event, be sure to incorporate the strategies we've shared here today or reach out to my team for targeted advice." Kent tipped his branded coffee mug toward me. "It's been so good to collaborate again, Joy. I have a feeling we'll have many opportunities to stir up the magic again real soon."

"Thanks for having me."

I followed Kent's example and smiled until the red lights on the cameras turned off. He gathered up papers he had spread on the table and stood. I felt like a balloon stabbed by a pin prick and all the air whooshed out of me as I slouched in the chair.

"Great job, Sadness." Kent's use of my nickname and crooked half-smile grabbed my heartstrings.

"Thanks. I feel like I've run a marathon. How do you do this every week?"

Kent waved his hand. "You'll get used to it."

Before I could respond, Kent tucked his papers under his arm and grabbed his coffee mug. "Ready to debrief over lunch?"

"Um—" Kent walked out of the room. "Sure," I said to myself.

CHAPTER FORTY-SIX

"LET'S REFLECT," Kent said after relaying his food order and returning the menu to the waiter.

Kent sat at the end of a table for ten people in a narrow room. The restaurant normally only opened for dinner service, but Kent said he knew the owner and often held private lunches and meetings there. I sat to his right with my back to a floor-to-ceiling rack with wine bottles of every variety and year. In front of me, the wall of glass boasted a breathtaking view of Central Park. I had to force myself to look away and focus on Kent and the discussion at hand.

"How do you think that went?" Kent asked.

"I think it offered a perfect balance of personal and practical. Your audience will enjoy getting a glimpse of your past, but your questions led me to share strategies they can implement themselves—almost."

"Almost?"

"If they know what they're doing, they may have gleaned a new idea or two. If they don't, now they know they'll need to hire you."

Kent smiled wide. "Good answer."

My heart warmed. I felt a strange mix of confidence and craving his approval.

"How about the pace?" Kent asked.

"Of the interview?"

"Of the day," he clarified.

"To be honest, you and your team run at hurricane force. It's exhilarating and exhausting all at the same time."

The waiter set our salads in front of us and refilled our waters. As we ate, Kent barraged me with questions about John, his contacts, and my marketing vision for their companies based on what I knew about them.

"You have a gift I don't have."

I sat there dumbfounded for a moment. Kent shoved a forkful of lettuce into his mouth oblivious to the fact that I could not compute his statement. How could I possess something lacking in someone so successful?

"Not possible," I said.

Kent leaned toward me with his elbows on the table. "You are able to uncover the client's convictions. I know what they need, but you uncover their deepest desires. We can use that to get them to do what we want."

"I'm—I'm not sure I feel comfortable with that tactic."

Kent tilted his head back and laughed. "I forget you've been hanging around principled people."

"And that's a bad thing?" I set my fork down with a clank. I straightened the knife and spoon to the right of my plate. I shifted my glass of water to align with the knife, then looked up at Kent, who was looking down the table.

Kent pulled at his chin while he chose his response. "Limiting."

I tucked a curl behind my ear and picked at invisible lint in my lap.

"Let me put it this way," Kent continued. "You told me they didn't want to change the theme at first."

I looked up into his intense brown eyes and nodded.

"But you knew they couldn't achieve their financial goals without a way to compel the sponsors you had at your disposal."

I nodded.

"So you manipulated them into accepting a new theme."

"I didn't manipulate."

"I'm sorry. I missed the part of the story where they agreed to the theme change," Kent's sarcasm came off playful rather than accusing.

"But—"

Kent waved his hand. "It doesn't matter. Look at the results. With one more event like this one, they're going to get that preschool building that was a pipe dream before."

I could almost feel the preschool director's hug again—and her tears on my shoulder.

"I—"

"Your power move was one I've used over and over. But your gift—your gift was on full display when you uncovered that family and unity meant the most to them and then you pulled on that string. You said it yourself—you pulled that same thread out of the sponsors to weave their stories together to compel greater giving."

"I just wanted to tell a true story."

"And you never would have been given the opportunity without the courage you displayed in manip—er—nudging your client based on your expertise."

I let Kent's words settle over me as I gazed through the wall of glass. Building after building snuggled in next to each other and lined the edges of the park below. Each window represented people with stories in every room—stories that will never be told.

"Bring me up to speed on the status of your consulting firm," Kent said.

Grateful for the shift in conversation, I shared how I launched my own firm with the pro bono contest to build my portfolio. I left out the affair and deceit.

"So, they didn't ask you to consult? You asked them?" Kent confirmed.

"Right. I uncovered the opportunity during my time on campus working on the first promotional video."

Kent leaned back in his chair and clasped his hands behind his head. His grin reminded me of our time together at camp when he would throw out an idea that seemed harebrained at first, but always turned out in the end.

"Come to work for me," he said.

"What?" I dropped my fork and it clattered to the floor. I bent down, picked it up, and wrapped it in my napkin. I didn't need it anymore. I didn't think I could eat anything else now, anyway.

"Come to work for me."

"I—"

"You've barely launched your own firm. I'm sure I can convince John we'll take care of his friends, so you can bring those clients with you. Together we're a storytelling power-team. You can keep learning from me and we'll collaborate on new projects without financial limits."

"Wow. I—it's just that—I—didn't really know that'd be an option. And I've found my groove with my team. And—"

"Your team?" Kent raised his eyebrows. "I have all the resources you'll need moving forward—you can't expect Coates, Inc. to keep loaning out their equipment and staff."

I looked around the room. A table set to impress, wealth and grandeur screaming success, and a man I trusted offering me a dream job with no restrictions on my creativity.

"What would that look like? Would I have to move to New York?"

"Not at all. I want you to build our portfolio in the Northwest. However, we have clients nationwide and a few in-person team meetings, so it would entail quite a bit of travel."

I fidgeted with a loose string at the edge of my blouse. I knew Maggie's team wasn't my team. They had become friends, but they worked for Coates and now that the BCA projects were over, they wouldn't be working with me.

I looked up and stared out the window. I earned more than enough money to pay John back as a consultant on the gala. At this very moment, I was essentially back to square one. I spent a little bit on some graphics and a new website, but I could tuck those away for some future point if I ever decided to go out on my own again.

I turned my head toward Kent who looked at me with the expectancy of a kid who asked his mom for a cookie for breakfast. Kent's national presence would surely put me at tables I could never have dreamed of.

"What the heck. I'm in," I said.

"Yes!" Kent flung himself back in his chair with a loud clap. "Welcome to the team, Sadness."

CHAPTER FORTY-SEVEN

"GOOD MONDAY MORNING!" Mateo greeted me at the receptionist desk in the lobby of Coates, Inc. His bright red bow tie reflected the cheer in his voice.

He took the gift basket I balanced in one arm as I scanned my ID and had my photo taken for my visitor pass.

"What's this for?" Mateo lifted the basket.

"It's some of John and Sarah's favorite things from New York."

Mateo squinted his eyes and tilted his head.

"What?" I shrugged. "My momma raised me right. Despite our history, John's loan and influence is worth my gratitude."

Mateo and I hiked up the stairs and stopped at the coffee station. "Are we still on for tonight?" he asked.

"Yes, but it may be late if that's okay. I want to give Piper and Ruby a chance to say goodbye."

I placed a mug under the spout and pressed the preset for

Americano. The machine made a low grinding sound and released the coffee-water mix in a perfect blend.

"Are you sure about this?" Mateo asked.

"I'm sure."

"I thought you loved Piper."

"Do I?" I gave a half smile then waved my hand. "With all the travel I'll be doing for my new job, it doesn't make sense to keep her. She'd be at the kennel all the time."

Mateo handed me my mug and slid an empty one in its place. He pressed a button, leaned against the coffee bar, and asked, "What'd Aunt Mimsy say?"

"Her emotions are all over the map. She's devastated to lose Piper, but she loves it in Oregon. She asked me to put her house up for sale."

"Wow."

"Yeah. It's a lot."

Mateo retrieved his cortado from beneath the spout and added three packets of sugar.

I swirled the toe of my shoe in small circles on the carpet. "She's going to a good home, right?"

Mateo elbowed me in the side. "I thought you didn't love her."

I kept my eyes directed at the floor as tears welled up in them. Mateo tilted his head to look into my eyes and placed his hand on my arm. "Don't worry. I've got it all lined up."

We drank our coffee and talked more about my four-day trip to New York.

"Have you talked to Chance since you've been back?" Mateo asked.

"Not really. I told him we'd talk in person at the park tonight."

"You mean you haven't told him about your new job?"

I shook my head. "Or about Piper, either. There's too many ways the conversation could go sideways over text—or over the phone, for that matter."

I checked my watch and gulped down my last sip of coffee.

"I'll take that from you," Mateo said and lifted the mug from my hands.

"Thanks. I'll see you tonight if I don't see you after I drop this off to John."

I retrieved the basket from the counter, waved to Mateo, and strode down the hall to John's office.

I knocked on the open door. John waved me in as he pounded a few more times on his keyboard and then closed his laptop.

"What's this?" John asked as I extended the basket toward him.

John took the basket and tilted it to examine the contents.

"It's an offering of my thanks. I tucked in a few things for you and Sarah from New York. And that envelope there holds the cashier's check to repay my loan."

John pulled out the envelope and plopped the basket on the floor behind his desk. He slanted the envelope toward me like the tip of a hat. "Pleasure doin' business with ya'." He slipped the envelope inside a leather portfolio and lifted the lid of his laptop.

"There's another envelope in there," I sputtered.

John peered at me over the edge of his computer screen. "It's not a recipe, is it?"

"Open it and see," I said through pursed lips.

John swiveled in his chair slightly and reached back to grab the envelope. The back of his chair tilted as he leaned back and pulled out the handwritten card inside and read it aloud. "Here's my personal cell. Call me anytime. Kent Kingsley."

John placed the card on his desk and looked up at me with wide eyes and arched eyebrows, creating an exaggerated curve.

"You continue to surprise me, Joy Swallow," John tapped the card. "Thank you."

I gave a sharp nod. "Goodbye, John."

I looked at my feet and gathered my thoughts as I exited his office. I thought I would feel lighter with my debt paid and my burden lifted. Rather, I felt like I needed a shower.

I didn't notice someone approaching me until I bumped into them. They dropped the file they were holding. I reached down and saw the file and the Christian Louboutin heels before I connected with her face.

"Maggie—um—hi," I stuttered.

"Joy. It's good to see you. I'd hoped to see you at some point to say thank you for your work on the gala. Great job, by the way. You've made a lasting impact on BCA."

"Thanks." I tucked a curl behind my ear and fidgeted with the hem of my suit jacket.

"What're you—"

I looked into Maggie's eyes and motioned with my thumb to John's office. "Repaying a loan."

"Oh—yes—well—what's next for you?" Maggie must have left her mask in her office. Her tenderness threw me off.

I stood taller and thrust my shoulders back and chin out. "I took a job offer from Kent Kingsley with Power Story Incorporated."

"Will I see you again? Peter and I would—"

"I don't imagine that's in our future, Maggie."

Maggie hugged the file to her chest. "I understand. Well, for what it's worth, I'm really proud of you."

I gave a sharp nod. "Goodbye, Maggie."

CHAPTER FORTY-EIGHT

I PULLED INTO THE PARKING LOT of the dog park and cruised into the spot next to Chance's car. I left Scarlett running for an extra minute to finish listening to the weather report on the radio.

"We're smack in the middle of wildfire season and the haze you see is an indicator of just how close these fires are getting to Treasure Valley. Crews are cutting lines in case the fire shifts any closer to Idaho City."

"Idaho City is where Nanette lives," I said to Piper in the rearview mirror as I cut the engine.

Piper's head rested on the back seat. Her sad eyes reminded me of the first day we met.

How do dogs seem to know things?

I said a quick prayer for God's protection over Nanette's home and for the conversation I was about to have. I hopped out and opened up the back of Scarlett. I snapped Piper's leash to her collar and she jumped down and spun around and around. "You missed your friend, didn't you?" I scrubbed her head. "I missed mine, too."

When we crested a rise in the large green space, I saw Chance tossing the ball for Ruby. Check that. Chance hurled the ball for Ruby to retrieve. Ruby seemed none the wiser, but I sensed Chance releasing pent-up anger or frustration.

I unclipped Piper's leash and she took off after Ruby. Chance spotted her and swiveled toward me. He rubbed his hand on the back of his neck and stared at his shoes.

"What'd that ball ever do to you?" I joked.

Ruby and Piper barreled back toward Chance, and Ruby dropped the ball at his feet. Chance picked up the ball, reared back, and launched it into the distance. The dogs happily raced to fetch it.

"Did you watch my interview?" I asked.

"Oh, yeah. We all did."

His response was as cold as a glass of ice water in my face, and I stepped back. "Did I do something wrong?"

"Well, you really hurt Millie's feelings with your 'some people don't know how to bring the glitz' comment."

I bowed my head and dug in the dirt with the toe of my shoe. "I regretted it as soon as I said it. Live interviews are no joke."

Chance knelt down on one knee and untied and retied his shoe. He stood and stared at the dogs running back to him with the ball.

"Kent definitely has a message he's trying to get out to his audience. I could feel your prayers," I said.

Chance grunted. Piper skidded to a stop in front of him and dropped the ball at his feet. She chased Ruby around and between us in a figure eight pattern. They stopped their game and both sat looking at the ball and back at Chance. He bent down, picked it up, and pitched it again.

"Well, I'm glad you got what you wanted. A big magazine spread, a radio interview, and new clients for your new business."

A breeze blew my curls into my face. I swept them aside and pulled my hair back into a ponytail.

"That's what I started out wanting. But God gave me so much more—" I reached out and stroked Chance's arm, "—like new friends and—"

Chance yanked his arm away from my touch. "Don't even pretend you care about friendship," he growled.

Confusion swirled in my mind and stole the voice from my throat. I took a step back. "Chance, I can tell you're angry with me."

Chance's eyes blazed and his voice dripped with sarcasm. "It turns out John Clarke somehow found out that I applied for a job at Mount Horeb Bible College. He used that information to convince the board that I broke my contract and they have dismissed me from my position at Berean Christian Academy. And you're the only person I told about Mount Horeb—in confidence. So, yeah. I'm angry with you."

My knees gave out and I sunk to the ground. I rested my forehead in my hands and replayed the conversation with John in my mind.

I looked up at Chance, "I'm so sorry. I swear I did not tell John that you applied at Mount Horeb—"

Chance huffed and turned his back to me.

"—but I did say something about you planning to get your doctorate." I laid on my back in the brittle grass and spoke to the sky as much as to Chance. "He was taunting me and disparaging you and I fell for it."

"And now he's cleared the path for the board to change the naming policy so he can get his name on the field like he always wanted," Chance said. And then he walked away.

I scrambled to my feet and dusted my backside. I jogged to catch up to Chance. "Do you really think you could have stood in his way?"

"At least I stood my ground. You kept following his lead."

"Chance, I'm really sorry. Is there anything I can do?"

"Obviously not." Chance called Ruby to his side.

"What do you mean by obviously?"

"Over and over I've tried to help you. Nanette has helped you. Beth has helped you. And you follow our lead for a few steps then go back to following him."

"I didn't follow John's lead. I simply used his contacts. That's business, Chance. Don't you think God blessed the gala? We raised so much money."

Chance continued to walk on the path with Ruby by his side. Piper wanted to play and tried to distract Ruby. I struggled to keep up with Chance's stride.

"When was the last time you read your Bible?"

"What does—" I clamped my mouth closed.

I considered his question. I had not picked up my Bible since Nanette helped me with the first BCA video.

Scene after scene played through my mind. So much had happened since then—so much pretense and progress, chaos and community. I thought back to the Psalm I read and the prayer I lifted to God—that He would unfold His Word to me.

"I can't blame you," Chance continued without an answer from me. "I keep giving you credit for a level of maturity you don't have. You're blown around by the cunning craftiness of others and you don't even see it."

"What are you saying, Chance?"

"As a brother in Christ, I urge you to read your Bible so you get to know God and His ways, and so you'll be able to test the advice you're given against a reliable standard. But as your friend, I don't trust you. Goodbye, Joy."

Unable to move my tongue or my feet, I stood numb and watched Ruby and Chance jog away.

Piper came and leaned against me. My frozen frame could not withstand the pressure of her body and I slumped into a heap on the ground. Piper curled up next to me, put her head in my lap, and waited.

One by one, tears spilled from my eyes. Piper didn't budge when they splashed on her fur. She took a deep breath and nudged her nose deeper into my abdomen.

I knew today would be hard. I had no idea it would be tragic.

My phone buzzed with a text message. My heart leaped in anticipation. *Maybe it's Chance.*

The message came from Kent. *I just emailed over the employment contract. Look it over and get it back ASAP. I have appointments scheduled for you in a couple days.*

I sniffed and wiped my nose with the back of my hand. I wouldn't let things with Chance end like this, but I needed to do the next thing before I could formulate a plan. I couldn't allow myself to be overcome with emotion. I would call Beth and process all of this, soon. But for now, I needed to drop Piper off.

I cupped Piper's face in my hands and looked into her eyes. "I didn't want you, but maybe I needed you. I don't thank you for ruining my clothes, eating my furniture, or tearing up my Jeep. I do thank you for your unconditional love. Unconditional love seems to be the only kind I'm worthy of."

Piper licked my face. I gasped and then tilted my head back and laughed. "I'll allow it." Piper panted and her eyes twinkled with what, I had to admit, looked like a smile. "Only this once." I tapped her nose.

I scrambled to my feet and hooked Piper's leash to her collar. We walked slow and steady toward the parking lot. We both sighed as Piper hopped into the back of Scarlett and I closed the rear door and window.

CHAPTER FORTY-NINE

I PULLED INTO GONZALES BODY SHOP and texted Mateo.

Here.

I had arranged to drop Piper off at Mateo's. He insisted it would be easier if I trusted him to find and deliver her to a new family.

The shop looked different with the three large garage doors shut tight. Two spotlights shone on the sign with words in bright red, "Gonzales Body Shop: Quality Care for Your Car's Wear and Tear." A single bulb shone a soft glow on the glass lobby door with the business hours displayed in white letters. Bright streetlights lit up the empty parking lot.

As soon as I saw Mateo skipping down the stairs from his apartment, I got out of the driver's seat and walked around to the back of Scarlett.

When I opened the back window and swung the rear door wide, Piper laid down, crossed her paws, and rested her head on them. She gazed up at me with sorrowful eyes.

I clipped her leash to her collar and gave a couple of gentle tugs, "Come on, Piper." On the third tug she hopped out of the Jeep. Piper immediately sat on my feet and looked up at me, her eyes locked onto mine.

As I handed the leash to Mateo, the lump in my throat made it hard to speak. I whispered my final words of love and comfort in Piper's ear, feeling the weight of my decision in every heartbeat.

Like the bucket tower at a water park, this final goodbye tipped the scale of my burdened spirit and sorrow washed over me in a deluge I couldn't contain. Sobs escaped my throat and tears flowed freely.

Mateo embraced me in a full hug. "I promise, she'll be okay."

My body shook as I wept into Mateo's chest. I regained control and stepped away. Jagged breaths escaped in staccato puffs. I wiped my face with the sleeve of my hooded jacket. "I'm sorry."

"I promise," Mateo affirmed with another pat on my arm.

"I know. It's not just Piper." I opened the driver's side back door and retrieved the dog crate and a container of food from the back seat.

"Everything okay?"

"Not really."

How in the world did I think I could get away with aligning myself with John Clarke and not get burned…again?

"Chance?"

I nodded.

How could I be so blind to the damage the shrapnel would do to the people I cared about when it all blew up?

"Wanna talk about it?"

"Not really."

I wiped more tears and took a deep breath. I squatted down and scrubbed Piper's ears. "You behave better for your new family than you did for me, okay?"

Piper tried to lick me, but I hopped back. "I told you," I said with finger pointed, "that was a one-time thing."

Piper whined.

I patted her head, turned, and shuffled away toward Scarlett. Piper whined again.

I swung around and ran to Piper. I squatted down, clutched her tight, and buried my face in the fur of her neck. I breathed out, "I'll miss you." I stood and dusted fur from my blouse and jeans, gave a meek smile to Mateo, and climbed into Scarlett.

Driving away from the body shop, my sadness churned within me like a storm gathering strength. My helplessness crashed over me in waves. I blinked away the image of the sadness in Piper's eyes. Her whine seemed to cry, "Don't leave me."

I had to. For her. She deserved someone present.

It was my only path forward.

I replayed my encounter with Chance over and over in my mind, each scene plunging me to new depths of sorrow. He looked so disappointed in me. *"At least I stood my ground. You kept following his lead."*

Gradually, my feeling of helplessness morphed into something else. As if the knob on the stovetop had been turned up, my sadness gave way to a simmering anger.

I felt a sudden surge of energy. My hands gripped the wheel tighter until my knuckles turned white.

I had only been to the Clarke house one time on the day John and I called on sponsors. I thought I remembered the way.

CHAPTER FIFTY

A GAS LANTERN FLICKERED above an archway leading to the solid wood front door of the Tudor-style home. Soft light glowed from an upstairs window tucked into an eyebrow dormer.

Blooms and greenery spilled over the rims of two hand-thrown pottery planters that flanked the archway. The rim of the pots came up to my hips and the tallest grasses tickled my shoulder.

I pressed the doorbell then retreated slightly and fiddled with a stalk of rosemary in one of the planters. I loved the smell of rosemary. Aunt Mimsy grew it in a pot on her front porch, and I would always pluck some leaves, rub them between my palms, and then sniff my hands.

A muffled male voice called out, "I got it!"

Jackson opened the door. "Miss Swallow," he declared with wide eyes.

Sarah walked up behind Jackson. She held a small dog with pointed ears and silky fur the color of chocolate and caramel. The dog wiggled with nervous excitement as Sarah pet its head in long strokes. "Joy, how can—"

"I'm so sorry to intrude. I know it's late, but I need to speak with John, please."

"Jackson, go get dad," Sarah instructed and Jackson jogged off. "While he gets John, I wanted to thank you for your thoughtful gift of the macaroons from my favorite bakery in New York. How did you know?"

"You mentioned something at the gala and I put it in my notes." I looked at my feet because I couldn't look this kind woman in the eyes knowing what I knew. Burning tears rose to the surface.

I heard footsteps approach and looked up in time to see John standing behind Sarah. "Joy. What can I do for you?"

I sniffed and a tear escaped down my cheek. I swallowed hard and clenched my hands at my side.

Sarah stepped forward out of the shadow of the door frame. "Oh, dear. You've been crying. Are you okay?" She clutched the dog in the crook of her elbow and placed her free hand on my arm.

"Oh, I just heard," John remarked. He slid around Sarah and approached me in the entryway. He sidled up to my right side and wrapped his left arm around my shoulders, "It's a work thing. Don't worry, I'll go pray with her."

Sarah studied my face and then glanced at John. "I don't think—"

"Not only that, but she had to re-home her dog." My head snapped to register his forlorn look. *How did he know that?*

Sarah's face crumpled in sympathy. "Oh, Joy, that's so hard. Okay, dear. I'll be praying for you too." She caressed my arm one more time before going back inside the house.

John kept his arm around my shoulder and wheeled me around. His firm grip never loosened until we stood at the driver's door of Scarlett.

"How could you do that to Chance?" I seethed.

"Thanks for helping me remove the last obstacle to my legacy," John smirked. "I'm sure I would have found a way without you, but you really came through. A woman of surprises."

"I've never met anyone like you," I growled. I couldn't seem to formulate demands for the justice I sought. My blood boiled and restricted my vocabulary.

"I'll take that as a compliment."

"Don't. You are a self-serving manipulator and—and," I stomped my foot, "—and a big fat cheat."

John grinned, shoved his hand into his front pocket, and leaned against Scarlett. "I'm sorry to disappoint you, Joy."

"I'm not the only one who's going to be disappointed in you. When I'm done, everyone will know the kind of guy you really are."

John pulled his hand out of his pocket, looked at his fingernails, and crossed his arms. "Oh? What'll you say?"

"I'm going to tell them how you had it out for Chance from the beginning and manipulated me into achieving your goals."

"Are you going to do that before or after you tell them how you blackmailed me into giving you the contract for the gala marketing consultant?"

John stepped into a mulched flower bed with mounding mums. He pulled a couple of weeds and tossed them into the grassy area. Then he plucked a couple of dead blooms from the mums and flicked them into the darkness beyond.

"I wanted to help BCA!" A whine tinted the edge of my voice.

John stood and pointed at me, "And you wanted the money."

"No. I *needed* the money after you tricked me into taking the loan and completing a free video that benefited you."

John's voice lowered to a growl, "That's rich. When you made your proposal to me, you knew what kind of man I was."

"I sure did, and now everyone else will, too."

"Are you talking about exposing my affair?"

I didn't mean that, but maybe that's what I should have been talking about. I straightened my shoulders and tossed my curls with a flick of my head, "Maybe. If it comes to that."

Both of us turned toward the house at the sound of the garage door opening. Jackson lugged two trashcans to the edge of the driveway. He smiled and waved on his trek back to the house.

"Hey, buddy. Thanks for taking care of that," John said.

"No problem. Is everything—" a loud rumble interrupted Jackson's question. We all tilted our heads to the sky to see a large aircraft fly directly overhead.

"What's that?" Jackson asked. "They're flying awful low."

"That's a smoke jumper aircraft," John replied. "The forest fire must be picking up."

"What kind of plane was it?"

"A Twin Otter or a Dornier, I think," John said. "I didn't get a good look at it."

"I did. I'm gonna go look it up online."

Jackson slipped into the garage and the door closed panel by panel until it sealed to the ground with a thump.

"What do you want, Joy?" John's question brought my attention back to our conversation. "You wanna devastate that kid? You wanna ruin him? Is that what you want?"

Tears streamed down my face. I fiddled with the key fob in my pocket.

"Do you want to devastate Jackson?" John demanded an answer.

I kicked a small pine cone from the driveway into the close-cropped grass, sniffed, and shook my head "no."

"What do you want?" John punctuated each word with a force that felt like four taps of a finger in my chest.

I looked at John and pleaded with my eyes and tone, "I want Chance to get his job back. He did nothing wrong."

"You think Chance did nothing wrong?" John asked. "Oh, but you are mistaken. He stood in my way."

I opened my mouth but stopped when John took steps toward me. He tread closer and closer and I flattened my body against Scarlett. My heart raced when he placed both hands flat against Scarlett, on either side of my head. Then he leaned in so close I could feel his breath on my face.

"And now *you're* threatening to stand in my way." I fought the urge to squeeze my eyes tight and turn my head.

I breathed deep through my nose, "I'll find a way around you," my voice quivered.

"You've messed with the wrong guy," John snarled.

I clenched my jaw and looked directly into his eyes, just inches from mine, "You're a bully and a cheat and I'm done with you."

John's face remained in front of mine. My shoulder blades stung as I pressed my back further into Scarlett. The corners of his mouth lifted into a sinister grin and a puff of hot air assaulted me when he snorted, "You have no idea what I'm capable of."

John bent his elbows and shoved himself upright. He shoved his right hand into his front pocket and sauntered toward the front door. I didn't move a muscle, only my chest expanded in short, ragged breaths.

My back remained pressed against the driver's door of Scarlett when I heard John say, "Go home, Joy. I don't need you anymore." I heard the front door open and latch close before I crumpled to the driveway. I pulled my knees to my chest and sobbed—every moment of anguish from the day releasing in hopeless lament.

CHAPTER FIFTY-ONE

I LAID FLAT IN BED with my comforter tucked under my armpits. My head throbbed. I had tossed and turned all night replaying scenes from my conversation with Chance, my goodbye with Piper, and my confrontation with John.

I failed to pull my room-darkening shade when I went to bed, so I used the glow from the streetlight to examine the images that "appeared" in the popcorn ceiling. Like discovering images in the clouds as a child, it took my mind off the very real drama playing out in my life. I created an entire story in my mind about the troll who couldn't get to the cotton candy because of the tiger in the way. I finally gave in to the urge to check the clock—5:27 a.m.

I flung my covers back with both hands, sat up, and swiveled my feet to the floor. I made my way to the bathroom, shook two pain relief capsules into my hand, and swished them down with a cup of water from the tap.

I shuffled into the kitchen and poured water into the coffeepot and opted for pre-ground coffee rather than revving up the grinder.

Deadened by exhaustion and sorrow, I stared at the coffeepot. Clicks and gurgles accompanied the small stream of dark liquid that filled the interior of the carafe.

What do you want? John's question tormented me.

Long term, I still wanted to learn from successful people I admired. I had that opportunity on the horizon with Kent and his company. In the immediate, however, I wanted Chance to get his job back.

I thought of one more move I could make.

Maggie.

The thought of asking Maggie for help left a sour taste in my mouth.

I unplugged my phone from the charging cord and tapped out a text. *Can we meet?*

• • •

I sealed Scarlett up tight before heading to Berean Christian Academy—no open-air rides remained in the immediate forecast. Smoke from the forest fires hung in the sky like a veil, blurring everything in sight.

Maggie agreed to meet me at the school. Students remained at home because of the smoky conditions while a group of parents coordinated a food, clothing, and household goods drive for fire victims in nearby mountain communities.

I pulled into a parking spot on the side of the gym. I grabbed the box and oversized IKEA bag I brought with items to donate. My eyes stung from the smoke as I approached the lobby door.

The door swung open and a man in a ball cap ushered me inside.

"Oh, hi, Charles." His hat and my watering eyes kept me from recognizing him at first.

"Miss Swallow," he tucked his chin in a curt nod. "I'll take these." He took the items from my arms and walked away.

"Do you know where Mrs. Hensley is?" I called after him.

Charles turned his head slightly and jerked his chin toward the bank of doors leading to the gymnasium.

I hadn't been inside the gym since the academic pep rally. It turned out the bleachers could be tucked away, creating a flat wall of green with BCA emblazoned in white. This left the entire gym floor open to fill with sorting tables for the donated goods. I saw Maggie standing at a table along the wall under the "Inspiring Greatness Within" motto. She intercepted me as I walked toward her table. She wiped her hands on her jeans and ushered me through a door that led to a small conference room.

"I didn't expect to see you again," she said as the door closed behind her.

Maggie wore a green T-shirt with Berean Christian Academy Eagles plastered on the front. She had her cropped blonde hair tucked behind her ears and wore minimal makeup and simple pearl earrings. Her bright white tennis shoes looked like they had never been worn.

She looked so—normal. She didn't look like the monster I had made her out to be in my mind over these last few months. Nor did she look like the glowing goddess I fashioned in my mind when I placed her on a pedestal before. Normal or not, today I needed her to be indomitable.

"You have to stop him," I spouted.

"Who? John?" Maggie shook her head like Piper trying to dry off. "There's no stopping him."

"He can't do this to Chance, Maggie!"

At my raised voice, Maggie glanced at the closed door and lowered hers, "He can. And he did." Her expression held the same defeat as her tone.

"But you're on the board. You can convince the others."

Maggie shook her head.

I pursed my lips. "BCA shouldn't partner with someone like John. You need to tell them the truth about him."

Maggie's shoulders sagged and she sighed, "He'd find a way to destroy me. And to be honest, I think most of the board members would jump straight to forgiveness in order to accept John's money. Plus, I couldn't do that to Peter."

"Peter should already know," I grumbled.

The door to the conference room squeaked open. Millie popped her head in. "Sorry to interrupt, but I'm making a lunch run. Maggie, do you want anything?"

Millie's eyes grew round when she saw me. "Hi, Millie. Good to see you," I said. She blinked twice and looked at Maggie.

"A grilled chicken Caesar salad if they have it," Maggie replied. "Joy, are you staying? Do you want anything?"

"I'll—"

The door clunked closed. "I guess not," I mumbled to myself. I turned back to Maggie. "There's gotta be something you can do."

"Joy, I'm sorry. I wish—"

"It's not fair, Maggie!" I felt like a teenager whose mother told her she couldn't go to the party on Friday night. All I needed was a pillow to scream into.

"I know," she took a ragged breath. "But he's ruthless. He's got connections everywhere and he's not afraid to use them."

"Why would the board make a decision about the Bible teacher based on the advice of the Booster Club President?"

Maggie tilted her head and looked at me with sad eyes. She placed her hand on my shoulder and I jerked away. "You're not hearing me," I cried. "We have to get Chance his job back."

"You're not listening to me, Joy. John doesn't just have something on me, he has something on everyone. Not to mention the money he throws around to get his way. There's nothing we can do."

Maggie walked to the door and opened it as if asking me to leave.

"And to think I ever looked up to you," I seethed as I stormed out.

I ran straight into Liz. The stack of folded clothes she carried flew into the air and scattered on the gym floor. Millie, who stood at the table making notes on a piece of paper, threw her pen down and squatted with Liz to pick up my mess.

"Here. Let me help," I offered. I knelt on the floor and leaned back on my heels. I picked up a small white onesie and folded it on my knee.

Millie snatched it from my lap, "I think you've helped BCA enough, don't you?"

"Millie," Liz whispered.

I stood and dusted my knees. "At least I'm willing to try and clean up my messes." I glared at Maggie and stomped toward the exit.

I stopped before pushing on the silver metal bar on the doors leading to the lobby. There are times when you leave a place not realizing it was your last time. This time I knew.

CHAPTER FIFTY-TWO

I PULLED MY PHONE out of my back pocket as I climbed into Scarlett. When I tossed it onto the passenger seat the screen lit up with notifications of a missed call and an unread text. Both were from Kent. The text read, *Call me.*

Panic filled my chest. Had I missed an appointment? I checked my calendar and scrolled through my unread email. Nothing stood out to me. The only email from Kent or his staff was my employment contract from the Human Resources department. I planned to sign and return that first thing today. I tilted my head back with the realization that though it was still morning in Boise, it was almost noon in New York.

He's probably anxious to get the paperwork done before his trip into town.

I tapped on the missed call.

"Kent Kingsley," Kent said. His voice sounded distant, I heard papers shuffling on the other end of the line.

I projected my best singsong voice, "Good morning."

"Is it?"

I glanced at the clock. "In Boise?" I said with the end of the word rising in a question. Before Kent could respond, I added, "I have the employment contract right here. I plan to—"

"That's what I called about. John Clarke and I finally talked."

My stomach churned.

"Thanks for that connection, by the way. He's a real powerhouse."

You could say that.

"Anyway, he made a compelling offer I couldn't refuse. He only had two conditions. One was that he run point on his clients—which happen to be the referrals you were bringing with you. The other was that I rescind your offer of employment at Power Story Incorporated."

"You're firing me?" I placed my left hand on my forehead and held my breath with my mouth open.

"Technically, I'm not hiring you."

"Because of John Clarke?" I screeched. I hopped out of Scarlett and took a deep breath. The smoke burned my throat and I choked and coughed.

"I'm not going to get into the details, but from his perspective it's because of you."

I squeezed my temples with my free hand and paced the sidewalk in front of the Jeep. One step. Two steps. Turn. One step. Two steps. Turn.

"Kent, I think you should hear my side of the story."

"Honestly, Joy, I don't need it. You have mad talent, but John's experience and connections are the more strategic play for me right now."

"But you don't understand what kind of man—"

"I'll always be here for you. I'm just not offering you a job right now. Take care, Sadness."

The line went dead.

I could feel the pounding of my heart in my temples. The parking lot began to spin and I placed my hand on Scarlett to steady myself. I slogged back to the driver's seat, slammed the door, and banged my head three times on the steering wheel.

My tears remained pent-up like a dark cloud heavy with rain that refused to fall.

I screamed at the top of my lungs—the sound ricocheted around the interior of the Jeep as John's words echoed in my head—*"You've messed with the wrong guy."*

CHAPTER FIFTY-THREE

AFTER LEAVING BCA, I returned home, binged-watched trash TV, and ate peanut butter out of the jar for dinner. Another fitful night had me staring at the ceiling. I needed Beth, so at some point in the middle of the night, I threw on some clothes, backed Scarlett out of my driveway, and headed out. The sun had no intention of rising for another couple of hours when I pulled up and parked along the street in front of Cup O' Joe in Mountain Home.

I retrieved my butter-soft, hooded fleece jacket from the passenger seat, slipped it on over my Pepperdine University T-shirt, and zipped it up. I tucked my phone into the pocket of my sweatpants and held the brim of my baseball cap while I shoved a few curls that attempted to escape back under the hat. I hopped down from the Jeep and pressed the key fob until Scarlett let out a short beep.

I knocked on the front door of the café. It wouldn't open for another hour. Beth approached the door with caution until she recognized me and unlocked the door and swung it wide.

"Joy! What are you doing here?"

I stood in the doorway and didn't hold back my tears. "I've lost everything. Everything is gone."

"Get in here," Beth grabbed my arm, pulled me inside, and closed and relocked the door. She gave me a firm hug and then guided me to the booth by the front window. "Sit here. I'm gonna get us some coffee."

I slid into the booth and wiped my tears with the cuff of my jacket. I looked down at the 366th Fighter Wing seal and realized this was the same booth I sat in a few months prior. The motto—"*Audentes Fortuna Juvat*"—ridiculed me from beneath the glossy surface.

"Ha!" I exclaimed.

Beth placed a white mug of hot black coffee in front of me and slid into the other side of the booth. "What was that for?" she asked.

I pointed at the Latin phrase—"*Audentes Fortuna Juvat*"—fortune favors the bold. Not this time."

Beth placed her hand on top of mine. "Start at the beginning. Tell me everything."

"How much time do you have?"

Beth looked at her watch. "Forty minutes before my first staff member arrives."

I started at the beginning like she asked. I told her everything—the details she knew about, and the details I hadn't disclosed. When I got to the part about the trickery surrounding the contest, she reached out and touched my hand. When I got to the part about my proposal to John, she raised her eyebrows, but didn't comment.

When my play-by-play got to the part about my conversation with Chance at the park, I whined, "I didn't tell John about Chance's application to Mount Horeb. I didn't!"

Beth shifted in her seat.

When I got to the part about my confrontation with John, I wailed, "He threatened me!"

Beth sat and sipped her coffee, eyes focused on me. She never spoke, and I barreled on.

When I described my encounter with Maggie, I lamented, "I can't believe she won't just tell the truth."

Beth rubbed the back of her neck and broke her silence. "Have you?"

"What?"

"Told the truth?"

"Yes! I'm telling the truth. And it's awful. I haven't even gotten to the worst part. Not only have I lost my friend, but I lost my dog, my reputation with everyone at BCA, and get this—Kent called me yesterday and took away my job!" I slapped the table with both hands and looked at Beth with wild eyes wet with tears.

I heard scratching at the door and turned my head to see a girl unlock it and walk in. She looked about nineteen with a high ponytail and bright smile. "Good morning," she chirped.

"Good morning," Beth replied. "Go ahead and get started on the back of house opening checklist. I'll double check front of house."

"Sure thing." Beth's worker skipped to the back and I heard water run and dishes clang.

I saw movement through the window outside. I tilted my head to see a man park behind Scarlett and walk toward the front door.

"Listen, Joy—"

"Oh my gosh, Beth, it's Marshal," I whispered in panic. "Did you know he was coming?"

Marshal stopped abruptly and dug in his briefcase bag. He tilted his head back in frustration and stomped back to his car.

"No. Sometimes he—"

"He forgot something in his car. I'm gonna slip out the back. Can I go to your house so we can talk more after your shift?"

"Joy," Beth's tone startled me. It reminded me of when my grandfather would give me what he called a "talking-to."

"Yes?" My eyes darted to Marshal still digging in the back seat of his car.

"I don't know how else to say this, but I have nothing left to say to you."

I blinked. "Wh—"

Beth put up her hand like a cop stopping traffic. "Joy, this is difficult for me to say, but you are no different than John or Maggie."

I felt the air leave my lungs.

Beth continued, "Maggie won't tell Peter of her sin because she's afraid she'll lose him and her reputation, so she's keeping the truth hidden. You're doing the same thing with Chance. And until today, with me.

"John was so laser focused on what he wanted that he lost sight of how his words could hurt people, and he used whatever means necessary to accomplish his task. You've done the same thing.

"You've been given wise and foolish counsel but have determined in your heart what sounds best to you with no thought as to how else to evaluate it even though Nanette has taught you how to look at it through the lens of God's Word.

"I will always be your friend. I have not and will not stop praying for you. But until you confess your sin, turn from your ways, and choose to follow truth, nothing I say to you will make a difference anyway."

I couldn't breathe. Beth had never stood up to me like that. She stood and kissed me on top of my head and walked toward the back of the café.

Beth stopped halfway between our booth and the counter and spoke without turning around. "And stop running away from your past. You're as flawed as the people you cut off."

Before I could process any of what Beth said, the door to the coffee shop opened and Marshal walked in. I felt like I was free-falling with no parachute and no net. A conversation with Marshal felt more like being dashed on the craggy rocks than splashing into the forgiving sea.

"Joy, what a pl—"

I shoved past Marshal and stumbled to Scarlett. I revved the engine and sped away.

CHAPTER FIFTY-FOUR

I STOOD ON AUNT MIMSY'S FRONT PORCH and dropped keys to the house into the hand of the realtor. I should feel great. The house never looked better. The updated kitchen and bathroom counters transformed the spaces—out with the orange laminate and in with the white quartz. The house morphed from old-lady-bungalow into cozy-starter-home when I sold all of Aunt Mimsy's furniture and allowed the staging company to fill the space with rented everything. It looked like a magazine.

I should feel great. But my heart felt too tender to bear another loss.

I swept my fingers down the fronds of the green Boston ferns on the hooks of the freshly painted porch.

"Again, great job, Joy. Thanks for taking care of everything on the list. You'd be amazed at how many clients think they know better."

"A lesson I've learned the hard way," I admitted with a meek smile.

I walked her to her car. "I'll let you know if we drum up any interest with the open house this weekend," she said as she slid into the driver's seat.

"Thanks," I said, closed her door, and waved goodbye as she drove away. I dropped my raised hand to my side and sighed. The words FOR SALE on the sign in the yard mocked me. Beth was right. I put a FOR SALE sign on my integrity when I called John that day.

Now what?

For the past several weeks I had thrown myself into renovating Aunt Mimsy's house. She said I could split the equity with her, so I focused on the house rather than looking for a job or drumming up marketing clients.

I bent down to pluck a weed from the flower bed at the end of the driveway. "Joy?" I heard my name and looked up across the street to see Nanette standing on the sidewalk of a bungalow similar to Aunt Mimsy's.

"Nanette? What are you doing here?"

"This is my daughter Ann's house. I've been staying with her while Rick's in Africa on a mission trip and—" Nanette dropped her head to her chest and sniffed. I saw a drop of water leave a mark on her bright red knit top.

I glanced both ways before I jogged across the street. I gripped both of her arms, "Nanette, are you okay?"

"Not really," she sniffed.

"What—"

"The fire destroyed everything."

"The forest fire?"

Nanette nodded and wiped her eyes with the back of her hand. I pulled her into an embrace. "I'm so so sorry."

"I got word today that we can finally go back. But neither Ann nor her husband can take off work, and I don't have a vehicle. Even if I did, with Rick in Africa, I don't think I could bear to go see it alone."

"I could take you." I grasped both of her hands in mine.

Nanette's eyes glistened. "You would do that?"

"Of course."

As I waited for Nanette to gather her things, I questioned the wisdom of my hasty offer. With my own life in ashes, I didn't have much else to give beyond the ride. I had actually considered calling her for counsel, but had placed Nanette Verity squarely in the past. Now, it wouldn't be fair to ask her to help me make sense of the destruction in my life while she faced her own tragedy.

About fifteen minutes out of town Nanette bounced in her seat and turned to look in the back of Scarlett. "I just realized. I don't see Piper. She's not with you today?"

It was my turn for a drop of water to escape my eyes and splash on my blouse. "I took a new job with significant travel so I re-homed her."

"Oh, honey. That's so hard."

"And pointless," I mumbled.

"Pointless?"

"The job fell through. So now, no job and no Piper."

My tires created a drumbeat as they crossed lines in the road. Thump-thump. Pause. Thump-thump.

"Seems like we've both suffered great loss." Thump-thump. Pause. Thump-thump. "I've been clinging to Psalm 34. It says that the Lord hears the cries of His people and delivers them from all of their troubles."

"He didn't deliver you," I groused.

"Not in the way I had hoped, no. But the next verse is even more comforting. It says the Lord is near to the brokenhearted and saves the crushed in spirit. He's been so near to me these last couple of weeks."

I didn't respond, and Nanette allowed me to drive in silence. Crushed in spirit pretty much summed up my situation. I wondered how Nanette felt God's nearness in the face of such loss. I had never felt so alone.

As we traveled, Nanette sat content to look out the window in silence. Her serenity stood in stark contrast to the war inside of me. Here sat a woman with answers—and questions. I dreaded her questions. I longed for her questions.

I had skillfully avoided thinking about much of anything other than the next step in front of me. Choose a paint color, tape off the hardwood floors, paint the trim, paint the wall. I swapped my marketing podcasts for a true crime series about the murder and disappearances of people I didn't know.

Now face-to-face with another person dealing with loss, I could no longer avoid my own. I had to figure out where to go from here, but I was afraid to take the next step. I was afraid to consider what that next step might be.

The desert landscape gave way to foothills as we took a road north heading toward Idaho City. We crossed the bridge near the Lucky Peak Reservoir before Nanette broke the silence.

"What are you waiting for?" Nanette asked.

"I'm sorry, what?"

"I honestly don't know, Joy. I felt the Lord tell me to ask you what you're waiting for."

What am I waiting for? Direction. I'm always waiting for direction.

"A spotlight that shines a hundred yards ahead, I guess," I offered.

"I think you were the one to remind me that's not how God works. He is our light, His Word is our light, Jesus is our light, and we are to walk in that light. So what are you waiting for?"

"A clue as to my next step?" I shrugged. "I'm feeling a little gun-shy. I keep picking guides to take me where I want to go and they've all left me lost and alone wandering around in the darkness."

"God is light and in Him is no darkness at all."

"The people I've been following have all claimed faith in God."

"If we say we have fellowship with God while we walk in darkness, we lie and do not practice the truth."

Images of Maggie, John, and Kent flashed through my mind. "Yeah, they definitely don't practice the truth."

I slowed for a tractor inching along with a loader bucket in front. I had a dotted line to pass and I checked my mirrors before accelerating around it. I glanced in my rearview mirror one last time after I passed and caught sight of my own reflection.

You've done the same thing. Beth's words echoed in my memory.

"And I followed their lead, dug my own pit, and jumped right in," I admitted.

"So, what are you waiting for?"

"Didn't you hear me? I'm alone, in a pit, in the darkness. I can't see a way out. I'm waiting for a glimmer of light."

"Didn't you hear me? God is near to the brokenhearted and saves the crushed in spirit."

I tightened my grip on the steering wheel. "I don't want to be rude, but I don't think we're speaking the same language. I. Am. Stuck. God is not saving me. I'm alone."

"Are you crying out?"

"Yes. I'm crying out! Are you not listening? I'm crying out."

"I haven't heard you crying out. Right now all I hear is wallowing."

I pressed my back into the seat and glanced at Nanette with my mouth frozen open.

Why is she taunting me?

"What do you know about it?" I spat.

"I recognize it because I've been there," Nanette spoke calmly. "I'd been rehearsing my sorrows more than God's goodness. I wallowed instead of crying out. But when I came to my senses, I confessed my sin of self-pity and saw the ladder clinging to the side of the pit all along. Jesus is the light and the path to light."

I shook my head as a tear escaped down my cheek. I whispered, "I can't see the ladder."

"We've suffered great loss, you and I. We are struck down, but not destroyed. Confess your sins and He is faithful and just to forgive you and cleanse you from all unrighteousness."

"Nanette, I really like you. You've taught me things I didn't know that I didn't know. I feel something different when I'm with you. But it's like you're speaking a foreign language here. I really don't know what you're getting at."

"If you want to be able to see your next step, you have to walk in the light. If we claim to be without sin the truth is not in us and we remain in darkness. The way out of that darkness is confession. So, I'll ask you again—what are you waiting for?"

I tucked a curl behind my ear and took a deep breath. Despite my best efforts to avoid thinking about it, I knew exactly what I needed to confess. Beth had basically given me the list.

"I confess my sin."

"What sin? Don't tell me, tell God. Name it, Joy."

"God, I confess I've been following whatever path seems right to me at the time."

"Is that all?"

I wiped one palm on my thigh. Then the other. "I confess the secrecy, the manipulation, the greed, the pride, and the dogged commitment to my own goals."

Nanette patted my shoulder. "Thank you, Father, for Your faithfulness to forgive. Shine Your light on Joy's next steps so she can walk with You."

CHAPTER FIFTY-FIVE

GREEN TREES AND FALL GRASSES gave way to scorched earth as we traveled the road to Nanette's cabin. Periodically a lodgepole pine stood tall and strong amidst the ashes—as if the closer it reached to heaven, the better its chance of survival. Some scorched trunks gave way to branches seemingly untouched. Other trees succumbed completely to the flames and looked like black spikes emerging from a sea of gray.

Nanette folded her hands in her lap and closed her eyes as we crossed the stone bridge nearest her property. The bushes that blazed with fall foliage weeks before had yielded to the flames of the wildfire. Only mounds of ash and sticks remained. The water that danced and sparkled in the stream below now murmured and sighed, a melancholy survivor in the midst of devastation.

I stopped at the base of Nanette's driveway. Her black metal mailbox stood firmly planted in the ground, but the red paint on the flag had blistered in the heat. I touched Nanette's hands in her lap. Her eyes remained closed. "Are you sure you're ready?" I asked.

"In my weakness He is made strong."

I blinked. "Does that mean 'yes'?"

Nanette opened her eyes and looked at me with a soft smile. "Yes."

I put Scarlett into first gear and slowly let out the clutch while I pressed the gas. The tires slipped a little as we crested the steep drive.

I heard Nanette whimper before she slapped her hand over her mouth. I pulled the parking brake and turned off the engine and watched Nanette take in the scene. The wail that escaped her lips rose from the depth of her soul and seeped out from between her fingers until it filled the interior of the vehicle.

Shared sorrow overwhelmed me as I surveyed the property. The entire homestead looked like a war zone. Gray ash covered every inch of everything. The green metal roof lay in a twisted heap where the cabin once stood. Only the stone chimney stood proud.

Nanette's hands shook as she opened the door to get out of Scarlett. I hopped out and ran around to the passenger side. I wrapped my arm around her to steady her quaking frame. We shuffled to a grove of aspens that remained adjacent to where her wooden deck once stood. Whatever tissue-thin leaves lingered in the autumn season had been burned off, and patches of white bark contrasted against the charred trunks.

Nanette ran her hand along a trunk, "This was my choir."

"Your choir?" I asked.

"The leaves of the aspen rustle together like applause in the mountain breezes. They always made me think of that verse that says 'the mountains and the hills before you shall break forth into singing, and all the trees of the field shall clap their hands.'"

Nanette rotated a small step. Then another. Then another. I had seen feeble residents of the local nursing home move faster. Her slowness was not frailty, rather reticence. At long last she pivoted completely from the grove of trees to face the desolation before her.

I gently grasped her elbow, "Let's go. There's nothing left here but heartache."

"I think I see the corner of a frame right there," Nanette pointed and stumbled as she reached to move a sheet of metal out of the way.

"Wait, you could hurt yourself," I said. "I have some work gloves in the back of Scarlett. Let me get those."

I made my way back to the Jeep and noticed another pile of twisted metal. Nanette's burned-out car peeked from underneath the green roof that once graced the detached garage.

I retrieved the gloves from Scarlett and put them on. I walked over to where Nanette stood and lifted the corner of green metal. Nanette tugged on the frame. The charred wood bordered one of her husband's landscape paintings. The heat from the fire bubbled the paint and distorted the image. She hugged it to her chest.

"Wouldn't you rather remember things as they were?" I asked.

Nanette turned to me with raised eyebrows.

"That painting is ruined," I explained.

"It's scarred, but not ruined. Scars remind us we're stronger than whatever tried to hurt us."

There were very few items we uncovered that had not completely been consumed by the fire. Even fireproof items like dishes lay in a broken heap. Once the wood cabinets supporting them collapsed, they broke into a thousand pieces.

We had a small selection of cast iron pots, a few ceramic items, and some silver serving dishes and flatware sitting on and around a boulder we used as a table to collect our rescues.

"I need to sit down for a minute," Nanette said. Her body hunched over in weariness.

"I think we should go."

"I'm not ready. There's something else to uncover. I feel it. I just need to rest for a minute."

"I have a couple of folding chairs I keep in Scarlett. I'll grab them." I took my gloves off and slapped them together to rid them of ash. I retrieved the chairs and set them up in the sun. Now that we weren't moving around as much, the breeze chilled me.

"Even though I walk through the valley of the shadow of death, I will fear no evil, for you are with me." Nanette spoke aloud with hands folded in her lap.

I sat for a moment, but nervous energy pulsed through my body. I didn't want to think deeply, I wanted to do something. "Do you mind if I keep poking around?" I asked.

"Sure."

I walked around to an area we had not yet explored. I shifted a sheet of metal to reveal a pile of jars of fruits and vegetables broken and spilled out. "I think this might have been your pantry. Did you preserve all this food yourself?"

"Oh, yes. My grandmother taught me. My grandparents were hard workers. They always had a big garden. They'd share with their neighbors and can the rest to eat throughout the winter. I have—" Nanette stopped and took in a jagged breath "—had a much smaller garden."

I pushed aside some of the broken jars and located a large batch of unbroken treasure. I retrieved each unbroken jar and lined them up. I uncovered enough jars to fill a grocery cart.

I stood with my hands on my hips and surveyed my bounty. "It must have taken a huge amount of time to can this much food."

"A labor of love. And a picture of God's provision." Nanette shifted in her seat and clapped her hands. "That's it! I want to bring this food to my neighbors."

"You don't want to keep it for yourself?"

"We have family and friends to help us. Some of our neighbors up here don't have that kind of support. Plus, I don't want to lay up treasure for myself and not be rich toward God."

I didn't know what she meant by that, but I knew how to get the food to the neighbors. "I have a few boxes in Scarlett left over from moving stuff at Aunt Mimsy's. We can put the food in there to give away."

Nanette laughed. "Scarlett is like Mary Poppins's bag. You have everything we need in there today."

"It seems so." It felt good to smile. I pulled out the flat cardboard and a packing tape dispenser and folded them into usable boxes. Nanette rose from her chair to help me load the jars.

"I don't know how you can think of others at a time like this," I said, taking a jar from Nanette and placing it into a box. "I lost a few friends and a job and haven't been able to think of anyone else but me."

Nanette laughed. "I do love your candor, Joy Swallow." Nanette placed her hand on my shoulder. "Plus, that's not entirely true. You're here with me."

CHAPTER FIFTY-SIX

AS WE LOADED THE LAST BOX into the back of Scarlett, I heard the crunching of tires behind us. We turned to see a white minivan and a truck with a trailer pull up on the road and stop at the base of Nanette's driveway. Eight people emerged from the vehicles. I only recognized Liz, Millie, and Jeremy from The Remnant. Jeremy trudged up the steep drive to greet us while the others pulled items from Liz's van.

"What's this?" Nanette asked with her hands clasped at her heart.

"We heard you might be able to use a bit of help today," Jeremy said. He gave Nanette a hug and raised a hand of greeting toward me before stepping back in shock at the devastation.

I heard scuffles behind me. Liz and Millie lugged an ice chest up the steep incline with huffs and puffs. A few men and women I had never met followed close behind hauling a table, large bags, and camp chairs slung over their shoulders. Within minutes, the chairs were arranged around the table loaded with buckets of fried chicken and Styrofoam bowls of coleslaw and mashed potatoes. Millie walked over, took Nanette by the hand, and led her toward the others. I followed and stood between Nanette and Jeremy as everyone held hands around the table.

"Jeremy, would you bless the food?" Liz nudged.

"Dear God, we ask for Your blessing today—on this food, on our efforts, and on our dear friend, Mrs. Verity. Help us look beyond the sad scene before us to see all of this through Your eyes. Help us move from trauma to trust. Be our comfort today. In Jesus's name, amen."

I remained silent while conversation bubbled and swirled like a spring creek. I gnawed on a chicken leg and ate too many mashed potatoes as everyone talked about anything but the wildfire. I watched as Nanette nibbled at her food and stole glances at the pile of debris.

Jeremy reached over and touched Nanette's hand. "I know you're anxious, but—"

The crunch of wheels on gravel stole Jeremy's attention. He stood and looked down the hill. "Perfect timing."

"Who's here?" Nanette asked.

"The adjuster. Rick contacted me from Africa to arrange it all. Once the adjuster makes note of the damage, we can start cleaning up."

Jeremy and Nanette greeted the adjuster at the top of the steep drive and he began taking photos and documenting his findings on a tablet. I turned to see Liz and Millie and a few other ladies packaging up the leftover food.

"Can I help clean up?" I asked.

Millie snapped lids on containers and turned her back to me. Liz offered a gentle smile and handed me a tablecloth to fold.

Jeremy walked over and tapped the table. "We're set. Joy, if you'll move your Jeep down to the road, I'll back my trailer up here and me and the guys'll load up the metal from the roof onto it. That should give you ladies access to sift through everything to see what else you can salvage. I already called a buddy of mine to come up with another trailer to load up the car and take it to a yard in town."

"Before we get to that, can we do something?" Nanette asked.

Jeremy glanced at the piles of debris and tucked his hand in his front pockets. "Sure."

Nanette waved her hands for everyone to gather. I set down the folded tablecloth in my hands and joined the circle.

Tears streamed down Nanette's face. She opened her mouth to speak and then tucked her chin. She opened her mouth again, "I've—" Nanette sniffed and patted her cheeks to disperse the tears. "I've been thinking a lot about all that we've lost. For weeks I sat in the unknown, but now I see. We've lost our wedding photos and Ann's outfit she wore home from the hospital. We've lost Ricky's art and the library of commentaries he's collected all these years."

I looked around the circle. Many people looked at their feet. A few had the courage to look Nanette in the face and take in her agony. The sounds of sniffs and shuffled feet accompanied the songs of the birds I had not noticed before.

"In Psalm 103, David gave his soul a good talking-to when he said, 'Praise the Lord, oh my soul and don't forget God's benefits.' I've been rehearsing my loss more than God's benefits. Before we continue, my soul needs to praise the Lord."

A song trickled out of Millie, "Great is Thy faithfulness, O God my Father—"

Another female voice joined in, "There is no shadow of turning with Thee—"

A baritone voice prompted the others to grow in strength, "Thou changest not, Thy compassions, they fail not—"

"As Thou hast been, Thou forever will be," the choir of voices overpowered the forest chorus of birds.

When the hymn had been sung, the voices stopped with the exception of Nanette's. She sang the refrain one last time.

"Great is Thy faithfulness

Great is Thy faithfulness

Morning by morning new mercies I see

All I have needed Thy hand hath provided

Great is Thy faithfulness, Lord, unto me."

The birds picked up their chorus as a gentle breeze rattled the charred branches of the remaining trees. I felt heavy, but not burdened. Where I would normally seek to fill the silence, I stood mesmerized in the tranquility of the moment.

"I confess I feel very—" Nanette choked back a sob. My heart lurched toward her, longing to offer comfort "—alone. With all this and Rick in Africa, I need to remind my soul of God's benefits. Does anyone have a testimony of God drawing near in your solitude?"

Liz shared a childhood story of being left behind at a rest stop on a church trip. She got emotional recounting the traumatic experience and how God showed up. "I'd go through it again, though," Liz added. "I never questioned God's presence after that. I'd like to pray for you, if that's alright."

Nanette nodded and clutched her hands to her heart. Liz lifted a heartfelt request that God would convince Nanette of his nearness.

"Thank you, Liz," Nanette said, then looked around the circle. "I'm also feeling adrift. Does anyone have a testimony of God's anchoring?"

Jeremy shared a story about a time he and his buddies went fishing and their boat took on water. They ended up getting rescued by the

Coast Guard after drifting for hours in emergency life ring buoys off the coast of Vancouver Island.

He, too, ended his story with a prayer for Nanette to cling to the hope she has in Christ as a strong and trustworthy anchor for her soul.

Nanette nodded and wiped more tears from her face. "And one more. I can't see past this ash heap today. Does anyone have a testimony of God restoring?"

Millie sniffed and wiped her nose with the back of her wrist. She told stories of her alcoholic mother. One time, her mother threatened to run her car off the cliff with her children inside. Millie endured other abusive rampages that ended with her mom kicking the kids out of the house alone at night to fend for themselves. "But God restored our ash heap of a relationship over time after He radically saved her a few years ago." Liz grasped her friend's shoulder in a tight side hug.

"Thank you all," Nanette said with her hand over her heart. "I am encouraged. I mean it. I am stepping out *in* courage. God is here in this place and He has graciously comforted me through you."

Our circle broke up and I moved Scarlett down the hill. Jeremy backed the trailer up to where the cabin once stood. The men cut and moved large sheets of roof metal to the trailer. This gave the women access to surprising treasures preserved underneath. A glass figurine Nanette's great-grandmother passed down remained untouched by ash or flame. The Bible Rick took on his first mission trip had a tattoo of a doorknob marring the cover, but otherwise no real damage.

The emotion of the day pulled on me. I wandered off behind the homestead and took a path up a slope. I slumped onto a boulder and tilted my head toward the sky as tears spilled from the edges of my eyes. I mourned the beauty of nature so ravaged by the fire. I took a deep breath and then gasped when I saw the stones at my feet. I buried my head in my hands and mourned the losses I experienced since the day Beth, Chance, and I nestled those stones into the earth.

I thought back to the stories shared with Nanette and the prayers lifted. I wondered if I could ever feel the nearness of God in my aloneness and pondered how God might anchor my drifting life. Would He be willing to restore?

The snap of a twig alerted me to Nanette's presence. "Mind if I sit?" she asked.

"Of course."

"BJC?" Nanette tilted her head to read the stones.

"Beth, Joy, and Chance," I smiled.

"Hmm."

"Something I would do as a kid with my cousins in the woods. We always wanted to leave our mark," I said.

Nanette sat with her hands folded in her lap. I reached down and dusted the ash off of one of the stones.

"I feel like the mark I've made on BCA is more like the destructive flames of the wildfire than anything," I blurted.

"They've been throwing kindling on a pile for a while now."

"But I handed John Clarke a match."

We sat in silence. The birds chirped. A breeze rattled the empty branches over our heads.

"You should see these as stones of remembrance," Nanette said. "In the Bible, God would have His people set up stones to remind them of the hardships of their journey coupled with the Lord's deliverance."

"What deliverance?" I snorted.

"Well, that's what we'll begin praying for. You heard the stories today, and the Bible is full of them, too—God is all about making the impossible possible."

I stared at my feet and kicked at the dirt. "I wouldn't even know where to start."

"Let's get together and I'll show you."

I looked up at Nanette as hope welled within me.

"Julia insists I stay at her house in Boise for the foreseeable future because she lives full-time in San Francisco anyway. Let's plan to meet in a couple of days and start praying in earnest for Berean Christian Academy. It's God's school and I'm not ready to give up on it yet."

I agreed with a nod.

CHAPTER FIFTY-SEVEN

I COULDN'T WAIT to tell Beth about—well—everything. As always, she came when I called. She said she could stay for a couple of days, and so I busied myself in preparation for her arrival. The guest room had fresh sheets and I bent over the bathtub coated with blue Comet powder. I wore yellow rubber cleaning gloves with cotton lining like my mom used to use, and scrubbed in circles with a green abrasive pad.

The doorbell rang and I stood and wiped my brow with the crook of my elbow to avoid getting cleaning residue on my face.

Strange. Beth has a key, why would she ring the bell?

I hoped it wasn't a precursor to an awkward meeting where we had to start over as friends. I peeked out the window overlooking the carport and stood on my tiptoes to see that Beth's car was not parked behind Scarlett in my driveway.

The doorbell rang again.

Front door.

I walked to the front door with my hands held upright like a doctor who had just scrubbed in for surgery. I didn't want to take the gloves off if it was someone trying to sell me something.

I peered through the eye hole in my front door and saw Mateo. I flung my back against the door and slid to the floor as if he could see me. My heart raced.

I didn't want to see Mateo again. His friendship brought me great joy and great sorrow, but at this point I didn't want to have anything to do with him. Especially as long as he worked for John.

I ignored the bell and returned to the bathroom. I rinsed the bathtub thoroughly and then I rinsed my gloves. I pulled each finger of my gloves to release the rubber suctioned to my hands and laid them on the side of the tub to dry.

The doorbell rang again.

I couldn't imagine what Mateo wanted to say to me, but I knew I didn't want to hear it. As long as he followed John's lead he could not be trusted. And I wanted to keep as much distance from John as God would allow.

I looked at myself in the mirror and tucked my curls behind my ears. I heard a key in the carport door.

I came out of the bathroom to see Beth walk in the door, rolling her suitcase over the threshold. "There's a guy in a bow tie standing on your front porch with a dog that looks an awful lot like Piper."

"What?"

I flew to the door and flung it open. Mateo stood in a brown suit and rust-colored bow tie and held a leash with Piper on the end of it.

I looked up at Mateo with wide eyes filled with questions and tears as I squatted down to embrace Piper who wiggled and jumped and whined.

I slumped on the steps and buried my head in Piper's fur. This was a reunion I could never have dreamed of.

"What—how— oh!" Piper licked my face over and over. I tilted my head back and released laughter entombed over the last few weeks.

"Okay, okay," I said as I pulled Piper away from me and stood to talk to Mateo. "What's going on? Did the family not want her anymore?"

"I never gave her to a family. Well, not technically anyway. Maria kept her."

"But—why?" My eyes narrowed, "Unless—" I pulled Piper behind me like a mother protecting her child, "—you knew John would take my job away from me."

Mateo put both hands up in surrender, "No, Joy. I swear I didn't know that would happen. I just felt like you pulled the trigger too quickly to re-home Piper, and once the dust settled you'd regret your decision."

Mateo reached his arm out to place his hand on my shoulder, "I'm truly sorry about the job falling through."

I took a step back. I didn't know what to do with the feelings at war within me. I couldn't trust Mateo, yet he brought me a gift I didn't deserve and would never have thought to ask for.

Mateo shoved both hands in the front pockets of his slacks. "Anyway, Piper and I have come over every day for the last three weeks. Where've you been?"

"In Mountain Home fixing up Aunt Mimsy's house for sale."

"Ah," he said with a nod. "Well—" Mateo leaned over and scrubbed Piper's head "—bye, Piper. Bye, Joy." He flicked his hand in a small wave as he turned to walk down the sidewalk toward his car parked on the street.

"Mateo," I called. He paused and turned his upper body toward me. "You've been the best of friends and the worst of friends. This goes in the best of friends column. Thanks."

Mateo looked at his shoes and then back at me with a smile. He turned and walked away.

"What just happened?" Beth asked, as Piper and I went inside.

"Restoration."

CHAPTER FIFTY-EIGHT

BETH AND I spent two days discussing the details of the previous weeks since our last encounter at the coffee shop. It was the longest we had ever spent not talking to each other. We laughed, we cried, and Piper got to be a part of all of it.

I planned to spend the evening with Nanette to start praying for BCA.

"Are you sure you don't want to come? I know she'd love to see you again. You two hit it off so well the last time I brought you with me."

"I think this is something you need to do for yourself," Beth replied. "I brought my Bible, my journal, and a book I've been reading. I'll have plenty to occupy myself." She was already tucked into the corner of the couch with a blanket and a cup of tea and her Bible open on her lap. "You sure I can't babysit Piper for you?"

"No, I don't want to be apart from her right now. I'm going to the park to play with her and read my Bible for a bit before my meeting with Nanette."

Beth's eyes welled up with tears. "Good," she choked out.

• • •

I scanned the parking lot of the dog park for Chance's car. I didn't know if I was ready to see him, but obviously part of me wanted to because I felt a wave of disappointment wash over me when his car wasn't there.

Piper and I walked the entire trail around the park before finding a spot in the sunshine to lay out a blanket. Piper lay still—content to rest her head on my lap as I read the Psalm Nanette mentioned about David talking to his soul.

I read the text aloud to Piper.

"Bless the Lord, O my soul,

and forget not all His benefits,

Who forgives all your iniquity,

Who heals all your diseases,

Who redeems your life from the pit,

Who crowns you with steadfast love and mercy,

Who satisfies you with good

so that your youth is renewed like the eagle's."

I stroked Piper's fur and kept reading to myself. Piper flinched as I jumped at the words a few verses down.

"He does not deal with us according to our sins,

nor repay us according to our iniquities.

For as high as the heavens are above the earth,

so great is His steadfast love toward those who fear Him."

I laid back on the blanket and stared at the sky. *As high as the heavens are above the earth, so great is His steadfast love toward me.*

"This is quite a list of benefits, Piper."

Piper got up and shoved her nose in my bag. She found her ball and dropped it on my stomach.

I propped myself up on my elbows and laughed. "Bible time's over?"

Piper sat and whined, then stood and spun in a circle and sat down again.

"Okay, we have a few minutes."

I sat up, crossed my legs, and flung the ball into the distance. Piper raced to retrieve it and trotted back and dropped it in my lap. We repeated the process over and over again. I knew what to do, and she responded as she should. Why couldn't the rest of my life be so ordered?

"You throw like a girl," a familiar voice sounded over my shoulder as I saw a streak of black and white blaze by to catch up with Piper.

My stomach did a flip-flop as I tilted my head up to see Chance standing there, coiling Ruby's leash in his hand.

"I am a girl."

He smiled and looked at his shoes as he pushed his black glasses up his nose. "Doing some reading?" he stared at my open Bible on the blanket next to me.

"Learning to rehearse God's goodness more than my sorrows. That David sure knew how to give his soul a good talking-to."

"Mmhm."

I took a breath and a gamble, "It turns out God doesn't deal with us according to our sins." I blinked at Chance. "That's a relief."

"Yes. Yes, it is."

The dogs barreled back toward us and twirled and yipped until Chance picked up the ball and flung it into the distance.

"Chance, I'm sorry for the part I played in you losing your job. But more than that, I'm sorry I didn't listen to your warnings along the way." I twisted a ring on my finger. I took a deep breath and tilted my head to look at him. "Can you forgive me?"

"Thank you for saying that. And I already have."

Relief washed over me and I felt lighter. "I'm actually headed over to Nanette's—well—Julia's house where Nanette's staying. We're going to pray for BCA. Wanna come?"

Chance pushed his shoulders back, shoved his hands in his pockets, and looked into the distance.

"I shouldn't've—"

"Sure."

"Really?" I wanted to spin in a circle like Piper.

"Really," Chance gave a half smile. "I'll follow you."

CHAPTER FIFTY-NINE

I LOOKED AROUND Julia's perfectly manicured backyard. Trimmed grass curved toward flower beds featuring native grasses, boulders, and blue rug juniper bushes. The landscape reminded me of some of my favorite hiking trails. A redwood fence served as the backdrop to a waterfall tucked in the corner. The water bubbled and splashed—nature's serene soundtrack. The fireplace behind me flickered and warmed the entire patio area enclosed on three sides by the house. The smells of sweet and savory treats wafted from a buffet table off to my right.

I may not have been sitting at her kitchen table, but I sat at Julia's patio table in awe of what God had done over the course of a few weeks. Of course, Julia didn't live here. Nanette and Rick did while construction crews rebuilt their cabin, but it had become a place of growth for me.

The first night of prayer with Nanette and Chance turned into another night and then another. At first, Nanette and Chance mostly taught me about prayer. We read Scripture aloud, turned what we read in the Bible into prayers, and sang worship songs.

We focused our prayers on Berean Christian Academy, and not too many days into our small gatherings, Nanette encouraged us to invite others to join us. Chance invited members of The Remnant. While we prayed together in unity, some of them remained cold and distant from me.

"Trust takes time to rebuild," Chance encouraged.

"You don't hold everything against me."

"I know you better."

I wanted everything to go back to when it felt like I belonged—when it felt like I was a welcome member of their family—honored even.

Two days before, we had read in II Chronicles about the dedication of Solomon's temple. Nanette challenged us to consider what God confirmed to Solomon in a dream, that if the people found themselves in opposition to God that the way back was to humble themselves, pray, seek His face, and turn from their wicked ways.

"That's what we've been doing," Charles insisted. Mr. Prayer-Walk himself snapped, "We have specifically prayed for administration to return to the policies that made our school distinctly Christian."

Millie chimed in, "We know they've hired non-Christians as coaches."

"And teachers are cursing in the classroom," Liz added.

"Yes, but I'm talking about *our* wicked ways," Nanette said. "I believe God wants us to personally confess. Before He heals the land of Berean Christian Academy, He wants to heal the land of our hearts. We need to name our specific sins. Next time we meet, come prepared to do that."

My stomach dropped. I wondered what God would have me confess to this group of people. Technically we were on the same team, but so far it didn't feel like a safe place to "air out my dirty laundry" as Grandpa used to say.

I looked around the table. Millie scraped something from the tabletop with her fingernail. Charles crossed his arms and shifted his shoulders back and forth. Liz straightened the rings on her fingers. Everyone seemed as uncomfortable with the idea as I was. Even Chance shifted in his chair a bit, but nodded in agreement.

"The kind of prayer we are engaging in is warfare. We have to get battle-ready by shedding anything that will weigh us down—unconfessed sin keeps us from walking in the light."

I left that session committed to prepare for our confession night. I posted II Chronicles 7:14 on sticky notes on my computer screen, my bathroom mirror, and my windshield. I rehearsed God's instruction to humble myself, pray, seek His face, and turn from my wicked ways. Over time, I knew what God had called me to confess.

. . .

Chance and I walked the dogs at the park before the gathering. I confessed to him that I started out thinking the most painful thing about the evening would be that I would feel ashamed of my sin in front of other people. I admitted, however, that once I knew how God wanted me to respond, I ached with the pain of loss.

"Are you sure?" Chance asked.

"Yes. I'm sure. I've made it an idol."

Now I sat with my back to the flickering fire wondering if I could really do it. I watched the dogs wrestle in the grass. We had not brought the dogs to meetings before, but Nanette insisted it would be fine since we never met inside Julia's house. I smiled at the comfortable way they played together.

"Are we ready to get started?" Nanette sat at the head of the table.

Side conversations wrapped up and a hush fell over the group.

After opening in prayer, Nanette spoke. "God is calling us as a community of believers to raise the bar. Our numbers need to grow, but before we add to our number we must set aside our grumblings of anger and accusation as if 'they' are Berean Christian Academy and not 'we.' So tonight we will confess our sins individually even as we seek God to rescue us from our communal sins."

"I'll go first," Chance offered. He stood and wiped his hands on his pants. "It's always easy to spot problems in other people. It's clear how certain people have exchanged God's ways for football victories and naming rights. It's easy to point our fingers at them—er, to point my finger at them—as if I'm somehow superior. So, I confess my sin of pride and arrogance. I may have been treated unfairly, but I have not reflected Christ in my feelings, words, or actions toward John Clarke specifically. I commit to seeking God's face in praying for Mr. Clarke and BCA."

Chance sat down and Nanette patted him on the back. He let out a sigh. He sat a little straighter and the air around him felt lighter somehow. I fidgeted with my fingers in my lap and stole glances at the others around the table. Some twisted their hair, others tugged at their clothes, while others stared at their shoes.

It's time.

My stomach flitted and flipped. "I'll go next," I took a deep breath and reached into my bag at my feet.

A yip pulled my attention to the dogs. Piper splashed in the waterfall and bit at the stream of water flowing from the rocks. Ruby sat at attention in the grass with her head tilted like she wondered what had gotten into her friend.

"Piper!" I leaped to my feet and raced toward the waterfall. Piper looked up and stood like a statue in the water. "Get out of there!"

Piper jumped out of the waterfall and then shook the water from her coat. I cried out as the spray of water droplets soaked me. Chance walked up and Ruby hid behind his legs.

I looked across the yard at everyone staring at me. "I'm gonna go," I said. "You guys go on ahead. I'll share next time."

"This is just a distraction."

"It's not a distraction, it's a disaster. Piper has made a mess of everything. Plus, they don't really want me here anyway." I stabbed my thumb toward the patio and started to cry.

"It's only a little bit of water," Chance replied.

He didn't understand. Piper's actions reflected my own. A good group of people, united and following the Lord, sat at that table. My presence among them only made a mess of things. I was the distraction.

"Stay," I snapped at Piper who laid in the grass with her chin resting on her front paws folded one on top of the other. She looked up with repentant eyes.

I trudged over to the patio. "I'm sorry for the disruption. I'll get out of your way," I mumbled as I bent down and retrieved my bag from beneath the table.

When I stood upright, I flung my bag over my shoulder and stood face-to-face with Millie. She handed me a towel. "I confess I've been unforgiving and cruel."

I blinked.

"To you," she added.

My nose burned and tears dripped from my eyes. I sniffed and wiped at my nose with the towel. "But I made such a mess of things. You were better off before I ever came to BCA."

"I thought that for a while," she agreed. Her words came out uncharacteristically measured. "When they dismissed Mr. Easton, I couldn't understand what good more money for the preschool did us if we sacrificed the very people who fill the hearts and minds of children with truth. It felt personal."

I looked at my feet. I knew it. They were better off without me.

Millie leaned over and caught my gaze with her own and I lifted my head. "But like Mr. Easton, I chose to walk around in the dark asking God to shine a light on 'your' darkness. Tonight I confess my anger, blame, and unforgiveness. Will you forgive me?"

I felt my throat constrict. I blinked more tears from my eyes and nodded in agreement.

Millie wrapped her arms around me in a hug. "Good, because in my pettiness I've refused to make your banana pudding—and it's so delicious."

We all laughed together.

Jeremy stoked the fire while Liz gave Millie a side hug. Everyone returned to their seats around the table.

Chance returned to the patio and said, "I don't think Piper will try that again. Are you ready?"

I nodded and tucked my curls behind my ears. I reached into the bag hanging by my side and pulled out a piece of poster board I had folded into quarters to fit into the tote. I stood and let the empty bag fall in a heap at my feet.

"This is my vision board," I said as I unfolded it. "I made it in high school with my best friend and added to it over time. I've used it over the years to stay focused on my goals. In a roundabout way, it's what led me to BCA to begin with. I confess I've made my vision for my life an idol and haven't left room for God's vision."

I tore a corner off of the poster board. I smiled at Millie's gasp. She got it on some level. This was a heart-tearing of sorts. I turned and tossed the scrap into the fire behind me. "Tonight—" I said, tearing another chunk of the poster board, "—I give it all up to God. May His ways consume my life." I tossed that piece into the fire and watched as the flames devoured it.

Piece by piece everything went into the flames. Piece by piece I dedicated my past accomplishments and my future goals to the Lord.

The final fragment of the vision board I tossed into the flames held the picture of the kitchen table. From here on out, the only table I wanted to sit at was the table God prepared for me.

CHAPTER SIXTY

THE SECRET PRAYER MEETINGS played havoc with my diet. Each time we met, more and more people came, and the food table overflowed with more and more sugar-filled, carb-laden delights.

Several staff and teachers from BCA had joined our number, a few more parents, and some students, too. I saw Jackson and Olivia arrive hand-in-hand, and Olivia's ponytail swung back and forth with the same joyful energy she brought to each meeting.

When Jackson and Olivia first started coming to the prayer sessions, I worried John would find out and figure out a way to shut the whole thing down. Chance assured me that while Jackson loved his dad, he knew what kind of man he was. I remained skeptical. Chance still didn't know about John's affair with Maggie. I no longer kept the affair as a secret to promote or protect myself, but figured it still wasn't my story to tell.

Whether Jackson knew everything about his dad or not, he didn't reveal the underground prayer meetings to him. He did, however, recruit other students to come and pray for their school. I couldn't believe it. I never could have imagined young people giving up multiple evenings every week to gather with adults to pray for their school. I remember the middle school girls at camp getting excited about Bible study and prayer services, but I always chalked that up to "camp high." Some of the kids at our gatherings were more fired up than the adults. Even so, a good mix of kids and adults remained cautious in their engagement at the meetings, but I felt good about how things were going.

My hand hovered over the vegetable tray for the briefest of moments before I spotted the powdered sugar donuts. I didn't want to get the white coating all over my black sweater, so I shoved the whole mini donut in my mouth. I turned my back to the gathering to hide the fact that I barely had enough room in my mouth to chew.

I felt a tap on my shoulder. "Joy?"

I turned to face Maggie and Peter standing side-by-side, holding hands. My surprise induced a cough that spewed white powder from my mouth in a cloud. I held up one finger and choked down whole bits of donut and chased it with water from an open bottle I snatched from Chance as he walked up beside me.

Chance spoke as I gulped. "Mr. and Mrs. Hensley, what a n—"

"Shock," I interrupted with narrowed eyes. I didn't try to hide my sharp distaste. I couldn't pull my eyes away from their interlaced fingers.

"Can we talk to you alone before the meeting starts?" Peter asked. I looked over my shoulder away from Chance and refused to make eye contact with Peter.

I felt Chance touch the small of my back.

Be kind.

After several sessions of public confession, I praised God daily for the kindness and compassion showed by this growing remnant. Tender hearts and encouraging words made our meetings a safe place for more and more confession to take place. But every bit of joy and freedom God fanned into flame felt snuffed out by Maggie's presence.

I looked directly into Peter's eyes and said, "For you."

I clomped to an empty corner of the yard and wrapped my arms around myself. The chilled air penetrated my sweater as I stepped away from the fireplace.

Maggie spoke first. "Joy, I—"

I held up my finger, "I'm here for Peter."

Maggie pressed her lips together and gave two short nods and looked at Peter to continue. I hugged myself tighter and rubbed my hands on my arms to generate warmth.

"We've heard about what's been happening at these meetings," Peter began. "It seems like God is really healing BCA from the inside out."

"Mmhm." I scanned the yard and made note of who arrived.

I did not want to discuss the move of God with Peter while he held the hand of a traitor. He brought an enemy into the camp.

"Peter knows about my affair, Joy," Maggie blurted.

My eyes grew wide and I looked at Peter for confirmation. He squeezed Maggie's hand and attested to her statement with a nod of his head.

I didn't know what to say. I wanted him to know, but I wanted him to be as disgusted and angry with her as I was. "Finally," I muttered and shoved my hands in the front pockets of my pants.

"Maggie told me you've been bearing the burden of this secret for a while now."

"Yep."

"We've come tonight to publicly confess," Peter said.

The yard began to spin and I felt like I needed to sit down. So far I had listened to people I didn't know confess their hidden sins. Even what I had confessed so far was vague. What if Maggie's confession exposed me? What would Chance think of me then?

"But I wanted to ask for your forgiveness privately," Maggie added.

I looked at Peter as if he could guide me to the right response.

"I've forgiven her, Joy."

"Just like that?"

Peter huffed with a half-laugh and half-sigh. "No. Forgiveness is a choice *and* a process. But we want complete healing in our marriage, so we're going to add public confession to the therapy we're already participating in. Plus, we don't want our hidden sin to impact what God is doing at BCA, especially with Maggie's position on the board."

"Did you tell him who?" I scowled at Maggie.

Maggie's entire body slumped. "I know it was with John," Peter confirmed.

A crowd of students arrived and descended on the food table like a swarm of locusts. They laughed and shoved, completely oblivious to the tornado of emotions swirling in my corner of the yard.

"What about Jackson?"

"I'm not going to share publicly who it was with," Maggie said.

"Are you going to tell everyone I knew all along?"

"Of course not." Maggie sounded hurt.

"What exactly do you want me to forgive you for, Maggie?"

"I—"

I put my hand up. "You know what? Don't answer that. The meeting is about to start."

I started to walk away and Peter caught my arm. "Joy—"

"I'll get back to you," I patted Peter's hand. "I promise."

The grassy area of Julia's backyard held groups of people setting up camp chairs and laying out blankets. Nanette called the meeting to order and someone with a guitar started to play.

I tried to calm my spirit with deep breaths and surrender to the songs of praise lifted around me. My voice repeated the words of worship, but my mind flitted from scenes in my head to a dull gray nothingness.

After singing a few songs, Chance read Scripture aloud and then called for a time of public confession. I let out a trapped breath when several students stood to confess. The student confessions were always my favorite—so unrestrained.

Then Maggie stood and I sucked in and held my breath again.

"Hello. As most of you know, I'm Maggie Hensley and Peter and I want to thank you for welcoming us to this gathering this evening. I know they've been secret because of feared blowback from the board and administration. It is my full intention to keep them secret."

The audible collective sigh shifted the air in the yard. While God was showing up in big ways in the lives of the people gathered, they still feared future retribution—especially for their kids in the classroom and on teams.

"We're here tonight for more personal reasons," Maggie continued. "We agree that healing for the school starts with our individual healing. And we also agree that the enemy of our souls wants to keep us walking in darkness."

Several people agreed verbally with "amens" and "mmhms".

"I have been walking in darkness and want to confess my sin to bring it into the light. I have personally confessed to my husband and friends—"

Maggie allowed her gentle gaze to linger on me.

"—but I believe God is calling me to confess publicly and to ask your forgiveness. You placed your trust in me to serve as a board member of BCA. In that role, I am to seek God and His ways in my decisions. Instead, I elevated protecting myself and hiding my sin over truth. My desire is to seek forgiveness, but if after this, you believe I should step down from my position as a board member, I will do that."

A rumble echoed through the gathering. *She knows how to build the drama.*

"For the past year and a half—" Maggie paused and swallowed hard "—I have been having an affair. I have confessed this sin to my husband who has been gracious to forgive me and walk with me down the path toward restoration."

Maggie looked at Peter with a look of affection that matched his gaze toward her.

Maggie surveyed each person, "Please forgive me. I long for my marriage to be healed and for healing to come to our school."

I watched as some whispered to each other. Others plucked at the grass. Chance pushed his glasses up his nose and ran his fingers through his hair. Peter held Maggie's hand so tight his knuckles turned white.

Nanette rose and stood next to Maggie with an arm gripped around her waist. She called Peter to her other side with a wave of her hand. She pulled him tight to her other side in the same manner.

"Maggie, Peter, thank you for your display of courage and obedience. We know that God is faithful and just and will forgive you and purify you."

Nanette squeezed them tighter. "Is there any among us who refuses to forgive?"

Refuses. Is that what I'm doing?

"I know this is not easy for some of you. On previous nights, our confessions were personal to the one confessing, but not affecting all of us like this one. Maggie has said it. She was supposed to represent the needs of BCA in light of God's truth, yet she walked in darkness. But now you have a choice. You can, in turn, walk in darkness in unforgiveness, or you can join Maggie and Peter in walking in the light."

I had been building Maggie's judgment table in my mind for a while now. Detailed, intricate carvings graced the gavel. *God, I'm just supposed to let all this go?*

"God's ways are hard sometimes," Nanette continued. "Forgiveness is a big deal to God. I think you can see why. He endured great personal sacrifice to bring you forgiveness. So when He says that if you don't forgive others He won't forgive you, it's not because He's being petty—it's because it's important as a child of God to look and act like your Father. And Father God is a forgiving God."

Nanette called for everyone to circle up. As with every other meeting, those who confessed grouped in the middle for us to pray a prayer of blessing over them. I knew God wanted me to drop my gavel, but I had held it for so long, it felt comfortable in my hands.

I edged my way through the circle to join those standing in the middle. As I stepped up to Peter and Maggie, it felt surreal, like everything else faded away and the world spun in slow motion. I took a deep breath, dropped my gavel, grasped Maggie's hand with my right hand, and grasped Peter's hand with my left. And then I bowed my head.

CHAPTER SIXTY-ONE

WHEN NANETTE SAID "AMEN," people gathered their blankets and chairs, but lingered. I overheard some of the students talking about tests they had the next day, but they remained at the food table. I saw Jackson give fist bumps and he and Olivia waved to me as they left through the gate. Pockets of people continued to chat. It was like that every week. No one wanted to leave.

I grabbed a trash bag and walked up to people like a flight attendant collecting trash before landing. Jackson burst back into the yard with a slip of paper in his hand, wild eyes, and pale face.

"What is it?" Chance asked as he placed his hand on Jackson's shoulder.

"There's a pile of poop next to the driver's side door of my truck and this note tucked into the window. It says, 'You've really stepped in it.'"

"Eww," Liz said.

Millie's face puckered. "Who would do such a thing?" she asked.

"I think I have a pretty good idea," Jackson said. He furrowed his brow and Olivia touched his arm. "I overheard some of the guys talking about wanting to stand up to people who are against my dad's project. I didn't think anything of it because that's not what we're doing here, but obviously that's not what they think."

Chance and I exchanged glances.

"Oh!" Maggie's exclamation called our attention. "I just got a text from a friend on the board. They met tonight without me and crafted a letter forbidding groups of ten or more people to gather off campus without board approval if they're conducting BCA business."

Maggie touched her lips and looked at Peter with wide eyes. He rubbed the back of his neck.

"I see the email here," Liz confirmed as she tapped the screen on her phone. "Sent four minutes ago. It shows a unanimous vote with Maggie Hensley as absent."

"I knew this would happen. They know who we are and they're going to start targeting our kids," Millie lamented.

"Mrs. Hensley, do you think the board will fire us like they did Mr. Easton?" a preschool teacher asked.

"Not if I have anything to do with it," Maggie replied.

I pulled Nanette and Chance to a dark corner of the yard and asked, "What do we do now?"

Chance turned from our circle, tilted his head back, and blew out through pursed lips. Nanette looked at the ground, and her eyes darted back and forth.

"Why would the board of a Christian school block people from praying?" I asked.

Chance's face turned red, "Why would—"

"That's the wrong question," Nanette declared. "How can we play by their rules and keep praying? That's the question."

"I'm with Joy," Chance said. "Their demands are ludicrous."

"Chance, what we have going here is special," Nanette placed her hand on Chance's arm. "I don't want to stop, but I don't want to put the families at risk, either. I have an idea."

Nanette left our little circle and walked back toward the others in the yard. A low murmur came from those remaining. Nanette raised her voice, "Based on the guidelines from the board, the solution is to scatter."

My stomach fell. Scatter? I didn't want to scatter. There's strength in numbers. Isn't that giving in to the bullies?

"This way we are submitting to the authority over us and yet staying true to what God has called us to," Nanette continued.

"I agree with Nanette," Chance chimed in. My heart raced as I felt Chance gave in too quickly. "This solves a problem we've already identified. It's hard to invite new people to a group that's maxed out and intimidating because of the size."

Nanette clasped her hands to her chest. "It's settled. Give me a show of hands of those who are willing to host a group in their home."

I counted seven hands.

"Look around and see whose group you will join, and we'll stay in touch."

The previously vibrant atmosphere dissipated, taking away all the joy and vitality that had been present moments before.

"I'm confident this is part of God's plan. Let's trust Him, okay?" Nanette encouraged.

Mumbles of agreement rippled through the group as people trudged to their cars.

CHAPTER SIXTY-TWO

I DIDN'T BUY NANETTE'S THEORY that we would grow even more once we divided into seven groups. I joined Chance at his house. Nanette joined Maggie and Peter who volunteered to host a group at their home. Millie overcame her fear of retribution for her children and agreed to host a group at her home. Several other members of The Remnant opened their homes to groups.

The next Tuesday evening, as the sun was just beginning to kiss the rooftops, I parked Scarlett in front of Chance's detached garage and made my way to the front entryway. I turned at the sound of car doors slamming.

"Miss Swallow," Olivia called out with an energetic wave.

I stopped on the sidewalk and waited for her. A blonde woman and tall, thin man with short brown hair followed her. While Olivia wore a vintage Barbie graphic T-shirt, the couple with her looked like they were headed to a school event. The woman wore a long-sleeved BCA T-shirt and the man's green quarter-zip sweater had an embroidered BCA eagle near his left shoulder.

"Miss Swallow, these are my parents, James Conrad and Carla Stewart."

I extended my hand with a broad smile, "I'm so glad you could come. Olivia is precious."

Olivia's mom shook my hand and said, "My sister pays for Olivia to go to Berean. We're not into all this church stuff, but Olivia's been begging us to come for a while now."

"Oh," I struggled to find words. I looked to Olivia for help, but she looked at her shoes. "Well, to be honest," I shrugged, "what we've been doing is all pretty new to me, too. So, you're in good company."

I welcomed them into Chance's living room and glimpsed Chance rinsing a pitcher in the kitchen. Olivia's mom kept looking around the room like she might bolt any minute.

"Can I get you something to drink?" I asked.

"No, thank you," Olivia's dad said as he and Carla sat stiffly on the love seat.

Olivia slipped out the front door and reentered moments later with Jackson at her heels.

"Hey, there," Jackson greeted James with a handshake and Carla with a quick hug. "Glad you came."

Carla's expression softened and Jackson went into the kitchen to greet Chance and grab two bottles of water. When he returned to the living room, he handed the bottles to Olivia's parents who took them, removed the lids, and sipped.

Two other high school students and a single mom arrived. All had come to a meeting before except Olivia's parents. Chance and I acted as hosts and got everyone settled.

"I'm really glad you came," Chance began. "As many of you know, I'm no longer the Bible teacher at BCA, but God has laid it on my heart to join with all of you to pray for the future of the school."

"Why all the secrets?" James asked.

My shoulders tensed. Chance tilted his head and looked for clarification from James.

"Olivia tells me this—" James swept his hand around the circle "—is secret. I want to know why." James's jaw tightened.

I held my breath. Others shifted in their chairs. Olivia played with a hot-pink scrunchie on her wrist.

"I'll speak for myself," Chance answered. "I agreed to meet and pray for the school because I care about the students and the families. But if I'm completely honest, I also wanted God to straighten out administration. I believe they've put our school on a crooked path, and I wanted God to intervene."

"Wanted? Past tense?" James narrowed his eyes and leaned forward with both elbows on his knees.

Chance pushed his shoulders back and paused as if to consider his response. "Yes. Past tense."

What? What is he saying?

Chance took a deep breath. "When I started praying for BCA, I wanted to be proven right. I wanted God to show 'them' how wrong they were. But as usual, God's thoughts have proven to be higher than mine."

James raised one eyebrow.

"The more we prayed for our school, the more God revealed our prayers were not being answered because of our own unconfessed sin."

James huffed and rolled his eyes.

Chance continued, "God then called us to a season of personal confession. It's through this that I've learned to allow God to change me before I ask Him to change others."

"You still haven't answered my question. Why are they—uh—

were they secret?" James's sarcasm crackled like the half-empty water bottle he squeezed in his hand.

"Our meetings started out secret because we didn't want what we were doing to be construed as rebellious. It's radical, but not rebellious. God will begin to change the way people think. Some are threatened by that and will shift blame from God to innocent people. Some of the parents have indicated fear of retribution in the classroom or athletic teams for their students. Staff members fear losing their jobs."

"Like that would happen," James snorted.

"It happened to me." Chance stared at James with unblinking eyes.

James pursed his lips, but didn't say anything else.

"So, let's get started," Chance looked around the circle greeted by faint smiles and timid nods. Chance went on to describe the format for the evening—singing, Bible reading, personal confession, and then praying together for Berean Christian Academy.

James and Carla cupped their water bottles and sipped during the songs and Bible reading. When Chance called for personal confession, they shifted in their seats. Jackson's leg bounced and Olivia sat up straight and pulled her blonde ponytail through her hand. Her voice shook as she said, "Jackson and I have something we've repented of that we want to confess publicly."

Carla's head snapped toward her daughter. I recognized her "don't say anything" Mom look.

Jackson grabbed Olivia's hand as she continued, "Mr. Easton says part of repentance is confession. And—um—you have to know what you're turning from to—like—head in a new direction. Jackson and I have been coming for awhile now. We kind of thought—like—confession was for other people. And—like—what we've been doing isn't that bad, but —"

"Livvy—" Carla spoke up, but Olivia put her palm out to stop her.

"I'm sure you would call us 'good kids.' Like—some of you have called us that to our faces. But we want healing for our school and we don't want anything we're doing to stand in the way of that."

Olivia looked at Jackson, he gulped and he squeezed her hand and said, "Olivia and I have been lying—a lot." Jackson swallowed hard. "I tell my parents I'm at a friend's, and Olivia does the same, and we meet up to be together. We've even snuck out a few times in the middle of the night." Jackson leaned forward and turned his head to look at James and Carla. "God wants us to honor our parents—and—um—well—I'm sorry. And we're not gonna do any of it anymore."

Carla touched Jackson's leg and turned to look at James. James's neck turned red as he put the cap back on his empty water bottle and set it on the floor at his feet. Chance smiled at Jackson and Olivia.

"I've had enough," James slapped both thighs and stood. He grabbed Carla's hand and yanked her to her feet. "I don't know what kind of cult you guys have going here, but it's perfectly natural for young people to—to explore—and you're making them feel bad for it. I'm going straight to the board with this. Let's go, Olivia."

The screen door slammed behind them as James and Carla stormed out. Olivia looked at Jackson and then at Chance. Chance indicated she should leave with her parents with a slight nod. Tears streamed down her face as she shuffled out with shoulders slumped.

I sat and stared at my feet as an urge boiled up inside of me. I sprang to my feet and burst out the screen door after them. "Mr. and Mrs.—er—Carla. James. Wait!"

James spun around with fire in his eyes.

"Listen. I know this all seems strange, but I can personally attest to the freedom you feel on the other side of confession."

James pointed at me, "Listen, lady—"

"Daddy, please," Olivia cried.

My words rushed out before he could stop me—or leave. "I'm the poster child for doing things my own way. Even when I surrounded myself with people who knew more than I did, I would pick and choose which part of their advice to take."

I searched my mind for a good example.

"Like when I hired a dog trainer," I spouted. "The trainer gave me clear instructions and I would adjust them however I wanted. And it didn't work. Piper responded great to the trainer and not to me. I took it personally instead of seeing that I didn't really listen."

"You're equating what just happened in there with dog training?" James seethed.

"No. I mean—it's only an example of how we turn away from what's right. We do that with the Bible, too. We try to put our own spin on things, or cherry-pick the parts we think sound right. We're not really listening, and the chaos of our lives and lack of integrity shows it."

"Are you saying I lack integrity?"

"No, no. I'm saying I lacked integrity and could see it clearly in others, but not myself. And I sought wisdom from every source except God's Word and—"

"Miss Swallow, I've had enough. John Clarke was right." James took two steps toward me with his index finger pointed at my nose. "You and that Mr. Easton are nothing but trouble. BCA is better off without you. Stay away from Berean Christian Academy and stay away from my daughter." James grabbed Carla and Olivia by the hand and practically dragged them to the car.

As they sped away, I felt like someone had punched me in the gut.

I actually bent at the waist to try to catch my breath. What did he mean 'John Clarke was right'?

Chance and Jackson walked up behind me. "What happened?" Chance asked.

"I think I made it worse," I whispered.

I didn't want to voice my other fear in front of Jackson—that James was sent by John to spy and report back.

CHAPTER SIXTY-THREE

SO MANY CARS lined the street outside of Peter and Maggie's house that I had to park around the corner. I shut the driver's door to Scarlett and dug in my purse for the key fob to set the alarm and lock her doors.

I bumped into someone as I slung my purse over my shoulder. "Oh, I'm so sorry. I didn't even see you," I said as my cheeks flushed. I tucked a curl behind my ear and looked up to see I had run into BCA's Athletic Director, Jacob Vidal.

What is he doing here?

"Miss Swallow, right? I haven't seen you since the gala. John said you wouldn't be coming around BCA anymore."

I tried to decipher the meaning behind Mr. Vidal's words. His tone sounded friendly, but any mention of John Clarke set me on edge.

"I'm a personal friend of the Hensleys."

Saying those words—and meaning them—warmed me from the inside out. That feeling was short-lived as I looked over at Mr. Vidal and bristled. Did John send spies to every meeting?

One reason I came to Maggie's meeting tonight was because I wanted to tell Nanette in person about my encounter with Olivia's parents the night before. Another reason was because I hated splitting up. Once I reestablished the sense of family with these people, I didn't want to let it go to start over.

"Why are you here this fine evening?" I wanted to slap my forehead. *This fine evening? Could you sound any more fake?*

"One of my athletes invited me. I've never been to a prayer meeting before," he admitted.

At least he knows he's coming to a prayer meeting.

"How are you liking BCA?" I asked.

"Oh, I love it, everybody's been so supportive."

We walked by a house that looked like it came out of a horror film. Skeletons, gravestones, and spiderwebs filled the yard.

"What church do you go to?" I asked as we walked by another house with glowing jack-o'-lanterns lined up on the porch.

"No time for church. Too busy. I'm usually working on schedules on Sunday, but I might have to visit some churches in the area soon."

"Now that you're working for a Christian school?"

Mr. Vidal shook his head, "To recruit kids who might want to come to BCA."

We turned the corner onto the Hensley's street. We both had to step off the sidewalk as a young boy barreled toward us on his classic red, yellow, and blue Big Wheel trike.

I watched him career around the corner before I turned back and asked, "So what's your grand vision for the athletic program?"

Mr. Vidal laughed and tucked his hands in the front pockets of his jeans. "Are you writing an article, Miss Swallow?"

My cheeks burned and I tucked a curl behind my ear. "No. I just try to stay curious about leadership styles."

"I'm a simple guy. My vision is to win."

"Of course. I guess what I'm asking is what is your vision for the students. I've heard it said that athletics is a vehicle to gain access to students' hearts to develop their character," I offered.

"Exactly what inspiring greatness within is all about."

"The phrase you installed in the gym?"

"Yep."

I motioned to the Hensley's house across the street. We looked both ways before crossing the narrow street.

"Whose greatness are you inspiring?"

"The students', of course."

Maggie had her front porch decked out in fall mums and pumpkins. Her front door displayed a wreath made of faux autumn leaves and a sign that said "Welcome" in script font.

As we walked up to the door it flung wide open and Peter stood in the opening with a cheesy smile, "Greetings!"

I smiled and raised my hand in a brief wave, "Peter, have you met Mr. Vidal, BCA's new Athletic Director?"

Peter raised one eyebrow at me before pumping his arm, "Great to meet you. Welcome to our home."

"Thanks." Timidity replaced Jacob Vidal's confident demeanor as he leaned into the doorway.

"Coach! You came!" I heard a voice from inside. Mr. Vidal straightened and pushed his shoulders back. He shoved his left hand in his front pocket, waved, and sauntered into the house.

"Well, okay," Peter said.

"You think he's a plant?" I asked.

Peter shrugged, "I don't think it matters. What the enemy intends for evil God intends for good."

I shook my head and crossed my arms, "Well, we had a guy who came to our meeting last night who was definitely a plant. He mentioned John, called us a cult, and threatened to go to the board."

"He should have come to tonight's meeting then."

I furrowed my brow, "Why?"

"Because half the board is here."

"Really?" I leaned into the open doorway and looked around the room. I looked back at Peter and my mouth fell open. "How?"

"Oh, Joy," Peter gave me a side hug and shook me a little. "Our God is a God of miracles."

The house smelled of pumpkin spice. Maggie had an entire coffee bar with special syrups and sauces along with mini pumpkin Bundt cakes on a tiered platter. I fixed a cup of coffee, balanced a cake on a fall-themed napkin and gave a few lean-in hugs before settling into a corner chair. Nanette slipped into the seat next to mine and patted my leg. My anxiety about John planting spies diminished with Peter's encouragement and Nanette's presence. Now, I wanted to fade into the background and see what God might do.

Like so many nights before, I could feel the presence of God in the room—like if I opened my eyes during worship He'd be sitting right in front of me smiling. When the music tapered off, Maggie stood and called for a time of confession. She repeated the same instructions Nanette had given so many times. Her gift of communication rivaled her flair for hospitality.

It feels good to think nice thoughts about Maggie again.

God confirmed Peter's prediction when board members shared their sorrow for wandering from the ways of God in tears. Some confessed personal sins against their friends and family. Others confessed the ways they had not served BCA well.

"I confess I've slipped into humanism," one board member said. "And I know better. I've studied this." He put his head in his hands. The room remained quiet. Then he added, "How could we allow things like that phrase in the gym to stand? We've put our students at risk."

I had a clear view of Mr. Vidal situated behind the group of students. He had been silent all night, so perhaps the board member hadn't seen him. Perhaps he didn't care.

I saw Mr. Vidal lean forward with an elbow propped on one knee as he raised the other hand. "Excuse me," Mr. Vidal cleared his throat. "How does the phrase in the gym put our students at risk?"

The board member blew his nose into a tissue. "We're drawing them away from reliance on Christ and luring them into depending on their own strength."

Mr. Vidal opened his mouth, then closed it. He tapped a finger on his knee, then asked, "So, is that what humanism is?"

"Yes. Throughout history, humanism displaced the preeminence of Scripture with reliance on human intellect."

Some of the students shifted in their seat to see Mr. Vidal and the board member at the same time. Others played with their fingers in their laps.

A female student piped up, "Mr. Easton says it's the same strategy Satan used in the garden of Eden. Like, 'You don't need God, you are enough.' 'Forget God's words, He's holding out on you.' 'He's trying to limit you.' Stuff like that."

The board member smiled. The other students nodded. The rest of the room acted like they were watching a poker match—focused, quiet, and tense, with an occasional whisper in their neighbor's ear.

Nanette interjected, "At its core, it's putting faith in human effort over faith in God."

A shadow passed over Mr. Vidal's face. "I just wanted kids to be the best version of themselves."

The board member's head swished back and forth like windshield wipers in a rainstorm. "I'm not blaming you. I can tell you care about the kids. It's just the small things sometimes, that's where the enemy catches us. It's not your fault. We're supposed to keep an eye out for these things."

Nanette extended an open palm toward Jacob. "Coach Vidal, I don't mean to call you out on this, but may I ask whose greatness you're wanting to inspire?"

Mr. Vidal's head remained tilted toward the floor. The corners of his mouth curved up and he lifted his eyes to mine before shifting them toward Nanette. "Interesting you should ask that. Someone else asked me that recently, but now I'm beginning to think my answer is wrong."

Nanette surveyed Mr. Vidal with her head tilted and her hands folded in her lap. I felt for the guy. As a former victim of Nanette's probing and uncomfortable questions followed by long silence, I knew there was no escape.

Mr. Vidal shifted his gaze toward the floor and then back to Nanette. "I want to inspire greatness within the students. I think they all have value and potential, and I want to bring that out in them," he muttered.

"So does God," Nanette said.

A quick scan around the room showed more than one person with their head bowed and lips moving silently in prayer.

"Then where did I go wrong?" Mr. Vidal pleaded with his eyes and his tone.

"The problem with humanism isn't where it starts, it's where it ends up. Ultimately, when you take humanistic thinking all the way out, it says you have everything you need within you. And if you have everything you need within you, you don't need God. And if you don't need God, you don't need to study a book about Him. Eventually, the Bible is disregarded completely," Nanette explained.

Mr. Vidal's eyes widened and he raised his palms, "That is *not* where I was going with that."

"I believe you," Nanette said. "But the Bible teaches that all of the treasures of wisdom and knowledge are hidden in Christ. Not in ourselves."

Mr. Vidal stared at the floor and blinked a few times. He furrowed his brow and nodded.

Nanette turned to Maggie and asked, "Shall we pray for the school now?"

When the meeting ended and people stood in small groups, I brushed past a group of students when one reached out and grabbed my elbow. "Do you know how we could get into the gym?" one of the boys whispered.

"Um—I don't think so. Why?"

"We think it's time to take a stand. We've been wanting to paint Bible verses over that phrase in the gym, and—well—after tonight, we just have to."

"Isn't that vandalism?" I asked with a tilt of my head.

One of the girls shook her head, "It's civil disobedience."

"Yeah. We've been learning about that in history," a boy added.

"Plus, we don't want to make a mess of it, we want to make it better and take back the messaging of our school like that board member said. Isn't that what we've been doing all along in these prayer meetings?"

I couldn't argue with that. "Let me check with Mr. Easton."

After a few texts back and forth I confirmed that Mr. Easton still had a key card, but had no idea if it still worked.

"He really doesn't think it will," I warned.

"It's worth a shot." The kids all murmured their agreement. "Can you meet us tomorrow night at 9 p.m.?"

"I'll be there," I said as I felt someone touch my arm. I glanced over my shoulder to see Mr. Vidal. My mouth went dry and my eyes widened.

"I'm heading to my car and thought I'd offer to walk you to your Jeep."

"Um—" I couldn't find my words.

"I know if my wife were parked around the corner after dark, I'd appreciate someone walking with her."

"Of course. Yes. Thank you." I turned to the kids with a knowing look, "See you soon."

As we stepped out on the front porch, the brisk air took my breath away. I zipped my jacket and skipped down the steps after Mr. Vidal.

We walked past three houses before I said, "You seem quiet."

"That was quite an experience."

"What did you think of it?"

"I'm not really sure. I'm gonna have to process it some more."

We walked past a house with the empty Big Wheel tipped over in the grass.

"You handled the humanism conversation well," I said.

"Yeah. I need to process that, too. I don't normally handle situations like that so calmly. I don't know what came over me. It's like there was a hand on my shoulder telling me to just listen." He shook his head as if he'd walked through a mess of cobwebs. "That sounds crazy."

"Not at all."

CHAPTER SIXTY-FOUR

CHANCE AND I WALKED UP TO THE GYM DOOR and students came out of the shadows like they were special forces operatives. To them this was an adventure. I couldn't decide if this was an adventure or an escapade, but I had roped Chance into it as well.

"Thanks for coming, Mr. Easton," the kids whispered. I saw the students from the meeting at Maggie's along with Jackson, Olivia, and a few others who had attended past prayer meetings.

"Isn't that a camera?" I asked pointing to a device aimed at the very door we were trying to break into.

"It's okay, Miss Swallow," one of the students said. "We're ready to take full responsibility. But we'd rather ask for forgiveness than permission."

I shot a worried glance at Chance. He smiled and shrugged, "What are they gonna do—fire me?"

I took a deep breath as Chance walked up to the door and swiped his key card.

Red light.

A moan rose up from the group. "Aw, man!"

"I was afraid of that," Chance said.

"Having some trouble?" a voice came from behind us.

I whirled around to see Mr. Vidal standing in the parking lot. My stomach sank to my feet. He must have overheard our plans the night before.

"Mr. Vidal, I can expl—" I began.

He held up his hand, walked up to the door, swiped his key card, and held the door open, "After you."

Everyone in the group stood immobile and stole glances at each other. Jackson moved first, "Thanks, Coach," and sauntered inside. The rest of us followed.

Mr. Vidal propped open the doors between the lobby and the gym and turned on the lights. The large halogen bulbs came to life bit by bit. The bleachers were open and empty. The floor gleamed. Smiles and fierce expressions looked down on us from the senior athlete banners.

I gazed at the phrase "Inspiring Greatness Within" and saw the danger it posed in a whole new way. This must have been the same feeling Chance had when I tried to get him to agree to naming Clarke Field. He knew something I didn't know that day. I was glad to know more today than yesterday.

"Before I let you go and start painting my gym, I need to know the plan," Mr. Vidal said.

"I brought the drop cloths," a boy piped up.

"And I brought the paint," another said.

Olivia rolled her eyes at the boys and shook her head. She flipped her ponytail and stepped forward, "The plan—" she emphasized the word and shot another glance at the eager boys "—is to paint over—

um—your phrase." Olivia's words trailed off and her neck turned red. She paused and kicked the toe of her shoe on the gym floor.

"Go on," Mr. Vidal prodded.

"We plan to protect the floor and tape out a rectangular section that we'll paint in Eagle green. My aunt helped me cut letters on her vinyl cutter so they'll be nice and crisp." Olivia's words began soft and meek and ended strong and decisive.

"What phrase did you choose?" Mr. Vidal asked.

Jackson spoke up, "We chose words out of First Corinthians. It's five phrases actually. Be on your guard. Stand firm in the faith. Be courageous. Be strong. Do everything in love."

Mr. Vidal slowly nodded.

"We want this to become our new student code of conduct."

Mr. Vidal looked up at his slogan and then back at Jackson.

"We have ideas if you'd like to hear them," Jackson added with earnestness.

"I think I would very much like to hear them. But for now, you guys have a job to do. That paint has to dry before you can slap vinyl on it, so you better get after it. I'll be in my office if you need me."

Mr. Vidal walked back into the lobby toward his office.

One of the boys ducked into a janitor closet and retrieved a ladder. The students began taping a large rectangle on the wall around the phrase John and Mr. Vidal had revealed a couple of months prior. Olivia consulted a sheet with measurements and barked orders to those measuring and taping. Chance and I pitched in and filled paint pans.

After the first coat of green, Chance and I made a run to Taco Bell for provisions. The second coat of paint covered perfectly. The kids set a timer and sat down to play cards. A few of them laid their heads on bunched up sweatshirts and took a nap.

I wandered over to the bleachers and sat down. I watched Chance play cards with the kids. After a couple of rounds, he came over and plopped down next to me.

"Watcha thinkin?"

I swiveled on the bleacher to face Chance and pulled one leg under me.

"I'm thinking about the words these kids are about to put up on the wall. Every interaction I've had with BCA up to this point has been the opposite.

"I was not on my guard.

"I did not stand firm in my faith.

"I was not courageous.

"I was not strong.

"I did not do everything in love."

Chance furrowed his brow and pinched his lips, "You're being too hard on yourself."

"I'm not," I said with my head down as I played with my fingers. "You don't know everything."

"I'm listening if you want to tell me."

I refused to lift my head. "I'm afraid."

"Of what?"

I looked directly into Chance's blue eyes. "That once I tell you the whole truth it will be a final blow to our friendship that proves fatal."

Chance held my gaze, "If I've learned anything over these past weeks of prayer and confession it's that God's a forgiving God and expects me to follow suit. I can't promise exactly how I'll react, but I can promise my eyes are fixed on Jesus and not you."

I turned and placed my feet flat on the step under me. I stared blankly at the big green rectangle drying on the opposite wall. I didn't deserve to be in this place. God was so gentle in leading me to this moment despite my blindness.

"Maggie's affair was with John Clarke and I knew about it from the beginning."

Chance blew out a long breath through pursed lips. He leaned back and propped his elbows on the bleacher behind him. He did not turn to look at me, but stared straight ahead.

"Wow. Okay. Wow," Chance said.

"John didn't know that I knew for the longest time, and Maggie insisted that the pro bono project for BCA was the best choice for my career because it was for a contest that included podcast and magazine promotion as well as a personal retreat with Julia Coates. I knew Maggie believed in me because she loaned me fifty thousand dollars to make up for the time I'd be spending on the BCA promotion video."

My words came out fast and furious.

"I've gone over it a thousand times in my head. If I could go back and tell Maggie to 'shove it' once I uncovered her affair, would I? I don't think I would. Because then I would never have met you and—"

I turned to look at Chance. He continued to focus his gaze on the students playing cards.

"—and your relentless commitment to biblical worldview. Which led me to Nanette. And then you welcomed me into The Remnant. And God has seen fit to bring me all of these good things in spite of me."

I turned back to watch the students and let out a long sigh. Chance's hand on top of mine startled me. "And I'm glad he did."

I wanted to leave the story there—and leave my hand there—but the whole truth had yet to be revealed. And I needed to reveal the whole truth. I slipped my hand out from under his.

"I wish that was all."

"Okay."

My spigot of words opened full throttle again. "John found out that I knew about the affair and got me booted from the project. But he broke up with Maggie soon after and she invited me to finish it out to spite him. I ended up winning the contest, but the joke was on Maggie and me because John had lied to Maggie about what the contest was really for."

"I really don't like that guy," Chance seethed.

"Yeah. Me either. It gets worse, though. It was in San Francisco at the reveal of the contest winners that John told me that the fifty thousand dollars Maggie loaned me was really his money and he was calling my loan immediately."

"Did you still have the money?"

"Not all of it. So, I leveraged what I knew about John and Maggie to secure the marketing consultant position for the gala. I knew I could raise way more money than you guys had in the past and then I could repay my debt, still work with you, help BCA, and hopefully launch my career as planned."

"You blackmailed John."

"Yes."

I knew it. This was the end of our friendship. He called it. Even in my confession I wouldn't name what I had done. Chance couldn't associate with someone like me. He deserved better anyway.

"Ha ha! I win again!" one of the students shouted. He slammed his cards to the floor in victory. "It's you and me, Clarke, for the championship."

A timer alarm sounded. "We'll have to finish this later, man," Jackson shrugged. "We've got a job to finish."

"I would have beat you. In fact, let's just say I won."

Both boys laughed and slapped each other on the backs as they got up from the floor. Olivia laid out the vinyl phrases in order of installation.

"But John helped you." Chance's words encouraged me to continue.

"That's what I mean, though. I was not on my guard. I didn't calculate the cost of working with someone like John. And I didn't stand firm in the faith. I stood firm in my dream of sitting at tables with people of influence. That's why I burned my vision board. My vision caused me to blur the lines."

"And cross them."

A tear slipped down my cheek and I tucked my chin to my chest. "Yes. And cross them."

"Is John the one who got you to ask me to change my stance on naming the field?"

"Yes, but I truly didn't understand where you were coming from at the time. All I could see is that it would benefit Berean Christian Academy. I see it differently now, if that counts for anything at this point."

Chance stood up and stretched his shoulders back. He reached out his hand, "It counts. Let's finish helping these kids stand firm in their faith."

CHAPTER SIXTY-FIVE

CHANCE, NANETTE, AND I huddled by a service door at the back of the gym. The only sound came from the chatter of our teeth. I tugged at the zipper of my coat as if it could go any higher than the very top. I tucked my chin into the neckline and breathed hot air into the cavity to warm my neck. Almost immediately the cold crystallized the warm wet air and I had to breath out again. I couldn't tell whether the shiver down my spine was a result of the cool breeze, or the anticipation of what was to come.

I got Mr. Vidal's text over an hour before. *We got trouble. Call me immediately.*

My hands shook as I tapped his number. A thousand options spun through my mind. Mr. Vidal got canned. The school was on fire. The students—

"Hello?"

"Um—Coach Vidal, hey, it's me. What trouble?"

"My phone was ringing when I walked into the office this morning. Dr. Scott called an emergency all-school meeting. I was literally hanging up when John stormed into my office promising to 'get the little vandals' that painted over my sign," Mr. Vidal said.

"You didn't—"

"Ah, I didn't have the heart to tell him."

I didn't muffle my sigh of relief.

"Anyway, I'm not sure how all of this works, Miss Swallow, but if you have some friends who want to come and do that prayer thing you did the other night, I think this might be a good time."

"Mr. Clarke won't allow us anywhere near that assembly to pray," I scoffed.

"You're probably right. So, why don't we do this? You gather up your friends and meet me at the service door at the back of the gym at 9:50. It leads to a space under the bleachers. You'll be able to hear everything, but he won't know you're in the room."

"Why are you doing this?"

"You know, I'm not really sure. It just seems like the right thing to do."

"You realize John may pull his funding for the new field."

"Maybe. But there's somethin' about those kids you brought in last night. They have the kind of greatness in them that I want to foster—and John Clarke doesn't."

Images flashed in my mind like a social media reel. John Clarke flashing his charming white smile. Olivia and Jackson laughing with heads tilted as Piper jumped all over them and licked their faces. John working the room at his lake house. The students holding hands and praying at a backyard meeting. John sneering in my face in his driveway. The students working together to paint the gym.

I agreed to meet Coach Vidal at the service door and ended the call. Then the scramble ensued. Chance, Nanette, and I got on a group call where we decided to contact all the people from our prayer meetings. Parents wouldn't have to hide. Berean Christian Academy had a standing policy that parents were allowed at any public gathering. At least that policy hadn't changed yet.

We divided the list and started reaching out. Many of them said it was too short notice, but a good number headed straight to BCA. Some even said John Clarke had already invited them to attend.

Chance, Nanette, and I rode together to the school. I called Maggie on the way.

"What do you think John's up to?" I asked after I had filled her in on the details.

"I really don't know, Joy. I know he likes to be in control—pulling all the strings. I'll be praying, but I don't think I should go. Let's see what he's up to first."

We stayed in hustle mode all the way to the school parking lot. "Did you get a hold of so and so?" "What do you think this is all about?" "Why would John call some, but not all of the parents?" "Do you think the staff's jobs are at risk?" "Father God, be with us all."

All the words had been said by the time we stood shivering outside the service door. Mercifully, the door creaked open and Jacob Vidal greeted us with a whispered "good morning" and a smile. He cautioned us to watch our footing as we climbed over the support structure undergirding the bleachers.

Mr. Vidal left us amidst dust bunnies and a smattering of candy bar wrappers and empty chip bags. I spotted long horizontal cracks of light between where the seats of the bleachers met the risers. I creeped forward to find a spot I could peek through. I only saw the feet of students finding their seats. The hushed rumble of their conversation stood in stark contrast to the easy banter and laughter I heard at the last assembly I attended.

I climbed over the scaffolding to get to a place where two sections of bleachers met. The vertical space between the bleachers provided the view I sought. Dr. Scott stood at the podium. John stood to his right and Olivia's father, James, stood to John's right. A board member I recognized from the prayer meeting at Maggie's stood to Principal Scott's left. He stood with hands clasped behind his back, his chin protruding forward, and a smug look on his face.

Someone sat down and blocked my line of sight. I shifted to my left and whacked my shin on a metal bar. I swallowed a yelp and rubbed my leg until the sting subsided. I looked back at Nanette and Chance who held hands with heads bowed. Their mouths moved, but I couldn't hear them. I carefully chose a new spot with a clear line of sight to the podium. Mr. Vidal walked up and shook hands with those gathered and stood on the other side of the board member.

A few parents arrived and shook hands with the line of men. John's broad smile dimmed when parents from our prayer meetings walked in and shook his hand.

The principal cleared his throat and made a palms-down motion in the air to quiet the chatter. "Students, staff, and parents, thank you for gathering today on such short notice." His tone was gracious, but his attention was on a stack of papers on the podium. He picked up the papers, tapped them on the surface to align them, and laid them back down. He gripped the sides of the podium and turned to look at John. John nodded. The principal blinked twice, cleared his throat again, turned to the crowd and said, "Today, I have called all of you—"

"Excuse me, Dr. Scott?"

I couldn't see where the voice came from, but it sounded like a student. John frowned and Dr. Scott blinked several times.

"Dr. Scott, we didn't open in prayer. As the student chaplain I'd be happy to open in prayer if you'd like me to."

I swung around and looked at Nanette and Chance with wide eyes. Nanette closed her eyes, tilted her head back and mouthed, "Thank you, Father," and pumped her fists in victory.

"Um. Er—" I watched the student walk up to Dr. Scott and stand there. I recognized the boy as Elliot from our prayer meetings. Dr. Scott blinked again and backed into John to make room for Elliot to step up to the microphone.

Elliot stepped up to the microphone and bowed his head, "God, You're all powerful, all knowing, and completely trustworthy. Thanks for inviting us to be a part of what You're doing at BCA. Be with us today. We just want to please You. In Jesus's name. Amen."

Amen.

"Um. Thank you, Elliot," Dr. Scott said as he leaned into the microphone. He straightened his tie and looked at John again, but John leaned toward James, who whispered in his ear.

Dr. Scott cleared his throat, "It has come to our attention that someone broke into Berean Christian Academy and vandalized our school. As you can see by the wall behind me, Mr. Vidal's slogan has been painted over. We have reason to believe a group of our own students has perpetrated this crime. We ask that the guilty party please step forward."

I turned to look at Chance and Nanette who blew out silent breaths through pursed lips. I wondered what the kids would do. They said they would take responsibility. The bleachers creaked as people shifted in their seats.

John leaned over and whispered into Dr. Scott's ear. "Yes. Right," Dr. Scott said to John and then leaned into the microphone. "Mrs. Carrol are you in here? Ah, yes. There you are. Could you please go check the tapes?"

"Now?" I heard Molly ask.

Dr. Scott looked at John who straightened his shoulders and swept a hardened gaze across the stands, "We'll wait."

My heart nearly stopped. Not only would those tapes reveal the identity of the students involved, but Mr. Vidal, Chance, and myself. Mr. Vidal stood expressionless.

It felt like Molly might never return. My nerves were raw. What was I doing here anyway? How did this become my fight?

I knew how.

This had become a family to me. What The Remnant had at BCA was special and worth fighting for. I felt so connected to this place now. The BCA family Peter described during my mentorship with Maggie I had now experienced for myself.

I waffled between wanting to protect my new family and sticking my fingers in my ears. I purposefully kept away from some of the conversations that had started bubbling up at our prayer meetings. Real fervor grew around protecting the teachers and staff and returning to the guardrails that made BCA so unique — things like only hiring Christians and not accepting donations in exchange for naming rights.

The opening of the gym door broke through the uncomfortable silence. Molly's high heels clacked as she walked toward the podium. John stepped forward and raised his hands, "Well?"

Molly stopped and looked at her shoes, "The cameras didn't record last night."

"What?" John didn't hide his incredulity.

"The system's been a bit glitchy lately. I'll put in a service request to IT," Mr. Vidal offered.

I smiled to myself.

John huffed and waved his hand, "Well, it's obvious someone vandalized this gym. The evidence is right before our eyes." His voice was a little too loud and his hand motion a little too fierce. John Clarke teetered on the edge. "And that's not all. Dr. Scott, go on."

John returned to his position between James and Dr. Scott. He stood with his legs shoulder width apart and his hands clasped behind his back as if in roll call at boot camp.

"Yes. Um. Well, it has also come to our attention that students and parents have been gathering in direct opposition to the directive from the board. Mr. Dawson, would you please speak to the board's concerns here?"

"Gladly," the board member changed places with Dr. Scott. Mr. Dawson could straighten his shoulders all he wanted. He would still be a good four inches shorter than Dr. Scott. The podium only amplified the deficit in stature. The microphone screeched as Mr. Dawson pulled it down to speak into it. "It is the opinion of the board that this act of vandalism is an outcropping of the ongoing subversive meetings carried out by former staff and consultants of Berean Christian Academy. These people have led our students, parents, staff, and even board members astray, and it has to stop."

I backed away from my viewing station and climbed over pipes to cower in a dark corner. I pulled out my phone and turned down the brightness of the screen and tapped out a frantic text message to Maggie. I tried to send her word-for-word what Mr. Dawson had said even as he continued to pontificate.

"There have been reports of disparaging key donors, maligning our staff, and participating in cult-like activities. I realize we all come from different backgrounds and religious practices, but as a school that bears the name of Christ, we need to avoid the appearance of impropriety. These actions are a poor representation of Berean Christian Academy."

I tucked my phone into my back pocket and wedged myself back into a position to see the podium.

"I attended one of these so-called prayer meetings," Mr. Dawson continued. "It was merely a ruse to provide cover for the real discussion of overriding the board and administration. I say to you staff members who have perpetuated this malcontent, you are in a position of leadership and should use better judgment. To you students who have been swept into this defiance, you have been misled. And to you parents, we covet your partnership. It is an act of protection of the board that we demand these meetings cease."

Mr. Dawson stepped back from the podium and bowed his head to Dr. Scott with a formality that seemed out of place. He returned to the spot between Mr. Vidal and the podium.

John whispered in Dr. Scott's ear before he stepped back up to the microphone. He lifted the microphone with another screech. "We are not going to leave this gym until we know who vandalized it."

John jutted out his chin and smirked.

"Excuse me, Dr. Scott," the voice sounded like Jeremy from The Remnant, but I couldn't see him. "Mr. Dawson questioned the motivation of our prayer meetings. As a point of clarification, we've been praying for the light of Christ to shine brighter than anything else. Unless you want to shine brighter than Christ, we have not been praying against you."

I struggled to swallow the giggle that arose in my throat.

John shot a stern look at James who walked up to the microphone. "I'm James Conrad. I am the president of the Parent Teacher Association here at BCA. My daughter, Olivia, is a junior and co-captain of the cheer squad. We need to stand in solidarity behind our hardworking teachers and staff—especially our newest members of the BCA team like Coach Vidal here." James nodded to Mr. Vidal with a smile. "And as such, we should—"

"Even if they're not Christians?" an adult female voice questioned from the stands.

James stood speechless.

"Because BCA has always been committed to hiring qualified teachers, staff, and coaches who actively follow Him," the voice added.

John whispered into Dr. Scott's ear and nudged him with his elbow.

Dr. Scott stepped up to James's side and leaned into the microphone, "We're still committed to hiring Christian teachers."

"No offense to Coach Vidal, but he told me himself his faith was a low priority," a male voice rang out.

Jacob Vidal continued to stand motionless and expressionless.

John wedged himself in front of the microphone. "Our student athletes need to win games to prepare them for opportunities in college. And I think it's offensive to question someone else's faith in such a public way."

"The Bible says a little yeast leavens the whole loaf."

John smirked, "If I remember correctly, your students are still in elementary grades, right? You'll understand better when they're older."

"Yeah!" a male voice shouted from the stands. "Coach Vidal's already made a huge difference for our family. Not only are we winning games, but we've had more college recruiters seeking out our players."

Mr. Vidal gave a slight nod toward the male voice.

"See. That's what I'm talking about. We brought our kids to BCA because of its commitment to God's way, not the world's way. And is anyone going to point out that the supposed vandalism was to paint over a worldly phrase and replace it with Scripture?"

"The ends don't justify the means," Dr. Scott said. John clapped his hands in approval.

My blood boiled. I wanted to jump out of the shadows and shout, "You hypocrite!"

"We want to be known for loving Jesus and thinking His thoughts, not our own," a student voice rang out.

John marched back to the podium and Dr. Scott stumbled back to make room for him. John leaned in until his lips almost touched the microphone. "It's time to stop the nonsense. I'm looking at you, parents and staff. We are leading these students into chaos. If we can't find unity on this, I'll have no choice but to pull my funding. I don't want to do that to Coach Vidal who has big dreams, or our kids who have bright futures. We are a family and need to start acting like it. It's time to join together, not tear each other apart."

John said all the right things. Kids first. Unity. Family. John used the same words Nanette used in our prayer times, but for him they were just talking points. The only unity he wanted was people united around his way of thinking.

"What do you know about acting like a family?" Jackson's words rang out and it sounded like everyone in the room gasped at the same time.

John's eyes grew wide, then blazed with fury. "Son, this is not the time," John waved his hand as if to dismiss Jackson.

I watched Jackson and Olivia approach the podium hand-in-hand.

"Dr. Scott, we painted over the slogan," Jackson said.

"And me," I heard feet slam as someone jumped from the bleachers.

"I was there, too," I heard feet barreling down the steps above my head.

A few more "me, toos" rang out and John and James both turned the shade of an overripe tomato. Dr. Scott blinked and blinked at the pack of students before him, then looked at John and blinked and blinked.

"I'm disappointed in you, Jackson," John growled.

The doors from the gym lobby opened and Maggie and every member of the board walked in with her—minus Mr. Dawson who I didn't think could appear much smaller, but managed to shrink before my eyes.

"Mr. Clarke," Maggie said with pursed lips. "I'm not sure what you're trying to accomplish here today, but the board just met and agreed to remove you from your position as Booster Club President on the grounds that you are using your influence to subvert the convictions of Berean Christian Academy. We have also reinstated our policy of not attaching naming rights to any donations to BCA."

Chance, Nanette, and I scrambled from beneath the bleachers to watch the scene unfold. We stood at the opposite end of the gym from Maggie and the board. Murmurs rumbled through the stands and John's eyes swept across the room.

John saw us, narrowed his eyes, and pushed his shoulders back. "Then I'm pulling my funding," John said as his eyes bore a hole through mine.

"That is your prerogative, Mr. Clarke. We have faith that God will provide what we need."

"You're being short-sighted and vindictive, Mrs. Hensley," John seethed.

"No, sir. We have our eyes firmly fixed on Jesus who emptied Himself of the honor due Him to serve those He loves."

John looked to the stands as if seeking defenders. Then he looked over his shoulder at James who looked at his feet. "Jackson, let's go," John said with a huff as he shook his head and raised both arms in mock surrender.

"Sorry, Dad. I still have work to do here. With the board all here, the students want to see if they'll agree to our new student code of conduct."

John stood and stared at his son for long enough that even I started to feel uncomfortable. I wriggled and shifted, but Jackson held his ground. John turned his head toward Jacob Vidal. "Coach, I apologize for the actions of my son and the so-called Christians around here. I got you into this mess. I'll be happy to use my connections to get you out of it."

"No need, Mr. Clarke. I'm with them. They didn't vandalize the gym, I let them in."

Astonishment, then humiliation, then anger flashed across John's face.

"You have a remarkable son, John Clarke," Mr. Vidal continued. "He will be a greater legacy for you than any turf field ever could."

John Clarke let the door slam behind him and the entire gym erupted in applause.

CHAPTER SIXTY-SIX

MY STANDING MIXER RAN AT FULL BLAST. I didn't hear the notification bell on my oven to tell me it had come to temperature because my music also played at full blast. Piper came into the kitchen and barked at me. Piper rarely barked in the house.

"What?"

Piper barked again.

I muted the music and turned off the mixer and heard the ring of the doorbell.

"Oh. Thanks," I told Piper as I wiped my hands on the black apron Aunt Mimsy gave me for Christmas that read, "Don't Worry, I Can Do This. I Watched a YouTube Video."

I opened the door and almost fainted. Julia Coates stood on my doorstep. Her beauty and presence captivated me as it had every other time we'd met. She topped her black, full-length wool-blend coat with a black scarf looped and tightened around her neck. A black Lady Dior handbag hung from the crook of her left arm. With her right hand she took off her large black sunglasses and smiled, "Hello, Joy."

I bumbled my words and eventually mumbled some semblance of a greeting and welcomed her inside. I took her coat, scarf, and bag and laid them on the guest room bed, wishing I had a coat rack or closet of some sort. Of course, I rarely had guests and I had never offered to take anyone's coat before.

"Can I get you some tea?"

"That would be lovely."

I used the time it took to fill my electric kettle with water, bring it to temperature, and steep my favorite loose-leaf blend to think through what to say next. I eliminated "What brings you to the neighborhood?" "What a pleasant surprise," and every version of hello that required a British accent. The phrase "What say you, madam, on a day such as this?" actually passed through my mind.

I went with, "It's so good to see you again, Mrs. Coates." I handed her the steeped tea with a spoonful of honey stirred in and perched in the armchair across from the corner of the couch where she sat.

"Please call me Julia."

I crossed and uncrossed my legs. "How are you?" I asked as I sipped my tea.

"You mean since I had to fire my Chief Marketing Officer?"

I choked on my tea and fought to keep from spewing it all over Julia's lap.

Julia's hand covered my knee. "It's always best when the light shines in the darkness, no matter how inconvenient," she encouraged.

"I heard Maggie stepped into that role and she and Peter are moving to San Francisco," I said, wiping the back of my hand across my chin.

"Yes. I'm delighted. Now to install a new Director of Marketing for the Boise location."

I coughed and sloshed some tea on my pants. "You want me to be the Director of Marketing for the Boise location?" I blurted.

"No."

I felt heat rise in my cheeks and I jumped to my feet. "I need more honey. Do you need more honey?"

"No, thank you," Julia called over her shoulder.

I walked into the kitchen and added honey to my tea. I swirled the spoon and took a few deep breaths to calm my swirling thoughts.

"Tell me about the project John planned to fund at BCA," Julia prompted as I returned to the living room.

I planted myself near the edge of my chair and straightened my back. I tucked a curl behind my ear and launched into the details of the sports complex. Julia sipped her tea as I described the turf field, updated visitor stands, new bathrooms, new concession stand, updated press box, and new lights and scoreboard John had planned.

I took a risk and added, "But the real opportunity is to finish funding the new preschool."

Julia raised her eyebrows. "Oh?"

"No one ever wants to fund a preschool except the parents of preschoolers who generally can't afford it because they're still early in their careers. By the time they have more disposable income, the money goes to shiny projects like athletics."

"You don't think the updated sports complex is a good idea?"

"I wouldn't go that far. While I didn't appreciate John's tactics, I always thought the sports complex was a good idea. I think both projects would attract new families to BCA. An investment in either project will give BCA access to the hearts of students and families.

And with a renewed commitment to their roots, real transformation is possible.”

"How would you describe its roots?”

I snuggled back into the armchair and encircled my mug with both hands.

"Rooted in Christ and loyal to God's way of seeing things both in leadership and the classroom. I've never seen such courage in the face of real opposition. There is a remnant of Christ-followers at BCA who stood firm in their faith in love—staff, students, and parents alike. Not everyone's happy about it, but the tide is definitely shifting.”

"What do you think about that?”

I shrugged, "When I was a kid I only thought of myself." I let out a chirp of a laugh. "Who am I fooling? I still fight the urge to only think of myself.”

Julia smiled and I continued, "The students inspire me. And I've learned so much being around everyone at BCA. I know transformation is possible because I'm transformed.”

I found myself looking off into the distance, enveloped in my own thoughts and memories. When I "came back" Julia sat with proper posture and her mug resting in her lap. Even in my plain living room she looked elegant. Her silence made me nervous, so I added, "You've got an amazing best friend, by the way.”

"She thinks quite highly of you, too.”

I leaned over and straightened the rug at my feet. I sat up and twirled a curl of my hair around my finger. "Are you thinking about donating to Berean Christian Academy?”

"Yes," Julia said as she placed her empty mug on the coffee table. She folded her hands in her lap and looked into my eyes, "But that's only part of why I came today.”

I resolved to stay silent since everything came out wrong. I placed my mug on the table and immediately regretted it because then I didn't know what to do with my hands. I folded them in my lap like Julia, hoping she didn't think I mocked her.

Then she tilted her head and laughed. "I came to offer you an opportunity, but now I think I might offer you a job," Julia said.

I coughed and blinked.

"You are a wonder, Joy. Nanette promised you'd keep me on my toes, and it's already begun."

"I'm sorry. I don't follow."

Julia waved her hand as if to swat away the confusion. "I came here to offer you a seat on the board of my foundation. I believe your marketing experience and biblical worldview will be a perfect fit. Not to mention that the first project you would be a part of would be Berean Christian Academy."

"But now you don't want to offer me a seat on the board?" I squeaked.

"No. Actually, I'd like to amend my offer. Would you take the seat on the board *and* apply for the Director of Marketing position Maggie has left vacant? I can't believe it didn't occur to me before you suggested it."

Before I suggested it? Now I wanted to laugh out loud. That wasn't a suggestion, that was a blooper.

Then a sensation settled over me so soothing and all-consuming that I actually looked up. I felt as though an invisible pitcher of peace poured out and coated me from head to toe. I thought of a phrase I read in Deuteronomy when God declared the blessings for obedience—"all these blessings shall come upon you and overtake you, if you obey the voice of the LORD your God."

That's it. I've just been overtaken by the blessings of God.

"So?" eagerness tinged Julia's question.

"Yes," I declared. "Yes, to both."

404

CHAPTER SIXTY-SEVEN

THE PRESCHOOL DIRECTOR hugged me tighter than she had the night of the gala. "Today is a good day. I thought for sure it would be years until I saw this day, not *a* year. I'll never forget the day Mr. Easton came back to BCA, ran into me in the coffee room, and told me you now sat on the board of the Coates Foundation and would complete the funding for the new preschool."

We stood outside of the new preschool building on a mosaic patio adjacent to the covered drive. Parents pulled up and stopped. Staff members opened the back doors of the vehicles, helped students un-buckle, and held their hands as they hopped down with backpacks bouncing on their backs.

"It's an honor to be here, Mrs. Carlson," I said.

"The honor is all ours, Miss Swallow." She linked her arm in mine and turned me slightly and pointed in the distance. "Have you seen the new sports complex?"

"That's it, over there?" I asked so I didn't have to lie.

"Someone must have been inspired by the generosity of the Coates Foundation because within weeks of the donation to the preschool another anonymous donation came in to fund the entire sports complex just as John Clarke designed it. You don't happen to know who the donor was, do you?"

My mind whirled with how to spin my answer without giving away Julia Coates's anonymity. *You're a marketer, Joy. You can do this.*

A child with blonde curls and a giant pink bow skipped up to us and stopped abruptly.

"Well, aren't you adorable?" I squatted down to look at the child eye-to-eye.

"My name's Phoebe. What's your name?"

"My name's J—"

"This is Miss Swallow," Mrs. Carlson saved me.

"Like the bird?" Phoebe asked.

"Just like the bird."

"You have curly hair like me, but mine is yellow and yours is brown."

Before I could respond, her teacher called her inside and Phoebe skipped away.

Linking arms again, Mrs. Carlson spun me toward the door. "I'm glad you agreed to come early. Let's go inside. There's some people waiting to see you."

A small group of parents I didn't recognize stood on one side of the large multi-purpose room chatting and sipping coffee. A group of high school students crowded together on the other side, and I spotted Olivia among them. She grabbed the arm of a young man and they peeled away from the students and ran up to me. They embraced me at the same time in a group hug.

"Jackson, what are you doing here? You're a long way from Portland."

"He's home on fall break," Olivia answered for him with a quick squeeze around his waist. "We're all planning to be at the ribbon cutting later today, but my aunt is friends with Mrs. Carlson and she said you were coming early for a walk through, and I'm one of the tour guides."

"I'm so glad to see you both," I gave each of them another side hug.

Mrs. Carlson called the room to attention. "Thank you all for coming this morning. As you know, later today is the official ribbon cutting of our beautiful new preschool. Parents, your students have been enjoying the facility for a few weeks now and we are getting ready to start tours. Our high school tour guides have been learning their talking points, but today will be our dry run, so ask questions of your guides as if you were a prospective family." Mrs. Carlson smiled brightly at the high schoolers, "Students, you're ready for this." Then she stretched her arms toward everyone in the room, "Let's pray and ask for God's continued favor over this entire day."

After the prayer, we made our way through various classrooms. I reveled in the details of every room—the way the sunshine poured in through the windows, the brightly colored carpets, the soft music playing in the background, the Scripture on the walls, and the curious students practicing their math facts or singing and dancing.

Olivia brought us into a classroom where the students were playing in groups of two or three around the room. She described how the students learned through play at the various learning centers around the room while other students practiced their sight words one-on-one with the teacher.

"I know what the eagle means," a small voice drew our attention. Phoebe sat at a table with another student tracing letters on a worksheet.

"This one?" Olivia pointed to the eagle logo on her shirt. Phoebe nodded and continued tracing. "What does it mean?" Olivia asked.

"Our teacher said we are the Eagles and the eagle reminds us to trust in God. She said when we trust and obey God He'll give us what we need to soar like an eagle."

I smiled to myself. I could learn a lot from this little one.

"Miss Swallow," Phoebe called out.

"Yes?"

"Would you like to sit at my table?"

EPILOGUE

AT OUR LAKE HOUSE in northern Idaho, the leaves have all
turned brilliant shades of fall and I'm mesmerized by the hues of
autumn reflecting off of the glassy water. We named our house
Gahni Baa'—literally "Water House" in Shoshone. But still not so
clever. It's like when children name their stuffed bear "bear" and
their cat "cat."

We have great neighbors here. It's a retirement community, but
word has gotten out that it's a quiet place to vacation, too, so there
are a lot of short-term rental properties dotting the shores. We're
lucky most of our neighbors live here full-time. Anna always puts
fresh baked goods on our stoop the morning after our arrival when
we come up to visit. Randy still has a flip phone that he calls his
"walkie-talkie." There are two Elizabeths but one goes by Liz even
though "she was here first." There's a Dawn and a Don, so they
nicknamed one New Dawn and the other Colonel Don. Will Nelson
lives here and Michael Jordan, too, but let's just say they don't have

a social media account with a blue check. While they aren't @official, they officially look out for our property when we're away and are the best neighbors.

This chilly morning I'm reminded how Elizabeth (not Liz) taught me how to clap loudly to chase the Canadian geese from our yard. A family of them sit comfortably on the edge of our property, basking in the sun. As a visitor to the lake for decades, I always delighted in seeing the Canadian geese. Now, as a homeowner, I know them to be obnoxious and quite messy.

Today I choose to keep my clapping to myself and simply watch.

There's an alternate way to get a group of geese to move on, and that is for another group of geese to come and take their place. I spy a fresh flock soaring into our little cove. They're like large airplanes looking to overshoot the runway—angling their wings at the last minute and splashing into place.

It takes seconds for the lead guy to swim over to the edge where the other geese lay comfortably on the bulkhead. With insufferable honking and an arched neck ready for a fight, he chases those other geese away.

These geese all look alike to me. They sport the same colors. They have about the same number in each group. But they all know which family they belong to.

Methodically the lead goose of the new group approaches, threatens, and pursues each goose in the other group until one by one he displaces them from their previous spot of comfort. Then his family members each find their own place to settle in and bask in the sun.

"Bad ideas settle into the edges of our mind like that first family of geese," I say. "Sometimes you have to get a little aggressive to make room for the right ideas to bask in the sunlight. They may look alike, but make no mistake they are quite different. And there's not enough room lakeside for both."

My young guest nods silently as she stands beside me at the water's edge watching the sunlight shimmer and sparkle on the water like a disco ball. I laugh at the idea that I think Faye is young because she isn't much younger than I was in the stories I had been telling her.

"It's ironic," Faye comments. "Your story started out with you wanting to go to Julia's lake house in Tahoe to be mentored by her. And here we stand. You doing the same for me."

I turn to her and smile softly. I motion to the red Adirondack chairs facing the water. "Shall we sit out here, or is it too cool?"

Faye smiles. "I was hoping you would suggest that."

I settle into my chair and gaze at the water. It's so peaceful.

"Can I ask you a question?" Faye inquires.

"Of course."

"With all of the voices out there, how do you know which ones to listen to?"

I turn my head and look at her, "What voices—"

"Friends, podcasts, self-help books, online videos—as soon as I find one way that works, another voice pulls me in a new direction."

I see a fish jump in the distance and watch the ripples spread.

"The first bad idea we need to chase away is the one that says we can measure our thoughts or direction against anything but God's ways—and those ways are found in the Bible."

I see Faye pick lint from her pants.

"Jesus is our best example," I add. "He battled bad ideas and temptation with Scripture. He didn't use His own thoughts or the prevailing arguments of the day. He didn't say, 'I think…' or 'I heard a sermon this last Sabbath…' or 'It's like my favorite song says…' No. When He was tempted by Satan in the wilderness, His reply to every bad idea was, 'It is written.'"

Faye nods.

"It probably sounds silly to you that when I was your age I set my direction based on a craft project," I say.

"I actually thought the vision board was a pretty good way to stay focused until the part where God told you to burn it."

I laugh. "The bad idea wasn't keeping the end in mind, it was keeping the wrong end in mind. I literally shoved God's Word to the back of my shelf. I believed the lie as old as the Garden of Eden that God was somehow holding out on me. So I took things into my own hands and let my own idea of success take center stage."

"But didn't you end up at the kitchen table—and the board table—of Julia Coates like you always wanted?"

"Yes. Isn't it kind of God to give me my dream despite my crooked path? But—" I tap my finger on the arm of the chair, "—our steps are as important to God as our destination."

A few of the geese hop up onto the bulkhead and start pecking at bugs in the dirt. Faye props her feet on the stool in front of her. In my peripheral vision I see her look at me, but I keep my gaze ahead.

"So, we chase away the bad idea that God is holding out on us and replace it with the truth that He is generous with His revelation and wisdom. We simply have to open the pages of His Word and ask Him to help us understand."

"Can I be honest with you?" Faye asks.

"Of course."

"The Bible is hard to read and I'm not sure how detailed family trees or archaic sacrificial laws teach me or help me. Some of it just doesn't seem very—relevant."

Two mallard ducks drift silently by, leaving a small ripple behind them marring the otherwise glass-like surface.

"Would you say the Bible is irrelevant?"

"Well—no. I wouldn't go as far as that."

"Why not?" I ask.

Faye twitches her lips in thought and finally says, "Because that's what I've been taught in church." She shifts in her seat and tilts her head back. "That's a dumb answer."

I place my hand on the arm of her chair and look her in the eyes. "No. It's not a dumb answer."

Faye's shoulders release their tension and she offers me a meek smile.

"You've been taught well," I say. "The Bible is relevant—not always fashionable—but relevant."

I let the silence linger.

"Can I be honest with you?" I ask Faye.

Faye snaps her head toward me with wide eyes and a silent nod.

"I still struggle to read and understand parts of it, too. Here's what I know, though. The Bible is a grand story that leads to Jesus. It's how we get to know Him, and what's important to Him, and how to look like Him. I can't call myself a Christ-follower and not read my Bible."

Faye nods and turns and stares at the shimmering lake.

I'm enchanted by our ability to weave in and out of conversation yet sit comfortably in silence in between.

"The water is so sparkly," Faye says.

"Hmm. The reflection can be blinding at times. It reminds me of how Scripture says God is light and in Him is no darkness."

"You win," Faye says.

She startles me. "What?" I look at Faye.

She raises her hands in surrender. "You win. I surrender. I get it. The Bible's important."

"Subtlety is not my specialty," I smile. "I told you my story because if you can get the authority part right, your feet are on the right path for the next step and the next and the next."

"Authority?" I hear displeasure in her tone and see her face scrunch.

"I know submitting to authority is not a popular notion these days, but even when you think you're submitting to nothing you're submitting to something.

"Take my story, for example. The irony is that in submitting to the ways of others I bound myself to them instead. Paul asks, 'Don't you realize that you become the slave of whatever you choose to obey?'"

The breeze picks up and I shiver in the cold. I throw my blanket over my legs and throw up a prayer that I haven't overwhelmed my guest. "My husband should be home from dropping off the grandkids soon."

Faye's smile lights up her face, "I can't wait to meet him." She wraps her blanket up around her chin to ward off the wind.

"Let me finish with this," I sweep my arms in an arch over my head. "Picture God's Word as a giant tent. It covers everything else. All the other voices need to come under that covering.

"Scripture becomes your guide *and* your standard to measure every idea against.

"Once I submitted to the authority of Scripture, my interpretation of everything shifted. The Word of God became more than just promises to stand on, or metaphors to teach from, it transformed the way I thought and ultimately the way I lived."

I reach out and wait for Faye to place her hand in mine. She slips her arm from beneath the blanket and takes me up on the offer. I squeeze her hand. "And that's what I want for you, too."

"Will you help me with, like, how to read it and understand it?" Faye asks.

"We can start tomorrow after breakfast…at the kitchen table."

We both turn to the sound of footsteps behind us.

"Oh, hi honey! I'm so glad you made it. I'd like you to meet my friend, Faye."

He reaches out to shake her extended hand.

"Nice to meet you, Faye. I'm Chance."

AUTHOR'S NOTE

What this book became is different from how it started. I'm a Bible teacher. I generally teach at events, in classes at church, or through my podcast, *More Than a Song*, which I've been producing since 2014. My passion is to inspire people to discover and meditate on God's Word for themselves.

Initially, I thought this book would be half fiction and half nonfiction. I've learned a lot from business books designed like that. But, honestly, the narrative side of those books tends to be a little lame. While the story gives you pegs to hang knowledge on, I wanted to write a story that could stand on its own. Jesus taught through parables, and we can understand Kingdom things because he used everyday encounters to teach us. I want to do the same.

If you're reading this, I assume you've finished the story. There are hints in the narrative of what to do with your Bible. Nanette gives Joy hints, Beth helps, and Chance and The Remnant open Joy's eyes to the possibilities of thinking in new ways. That's nice for a fictional character. But what does that have to do with you? I've put together some online sessions to teach you what Nanette taught Joy and take the themes introduced in the book to dive deeper into Scripture and theology. You can find these sessions at michellenezat.com/storysessions

One more thing.

For this first book, I wrote from my own experiences. I was born and raised in Idaho. I'm a marketer. I teach the Bible. I worked for over a decade in a Christian school. And while it's perfectly natural for an author to tuck aspects of real people into their writing, don't read too much into it. If you know me personally, there are whispers of people and places in this book, but all the characters are entirely fictional.

Now, go read your Bible. Psalm 119 is a great place to start.

Michelle

P.S. I have a special copy of Joy's banana pudding recipe just for you. My daughter Emily designed it.

Just go to michellenezat.com/puddingrecipe and I'll send it right over.

ACKNOWLEDGMENTS

I know that sometimes authors wait until the end to build to a crescendo and then give their ultimate praise to God. But I can't wait. I must "acknowledge that the Lord is God" and come before Him with joyful songs. So, here goes. "I love you, Lord! Please take these few loaves and fishes and multiply them for Your kingdom. Thank you for inviting me to be a part of drawing others to Your Word. In the name of Your Son, Jesus Christ."

Now for the people—instruments in the hand of my loving Father.

I cannot thank my husband, Ron, enough. He really believes in me. He is a shameless supporter of everything I do with prayer, finances, words of affirmation, and even pulling on the reins when I get a little ahead of myself. He is the best love, friend, and head of our family a girl could ask for.

I want to express my gratitude to both of my daughters: my artistic daughter, Emily, who has a knack for keeping it real even if it hurts, and my avid reader, Meredith, who sometimes didn't even roll her eyes when I read her a scene and asked for her advice.

To my friends who have prayed more prayers over this book than I even know. To the original Board of Directors, Liz, Sonya, and Teri. You are a Remnant in your own right.

To Bill and Teri, who, next to my husband, are my biggest fans and sources of support. I'm tearing up just thinking about all the practical things they have done to make this book a success, not to mention all the ways they infuse me with courage.

To my very own white-minivan-Liz. She might drive a different vehicle now, but her heart is still rooted in Christ, and her friendship and wisdom hold me up in my writing and life.

Thanks to my mom, whose praise I can't always trust because her unlimited love for me blinds her.

To Mrs. Brooks, my very own Nanette Verity, guiding me with grace and truth.

I want to thank all the professionals and on-the-same-journey writers I've learned from over the years—my *Compel Training* friends, the campfire-writing-sessions-friends and teachers at *The Red House Writers Collective*, and the invaluable people and resources at *The Company*. I especially thank my book coach, developmental editor, and prayer warrior friend, Brad Pauquette. He understood my vision and heart and ensured I achieved it through a story that works.

Thank you to all the prayer warriors—the ones I'll remember to name (some who are no longer with us), the ones I'll inevitably forget, and those who prayed for this project and never told me. I offer special thanks to Christina, Amanda, Debbie, Allan and Ruth, Joni, Sarah, Jen, Pennie, Marshal and Apple, Susan, Keith, my CLC girls, Emily's Young Life girls, Mr. Davis, Grandma, and all of the precious advance readers and members of my release team.

May God's Word accomplish His purpose and succeed in the thing for which He sent it. (Isaiah 55:11)

THANK YOU FOR READING
MY DEBUT NOVEL

It's unbelievable that you've invested the time to read the (many) words I wove together into a story.

If you liked it, will you help others find this story?

Piper is asking for a friend!

How can you resist this face?

Here are two ways you can help others find this story:

1. Leave a review. Take two minutes to leave an honest review on Amazon or Goodreads.

2. Tell a friend. I'm more likely to read a book recommended by a friend, aren't you?

Thanks in advance,
Michelle

What if your next novel not only entertained but opened the door to wrestle with bigger ideas?

What if, when you're done reading, you're inspired to learn deeper truths from God's Word?

That's what *Story Sessions* are all about. *Story Sessions* are online sessions embracing the themes introduced through story and guiding us to study God's Word.

Check it out at michellenezat.com/storysessions
or follow the QR code below!

More Than a Song is a bi-weekly podcast dedicated to helping you discover the truth of Scripture hidden in today's popular Christian music.

My goal is to teach you to connect portions of God's Word with the songs you are singing along with on the radio; to help you meditate on Truths that will transform your way of thinking and ultimately your life.

Check it out at michellenezat.com
or follow the QR code below!

NEED A SPEAKER AT YOUR NEXT EVENT?

"Michelle is a gifted Bible teacher and speaker. I had the pleasure of hearing her speak at a women's conference and have never left a conference feeling more encouraged in my spiritual walk! She taught the Bible and gave practical tools that I have learned to apply in my Bible reading. Her insight into how to read and study scripture was new and refreshing. Michelle continues to encourage me weekly as I've listened to her podcast episodes and sought to grow in my own knowledge of God's Word."

- Emily M.

I only take a few speaking engagements each year so I can create custom presentations for my audiences.

Reach out and let's start a conversation at michellenezat.com/speaking or follow the QR code below!

ABOUT THE AUTHOR

Michelle Nezat writes Christian fiction with a purpose. The themes in her novels mirror the themes in the Bible and serve as a jumping-off point to study Scripture and theology in a new way.

She's a Cajun girl born in Idaho and living in Louisiana, and she has the best gumbo and sweet tea in the neighborhood (according to her husband and two daughters). Her passion is God's Word and inspiring others to discover and interact with Scripture for themselves.

Drawing from over a decade of Bible teaching through her podcast *More Than a Song*, she's turned to stories to inspire readers to explore deep theological truths. Learn more about her and her books at michellenezat.com/books